Women of the
DARK STREETS
LESBIAN PARANORMAL

Visit us at www.boldstrokesbooks.com

WOMEN OF THE
DARK STREETS

LESBIAN PARANORMAL

edited by

RADCLY*f*FE and
STACIA SEAMAN

2012

WOMEN OF THE DARK STREETS:
LESBIAN PARANORMAL

ISBN 13: 978-1-60282-651-9

This Trade Paperback Original Is Published By
Bold Strokes Books, Inc.
P.O. Box 249
Valley Falls, NY 12185

First Edition: March 2012

___

Credits
Editors: Radclyffe and Stacia Seaman
Production Design: Stacia Seaman
Cover Design by Sheri (graphicartist2020@hotmail.com)

CONTENTS

INTRODUCTION 1

LUCKY NUMBER SEVEN
Merry Shannon 3

COME TO ME
Sam Cameron 17

FULL MOON WEEKEND
Meghan O'Brien 33

TEMPORA MUTANTUR
Jane Fletcher 51

THE TRICKSTER CODEX
Jess Faraday 63

FOR ALL ETERNITY
Victoria Oldham 80

SOLSTICE
Karis Walsh 90

THE OTHER SIDE OF THE MIRROR
Valerie Bronwen 102

SKIN WALKERS
D. Jackson Leigh 115

FORGET ME NOT
Rebecca S. Buck 128

THE OTHERS
Nell Stark and Trinity Tam 141

EMILY
    Ronica Black   153

STUDY BREAK
    Rebekah Weatherspoon   168

AWAY WITH THE FAIRIES
    Lesley Davis   179

IN THE BELL TOWER
    MJ Williamz   192

BLOODSTONE
    Sheri Lewis Wohl   200

PLAGUED BY DARKNESS
    L.T. Marie   217

RECYCLABLES
    Joey Bass   225

THE ORIENT EXPRESS
    Shelley Thrasher   241

ERIS
    Winter Pennington   254

BLOOD MOON
    Yolanda Wallace   268

CONTRITION
    Mel Bossa   283

DEADLY GLAMOUR
    L.L. Raand   290

FRESH MEAT
    Clara Nipper   297

CONTRIBUTORS   323

ABOUT THE EDITORS   327

INTRODUCTION

When we read about the paranormal, we question what it means to be human. In reading about the other, we confront our deepest fears about ourselves as a whole: *Is reality limited by what our senses can perceive? Is life defined by birth and death? Are we really at the top of the food chain?* and as individuals: *Is there someone out there for me? Am I worthy of being loved?*

This is a book filled with temptation and seduction, redemption and perdition. Join your favorite Bold Strokes authors on a journey filled with vampires and shape-shifters; previous lives, the afterlife, eternal life; angels and demons—the full range of paranormal, from bone-chilling terror to erotic and exotic encounters to the sweetness of everlasting love.

Radclyffe and Stacia Seaman 2010

Lucky Number Seven
Merry Shannon

The world was awash in blood and fire. Thick black smoke, flickered through with a dull orange glow, choked the night air. Sirens shrieked madly from multiple directions, blue and red flashes searing Kara's peripheral vision as she struggled to open her eyes. A single thought tore through her dazed brain, and she sat up in terror.

"Nic!"

Across the dark, hard-packed earth her wife's blood-soaked form lay prostrate atop a glittering spread of broken glass. Kara screamed and scrambled over to her, but even before she reached her, she already knew.

Nic was dead.

"Oh God, no. No!" Kara collapsed over her wife's broken body. She twined her fingers with Nic's left hand, their matching gold wedding bands glinting in the crazy colored lights of the emergency vehicles. "Nic, baby, oh my God…"

Her wife's strong, handsome features were scarcely recognizable beneath layers of blood and dirt. A large triangular shard of glass jutted from her torso, and a thick, hot puddle of blood had formed beneath it. Her close-cropped blond hair was singed and part of her scalp was burned away in a sticky mess. Other parts of her seemed blackened and unnaturally twisted, and Kara squeezed her eyes shut, grateful that the darkness spared her from the most grisly details. She crushed Nic's hand in hers and rocked back and forth in agony. This was not happening. How could this be happening?

She was only vaguely aware of footsteps crunching through the warped metal and glass all around them, the hiss of water hoses aimed at the burning remains of the train, the shouts of emergency personnel as they sifted through the rubble. A pair of black boots suddenly came into view as someone stopped and bent over them.

"We've got another body over here!"

Another set of boots arrived, and a stretcher dropped to the ground next to Nic's body. Gloved hands reached down and rolled Nic over so that Kara got a good look at the cruel blade of glass impaling her wife's chest just beneath the sternum. Kara screamed again.

"Stop, don't touch her! Nic!"

The strangers ignored her, seizing Nic's shoulders and feet, but they were arrested by a soft female voice.

"Wait a moment, gentlemen."

Kara looked up to see a woman gazing down at her compassionately. Unlike the emergency workers in their soot-smudged coveralls, she was wearing a trim khaki pantsuit and pink satin blouse that looked starkly out of place against the smoky chaos. Soft chestnut hair framed her face in gentle waves. An ID badge was clipped to her lapel, though from this distance Kara couldn't read it. The woman laid a hand on the shoulder of the nearest man and said quietly, "Will you give us a minute, please?" She bobbed her head in Kara's direction and fixed him with a long stare.

Both emergency workers gave the woman disgusted scowls, but they left Nic's body where it lay and stomped off.

The woman crouched down on her heels next to Kara and surveyed Nic's battered form. "I'm so sorry. Was she a friend?"

Kara shook her head, a bitter laugh rising through the sobs in her throat. "Nic is my wife." As usual the words came out defiantly, as if daring the woman to contradict her. But the woman only nodded all the more kindly.

"I'm so very sorry," she said again, with even deeper feeling. She paused for a respectful moment before introducing herself. "My name is Elsa Cramer. I'm a special investigator working with the FBI."

Kara could read the laminated badge on her lapel now, which confirmed the name. "Kara Stinson," she replied automatically.

"Kara, I know all of this has got to be overwhelming right now, but I need to ask you a few questions. Were you and your wife on the train when this happened?"

"I…" Sharp fragments of memory dazzled her with images. The groan of tearing metal. A deafening explosion. Glass breaking. Gravity shifting. A raging wall of fire rushing toward them, and the sudden horror in Nic's eyes as she grabbed Kara's hand and they ran through a disintegrating tunnel of metal and flame... Kara pressed her hands to her temples and shook her head. "I don't know. I think so." She stared at Elsa numbly. "What happened?"

"That's what I intend to find out."

"Nic's dead."

"And I want to catch the people responsible. I need your help, Kara."

For the first time Kara took a good look at the scene of destruction behind them. It was like something out of a macho action flick—one train car was completely derailed, lying on its side with electric sparks raining from broken wires above. It had crushed the chain link fence and concrete barrier that lined the light rail and was protruding dangerously into the oncoming traffic lanes of I-25, the freeway that ran alongside the train track. A second train car was leaning haphazardly against the first, with tongues of angry flame licking their way out of the broken windows. Several bench seats, with their tacky blue pleather upholstery, had been flung out onto the ground. Unidentifiable pieces of metal and plastic were scattered everywhere, and the air hung heavy with acrid smoke and the bitter smell of burning chemicals. All along the track, dozens of men were carting away sheet-covered stretchers just like the one they'd left lying next to Nic.

Kara felt sick. "Are you saying someone did this to us?"

"We believe someone set off a bomb, either on the train or on the track itself. The FBI received a bomb threat just before it was detonated. Tell me, did you see anyone or anything unusual?"

Kara tried to think back, but still all she could recall were jumbled flashes of panic, the other passengers screaming, the awful quaking of the train beneath her feet. "I can't...I can't remember. It's all in pieces." She reached down for her wife's lifeless hand again.

"That's all right. Don't try to force it. Try going back further, maybe to earlier in the evening. Can you remember why you were on the train?"

"We were on our way home."

"From downtown?"

"Yes. We went out to dinner for our second third anniversary."

Elsa blinked in confusion. "Second third?"

"Nic and I have been married in six states so far, all of the ones that have legalized same-sex marriage." With a trembling hand Kara tried to turn Nic's wedding band so that its single small diamond would be centered on her finger. She could not make it move, and wondered if Nic's fingers were too swollen. "It's kind of our thing. Since we can't marry in our home state yet, we make special trips to other places when it becomes legal there. We went to Massachusetts first, then California—though Prop 8's still trying to reverse that, the bastards—and two years ago today, we were married for the third time in Connecticut. So today is our second third anniversary." Kara reached into her jacket pocket and pulled out a little colored envelope. Tears blurred her vision as she handed it to Elsa. "This was Nic's anniversary gift to me."

Elsa opened the envelope and withdrew its contents. "Tickets to New York?"

"She proposed tonight. For the seventh time." Kara turned back to Nic's body and a sob racked her insides. "But we won't get to go now, will we?"

Elsa said gently, "Can you tell me what happened after you and Nic got on the train?"

"We were excited, talking about all the things we wanted to do in NYC. She wanted to go to a Giants game. We wanted to hold our little wedding right in the middle of Times Square. Something simple, just us and an officiate. I wasn't really paying attention too much, you know? I mean, we've taken the light rail a hundred times. The train runs. It stops. People get on, people get off, it runs again. We were almost home, and then everything just…blew up." Shock was quickly giving way to rage. "If someone did this to us—if someone took her away from me, I want that person to pay."

"And I don't blame you one bit."

"But I don't know anything," Kara said in frustration. "I can't remember anything out of the ordinary at all."

The two rescue workers returned then, one of them grumbling under his breath while the other said gruffly, "Sorry, Ms. Cramer, but we've gotta take this one now." His companion had already halfway dragged Nic's body onto the stretcher.

Kara ground her teeth and turned to Elsa with a determined stare. "I'm going with her."

"I understand." Elsa held out a neat white business card. "If you think of anything else, here's where you can find me."

The rescue workers gave the FBI woman strange looks. Kara didn't even glance at the card. She just turned to follow as the men carried her wife away.

❖

The day of Nicole Stinson's funeral was just another cheerily sunny summer morning in Denver. The cemetery grounds were lovely, with dragonflies and bees humming happily between the sedate headstones, enjoying the lavish flower bouquets set out by the residents' loved ones. The other mourners were sweating profusely in their prim black dresses and suit jackets, but Kara's fingers felt like ice, as did her soul. Maybe Nic's death hadn't truly sunk in yet, because she couldn't seem to feel much of anything since the train wreck. A deep, aching cold had settled in her bones, and it made every part of her feel crystalline and numb.

Nic's sleek dark casket was lowered, inch by inch, into the neatly framed grave. Directly across from Kara stood Nic's parents, who hadn't so much as looked in Kara's direction throughout the service. Not that their disdain was much of a surprise. In spite of the six marriage licenses that hung proudly on the wall of their little condo, in spite of the fact that Kara's Social Security card and driver's license both stated proudly that Kara shared their family's last name, the Stinsons had always refused to acknowledge their daughter's relationship with another woman. Even now they stood there, tossing flowers after Nic's casket, weeping, and still managing to pretend that Kara was invisible.

Kara's sister Lexi was there, but Kara had no desire to go to her for comfort. Lexi was one of those women who positively thrived on the drama in others' lives. She liked nothing more than a good funeral or a scandalous affair, the more tragic the better. Oh, Lexi would be more than happy to lend Kara a shoulder to cry on, but she had a way of appropriating other people's pain as if she was just as much a victim of their suffering as they were. Lexi called it being empathetic, but Kara knew her sister just thrived on the attention. She didn't want Lexi leaching her feelings for her own personal entertainment right now.

Still, Kara was beginning to feel profoundly lonely as she stood at her wife's graveside. Though many of their friends had come to pay their respects, it seemed they were all too self-conscious to approach Kara either. Not one had offered her a sympathetic hug or even a trite muttering of condolence.

Nic had always been the outgoing one. Kara was usually content to sit shyly in the background and watch her charismatic wife socialize. Nic's sharp sense of humor and easygoing nature had a way of making everyone around her feel instantly comfortable. She drew people to her naturally, but Kara didn't possess that talent. Now Kara realized that the people she'd always thought of as their mutual friends had only ever really been Nic's friends, and with Nic gone, no one had any interest in her anymore. Was this what her life would be like now, isolated and frozen with grief? Never in her life had Kara felt so alone.

"I was hoping you'd be here."

Kara turned to see Elsa Cramer at her side. She was so grateful for the warmth of another person's voice that she very nearly hugged her, and a hard lump rose in her throat as she realized out of all the people here, only this virtual stranger seemed to have the heart to acknowledge her.

"Where else would I be?" she asked miserably. "My wife is here."

"I know. I'm deeply sorry for your loss, Kara."

"Have you caught the bastards that did this yet?"

"I'm afraid not." The FBI agent's eyes were troubled. "And we received another bomb threat today. The Bureau is certain it's from the same group that attacked the Denver light rail. We think their reign of terror is just getting started, and the train bomb was only a warm-up."

Kara felt her rage surge again, shattering the delicate ice that had held her emotions so carefully suspended. "No!" she hissed, and surged forward until her face was just inches from Elsa's nose. Elsa's hair was suddenly tossed about her face as a frosty breeze whipped through the cemetery. Surprised gasps went up from the gathered mourners as the brilliant summer heat was interrupted by an unseasonal chill.

Elsa, however, did not appear fazed. She returned Kara's furious stare grimly. "We don't know what their next target will be, just that it will most likely happen in another of the U.S.'s largest cities. Los Angeles, perhaps. Maybe New York or Boston."

Their first two marriages had been in Boston and Los Angeles.

Their seventh, the one they'd never have, would have been in New York. Kara couldn't bear the thought of any of these places undergoing the kind of tragedy she had just been through. "You can't let that happen!"

"Believe me, we're doing everything we can. But these terrorists seem to be ahead of us at every turn."

"Well, they probably have a whatchamacallit—a weasel? Inside the FBI."

"Do you mean a mole?"

"Yeah, that's it, a mole. I bet they've got one."

Elsa paused. Very slowly she said, "What makes you say that?"

"Don't you watch television? There's always some inside guy."

The look that Elsa gave her then was very strange, like she was trying to peer inside Kara's head. "Kara, I want you to think for me now, very carefully. Do you really believe the FBI has a leak?"

Kara snorted. "Why are you asking me? You're the special agent, isn't it your job to make sure things like that don't happen?"

Elsa gave her a wry smile. "I have a very different job description, actually. And asking you these questions is the most important part of it. Please, Kara, I want to know what your gut is telling you. Do you believe someone within the FBI is helping set off these bombs?"

"Why in the world would it matter what I—"

"Just answer the question."

Kara hissed again, a long, low sound that was eerie even to her own ears. But at last she nodded. "Yes. I do."

Even as she said the words, she felt certain of them. In fact, she could almost see him in her mind's eye, a squirrelly little fellow with thick tortoiseshell glasses and a bald patch, working behind some FBI desk somewhere, slinking off to dark corners of the office to make covert calls from a disposable cell phone. There was money on his mind, she decided. Someone was paying him massive sums of cash to keep them apprised of the FBI's movements, and he didn't care how many innocent lives might be lost because his focus was entirely on the Caribbean paradise he planned to escape to once he'd received his final payout.

Kara drew back and shook herself, startled. Clearly she had let Nic talk her into watching far too many episodes of *Alias* and *24*, because her imagination was definitely getting the better of her.

But Elsa was watching her intently. "Did you see something? Tell me."

"It's nothing. I told Nic she watched too many of those spy shows."

"I want to hear about it anyway."

"Why?"

"Because I think you know more than you think you do. And if there really is a mole within the FBI, you're our only hope of discovering them in time. You can see things, Kara, things that we can't."

She didn't like the way Elsa was looking at her so eagerly, as if she expected her to produce a crystal ball at any moment and start rattling off a list of the terrorist's names. Something clicked in Kara's head then, and she licked her lips nervously. "Just what exactly do you do for the FBI, Ms. Cramer?"

Elsa sighed heavily, and Kara wondered if she'd been expecting the question. "I'm a paranormal investigator."

"I see." Around them the crowd had begun to disperse, but Kara paid them no attention as she scowled at the other woman. "So what, they sent you in to find out if my near-death experience has suddenly triggered some clairvoyant sixth sense? You think I can see the future now? Read minds? Speak to the dead, maybe? I've changed my mind, Ms. Cramer. I think you're the one who's been watching too much TV."

Her soft brown eyes were sad as she shook her head. "I'm afraid you didn't have a near-death experience, Kara."

"And I don't have any special powers either. So I think you should just leave me alone. I'm done talking to you."

"Kara," Elsa said firmly, "there's something you should see." She pointed over Kara's shoulder.

Kara turned around, determined to stalk away and leave this crazy woman alone with her absurd supernatural fantasies. But the scene she confronted made her draw up short.

A second fresh grave had been dug next to Nic's, and the mourners had moved to surround it. Another casket, this one in a pretty blond-colored wood and spread with a stunning arrangement of hydrangea, delphinium, and roses, was being lowered into the waiting cavity. The flowers descended past the headstone slowly, revealing the inscription.

Kara Stinson, 3/14/1978–6/26/2011. Then, in prettily curling script beneath: *Beloved Wife of Nicole.*

Kara staggered forward, her mouth agape. "That's not possible."

She watched Lexi, tears streaking her cheeks, tossing flowers into the opening. And then to her complete and utter astonishment, Nic's parents did the same thing, with expressions of utter reverence mingled with guilt. Nic's mom turned to bury her head in her husband's shoulder, and he held her with one arm while extending his other to embrace a distraught Lexi. They stood there in a grief-stricken family embrace, and Kara shook her head. "Now I know this isn't real."

"It is real, Kara." Elsa moved to her side again. "You and Nic died together in that bombing, along with dozens of others. But you were the only one who remained behind to help us catch the ones who did this."

"But they hate me," Kara whispered in disbelief as Nic's parents tenderly draped her headstone with a gorgeous wreath of roses. It was a perfect match for the one they'd left for their daughter.

"Death is a funny thing. It has a way of changing one's perspective, sometimes radically."

Understanding dawned and Kara turned to her slowly. "I'm not the one who can speak to the dead, am I?"

Elsa shook her head with a small smile.

"How long have you been, um…gifted?"

"A very long time."

Kara found that she didn't feel as horrified as she ought to at the revelation that she was, in fact, deceased. She didn't feel devastated, or sad, or even angry. In fact, all she experienced was a sudden surge of hope. "If Nic and I were both killed in that accident, then we can be together now, can't we? Where is she? When can I see her?"

"Soon, I hope. She's waiting for you on the other side."

"The other side of what?"

Elsa's cell phone beeped at her waist and she flipped it open, scanning her text messages. "The next bombing's supposed to occur in exactly three hours and fifty-two minutes, and we still don't know where or who's behind it." She looked up at Kara urgently. "We don't have much time. There's a reason spirits remain behind, Kara, especially when their death was particularly violent or traumatic. They need the circumstances of their death resolved in order to find peace. And that's what I do—I help you achieve that resolution, so you can cross over where you belong."

Kara felt a twinge of panic rise up in her throat as she considered Elsa's words. "You mean, unless these terrorists are caught I won't ever be able to leave here?"

"I don't know. But I think, if we can stop them, that you should be able to find the path. If not, I promise I will continue to help you until we figure out what's holding you here. But right now hundreds, maybe thousands of lives depend on the two of us figuring out what you know. I need you to tell me what you saw earlier, when we were discussing the mole."

"But it was just a flight of fancy. I've never actually seen him before in my life."

"You're a ghost, Kara. You exist on a whole different plane now, one that's much less limited than ours. I don't fully understand it myself, but in my experience spirits can see things they would never have been able to in life. Especially when it's something they need in order to find closure. Whatever you saw, I believe you can trust it." She laid a hand on Kara's forearm. "You can trust me."

Elsa's touch felt curiously foggy, more like a memory than an immediate sensation, and Kara found it disconcerting. But Elsa's gaze was entirely sincere, and so hesitantly Kara began to describe the impression she'd gotten of the man with the glasses and bald spot.

Elsa listened carefully and nodded. "Would you be willing to come back to the office with me? I'd like you to sit with our sketch artist."

❖

After a few more pencil strokes and a little smudging with the tip of his finger, the heavyset man pushed the drawing across the table toward Elsa. "That him?" Without waiting for an answer he picked up his cell phone from the desk and lazily scrolled through its text messages.

Elsa had said that Reggie Guest was one of the FBI's best sketch artists, but Kara didn't like him much. He made it clear he thought their entire session was an enormous waste of his time. Kara caught every one of his skeptical eye-rolls whenever Elsa turned to her to get the answers to his questions. She didn't suppose she could blame him, really. From his perspective, Elsa was carrying on a conversation with thin air, and it had to look strange. But from what Kara had seen, this behavior seemed to follow Elsa everywhere she went. From the moment they'd walked into the FBI office, people had steered politely clear of the paranormal investigator as if she had some dreadful contagious disease. Kara had caught a number of whispered comments as they passed.

Check it out, the ghost hunter's back!

Will never understand why the FBI wastes the taxpayers' dollars on these quacks.

Creepy Cramer says her new ghost BFF is going to help her catch a terrorist. What a freak.

Whereas that very morning she had been just as ready to ridicule the idea of communing with the dead, Kara now found herself wishing she could leap to Elsa's defense. She was impressed by the grace with which Elsa ignored the derision of her coworkers. Head held high, she'd just marched past their cubicles, seemingly blind to the stares and whispers drifting in her wake. She'd planted herself before Guest's desk and gestured to Kara to follow. The sketch artist appeared to be waiting for them, however reluctantly, and now lying on the desk before their eyes was a finely detailed composite of the man that Kara had envisioned.

She nodded at Elsa's questioning look. "That's him," she said firmly.

The man's image had sharpened in Kara's mind as she'd tried to describe him, until she could see his face as clearly as a photograph when she closed her eyes. And though she had no idea what his name was or even what FBI office he worked in, Kara had never felt so absolutely certain of anything in her life. This man was real, and he was collaborating with terrorists for personal gain. She stared down at his face and rage welled up inside her. This man was responsible for Nic's death. He might be responsible for hundreds more in the next few hours. Someone had to stop him, and Reggie Guest's not-so-subtle contempt for Elsa was really beginning to infuriate her. Elsa Cramer was the only one Kara could share this with, so she was the only one who could find this man before it was too late.

Elsa pushed the drawing back to the artist. "I want you to run this against the FBI's personnel database immediately. When you find the match, go pick him up. This man is our leak, and he's the only chance we've got at stopping this bomb."

He looked up from his cell phone with a sneer. "We don't have the resources to devote to a massive project like that, Ms. Cramer, just because you say some ghost told you…"

"Do I need to call Director Stevens?"

He bristled. "Don't you go name-dropping with me, Cramer. You may have the director convinced you're our nation's greatest secret weapon, but he's not going to start a witch hunt through the FBI based on a description from some loony psychic."

Livid, Kara snatched Guest's cell phone right out of his hand and threw it. It sang past his ear and smashed into the cubicle wall behind him, splintering into pieces on the carpet. The temperature in the room suddenly dropped at least thirty degrees as she shrieked, "Listen up, you asshole, this man murdered my wife!"

The sketch artist let out a surprised puff of breath that formed a cloud of mist in front of his lips, and he stared down in absolute shock at the fragments of his phone. A chorus of startled shouts went up throughout the office at the abrupt change in temperature, but Elsa only sat back in her chair, a smile playing at her lips.

"I think you're pissing her off, Guest." Elsa stood and cocked her head to the side as Kara spoke angrily in her ear, then nodded and turned to leave. "One more thing," she tossed breezily over her shoulder. "When you find the mole, grab *his* cell phone. It's a disposable, but there should still be more than enough evidence on it to prove his guilt. Maybe even help track down his terrorist buddies before they manage to blow anything else up."

❖

Nic's smiling face was the most beautiful thing Kara had ever seen, and her heart caught in her throat as her wife, tall and perfect and haloed in glorious brightness, extended a welcoming hand to her.

"I'm coming, babe," Kara called out. She could feel the light tugging at her, Nic's presence beckoning to her soul like irresistible music. She wanted to let go immediately and fly right into her wife's strong arms, and she knew without doubt that once she was there nothing would ever part them again. But she held back, because there was one last thing she had to do.

Kara turned to Elsa and wrapped her in a hug, even though she knew the other woman would barely feel more than a slight chill at her touch. "Thank you," she whispered.

"Oh Kara, no, thank you. Because of you we were able to catch not just the FBI leak but eight of his terrorist friends. The FBI disarmed the second bomb in Chicago's Union Station just seconds before it detonated, and we got our hands on plans for a third and fourth bombing that will never take place now. We never would have even gotten close if it hadn't been for your help. You've saved so many lives today." Elsa's eyes were sparkling with tears as she pulled back. "More importantly, though, I hope Nic knows just how much you love her."

"What do you mean?"

"I've never seen a spirit able to do what you did, throwing that phone. I've heard of it before, of course, but ghosts who are powerful enough to move objects within our world are just as rare as those of us who can see into yours. Your passion for Nic is what gives you such strength, and I've never seen anything like it. You certainly made a believer out of Guest today, and I never would have thought that possible." Elsa laughed. "This wife of yours must be one amazing woman."

Kara looked back over her shoulder and beamed at Nic. "She certainly is."

"What happened to you two just isn't fair. I promise you, Kara, the ones who did this will be held accountable for it."

Kara let herself slide backward, just a little, into the light. "You know, it really is all right," she assured Elsa happily. "I'm not angry anymore. Nic's here now, and I get the feeling that our adventures together are just beginning."

"I'm sure you're right." As the light pulled at Kara even more insistently, Elsa smiled. "Go on, Kara. Say hi to Nic for me."

"I will." Kara turned, flung her arms out, and surrendered to the light's coaxing. In an instant she found herself wrapped in Nic's strong embrace. Her wife's adoring eyes were as impossibly blue as ever, and a shiver of joy went through her entire being.

"About time you got here," Nic rumbled in amusement.

Kara captured Nic's face in her hands, greedily devouring the sight of her. "God, Nic, thought I'd lost you."

"Not getting rid of me that easily." Nic chuckled. "Six times you've promised me forever, Mrs. Stinson, and I'm holding you to every last one."

Kara snuggled contentedly against Nic's chest, love swelling golden and warm inside her. "You think maybe on the other side we can make it lucky number seven?"

Nic's grin stretched from ear to ear. "Let's go find out."

But before leading the way into the waiting light, Nic bent her head and captured Kara's mouth in a kiss, one so sweet and tender that it was guaranteed to outlast anything that might come next.

COME TO ME
SAM CAMERON

In other news today, the Transportation Security Agency is under public fire for the treatment of an elderly, wheelchair-bound grandmother with leukemia. The ninety-two-year-old woman was flying to a family reunion in Boston when she was subjected to a TSA pat-down, scanned with a portable backscatter unit, and then forced to remove her adult diaper. So far, the official government response is that the treatment of the elderly woman was "appropriate" and "within federal guidelines."—NBC 4, Columbus

Elsa knew from sad experience that most hotel gyms weren't worth the time it took to swipe a card key. Usually she exercised alone in her room. With the furniture arranged just right, she could mambo left and grapevine right without bashing into anything. Exercising alone was lonely, but it wasn't as if she was looking to make friends. She was in the business of constant travel. She had one small suitcase, very efficiently packed, and spent much of her time in the clouds.

But the very nice thing about this hotel at Columbus Airport was that it had an indoor swimming pool, and she'd bought a bathing suit in an overpriced shop two airports ago. Fifteen minutes after checking in on a gray Tuesday afternoon, she was sticking her toes into the blue-green water and taking the plunge.

Warm, but not as warm as bathwater. Filled with chlorine, but not so much that her eyes stung. The maximum depth was only three and a half feet. It was designed for recreation, not lap swimming. The area was empty except for herself, the water, and some fake palm trees and white deck chairs. Elsa swam east to west, then north to south, and that was maybe twenty-five yards total. She figured she could get a mile done in thirty-six circuits.

She had just passed the quarter-mile mark when the glass door opened and a woman in a white bathrobe came in. Her long dark hair was very curly, and her heart-shaped face open and friendly. Elsa met her gaze, nodded politely. The woman smiled back with dimples that made Elsa dead jealous—she'd never had dimples, herself. Just acne-prone skin and a tendency to sunburn.

The other guest slid out of her bathrobe. Underneath was a very nice green bikini clinging to a very nice body—tall but shapely, not so skinny that you'd want to sit her down and force feed her a plate of pasta. Elsa could think of more enjoyable things to do with her, frankly. Which reminded her that she hadn't had a date in seven months, and that she had to work tonight, and wouldn't it be better to just get her swimming done? She didn't hook up with strangers in hotels.

"Is it cold?" the woman asked. "It's usually cold."

Elsa shook her head.

The woman stood on the top of the steps and stuck one perfectly manicured foot in. Purple toenail polish. Long leg, smooth and muscled—a runner, maybe.

"I'm a wimp when it comes to cold," the woman confided, wagging her foot. "I think I was supposed to have been born in the tropics. Near those fruity drinks with umbrellas in them. And those thatch buildings you drink the fruity drinks under. What are they called?"

Elsa stopped swimming. "Tiki huts?"

"Tiki huts," the woman said, and those dimples showed themselves again. "I'm a big fan of fruity drinks, tiki huts, and sunsets. All of which are sadly far away from Columbus, Ohio."

"We are at an airport," Elsa pointed out. "You could get on a plane."

"I've heard of these things called vacations, but they sadly don't exist in my world." The woman stepped down and let the water rise up to her knees, then her firm, smooth thighs. She was only five or six feet away from Elsa now. She wore no jewelry, and only a little makeup to show off her dark brown eyes. "What about you? Don't tell me Columbus is your idea of a relaxing retreat."

Elsa was torn between chatting or continuing her swim. She

glanced at the clock hanging over the complimentary towels. Her crew wouldn't pick her up until midnight. There was time for chatting and maybe even dinner, and was that hope flaring in her chest? A little romance? No, probably just heartburn from swallowing chlorine.

"I'm not on vacation," she said. "Just passing through."

"Then you're lucky." The woman stuck out her hand. "I'm Lisa-Marie. Like Elvis's daughter. Sadly, without his massive fortune."

"I'm Elsa, like the British actress."

Lisa-Marie's face brightened. "Elsa Lancaster! She was in *Mary Poppins*."

"Most people wouldn't know that," Elsa said, amused.

"Most people don't have five-year-old nieces who watch it at least once a day, even when you beg her not to, because how many times can one person endure 'Chim Chim Cher-ee' without going crazy?"

"That's a rhetorical question, isn't it?" Elsa asked.

"Absolutely." Lisa-Marie showed her dimples again. "I have no intention of subjecting you to Dick Van Dyke or any faux Cockney accents. But as a longtime resident of Columbus, I feel terrible for anyone stuck eating hotel food when there's a great Italian restaurant nearby. How do you feel about fettuccini?"

Now it was Elsa's turn to smile. "Love it."

Near midnight, an unmarked black utility van pulled into the hotel parking lot. Andrew popped the side door for Elsa and she climbed in. He was sucking on the straw of an empty Frappuccino cup and had cinnamon frosting on his chin.

"We stopped for breakfast," he said, burping. "Late-night snack. Whatever."

"Saved you one," said Christopher from the driver's seat. He always drove because he liked being behind the wheel. As opposed to flying, which he hated. Andrew always teased him about that: a guy who hated to fly, and his job was to fly around and fix things.

Elsa said, "I had dinner. A real dinner. With vegetables. You've heard of them?"

Andrew burped. "Filled with radioactive fallout from that

Japanese reactor. It's spread all over the world by now, carried by the winds. Seeps into the earth. You're much healthier with artificial food substances."

Christopher checked his rearview mirrors, though traffic was non-existent at this hour. "You look different. Did these vegetables happen to come with some extra-friendly companionship?"

"None of your business," Elsa replied.

"You scored!" Andrew grabbed the last cinnamon roll. "We're proud of you."

"Shut up," she suggested. "I didn't score anything. Ships that pass in the night. I'm never going to see her again."

Which was a shame, really, because Lisa-Marie was bright and funny and they'd had a fabulous dinner. She lived with her parents, grandmother, sister, and two nieces because her job in legal aid didn't pay much. One of her former clients was a night manager at Elsa's hotel, and whenever she needed to escape the noise at home, he let her crash in one of the empty rooms. Lisa-Marie was a good flirt, but Elsa was accomplished at dodging. The dinner had ended with no promises, no exchange of phone numbers, but Lisa-Marie had sounded very sincere when she said, "Next time you're in Columbus, you should call me."

It had been the nicest dinner Elsa had experienced in quite some time, and if the memory of Lisa-Marie's bright eyes and pretty face still gave her a warm little glow, there was no harm in that.

While Christopher circled around the airport, Elsa pulled on a brown jumpsuit that smelled like laundry detergent. The airport IDs were still warm from the laminator. The service parking lot was empty but for some cleaning vans and three airport security cars. Their local TSA contact was a big, unhappy-looking woman named Dorothy Armstrong.

"I wish you guys could do this earlier at night," she said. "I've got to be back here at six a.m."

Elsa sympathized, but all she said was, "Not our rules, ma'am."

"Less chance of nosy tourists," Andrew added, eyeing the empty food kiosks.

Midnight was actually early for them. Elsa preferred two or three a.m., but scheduling this job had already been hard—Christopher was due to fly to Memphis for a cleaning there, and Andrew had to travel out to San Francisco to train some new technicians. The job paid well but the travel was grinding, and at the lower levels, employee turnover was high.

Columbus Airport had three security checkpoints for passengers. They headed directly for Concourse A, which had already shut down for the night. Four screening lanes, typical formation, with four traditional scanners and two enormous backscatter units. The machine that had alerted was a model AXB-78-09-DZ, one of the best out there, sometimes a little temperamental. Christopher powered it up, Elsa plugged her laptop into the control panel, and Andrew unpacked the containment unit.

Dorothy Armstrong was still complaining. "I don't understand why a software update can't be done remotely. I mean, does it really take three people?"

"It's very complicated machinery," Elsa said. "It'll take about an hour if it goes well. You don't have to stick around, if there's something you'd rather be doing."

"I'd rather be sleeping," Dorothy Armstrong said. "I'll be in my office, how's that?"

Elsa nodded. "Sounds good."

It was a relief when she left. Not that Elsa couldn't handle curiosity and questions, but the process went faster without distractions. She popped on her goggles and started scanning the AXB's memory. Thousands of images flickered by, naked or nearly so—the vacationing grandmothers and grandfathers of America, the harried moms and impatient husbands and frazzled business travelers, the teenagers who'd forgotten to unpack their MP3 players. The images captured pacemakers, artificial hips, metal pins in bones, and other surgical remnants. Sometimes she saw people who'd had transgender surgery. Or people wearing sex toys. The screening was more invasive than people knew, and always uncomfortable for Elsa.

The Class B image popped up. The passenger was a tall woman with nipple rings. Her body was shaded white against the black background. Elsa inverted the image. Black on white now, which highlighted the second image right behind her—a large, gray shape with two ominous wings, like a two-foot-wide bat.

"That's a biggie," Elsa said. She pulled off the goggles and toggled the view for Andrew and Christopher.

"Pretty girl," Christopher said.

Andrew glanced up while he screwed a transfer cable into the port under Elsa's right hand. "Sweet demon."

"Only you could call a soul-sucking destructive force of the universe 'sweet,'" Christopher complained.

Elsa glanced around. It was just the three of them, and no one could possibly be eavesdropping. But loose lips sank ships, or so her father liked to say.

Gleefully Andrew said, "You're violating your security clearance."

"Tell the mice in the wall," Christopher said. "How long's she been in there?"

"The demon is not a 'she,'" Elsa said. "Don't be sexist. Seventeen hours."

"Okay. Should be lulled into a nice sleep by now. Send her down."

The AXB hummed. The containment unit, which was the size of a large upright vacuum cleaner (and did a similar job, Elsa often thought), beeped as it began to work. The winged creature attached to the woman's image slowly began to fade. This was the best part of Elsa's job. Knowing that the technology that perplexed and aggravated so many travelers was, in fact, performing its job exceptionally well. Keeping the plane safe, and other passengers from infection, and preventing innocent people from who-knew-what disaster down the road.

The demon went into storage in just under twenty minutes. It took another fifteen for Elsa to match up the passenger record with a report for the Department of Homeland Security and file the necessary paperwork. It wasn't the woman's fault that she'd been a carrier, but her home environment would have to be scrutinized. Agents would break in during the day while she was at work and scan the place. Had to be done. Fifteen minutes after the report went in, Elsa and her team departed the terminal. Christopher and Andrew would take the containment unit to the nearest storage facility for indefinite safekeeping.

She thought about that sometimes: locked up forever, no chance of reprieve. Not exactly in keeping with the American justice system. But demons weren't Americans.

Tonight it was more satisfying to think about Lisa-Marie, and wonder if she was sleeping well, and imagine what she was sleeping in. Silk pajamas, maybe. Or a lacy gown, tight in all the right places. Maybe Lisa-Marie spent time that night thinking about her, too, because when Elsa woke, there was a note and e-mail address attached to the receipt under her door.

Elsa took the e-mail address with her to Boston, and then to Tampa, and then back up to Syracuse. But she didn't e-mail Lisa-Marie. Dinner had been nice, but she never expected to see her again.

❖

More complaints were voiced today about the TSA after a five-year-old girl was separated from her parents for a backscatter X-ray. This video shows the girl growing upset and crying while her parents voiced their objections. A TSA spokesman today said that all passengers, regardless of age and size, are required to comply with government regulations for national security.—WCVB, Boston

❖

Orlando was a tricky airport for extractions. International and delayed flights meant for a lot of late-night arrivals and departures at over one hundred and twenty gates. Even late at night, people were milling around—janitors, maintenance workers, security guards, stranded passengers in plastic chairs. This particular checkpoint still had two lanes open when Elsa's crew arrived. The conditions were not optimal. But the Class A had already been trapped for twenty-six hours, and the specs called for thirty hours tops, so here they were, Elsa and Christopher and Sam, who was a last-minute fill-in. Elsa didn't like Sam. He was cocky and rushed through jobs. She preferred Andrew, but he was stuck overnight in Houston with indigestion.

Their TSA contact was a short, stocky guy in rumpled white shirt, garish orange tie, and pants that needed to be hemmed. His name was Robert Henderson Clark and he talked a lot.

"These machines need more maintenance than my car, and that's saying a lot," he complained. "When taxpayers bitch about their money being wasted, I know what they mean. I should buy stock in the manufacturer. Or your company. You guys are the only ones who service them, right? Big monopoly?"

"I don't know much about the back-end," Elsa said vaguely.

Clark kept talking. "I hear that half of Congress owns stock in these machines. Easy for them, right? They all fly private jets and don't have to listen to the complaints I get."

"Hmm," Elsa said.

The image playback stopped at the scan of a woman Elsa's own size. The woman was wearing a clunky necklace and had a tampon inserted in her vagina. The Class A behind her had an extra-wide wingspan but what was extraordinary, really, was the fist-sized head with hooded ears. Elsa hardly ever saw heads on them.

She checked the size of the demon in the machine's storage bank and tried not to blanch. "Christopher, can you verify this?"

He sidled up to her while Clark continued his financial and investment speculations.

"That's a bigger allocation than usual," he said.

"Let me see," Sam said, bouncing over like an enthusiastic puppy. "Wow."

"Wow what?" Clark asked. "Is the machine really broken?"

"It's not broken," Elsa said, with a pointed look at Christopher.

"Let's take a look at your other AXB," he said, and steered the annoying man away.

Elsa double-checked the cables and triple-checked the storage unit, but Sam's work seemed okay. She initiated the transfer and watched as the demon slowly disappeared. She wondered what havoc it had wreaked in the tampon lady's life, or what it might have done if it had been left to board the plane. No one could officially say it, of course, but it was widely believed that the Brazilian jet that had recently gone down over the Atlantic had been a Class A. The sooner this demon was locked up, the better. At twenty-five percent the download began to slow. At forty percent, she realized that the creature was fighting the transfer.

"Sam, you're going to need power from the backup unit."

He was at her side instantly. "What? Nah. This one can handle it."

"If the download slows too much, we'll have a breach," she said.

Sam shook his head. "It won't. See, it's holding steady—"

The AXB began to shriek. Elsa tried an emergency abort, which should have sucked the demon right back up the pipeline into the backscatter machine. Instead, the storage unit jumped a foot into the air and emitted a spray of sparks. The terminal lights all flickered, and the warning sound turned into a whooping alarm.

"Oh, shit," said Christopher as he dashed back.

"That shouldn't have happened!" Sam protested.

Everyone was turning to stare at her. Elsa ignored them. Although normal vision was useless, she instinctively glanced upward. Where had it gone? Whirling over their heads, unseen and menacing? Racing down toward the gates to attach itself to a sleepy kid, a flight attendant, a pilot?

Damn it, they were going to have rescreen anybody who had passed through recently and was still at a gate.

And screen themselves.

And file a half dozen reports.

It was the first Class A she'd ever let escape.

She didn't get back to her hotel until nearly dawn. The front desk clerk let her extend her reservation. Elsa crashed hard on her pillows, waking near noon to a series of upset voicemails from her bosses in Philadelphia. Leftover pizza in the mini-fridge sufficed for lunch. After three conference calls and two aspirin, she changed into her bathing suit and went down to the outdoor pool. The weather was sunny and warm, and six or seven other guests were also swimming. Elsa ignored them. She wasn't in the mood to talk to anyone.

A friendly voice said, "Hey! It's Elsa Lancaster."

Elsa turned in surprise. Lisa-Marie was stretched out on a beige lounge chair. She was wearing the same green bikini she'd been wearing in Columbus four months ago and looked just as fabulously pretty. She lifted up her big brown sunglasses and gave Elsa a grin.

"Small world," Lisa-Marie said.

Elsa felt off balance. In both a good way, because the day suddenly seemed a lot less crappy, but in a suspicious way as well, because how small was the world, really?

"What brings you here?" Elsa asked cautiously.

Lisa-Marie waved her right hand toward the horizon. "Mom and Dad had a hankering for Disney World. I thought I booked us into a hotel over in Kissimmee, but I guess I clicked the wrong button. At least there's a shuttle bus. I had to leave them there, or one more trip through It's a Small World would have made me commit hari-kari."

Elsa relaxed. "I don't do theme parks."

"Smart woman," Lisa-Marie replied. "So what do you do when you have a day off in Orlando?"

"What makes you think I have a day off?" Elsa asked.

"Because check-out was hours ago, and you're in the pool, and you said you don't do theme parks." Lisa-Marie leaned forward, filling out her bikini top even more. Suntan lotion glistened on her skin. "Don't you want to spend a few hours playing tourist with me?"

Elsa had nothing to do until the Class A showed up again at the airport or she got her next assignment. She had the feeling that Philadelphia would punish her a little for this, maybe keep her cooling her heels for another day or two.

"I'd love to play with you," she replied.

They lounged by the pool, went for ice cream at Downtown Disney, and then walked around the lake and shops there while canned music played in the perfectly trimmed flowerbeds. Every now and then Lisa-Marie's parents called from the Magic Kingdom with updates on how much fun they'd just had in the Haunted Mansion or Pirates of the Caribbean ride, and Lisa-Marie would roll her eyes and grin. Elsa's own folks never left suburban Chicago. Certainly they wouldn't be walking around a theme park all day.

"They probably rented electric wheelchairs," Lisa-Marie mused. "Last time, Dad slammed right into a Mickey Mouse who was signing autographs."

They had a seafood dinner at a restaurant built to look like a steamboat, and afterward drank hot chocolate at a small table in the Godiva shop. Shoppers streamed in and out of the Disney Store next door. Elsa was feeling a bit like Snow White herself. She'd immensely enjoyed the day, and the way Lisa-Marie smiled at her, and her sense of humor about just about everything. But it couldn't last. Like horses turning back into pumpkins, Elsa had to return to her normal life.

Knowledge of that couldn't keep her from wanting to lean across the table and kiss Lisa-Marie. Just once for memory's sake, to see if those lips tasted as sweet as they looked.

They talked and talked and talked. Once their cups were empty Lisa-Marie said, "Be right back," and dashed off to the bathroom. Her phone buzzed as soon as she was out of sight. Elsa thought Lisa-Marie's parents would worry if she didn't pick up, so she scooped up the smartphone. But there was no call. Instead, it was a message and her own name was the subject line. That was odd. After further investigation she realized her name was attached to several messages, and documents were attached as well.

Her hotel itinerary for here in Orlando.

Her hotel itinerary for her last job, back in Atlanta.

Her hotel itinerary for the job before that, in Roanoke.

Shivers went down her back and left her feeling ice cold. Quickly Elsa dropped the phone, left the shop, and walked toward the nearest exit. She felt like she was thinking perfectly clearly, but also like she was moving through unseen bales of thick cotton. Dimly she heard Lisa-Marie calling after her.

"Elsa, wait!" Lisa-Marie was calling out. "I can explain!"

A long line of yellow cabs was idling in the parking lot. Elsa slid into the backseat of the first one and muttered her hotel's name. The driver, an elderly man with a shiny bald head, was pulling out when the other passenger door opened and Lisa-Marie climbed in.

"Hey!" protested the driver.

Elsa ordered, "Get out."

"I can explain," Lisa-Marie said breathlessly. "Everything. I'm not some stalker following you around the country."

"That's exactly what you are," Elsa retorted.

The driver was eyeing both of them in the rearview mirror. "Keep going?"

"No," Elsa said.

"Yes," Lisa-Marie told him. "Elsa, I know you're upset. But it's not what you think—"

"That you have my hotel reservations on your phone?" Elsa said, glaring at her. "That today wasn't a coincidence? That your parents probably aren't even at the park, are they? Who's been calling you?"

Lisa-Marie grimaced. "My secretary."

The cabbie turned, but the Cirque de Soleil show was letting out and the lane was jammed with cabs and vans. Exasperated, Elsa reached for her door handle.

Quickly Lisa-Marie said, "I'm a lawyer working on a class action suit against the Department of Homeland Security and their routine violation of American civil rights, especially electronic privacy issues and unreasonable searches. Your company is the only one that services backscatter machines and we need technical information. My firm asked me to contact you, to see if you could help us."

"Help you?" Elsa demanded. Anger boiled up in her head and heart. "Why? Do I look like someone who wants to be unemployed? I have a security clearance—"

Too late she shut her mouth.

Lisa-Marie asked, "Why does a technician need a security clearance? Why is it that the TSA went ahead and implemented this technology, as unproven and dangerous as it might be? At first we thought, backroom politics. Pork spending. Everyone knows that a real terrorist these days wouldn't go through security—there's a half dozen easier ways, from the food service people to the plane cleaners. So there's got to be some other reason for all this security theater, all this ridiculous pretense we can prepare for everything. Some reason why millions of passengers a year have to take off their shoes, why little kids get frisked, and why the TSA constantly lies about what the technology is or does. And you know what it is, don't you?"

"I don't know anything," Elsa said, squeezing the bridge of her nose. "Other than the fact that you lied to me and tricked me and made me think—well, that doesn't matter, because it wasn't true."

Lisa-Marie touched Elsa's leg. The expression on her face was almost as distraught as Elsa felt. "It was true. I'm not that good an actress. As much as I care about my job, I care about you, too. Do you know that they're starting to identify possible cancer clusters around TSA agents? Tell me you wear a dosimeter to measure radiation."

"I'm not worried about radiation," Elsa retorted. "I'm worried about lawyers who try to use me so they can win some frivolous lawsuit!"

"It's not frivolous!" Lisa-Marie insisted. "Backscatter and other screening machines could pose more dangers to the American public than we've ever seen before. I was supposed to ask you about your job, but I couldn't. I didn't want to ruin what we've got started here. Tell me you don't feel the same way."

The taxi inched forward. They were still stuck in the damned parking lot, and might be for an hour. The cabbie was watching them in the rearview mirror with unabashed interest. Elsa glared at him until he dropped his gaze and started fiddling with his meter.

"I don't feel anything," Elsa said. "How could I?"

She tossed a ten-dollar bill over the divider and slid out of the cab. Lisa-Marie followed, but it was easy to lose her in the crowd pouring from the theater. Elsa kept moving and kept her gaze down. She seemed surrounded by lovers walking hand in hand, laughing and kissing, all these happy people, while she suffered the hollow, queasy feeling of being humiliated.

When her phone rang with a text message she nearly threw it in the lake, but the number was Christopher's. The Class A had been caught again at the Orlando airport. Where should he pick her up?

Elsa squared her shoulders, wiped her face dry, and went back to work.

❖

A Freedom of Information lawsuit filed today against the Department of Homeland Transportation alleges that images of thousands of people entering federal courthouse have been saved and stored without consent or awareness. The backscatter technology involved is the same used in airport screening lanes. A separate lawsuit alleges that the zones around these machines can expose the population to radiation that exceeds the "general public dose limit."—WJCT, Jacksonville

❖

Norfolk. Hartford. Manchester. Albany. Elsa figured that Lisa-Marie had tracked her so easily because she preferred one particular hotel chain, so she started mixing up her choices. She kept away from any that had swimming pools. Her back started to ache from so many hours in airplane seats, and her clothes began to get depressingly tight, so she doubled the workouts she did in her room. In Boston she tripped over an ottoman while doing lunges and had to use crutches for three days.

Elsa knew that she was supposed to have reported Lisa-Marie to DHS but she didn't really want to call down that kind of scrutiny on her. Once the government started keeping files, it kept on collecting information and invading privacy. Better to just forget the whole thing. Elsa didn't answer e-mails or calls from people she didn't know, she ate alone in her room each night, and she went to bed resolutely not thinking about long dark hair, a heart-shaped face, and lovely dimples.

The last part would have been easier if she didn't turn on the news one night to see Lisa-Marie on TV, being interviewed about electronic privacy. She looked smart and professional in a black business suit, her eyes hidden behind glasses. Like Superman masquerading as Clark Kent, Elsa thought uncomfortably. Fighting for what seemed like civil rights, but only because she didn't know what danger America really was in.

"More people need to realize what information is being collected against their will," Lisa-Marie was saying. "More people with knowledge about these machines need to speak up."

Elsa turned off the TV.

An AXB machine in Newark alerted with a Class A. Christopher picked her up at a Holiday Inn parking lot with a new technician named Alice. "Andrew's out on disability," Christopher said tightly when Elsa asked about him.

"What for?" Elsa asked.

Christopher turned the van toward the terminal. "Stomach cancer."

"It's not job-related," Elsa said, though she wasn't sure if she was asking a question or not.

Christopher said, "Probably not."

"We're not exposed to enough," Elsa insisted. "You know the specs."

"I know what they tell us," he replied.

Alice popped her head up from the backseat of the van. She was short and dark-haired, with a pixie cut and purple eye shadow. "Are we there yet? This is my first big one."

Elsa sat back in her seat. Christopher said nothing.

The B1 security checkpoint was closed by the time they arrived.

Their TSA contact was a big ex-football player named Tyrone Graham who sat in a plastic chair, arms folded, and glared at them for making him work overtime. Elsa ignored him. She had a hard time locating the Class A image. She realized that someone on the local staff had been moving around images in direct violation of protocol—storing groups of them in a local folder instead of keeping everything in one place.

She opened a sub-folder. Over a hundred images had been saved there. Women, all of them, their faces blurred but their curvy bodies in clear view. Another folder had children, all of them standing with their arms raised over their heads in the same way as the adults.

"Ew," Alice said. "Someone's a creep, huh? I thought users weren't supposed to set up their little peepshows."

"They're not supposed to." Elsa angrily deleted the folders. She would report the incident, but didn't know if anything would come of it. Philadelphia was good at collecting information and not very good at passing it down. Meanwhile, whoever had been collecting images would just start all over again, with plenty of material passing by every day.

She tried to focus on the task in front of her. When the Class A image popped up, it was attached to the image of an overweight man with a prosthetic knee. Like that long-ago one in Columbus, this demon had a head perched above the spread-open wings. The head was round and small, tilted slightly as if quizzically looking at the scanner. Some kind of circle hung around it, like a ring around Saturn.

"What is that?" Christopher asked curiously.

"I don't know," Elsa said. Her heart thumped faster in her chest and her palms turned sweaty.

Alice snapped her chewing gum. "Looks like a halo. Pretty funny."

Elsa met Christopher's gaze. If you believed in demons, then why not their opposites? For a moment he looked like he wanted to say something, but then his gaze slid across the empty security lanes to their TSA guy.

"Let's do it and get out of here," he said.

Elsa couldn't help herself. "What if some of them are protecting people, not hurting them? What if everything we've been told is wrong?"

"It's not," Christopher said tightly. "It's not, because then you would lose your job. Do you understand me? You would lose your job and your income, and anything more would violate your security clearance, and how do you feel about a home visit from federal agents with guns? Because I, myself, would not like that at all."

Alice snapped her chewing gum again.

Elsa's fingers trembled as she started the download. She watched the creature slowly fade down the pipeline, its head tilted thoughtfully, its halo and wings disappearing into nothingness.

Later that night, Elsa herself disappeared.

❖

"I didn't know," she said, standing in the drenching rain outside of Lisa-Marie's front door. "I didn't know any of it."

Lisa-Marie was dressed only in a white bathrobe. It was just after dawn. Her hair was messy and her face creased from the pillow. "You're soaked. Come in."

Elsa shook her head. She didn't deserve to be warm and dry yet. "I want to help find out what's really going on. I want people to know the truth and what the government is doing. But I don't know how, and I don't know who to trust. What do you do when you don't even know if you're standing on solid ground anymore?"

Thunder rolled in the sky over their heads. The rain came down harder, but Elsa was beyond feeling cold.

"You come to someone who cares about you." Lisa-Marie stepped out into the rain with her arms open and Elsa buried her head against her shoulder. "You come to me, and we'll find out the truth together."

FULL MOON WEEKEND
MEGHAN O'BRIEN

A re we there yet?"

Dr. Eve Thomas chuckled. This close to the full moon, it was a wonder Selene hadn't asked three hours ago. Being trapped in a car was never easy for her shape-shifting girlfriend, but it seemed especially difficult around Selene's time of the month. A little over forty-eight hours out, the moon was already starting to turn Selene wild—she squirmed in her seat, radiating a curious mixture of desire and nervous energy.

Eve raised an eyebrow. "Are you asking because you want to know where I'm taking you, or because you're horny?"

"Both." Selene fidgeted and Eve caught a hint of a grimace in her peripheral vision. "I also have to pee."

"Think you can hold it fifteen minutes?"

"Yes." Selene folded her arms over her chest, clearly satisfied. "So we *are* close." Her amusement faded quickly, drawing Eve's attention away from the road.

"What else is wrong?" Eve asked.

Selene radiated grim resignation as she gazed out at the passing redwood trees. "We're in the middle of nowhere, darling, and you're so nervous it makes my stomach hurt. You've been on edge for the past week. Please tell me what's going on?"

Eve exhaled. Hiding things from Selene was impossible. With their empathetic bond, Selene would have known Eve was keeping a secret almost immediately, and yet she hadn't asked, though she'd obviously wanted to. Eve had expected to have this conversation days ago and had been rehearsing what to say for weeks.

Humbled, Eve opted for total honesty. "I wanted us to go away for the weekend. I know you don't like being far from home during the full moon, but I think it's time we change up your routine."

"My routine exists for a reason—"

"A reason we debunked as unfounded two months ago when you—as the wolf—saved my life." Eve chanced a sidelong glance at Selene, watching her react to the words. "I'm not going to lash you to that steel table anymore. I know you're worried that night was a fluke, which is why I agreed to follow your routine last month. But you're not dangerous. You're *not* a monster, and I won't treat you like one anymore."

Worry, fear, and mild relief emanated from Selene's tense frame, a complex tangle of emotions. "I know I didn't hurt you that night, but—"

"No buts." Eve kept her tone firm, trying not to dwell on her memories of *that night*. The first time she'd witnessed Selene's lunar transformation had been during a life-or-death struggle with a crazed killer. Wolf-Selene had saved her life, belying her lover's lifelong fear that the moon reduced her to a bloodthirsty, remorseless killer. Eve had imagined that the news that wolf-Selene was nothing more than a giant, fiercely loyal puppy would liberate Selene from her monthly ritual. Yet Selene still seemed too frightened to accept that she wasn't the monster she'd always feared. "This weekend is about unshackling you, literally and figuratively. I love you—everything about you. Even the wolf. More importantly, I trust you. So no more restraints. Okay?"

Selene's palpable fear hung over them like a dense fog, making it hard to breathe. Eve rested a calming hand on her tense thigh.

"If I ever hurt you…" Selene's voice caught. Her face tightened with her obvious effort not to cry. "I wouldn't forgive myself."

"You won't hurt me." Calling up a little of her own ferocity, Eve launched into her familiar, passionate defense of Selene's nature. "You *have* to trust me, sweetheart. I met the wolf. I know her. She won't hurt me."

Because Selene viewed her full-moon incarnation as entirely distinct from her human self, Eve talked about her that way, too. But she knew better than to believe that Selene was not the wolf and the wolf was not Selene—they were one and the same, and both very much devoted to Eve.

Selene sighed. "You know it's not you I don't trust."

"I know. Let me prove you wrong. Please." Eve perked up at the sight of their turn-off up ahead. "I rented the most remote cabin I could find. We're miles away from the nearest neighbor, next to a gorgeous river. I say we spend the entire weekend naked, fucking and cuddling and swimming and just having a good time. We'll have complete privacy. When the full moon comes, we'll spend the night indoors. I brought a romance novel I've been dying to read. I'm sure you'll be content warming my feet."

Eve drove into a long driveway so hidden she doubted that anyone who wasn't looking for it would find it. Selene was silent as they went deeper into the redwood forest, and for a moment, Eve worried that she'd crossed a line.

"I'm not upset with you," Selene said. "I'm just scared."

"I know. Don't be."

Selene barked a humorless laugh. "I wish it were that easy."

"It can be." In the distance she spotted their cabin, and beyond it, the river that had attracted her to this location. This late in the summer, she craved a refreshing break from the warm weather. Excited despite Selene's unease, Eve parked next to the cabin, then cut the engine. She turned to Selene and smiled. "I promise we'll have fun."

Selene's vivid green eyes were full of doubt. "The fucking and cuddling part *does* sound fun. I'm just not sure about the rest."

Eve unbuckled her seat belt and leaned over the console and kissed Selene, the deep, soulful kiss rapidly becoming so intense she nearly orgasmed. When she pulled away, she cradled Selene's face between her hands. "I brought you to the middle of nowhere so you can be your true self…with me. I want you to be *you* this weekend. I want to see all the amazing things you can do—things *nobody* else can do—because that's such a big part of who you are. It's part of the woman I love. And I desperately want to know everything about that woman."

"You do know me." Hurt colored Selene's whisper. "You can literally *feel* everything I feel. You know me better than anyone ever has, or ever will."

"Baby, I don't think you even really know yourself." Stroking Selene's cheek with the back of her hand, Eve gentled her voice. "You've never felt safe enough to explore who you are. But this weekend, with me, you're safe. Even when you're not in control, you'll be safe. I'll be here with you."

Selene closed her eyes, allowing twin tears to escape. "Promise?"
"Promise."

❖

Despite being shaken by Eve's surprise, Selene's mood lifted at the discovery of an absolutely massive king-sized bed in the cabin's master bedroom. She sat down, bouncing on the mattress with a contented sigh. So close to the full moon, this was a welcome sight. Attempting a seductive tone, Selene called out, "Eve, why don't you come in here so we can start the weekend right?"

Silence met her not-so-subtle suggestion. Perturbed, Selene closed her eyes and attuned her senses to her surroundings. As a human, she had only a fraction of the tracking and hearing ability that she could attain in other forms. But she scarcely needed those things to find Eve. Their minds and bodies had always been eerily in synch.

Sensing that Eve had wandered outside, Selene walked downstairs and out the back door. The smell of redwoods hit her first, then the clean scent of the flowing river only thirty yards away. As much as she wanted to be angry with Eve for taking her away from the security of home on a full moon weekend, she couldn't.

This place was perfect.

Eve turned around, hugging a backpack to her chest. "Happy?"

"I love it here," Selene admitted. She closed the distance between them and kissed Eve's nose. "You haven't even seen the bed yet."

Grinning, Eve backed away from the embrace she surely felt coming, then withdrew a rolled blanket from her pack. She spread it on the ground in front of them before nonchalantly tugging her T-shirt over her head. Selene gaped at the ease with which Eve displayed her lacy black bra.

"I told you, we're alone." Eve unhooked her bra and tossed it aside. "Let's go swimming."

Selene swallowed at the sight of Eve's bare breasts. Two months after surviving a brutal attack, Eve's body had healed. The only physical scar that remained was a thin slice along her cheek. Regaining equilibrium in a drastically changed life—one that included a supernatural girlfriend—had been more challenging. Yet at that moment, baring her body without hesitation, Eve glowed with a new, radiant energy.

"You're gorgeous." Selene dragged her gaze down the center of Eve's belly, eager for every inch of bare flesh. When Eve pushed her jeans to her ankles, Selene nearly pounced as the fragrant scent of desire mingled with the heady smell of the outdoors. "Let's swim later—and make love now. Here on the blanket or inside on that bed. Your choice."

Eve's eyes sparkled. "*My* choice is to swim now, make love later. Unless you honestly can't wait."

Selene would never take advantage of Eve's willingness to satisfy her uncontrolled full-moon cravings. "I can wait." Hearing the pout in her voice, she added, "I can't promise I won't be just a little impatient."

Eve slipped off her panties, now gloriously nude. "Swimming will be fun. Besides, a little anticipation always makes sex better."

Selene couldn't deny that. She quickly shed her clothing and followed Eve to the edge of the river, then laughed as Eve dipped a toe into the water and yelped. "Cold?"

"Refreshing."

"I see." Selene submerged her entire foot. It was cool, but not enough to provoke a reaction. "I don't think I'm as temperature-sensitive as you are."

"Just one more super-awesome thing about being Selene Rhodes." Taking a deep breath, Eve walked into the water until it reached her calves. "Yikes!"

Bolstered by Eve's words, Selene decided to show off. She charged into the water, diving beneath the surface and swimming a short distance away. Coming up sputtering, she laughed at Eve's incredulous expression. "Definitely not as temperature-sensitive."

"Now you're just rubbing it in."

"Come here." Selene held out her arms. "I promise to warm you up."

"I don't doubt it." Eve hissed as she took slow, torturous steps deeper into the river. "Seriously? You don't feel how cold this is?"

"Right now cold is the last thing I feel." Selene didn't bother hiding her blatant appraisal of Eve's pink nipples, which had pebbled and hardened as though begging to be sucked. Eve shivered, then slipped beneath the water to swim the short distance between them.

When she surfaced, Eve leapt into Selene's waiting embrace. "I appreciate the very *hot* thoughts you just had. Not sure I could've taken that little dip without them."

Selene kissed Eve's shoulder. "You felt that?"

"Of course." Eve tilted her hips, pressing their lower bodies together. "I feel *everything* with you."

Selene shivered, and not from the water. "You're doing a poor job of keeping my mind off sex."

"Sorry." Cuddling closer, Eve looped her arms around Selene's neck and made eye contact. "So what does it feel like to swim as an aquatic animal?"

"I'm not sure."

"Seriously?" Eve seemed genuinely surprised. "You've never tried?"

"No." Selene shrugged, holding Eve tightly against her chest. "Haven't really had the opportunity—it's not often that I can swim in complete privacy."

"Well..." Eve backed out of Selene's embrace, gesturing around them. "You can now."

Eve had already seen her shift a few times, but the prospect still flooded Selene with shyness. "I don't know..."

"Show me." Eve traced her finger down the length of Selene's arm. "Please."

Embarrassed, Selene said, "What do you want me to be?"

Eve's face softened. "Sweetheart, I don't want to force you. If you're not comfortable—"

"I'm comfortable." Selene started to say more, then stopped. Unable to explain how she was feeling, she allowed Eve to experience her conflicted emotions instead. Eve stood quietly, as though listening, then nodded.

"There's no reason to be shy. I'm not going to judge you, I won't freak out, and I definitely, *definitely* will not love you any less." Eyes shining, Eve said, "Honestly, Selene, don't you believe in us yet?"

She did. She believed Eve loved and accepted her, wholeheartedly. But years of shame weren't so easy to overcome.

Eve inhaled. "Oh, so that's it." She caressed Selene's arm. "You saved my life, more than once, because of what you are. Embrace it. Own it. To hell with what anyone has said—or made you feel—in the past."

Knowing Eve was right, Selene closed her eyes, recalled a recent article in *National Geographic*, and swiftly became a pink Amazonian river dolphin. Instinctively she sucked in a large breath through the blowhole on top of her head, then dove beneath the water and tested her fins against the river's gentle current. The sound of Eve's delighted laughter above the surface bolstered her enthusiasm, inspiring her to swim quick circles around her lover.

"That's brilliant, Selene."

Eve's unabashed joy coaxed Selene to the surface. Rolling onto her back, she flapped her tail fin in Eve's direction, as though waving. Thrilled by the giggles that move elicited, Selene surged beneath the water once more. After building up speed, she launched herself into the air, executing a flip that probably looked even clumsier than it felt. Deciding that practice makes perfect, she tried another flip, this one flawless.

Eve cheered as Selene leapt from the water one last time, reverted to human form at the apex of her leap, then splashed noisily upon reentry. She paddled over to Eve beaming so hard her face ached.

"Pretty good?" Eve clearly knew the answer.

"Pretty fucking awesome."

"I figured." Taking slow, deliberate steps, Eve approached Selene with a predatory glint in her eyes. "Want to check out that bed now?"

❖

They didn't actually make it inside until hours later, after the sun sank in the sky and the evening breeze raised gooseflesh on Eve's naked skin. Though they had been making love for hours, red-hot passion eventually gave way to lazy touching and murmured conversation.

"Let's skip dinner and go to bed," Eve said. She'd barely crossed the threshold when Selene picked her up and hoisted her over her shoulder. Laughing, Eve reached out to slap Selene's bare bottom moments before being tossed onto the mattress. Eve came up on her elbows, warmth blooming in her chest as Selene settled in at her side.

"I love you," Eve murmured.

Selene's hand fluttered to her chest. "I feel it." She rested her other hand on the slope of Eve's breast. "Do you feel how much I love you?"

The rush of Selene's adoration threatened to sweep Eve away completely. "Oh, yes."

Selene dipped her fingers into the valley between Eve's breasts. The soft touch curled Eve's toes in pleasure. Selene smirked.

"You look pretty pleased with yourself." Eve edged closer. "Feeling better about this weekend?"

Selene's mirth faded. "Sure. A little."

"You know you can't fool me, right?"

Selene snorted. "Tell me about it."

"Don't worry about the moon." Eve nipped at Selene's clavicle. "You were magnificent earlier, in the water. So beautiful." Mild disbelief rippled through Selene, making Eve frown. "I could've watched you forever."

Selene shook her head, but a ghost of a smile played across her lips. "I still can't get over the fact that you're okay with…everything."

"Okay with it? It's wonderful." Remembering how it felt to watch Selene, graceful and shimmering beneath the water, Eve sighed. "I'd give anything to spend even five minutes with your ability. The hard part would be deciding what to try first. To experience life from so many perspectives would be a dream come true. You're blessed, sweetheart, and I could just pinch you for not seeing that."

Selene projected a jumble of emotion—shame, embarrassment, and sheepish realization. Eve's goal for the weekend was to help Selene look at her ability in a new way. She sensed they were on the right track.

"I've been foolish, haven't I? Treating this like a curse?" Selene stared at the ceiling, tracing circles around Eve's navel with her fingertip. Melancholy shimmered from her to Eve. "Before the moon started changing me, I loved shifting. All it took was that first transformation to convince me I was a monster." She swallowed audibly. "I never even doubted it before I met you."

Eve met Selene's eyes. "How could something that allowed you to save my life twice be a curse?"

"It couldn't."

"You're a superhero, Selene." Eve kissed Selene's top lip, then the bottom. "Deal with it."

Selene kissed her harder, sliding her hand between Eve's thighs and stroking gently. She slipped inside Eve's folds with deft fingers, skimming across swollen, oversensitive flesh that had already been the source of so much mutual pleasure over the course of the day. Three months in, Eve was still astonished by their sexual connection. Having never been multiorgasmic before, she now regularly lost track of how many times she climaxed in a given day. Eve let her legs fall open and surrendered to the exquisite sensation of their otherworldly intimacy.

Selene broke away to breathe. Her hand never faltered, rubbing slow circles over Eve's labia, around her clit, before venturing lower to tease her opening. "I'm going to make us come again."

Eve grinned. There was something delicious about knowing that her orgasm would trigger one in her lover. She cupped Selene's breast, rubbing her nipple lightly. The stimulation would intensify their mutual pleasure, and quite frankly, she found it difficult not to touch Selene.

"Watch," Selene whispered in her ear. Eve gazed down at the sight of Selene's slim, feminine hand working between her thighs. She shivered, then giggled when Selene trembled in sympathy. "You are so sexy."

Selene pushed a single finger inside, both of them groaning at the snug fit. "And I am one lucky dog. Literally."

Eve's laughter turned into a breathy moan. "Don't stop."

"I won't," Selene said. She didn't.

The next morning, Eve woke to an empty bed. She immediately forced her sleep-fogged mind to the task of finding Selene. Though she didn't understand how their connection worked, she trusted it. Their bond allowed her to feel Selene's mood even at a distance, and worked almost like a magnet, pulling Eve to her at all times.

Dressing quickly, Eve went downstairs, then out the back door. She folded her arms over her chest and scanned the surrounding redwoods. Selene was close, but Eve didn't see her. She walked toward the river, then stopped when a good-sized turtle with yellow spots on its head climbed on shore. Her heart raced when the turtle morphed swiftly upward, revealing Selene in all her naked glory.

"The strange thing about being a turtle," Selene said conversationally, "is the breathing. Took me a minute to get used to that."

Eve loved turtles and happened to know a bit about their physiology. "Buccal pumping. Turtles pull air into their mouths, then push it into the lungs via oscillations of the throat floor. They also contract the abdominal muscles that cover the posterior opening of the shell to draw air into their lungs. Similar to the mammalian diaphragm." Noticing Selene's amusement, Eve corralled her inner geek. "Fascinating creatures."

"Complicated, sounds like." Selene stopped in front of her, lush and gorgeous in the morning light. "I don't like losing control. Probably never will. But you're right. If I don't embrace the good with the bad, I'll always be miserable."

"And we don't want that."

"No, we don't." Selene stepped closer, tracing her finger over Eve's chest. "Honestly, knowing that you love this about me makes it a whole lot easier to love myself."

"Good." Eve shivered beneath her touch.

Selene stepped away, leaving Eve cold with her absence. Seconds later, Selene returned and offered Eve the backpack that had been sitting on the riverbank. "Put this on."

Eve obeyed. She had no idea what Selene had planned, but she was breathless in anticipation. When Selene shifted into a large black horse with a long, wavy mane and tail, Eve gasped.

She was gorgeous—and intimidating.

Selene ambled closer and lowered her massive body until she rested on her belly. When Eve didn't react, she whinnied, tossing her head back and forth playfully.

Startled, Eve said, "You want me to ride you?" Selene neighed this time. "I'm actually a little…cautious about horses."

Selene literally rolled her eyes.

"Okay, now that's just fucked up." Chewing her bottom lip, Eve took a tentative step forward and petted Selene's mane. "This is the perfect opportunity to get more comfortable with horses, right? After all, I'm pretty sure you won't throw me or turn around to bite my ankle."

Selene tossed her head again.

Aware that Selene was trying to offer her a gift, Eve pushed aside her anxiety about riding such a large animal. This was Selene, after all.

"Okay," Eve whispered. Gathering her courage, she grasped a handful of mane and climbed onto Selene's back. Selene stood slowly, rising to her full height with conscious grace. "Okay." Eve tightened her grip when Selene took a few confident steps forward. "I can do this."

She didn't have to hear Selene speak to know what she would say: *We can do this.*

Selene had never had a rider. Hell, she'd never ever been a horse. So she was surprised how natural it felt, how comfortable. Even slightly arousing, carrying the woman she loved on her back and giving her access to an animal she had never been comfortable around. Eve nearly vibrated atop her, expelling bursts of innocent joy as she exclaimed over the beauty of the surrounding redwoods, one hand fisted in Selene's mane.

So much had changed since Eve entered her life. Loving, and being loved, made her a different person. One who simply couldn't hate herself the way she once had. Selene had no idea how to repay Eve for the gift of growing self-acceptance, but she planned to spend the rest of her life trying.

Eve rubbed a hand along Selene's neck. "Thank you, Selene. This is a moment I'll remember for the rest of my life."

The sincerity of Eve's hushed whisper sent shivers racing down Selene's spine, making her skin jump and twitch. She slowed for a step, overcome by the intensity of their emotional connection. Only a day away from the full moon, her senses were heightened. So was her physical need for Eve. She had no idea how to contend with the flood of almost crippling want that coursed through her veins, so she simply stopped and stood still.

"Why don't you let me dismount?" Once again, Eve was on her wavelength.

Selene knelt, taking care not to jostle Eve too badly. Her control was always tenuous during this stage of the lunar cycle, so she wanted to be extra careful with her precious cargo. Eve slid off and backed away a couple of steps.

Selene reverted to human form, enjoying the rush of shifting in a whole new way. Primal energy throbbed between her thighs. What had been desire exploded into need. It took every bit of Selene's willpower not to rush to Eve and claim her body. Eve had never complained before, but Selene didn't want to be too aggressive.

Eve removed her shirt, tossing it onto the dirt. Selene drank in the rise and fall of her heaving chest, her flushed skin. Eve beckoned her forward. "Come here."

Selene's feet moved automatically. She took Eve by the elbows and pulled her into a passionate but restrained kiss. Eve gripped her biceps and squeezed hard, holding nothing back. The fire in Eve ignited an answering flame in Selene, rendering her powerless against the crippling need to take Eve hard and fast.

Wholly in synch, Eve tore her mouth away and said, "Did you bring a blanket?"

Selene grunted, scrabbling at the backpack's zipper like a clumsy teenager. Giggling, Eve took over, quickly extracting and laying out their blanket. Then she grabbed Selene's arm and pulled her down onto the ground, where they came together with open mouths, dueling tongues, and roaming hands.

Eve rolled them over so she was on top, pinning Selene's wrists above her head. Then her hand was between Selene's thighs and she entered her roughly, in one sharp thrust. The intrusion stole Selene's breath and sent toe-curling pleasure rocketing through her body. Satisfaction glimmered in Eve's eyes.

"You like it rough?" Eve rasped, thrusting into her again, deeper.

Selene nodded. Eve had stolen her ability to speak.

"Good." Eve grabbed Selene's hand and guided it down the front of her pants. "So do I."

❖

Not long after, they lay on their backs and panted up at the trees, bodies slick and sore from their frenzied lovemaking. Sated, Selene turned her head and regarded Eve warmly. There were so many things she wanted to tell her, but words seemed inadequate. Luckily, she didn't need to say something for Eve to know it.

Eve grabbed her hand and squeezed. "I'll remember this, too."

Selene finally found her voice. "So will I."

"Do you think there are others like you?"

The question startled Selene. It came from out of nowhere, stirring emotions she hadn't felt in a long time. "I don't know."

"You must wonder."

"I used to wonder all the time. After a while it seemed easier not to hope. I've never seen any evidence of others. Then again, I don't make myself known to others. So perhaps there are more, hidden like me."

Eve looked thoughtful. "Seems likely that at least one of your birth parents was a shifter."

Thinking about that made Selene's chest ache, which was why she didn't dwell on those thoughts anymore. "I know. Can we not talk about this now?"

"Okay."

Selene waited, hoping that Eve would really drop the subject. When Eve simply stared at her, then smiled, Selene relaxed. Without thinking, she said, "I used to feel totally alone in the world. Yes, there may be others like me, but I'm not sure whether I'll ever know for sure. Luckily, I can live with that—because I'm not alone anymore."

Eve leaned in for a kiss. "Neither am I." When she pulled back, her inquisitive expression made it clear that she wasn't done asking questions. "Is there anything you can't become?"

Selene laughed. Now that she'd had some practice, she enjoyed talking to Eve about her ability. The visceral thrill of being able to share it with someone surpassed even her wildest expectations. "I haven't found anything yet, but then again, I haven't done a ton of experimenting."

Eve's face lit up. "Do you think you could become an extinct animal? Like a dinosaur?"

What an interesting idea. Curious, Selene sat up, scooted well away from Eve, then closed her eyes. This one took a bit more concentration than normal, as she scanned her memory for a suitable test case. It came to her in a flash. Pteranodon. Eve would go crazy for that.

Body tingling, Selene recognized that she was already shifting, instinct taking over. She opened her eyes to see Eve staring slack-jawed from across the blanket. Selene followed Eve's gaze down to stare at her body, then stretched out her wings, marveling at their leathery span.

"Holy shit," Eve whispered. Her hands trembled. She crawled across the blanket, stopping when she came within reach. "May I touch you?"

Selene cocked her head, hoping that Eve understood. *Always.*

Eve traced her fingertips over one wing, then the other. Then her hands were everywhere, examining Selene with boundless enthusiasm: the crest on her head, her beak, her limbs. After a breathless exam, Eve said, "Will you fly? Not too high…we don't want anyone to see. Stay under the canopy of the forest." She fingered one of Selene's wings. "I just want to know…"

Selene took a step back, then vaulted herself into the air, raising her wings as soon as she cleared the ground, then bringing them down to complete her launch. She hovered in the air for a moment before ascending to just below the treetops. Then she flew circles over Eve's head, thrilled by the sight of her naked lover watching in awe.

Selene swooped down and landed beside Eve, then reverted to human form. She grinned when Eve burst into wild applause. "You're easily impressed."

"Easily impressed!" Eve gave her a playful shove. "That was the single most incredible thing I've ever seen. Probably that *anyone's* ever seen!"

"It felt pretty amazing, too."

"Of course it did." Eve shook her head. "I'm not sure you'll ever top that one."

Surprised by the tingle of anticipation that crawled up her spine at Eve's casual comment, Selene said, "I'll consider that a challenge."

"Can you become another person?"

A chill ran through Selene's body. "I don't know. I've never tried."

"Do you want to?"

She didn't even have to think about it. "Not unless there was a *very* good reason. It doesn't…feel right. I don't like that idea." Her stomach twisted into a tight, painful knot. "No."

Eve nodded. "It wouldn't be cooler than a pteranodon, anyway."

Pleased that Eve wasn't going to push, Selene wrapped an arm around her shoulders and pulled her closer. "No, it wouldn't."

❖

After two days of playful exploration and lovemaking, the evening of the full moon arrived. Over the past two months, they'd established a routine for the hours leading up to Selene's transformation. Up until about an hour before sunset, they fucked energetically and nearly unrelentingly, taking breaks only to replenish with food and drink and to catch their breath. Throughout, Eve tried to keep Selene calm about what was coming.

As nervous as Selene was, Eve knew the weekend had marked a turning point. Selene seemed more at ease in her body, more confident. Shifting regularly, and for an appreciative audience, had clearly bolstered her self-acceptance. Eve doubted she'd ever be able to persuade Selene not to fear the moon, but at least she'd convinced Selene of the value of her ability. That would have to be enough.

With less than an hour before she changed, Selene started to panic. They were lying tangled up in the big bed when Selene's breathing increased. Her eyes had gone slightly wild and she seemed to struggle to stay connected to her human consciousness. Her face was still wet with Eve's juices after she'd spent almost forty-five minutes feasting on very willing prey. When she spoke, her voice shook. "You should restrain me."

Eve purposely hadn't packed handcuffs or rope. "With what?"

"We must have something in the car." Selene glanced at the bedroom door, then blinked as though trying to remember what she was saying. "I'm not safe."

"You're not dangerous." Truthfully, Eve had no idea how tonight's transformation would go. Neither of them did. From what she gathered, it had been years since Selene tried this without being tied down. But Eve knew that once the change happened, Selene would be harmless— at least to Eve. "It'll be fine, darling. I promise."

"How can you know?"

"I just do."

"But—"

Eve silenced her with a gentle kiss. Then she whispered, "Tomorrow when you wake up, it'll be to me saying, 'I told you so.'"

Selene buried her face in Eve's neck like an upset child. "You have no idea how badly I hope that's true."

Eve knew Selene didn't trust her "beast-self," as she called it, and maybe never would. Though she'd expected Selene to cut herself some slack after the night that "monstrous beast-self" saved Eve's life, it hadn't worked out that way. Which was exactly why Eve had a plan for tonight.

Running her fingers through Selene's hair, Eve murmured, "You would never hurt me, Selene. You'll see."

Selene awoke with a gasp, sitting up in bed with her heart pounding. She didn't know where she was or why she'd woken so abruptly, and it took a few minutes of sifting through her brain to get her bearings. She was at the cabin, alone in the big bed, naked. Her entire body throbbed with a moon hangover.

Eve was nowhere to be found.

Forcing herself to stay focused and not assume the worst, Selene closed her eyes and reached out mentally for her partner. She felt Eve's answering presence immediately, assuring her that she was safe. Then the bedroom door opened, and Eve came in carrying her laptop and wearing a shit-eating grin.

"Sleep well?"

Selene laughed, then flinched at the harsh sound. "I think so?"

Eve smiled. "You seemed to." Wearing only a T-shirt and a pair of cotton panties, she crossed to the bed and climbed in beside Selene. Despite her exhaustion, Selene couldn't help craning her neck to sneak a peek between Eve's creamy thighs. "I saw that," Eve said as she opened her laptop. "Hold that thought, okay?"

"If you insist." Though Selene was curious about her lost full-moon night, she stayed quiet. It was obvious enough that she hadn't harmed Eve, which meant that her biggest fears hadn't come to pass. Sensing that Eve wanted to show her something, she decided to wait before asking questions.

Eve double-clicked on a file and the video player window appeared on-screen. The frozen image was of Selene, naked. Lying on the ground.

Heat rose on Selene's cheeks. "Eve!"

"Wait. Watch." Eve clicked Play, and within seconds Selene was watching the beginning of last night's transformation.

No wonder she didn't remember Eve using a camcorder. She'd been out of her mind. Selene leaned closer, no longer embarrassed by the sight of her recorded nudity. This was something she'd never seen before.

It looked awful. She writhed on the ground, moaning, before letting out an enraged growl that made the camera shake. "This part was a little scary," Eve said. "But just wait."

Selene watched in horror as her body convulsed, then exploded outward into the monstrous shape of an enormous silver wolf. Her mouth hung open as she studied her beast form—this was her first glimpse of the thing she feared most. Hulking and freakishly large, she cut an intimidating figure. When the wolf stared up into the camera with shining green eyes, then leapt at Eve, Selene let out a startled scream.

Eve chuckled. "Calm down. Watch."

But Selene had already relaxed. On the video, Eve was laughing out loud as the wolf bumped its head against her thighs. Selene stared at the sight of Eve's hand, so small and pale, stroking silver fur as though petting the family dog. The video cut to a new scene. Eve sitting on the couch, a book resting open on her knees, as Selene's beast-self lay on the floor with her head propped on Eve's feet.

"Warming your feet," Selene murmured, recalling Eve's prediction at the beginning of the weekend.

Eve just grinned.

One more scene: Eve lying in bed, the wolf beside her. Eve running her hand up and down the wolf's—*Selene's*—belly, while Selene soaked it up. Then Eve spoke: "What a small price to pay for the wonder inside you."

The video ended. Eve deleted it immediately, then shut the laptop and turned to Selene. Eyes shining, Eve climbed into Selene's lap and held her tightly. It was only when Selene laid her face on Eve's shoulder that she felt her own tears.

And she realized that she'd never felt happier—or quite so free.

Eve made a joyful noise. "I told you so."

TEMPORA MUTANTUR
JANE FLETCHER

"Why did this happen to me?" The bleakness of my question matched the cold rain. Distant thunder reverberated through the shroud of black cloud, draped over the city. "Is this what it feels like to turn into a monster?"

The wind fractured into sharp gusts, slicing at exposed skin. I moved to the other side of the alcove, seeking shelter, but my eyes remained trained on the parking lot—on her car and the path she'd take from the staff entrance—never flinching, even when a hard salvo of rain stung my face.

I tormented the part of myself that so desperately didn't want to be there, playing the game that in another five minutes I'd give up and leave. A cruel hoax. I knew I wouldn't go. I couldn't. I stayed in place the day before, and I'd be here tomorrow.

Her schedule was imprinted on my memory. The subterfuge involved in getting it was one more reason to despise myself—fraudulent phone calls and timesheets snatched from notice boards. For a split second, I glanced down at my watch. Her shift had ended forty minutes ago, but she rarely left on time. More often than not, an emergency would delay her. She might not appear for hours, maybe all night. But I would wait, alone in the cold and gathering dark, just for one brief glimpse of her.

My own job took second place. I'd tweaked and cut my timetable so I could be waiting when she left work. Back in the early days, I'd occasionally missed seeing her. No longer. I couldn't stay away. Last week, when she was on an early shift, I'd called in sick, just to watch her walk those thirty yards from door to car. How much longer could I keep it up? I'd lost any hope the desperate need to see her would fade. If anything, it was getting stronger.

"How have I turned into a stalker?"

I no longer dared to confide in my friends. I knew what they'd say. And what they'd think, but leave unsaid. I was losing my mind, along with my self-respect. Maybe it was time to find a shrink. We could pry into the twisted recesses of my mind. Or would I only get the same bland reassurances my friends had offered? Dr Patricia Mallory saved my life. Of course she'd left an impression on me, a huge debt of gratitude. In the circumstances, an adolescent crush was no cause for surprise. It's only natural I'd imagine some deep bond between us. Everyone would feel the same.

But everyone wasn't waiting in the cold dusk, soaked by rain, staring at a car park.

I had no hope of getting her out of my head. The dreams made sure of that. They'd started while I lay, an inch from death, in the grip of swine flu. I've no memory of those days, but my family filled in the dramatic details, such as the nurse summoning them to say a final good-bye to my unconscious body. Everyone had given up on me, except Dr Mallory. She worked around the clock, a modern-day sorceress stealing me back from the underworld. Had my subconscious sucked my saviour into fever-racked dreams and buried her there so deeply I'd never be free?

Every night the same stories repeated, with each retelling growing clearer, more detailed, more convincing. The most common dream was easily explained—a simple fantasy of repaying the debt by saving her from the volcano. Others were fragments taken from films and books, a miscellany of trite travelogues, bodice rippers, bad B movies, and butchered classics that had no place in the imagination of anyone past puberty. Regardless of the source, the castles, cow-barns, fires, and sinking boats were becoming as familiar as the city I lived in. No common thread bound them, except the two of us together.

Always us together.

That morning, my alarm clock had torn me from a dream, less dramatic than most, but heart-stopping in intensity. We stood, inches apart, at the edge of a forest, overlooking the smoking chimneys of a town. A procession of horse carts clogged the roads. Distance softened the drivers' shouts into an accompaniment for the birdsong. Then she turned to me, staring centuries deep into my eyes. And I wanted to kiss her so much the world vanished; so much I would give my life for it; so much it made my fingernails ache. She leaned toward me, inclining her head, her eyes closing…

…and the diabolic alarm had sounded, calling me back to a day of lectures and seminars.

I shook raindrops from my face, wishing I could as easily shake away the memories. The shift in balance squeezed water from my socks. Cold, oozing between my toes, pulled my gaze from the car park. A puddle had formed in the alcove. How long had I been standing in it, oblivious? Three months had passed since I'd been discharged from the hospital. I'd stood watch in similar cloudbursts and knew the alcove would soon be a foot deep in oily water.

The rain hardened. I scuttled across the road, panicking I might miss her while dodging traffic. The bus shelter was my second favourite viewpoint. It was closer to the car park, but she'd be hidden until she rounded the corner of the outpatient block. A few seconds less of my pitiful daily dose of Dr Mallory.

I was now a bare ten yards from her car in its allocated spot. Despite the cold, my palms grew sweaty at the thought she would pass so close. Anticipation was tinted by the fear she might spot me, even though I was mostly hidden by bushes lining the hospital perimeter.

Behind me, cars splashed by, sending up walls of water. Most had their headlights on. The hospital windows shone in the thickening gloom, surrounded by glittering halos of rain. Autumn was advancing and the nights were drawing in. Stalking her in freezing snow wouldn't be fun, but I'd be there. My life was reducing to these few seconds of her each night.

If I gave up my job, I could watch her arrive at work and double my exposure. Or I could find out where she lived. Thoughts of following her home were growing stronger, and I couldn't hold out much longer. Still I battled the compulsion, refusing to succumb. My last line of defence. Because once I gave in, my descent into stalkerdom would be complete. I was so far beyond being able to help myself.

"What sick spell have you cast on me, Dr Patricia Mallory?"

The sound of footsteps. Her footsteps. Blindfolded, I could have picked them out of a passing parade, complete with marching bands. She'd left work.

A ripple of relief that I'd soon be able to go home and dry off crashed into a wall of misery. Once she drove away there'd be nothing to look forward to, until tomorrow. Both emotions were overwhelmed when she appeared, head down to shield her face from the rain, her hand fumbling in her pocket. Watching her became the only thing that mattered, the only activity holding any meaning or value. My eyes ached with the strain. She reached the blue sedan and pulled out her car keys.

A click came from my right, followed by buzzing overhead. I flinched at the sounds, although my attention didn't waver, as the fluorescent tube in the shelter canopy battered its way into life. The automatic timer had turned on earlier than in previous weeks, due to the shortening days. Light flowed over me. The flare caught Dr Mallory's attention and she looked up from her car door, straight at me.

Time stopped. My chest contracted. My body turned to lead. She also stiffened, staring at me through the driving rain. Only her hair was moving in the gusting wind.

Would she remember me? Had she recognised me? And how many times would she need to catch me out, stalking her, before she took the matter to the police? She continued to stare, clearly already knowing something was awry. A stranger at a bus stop did not warrant so much notice.

An eternity later, she dropped the keys back in her pocket and stepped away from the door. Fear gripped my stomach, certain she would flee back to the hospital in search of security guards. Instead, she moved around the car, edging through the gap between it and the wet bushes. Her eyes were fixed on the ground, avoiding puddles, but she was clearly heading for the pathway through to the bus shelter.

Fluorescent light glinted off raindrops on her cheek and eyelashes when she stopped, a scant three feet away. It was the first time since I'd been discharged that we were close enough to talk, close enough to touch. The weight of my longing tugged on muscle and bone, pinning my arms to my side.

At first, she too appeared uncertain. "It's Diana O'Rourke, isn't it? Are you waiting for a bus?"

I tore my eyes from her, trying to act as if my heart wasn't trying to burrow through my chest. Ragged, graffiti-covered remains of timetables flapped in the wind. Of course. Why did people normally stand in bus-stops? "Yes. My car has broken down."

A frown tweaked her eyebrows. "I thought you lived south of here, in Redford. Isn't this the wrong stop?"

"I'm not going home. I'm on my way to visit my…er… hairdresser."

"At this time of night?"

"She's ill. I'm calling by, to see how she's doing."

"Either a good friend, or an exceptional hairdresser. I'm not sure I'd come out on a night like this."

"We went to school together."

"Aren't you from California, originally?" Dr Mallory's frown deepened.

"Yes. So's she. She's just moved here. And she's ill. So I thought I'd…" I had to extricate myself from the hole I was in. The first thing was to stop digging.

"Can I give you a lift?"

"No." I yelped the word. I couldn't help it.

"Are you all right?"

"Yes. Mostly. I think."

"You think?" The edge to her tone was more worried than confused.

"No. I mean yes. I'm fine."

"We—" Dr Mallory broke off and looked down. She rubbed her forehead, as if easing a headache.

I waited, biting my lip.

When she looked up, her manner was more uncertain, but a decision had clearly been made. "Look. Would you like to go for a coffee, or something?"

She indicated the bar opposite the hospital entrance. Yellow light flooded from the steamed-up windows and reflected off wet pavement. The doors beckoned with a treacherous promise of warmth on a wet, cold night. I should refuse. The risks were too high. To pass through those doors was to lay my sanity on the line. Yet had they been the icy gates of hell, I could have done nothing else, other than to nod and follow her.

❖

I wrapped my hands around the latte. The warmth set my fingers tingling. I must have been colder than I'd realised. My nails held a blue tinge. On the plus side, this provided a convenient excuse for the trembling.

I tried to give a relaxed smile as she settled into the seat opposite. "Thank you, Dr Mallory."

"Please, Trisha. It's what my friends call me."

I swallowed. Would I be able to pronounce the familiar name? Or would I be reduced to stuttering juvenile jelly? A façade of formality might help keep my distance, and composure. A weak hope, but all I had. My reticence must have shown.

"Otherwise, I'll have to call you Dr O'Rourke." Her tone was teasing.

"I'm not a medical doctor."

"I know."

Of course she'd read my notes, with my profession and other details—height, weight, age. If she cared enough to find out, she was in a position to know vastly more about me than I knew in return. Even though her information was acquired legitimately, unlike my own prying, it eased the knots in my throat and stomach. Her privacy was more intact than mine, thanks to the flu bug.

"Di." I felt my face thaw into a proper smile. "That's my name. Not a threat."

She exhaled in a laugh. Only when I saw her shoulders relax did I realise she'd been holding herself taut. Why? Was she nervous? It would be justifiable if she knew I'd been stalking her, but in that case she'd hardly have invited me to join her for a coffee.

I sipped my drink, watching her. Her face both was and wasn't the one dominating my dreams. Now I thought about it, the women all looked so different. What was it that made me certain they were her? Yet they were. I knew it as surely as I knew the earth was beneath my feet.

This Patricia Mallory was in her mid-thirties. The etching of laugh lines was showing at the corners of her wide lips. Her face was firm and well balanced, strong rather than beautiful. Elegant, long-fingered hands danced to punctuate her words. She glanced up at me and opened her mouth as if to speak, but instead smiled. A tiny bit of her tongue touched her upper lip.

The world lurched as the sudden revelation knocked me off balance. That was the smile I knew from my dreams. The one that let me identify her, regardless of age, race or any other feature. Had she smiled that same smile at me, as I lay in the hospital bed. Was that where I'd picked up on it? The shock was so hard air solidified in my lungs.

"Is everything okay? Do you feel all right?" She grasped my wrist, back in doctor mode.

"I'm fine. Coffee went down the wrong way." I pulled my hand away and coughed a little for effect, buying time for my breathing to settle.

"You are completely over the flu, aren't you? I mean, I know you must be by now, but—"

"Yes. Weeks ago." I hesitated. "Except…"

Why not say something? She was a doctor, after all—better her than a shrink. Just be a little cagey on the details. Perhaps obsessive dreams were a well-documented side effect of my treatment.

"Except?"

"I'm getting weird dreams."

"Nightmares?"

"Not exactly. But they're unsettling. My head isn't back where it should be."

"The dreams worry you?"

"Not the dreams themselves, more the effect they have on me. I'm becoming obsessed. They're taking over my life."

"What is it about the dreams that makes you feel obsessive? Can you quantify it?"

Easy. You. Not an answer I should give aloud. "They're vivid and they repeat. I've never had that before." *Before I met you.*

"Do you ever—" She broke off and took a hasty mouthful of coffee. "The repetitions, are they details or just situations?"

"Both. There's the volcano that keeps erupting."

"What else?" Her eyes fixed on me, probing and intense.

I slumped in my chair, in relaxation rather than despair. I was waltzing around a pit of insanity, and yet felt absurdly at peace. For the first time since catching the flu, I was where I was supposed to be, doing what I was supposed to do. I was home, and everything was going to work out fine.

"Don't laugh. I dream about being on the *Titanic*."

"The *Titanic*?"

"Yes. Tell me, are dreams cobbled together from overblown B movies a side effect of flu?"

"In that case, I've had flu as well." Trisha continued staring at me.

"You've dreamed about it too?"

"Yes."

"Do you think it's something in the hospital food?"

"A catering assistant mistook the morphine for sugar?" Her smile returned, softer than before.

I matched it. I didn't know what the book was, but we were on the same page. "Stranger things have happened."

"Something stranger is happening, right now." Her voice was, at the same time, both decisive and wistful. She drained her coffee. "Not wanting to sound clichéd, but would you like to come back to my place? There's something I want to show you."

❖

Give or take an Art Deco poster, Trisha's apartment was exactly as I'd imagined. The living room was furnished with an emphasis on comfort and practicality rather than style. Underplayed pastels served as a background to a forest of houseplants. She'd always want greenery around—but how did I know that?

The bookshelf was more prominent than the TV, filling the wall opposite the door. I wandered over to check out the titles, wondering if I'd find any surprises. A longhaired white cat, sprawled on the coffee table, ignored me.

"Red or white?" Trisha called from the kitchen.

"Red, if you've got it."

"I wouldn't have offered if I didn't." She appeared, holding two full wineglasses.

Trisha had towelled off her wet hair and removed her raincoat and shoes. It was the first time I'd seen her without the doctor's professional veneer. In the hospital, her figure had always been concealed beneath her white doctor's gown. In the car park she had worn a coat.

Her uncombed hair stuck out in comically endearing spikes. The pattern of wear on her faded denims suggested the legs of a runner. Her hips were as wide as her shoulders. A plain yellow shirt clung to her just tightly enough to reveal full breasts and narrow waist. My heart thudded at the sight, while my stomach performed a familiar somersault. Was that all it was? The attraction was no more than simple desire?

No sooner had the idea snuck into my head than an immediate denial hit me. I've been in love often enough before—or thought I was, at the time. There had been a string of clever, witty, sexy women who had caught my attention. The relationships had rarely lasted a month before a hollow sense of wrongness had eaten away at the emotion, leaving a charade, going through the motions of an affair. The shams had ended in recriminations, with accusations of me being frigid, uncaring, or even straight.

This was going to be different. I knew it as assuredly as I knew Trisha and I would become lovers. It was ordained. Neither of us had a say in it—not that I was complaining.

"I thought about pouring two glasses for myself, but it seemed a trifle greedy." Her voice recalled me from my fantasy.

"Pardon?"

"One of these glasses is for you. Do you want to take it?"

"Oh. Sorry. I was um…"

"I noticed." Judging by her smile, Trisha was unbothered at my blatant gawping.

We sat on mismatched sofas, facing each other across the coffee table. Her gaze ran over me, an appraisal matching mine in its brazenness. After one more sip of wine, she shunted the cat aside and put the glass down. The cat gave an indignant sigh and twitched one ear, but made no other move.

"I was so frightened you were going to die. You know how close you came, don't you?"

"I know I'm only here because of you. My family told me all about it. You know they've elevated you to the sainthood?"

She pursed her lips. "As a doctor, you try to see all patients as equally important. You can't, of course. Wouldn't be human if you could. But I've never felt so desperate about anyone before. I've spent the last three months telling myself swine flu was the big news story, or you reminded me of someone, or I was having my mid-life crisis early, or whatever." She shrugged. "I've been lying to myself."

My heart started thudding. "You feel the bond too?"

"Yes." Trisha looked down at her interlaced fingers. "Yes, I do."

I started to move, to wrap her in my arms, but now was not yet the time—not quite. Trisha had more to say.

"I knew you lectured at the college, but I was surprised you teach math. I'd assumed you were in the languages faculty."

"Languages?"

"Latin, to be exact."

"Why?"

"You spoke it while you were half-conscious."

"I was? Are you sure?" I shook my head. "My knowledge of languages goes as far as being able to order beer in Spanish. That's it."

"*Tempora mutantur, nos et mutamur in illis*. You said that a few times, muddled in with all the other stuff. I couldn't make most of it out, but I was able to write that bit down. It translates as, *Times change, and we change with them*."

"I don't know where I picked that up."

"I do, now. In fact, I've known for a while but I haven't been listening to myself."

Trisha stretched toward the bookshelf. The sofa was just close enough for her to reach it without getting up. She slipped a book out with her middle finger. From the brief glimpse of the cover, it was a tourist guide book to somewhere European. Trisha flipped it open and removed a photo she'd been using as a bookmark.

"I went on holiday to Italy, last summer. This is from Pompeii. I spent hours there. They had to evict me at closing time. I just—" She broke off. "Well. What do you make of it?"

I don't know how long I stared at the photo. Time can be so very relative.

The photo was of an interior courtyard, lined with white marble columns. Most of the ground was dirt, but a few remaining patches of black and white mosaic tiles dotted the floor. The mural on the wall behind held only faded traces of what had been vivid blues and reds, but the picture was still distinct. The line of dancing girls was as clear as they had been on that last morning.

Flickers of déjà vu have jolted me before. This didn't fit into the same league. The dream fragments marched back into my head and lined themselves up, rank upon rank, linking and interlinking. They wove their stories around me, the warp and weft of a hundred lifetimes.

Trisha's voice broke through the engulfing wave of memories. "I felt so drawn to this house."

"It was yours."

"And you lived around the corner."

"When I wasn't in your bed." I looked up from the photo.

Her eyes met mine, dancing. "Maybe if the dreams hadn't been so much fun I might have taken them seriously earlier. I've been trying to persuade myself I've simply been celibate a bit too long, and working too hard. Then I saw you in the bus-stop, and it all dropped into place."

I had to confess. I knew she wouldn't mind. "I've been stalking you."

"I've got all your hospital notes in triplicate, and some photos of you."

"I thought I was going mad. I was thinking about seeing a shrink."

"Me too. I was so relieved when you mentioned the volcano." She grinned, and picked up her wine. "When you woke me, insisting we leave Pompeii at once—how did you know Vesuvius was about to erupt?"

"You expect me to remember that after two thousand years?" I shrugged. "Probably the same way you knew to get off the boat after the iceberg hit. I wanted to carry on dancing. You were the one who said ignore the captain and get in the nearest lifeboat."

We sat back and watched each other, remembering and readjusting. Trisha cocked an eyebrow. "How many times do you think we've known each other?"

"Not enough."

I slipped off the sofa and shuffled crablike around the coffee table. She met me halfway, so that we were kneeling, face-to-face.

"So how do you want to play it this time?" She was close enough that I felt her breath on my lips.

"Any way you want."

"My bedroom is next door, or we could take it slow. We have all the time in the world."

"Would you like me to court you properly?"

"That might be nice. Just no sonnets, please."

"You didn't like my poetry?" I feigned hurt surprise.

"I like poems to rhyme."

"That is just so seventeenth century of you."

Trisha grinned, and then became serious. She reached up and gently cupped the side of my face. The touch of her hand ignited a thousand memories and I gasped. I needed her. Through all my lives, through all the centuries, through all eternity, I needed her. Before I knew it, my arms had slipped around her back, pulling us together. Our lips met, as if for the first time.

The kiss was everything I knew it would be. My past, present, and future. By the time it ended my legs were shaking so hard I would have fallen, had I been on my feet. I clung to Trisha for support and rested my head on her shoulder.

I wanted to giggle, run around, shout, and dance. But most of all I wanted to hold her. The world was so utterly, perfectly as it should be.

Trisha's lips nuzzled against my throat and then found my ear. "Times change. Love endures."

"Always."

THE TRICKSTER CODEX
JESS FARADAY

A wise man once said that if a stranger's calling after you, don't stop, because he probably ain't about to hand you a winning lottery ticket. When I heard the whimper in the alley by my building, I knew I should have kept moving. But I'm a sucker for a pooch, and the one that was standing there, half in the darkness and half in sun, was the ugliest mutt I'd ever seen: ragged and hungry-looking, with spindly legs, a long, pointy snout, and a bushy tail that looked like the tip had been dipped in ink.

I'd been walking up Spring Street from the new courthouse, minding my own business, my day-old Danish in my hand. It was more doorstop than pastry, but considering how business had been lately, it was probably all I was going to get for the day. And now this scrawny mutt was eyeing it like it was prime rib.

"Don't even think about it," I said.

The beast sat on its haunches and turned on the charm. And believe it or not, the fleabag had charm. Just look in the dictionary under "puppy-dog eyes."

My stomach growled. I'd punched an extra hole in my belt that morning, and it wasn't so I'd look more like those dolls in *Vogue*. But the dog looked worse than me, no lie, and in the end I tossed the Danish.

"But you're on your own for lunch. You hear me?"

The mutt caught my breakfast in its toothy grin, bobbed its skinny head, and then winked at me before turning and disappearing into the shadows of the alley.

❖

"How's the morning treating you, Miss Archer?" asked the doorman as I ducked past him into my building, shaking my head. Funny the building owners could afford to hire a doorman, but not to fix my toilet.

"The morning," I informed him, "is going to the dogs. You might want to make sure your shots are up to date."

The infrequently patronized offices of Amelia Archer, Private Investigator—that is, me—sit on top of a squat brown brick building in downtown Los Angeles. It's a dump. The water is unreliable and the wiring downright dangerous. But between the war and the fact that nobody hires the city's only female dick with that bastard Philip Marlowe hanging around, I'm lucky to have it. My office is on the eighth floor, and the elevator is always broken. After a year and change, I had a caboose like a marble statue and I could run up the stairs in heels without breaking a sweat.

I like to look on the bright side.

That day, I'd barely had time to toss my hat on the rack, light up a smoke, and put my size nines up on my desk when she walked through the door. Now the dame hadn't been waiting when I got there, and I sure as Shinola hadn't heard anyone on the stairs behind me. But who was I to complain? My first walk-in in weeks, and she was five and a half feet of gorgeous, with shoulders like a general, black hair and eyes, and skin like red desert clay. She held herself straight and proud, and though she was wearing a tailored jacket and skirt, when I looked at her, I saw her barefoot and in buckskin on some high desert plain, that black hair no longer restrained by pins and fedora, but whipping free around her shoulders in the wind.

"What's up, Tiger Lily?" I asked.

She gave me a look that said she'd heard it before, and from better than the likes of me. Then she looked around my empty office as if she'd seen outhouses nicer than this. Or maybe it was the plumbing.

"My name is Lorena Claw," she said, turning back to me.

"Mel Archer." I stuck out my hand. She frowned at it until I put it away. I'd been trying to change over from "Amy" for months, but it never seemed to catch on.

"I trust I'm not interrupting anything," she continued.

"Sister, nobody comes to me unless they're desperate." I ground out my Lucky Strike in the ashtray on the corner of my desk. "You aren't, by any chance…"

"Desperate?" She flashed a pained smile. "Hardly. But I do believe that you're the right person for the job."

"What makes you think that?"

She flipped open the leather portfolio she'd been holding under her arm and began to pace. I craned my neck to get a better look, but she was like a high school principal gloating over my permanent record.

"Amelia Archer, former WASP ace pilot. On your way to a medal, but—"

"But my plane went down behind enemy lines and the president decided he'd rather pretend he didn't know me than answer tough questions about women in combat," I said as she slapped the portfolio shut. "But enough about me. Why don't you take a load off and tell your Aunt Amy what brings you here?"

I watched her pull up the only other piece of furniture in the room—a splintery schoolhouse chair with one leg shorter than the others—perch on the edge, and cross her long, long legs. Legs like that came from using them a lot. Between her muscle tone and her abruptness, it occurred to me that she might be military herself. I took my feet down.

"You attended cryptography school before applying to the WASP program," she began.

"Best in my class until they decided code-breaking was a boys' game."

It surprised me how much that still stung.

"But you understand codes, and you understand the military mentality."

"A little too well."

"Miss Archer, I'm a civilian consultant currently overseeing a project involving a new kind of code," she said. "Everything was going well until I started to pick up some unauthorized transmissions from my group to the officers in charge. These transmissions used our code, but in a way I couldn't understand. A code within a code. I have the transmissions here. I need you to try to figure out what they're saying."

"Whoa, whoa, sister," I said. "We're at war. Loose lips sink ships, and people who pass military secrets end up on the business end of a firing squad." My heart pounded, and not in a good way. Strictly small time, that was me: cheating spouses, lost kittens. Nobody gets shot over lost kittens. "I'm sorry. You need to leave."

"But I have nowhere else to turn!" She suddenly came across more doll than drill sergeant. My heart dropped to my panties. She widened her eyes—deliberate, calculated, but no less devastating. It had been a long time, and I've always been dizzy for brunettes. Especially when they were clearly trouble.

"Not my problem," I croaked.

"But you're the only one who can help me."

Oh, she was clever. She was good. She was sitting on the edge of the chair, pushing out her chest in a way that was as irresistible as it was obvious. I wondered if her little dossier had detailed my weakness for dames in distress.

"Cripes," I muttered. I dropped back into my chair.

"Miss Archer, my people were glad to take what I had to offer. Now I believe they're trying to cut me out without so much as a thank you. I can't let go of all my work without a fight. Can't you understand?"

Understand? Did I ever. That little shit Marlowe had been my right-hand man for a year and a half before turning around and stealing all my clients. My hard-won police contacts had been happy to go skipping off with him as well. It was the same story any time a woman tried to get ahead in a man's world. All the same, it was one thing to grouse about the world's unfairness, and something else to put yourself in the line of fire over it. And all I had was this dame's word for any of it.

"Of course I can show you my credentials," she said.

"I think you'd better."

She took a card from her purse and handed it across the desk. If her military I.D. was a fake, then Dr. Lorena Claw, Civilian Consultant, was a master forger as well as a spy. When I handed the card back, the little flutter of her lashes was unnecessary. I'd made up my mind.

"I'm going to need six hundred big ones up front, plus forty clams a day for expenses," I said. It was excessive, but I was broke, and if I took her case it'd be my tuchus behind the eight-ball.

She met my eyes. The clouds cleared from the desert sky. When she spoke again, the California sun seemed to flood through the blinds, chasing away the remaining shadows of doubt.

"Money, Miss Archer, will be no object."

An hour after she left, I was still running my fingers over the bills she'd counted out onto my desk, and fantasizing about what Dr. Lorena Claw might like for breakfast, when someone knocked on my door.

"Yes?"

"Miss Archer?" said the man as he stepped into my office—wrench on his belt, smokes rolled into the sleeve above his left shoulder, a plunger slung over his right. "Stanley Clements, Angel City Plumbing. I came to have a look at your u-bend."

❖

The delectable Dr. Claw hadn't told me anything about the code itself. Gave me a list of words and said I could figure it out from there. But the only reason Uncle Sam hires an outsider—especially a dame—is if she's got something he can't get anywhere else. During my short, happy stint as a trainee code-breaker, I'd learned that in the first war, we'd gotten around the Jerrys by sending messages in Chocktaw. Between my client's distinctive appearance, and her telling irritation with my little nickname, I'd bet dollars to doughnuts Uncle Sam was up to something similar this time around.

Problem was, there were a couple hundred Indian languages between Alaska and Florida. Of course, if Uncle Sam was using my future ex-girlfriend because she was an expert in one of those languages, it would narrow things down a bit. Given her unusual name, and the fact that she signed PhD after it, it didn't take more than fifteen minutes on the horn to find her: Dr. Lorena Claw, Adjunct Instructor of Navajo Language at USC.

With this information, plus the shiny new gold pen I'd bought out of my retainer, I went to see a friend.

❖

Sheridan Eliott ran the only Michelin-starred Italian joint downtown. Normally a place like Eliott's wouldn't let the likes of me within two blocks of the front door. But I'd helped him out a while back, and now he sometimes even let me eat there.

"Where'd you get this?" Eliott asked me as I took my seat at my favorite table. The table was in a little nook between the kitchen and the john. It was invisible from the front door, but an ingenious arrangement of mirrors let me see everyone who came in and out.

"If I told you I'd have to kill you," I said.

He picked up the notes I'd laid out—the three transmissions and Dr. Claw's little codex—and replaced them with a plate of heaven. I picked up a fork.

"What's this?" I asked, as he looked my notes over.

"*Involtine de vitello.* I'm considering it for the dinner menu. What do you think?"

I cut off a bite from a battered, fried roll of meat and let it melt on my tongue. Veal. Prosciutto. Garlic, cheese, sage, and butter. I washed it down with a mouthful of the cold white wine he had provided. Angels sang.

"Eliott, if they ever give me the chair, this is what I want for my last meal."

The broad, ruddy planes of his face remained impassive, but the edges of his dark eyes crinkled with smug satisfaction.

Eliott had come to Los Angeles to break into the movies. Westerns were hot again, and this time the Indians weren't always the bad guys. Unfortunately, Hollywood was only hiring Italians for the roles. So Eliott opened a restaurant. Now he makes money hand over fist serving up overpriced fettuccine to those same directors who didn't think a full-blooded Navajo was "authentic" enough to play Manuelito in their films.

He took the seat across from mine and read over my notes while I made sweet love to my dinner. When the food was gone and I'd loosened my belt, I pushed away my empty plate and told him my tale.

"I haven't read a lot of Navajo," he said after a few minutes. Like most of the kids on his reservation, he'd been sent to boarding school, where using his native language had been, shall we say, discouraged. "Some professor came up with an alphabet a few years ago, but it never really caught on." He handed the papers back to me. "Your client translated the words right, though. *Chicken-hawk,*" he said, pointing. "*Mosquito.* This one could be *intestine.*" He looked at me. "But together the words don't make any sense. The words are Navajo, but…"

"The client said it was a code within a code. She thinks her men are using it to pass information they want to keep from her," I said.

He looked up.

"*Her* men?"

"Dr. Claw. My client."

The heat that spread across my face gave away more than words could have. Eliott regarded me evenly. We did not, as a rule, discuss our personal lives. But after all the years we'd known each other, Eliott had to have figured I wasn't the fetching-my-husband's-slippers type. When he spoke again, the skin around his eyes didn't crinkle, but his forehead did.

"Be careful," he said.

"I always am."

Just as quickly as this window had opened onto my pathetic excuse for a love life, he slammed it shut.

"You've checked this woman's background, I take it."

"She was teaching Navajo at USC before going on sabbatical—to consult with the military, I guess."

"And the dog?" he asked.

"The what?"

"You said something about a dog tricking you out of your breakfast."

"It didn't trick me," I said. "It was looking at me with those big brown eyes...exactly!" I cried, as he put on an eerily similar expression. "How's anyone supposed to resist that? Anyway, what does that have to do with—"

At that moment two men entered the restaurant with a clatter and tinkle as the door jarred the string of bells hanging above it.

"Uh-oh," I said. Identical boring haircuts. Bad G-man suits. Dark sunglasses.

"You know those guys?"

"Not personally." I instinctively sank down in my seat. "They're Feds."

"They were in here earlier asking about you."

"Shit."

Feds were like mobsters. Never a good thing when they know your name. Even worse when they think they have business with you.

"Do you believe in synchronicity?" Eliott asked.

"What?"

"Never mind." He chuckled under his breath. "You sneak out through the kitchen. I'll see if I can interest them in a five-course FBI special."

"I owe you," I said.

He waved me off and strode toward the front of the restaurant. While my old friend made nice with the Feds, I slipped a five-spot under my plate, shoved Dr. Claw's portfolio back under my arm, and scurried for the kitchen.

❖

The G-Men must have already eaten, because I wasn't halfway down the alley when I heard the back door of the restaurant slam open with a vengeance and four flat Fed feet beat down the alley behind me.

"Stop, Miss Archer!" one called. "We just want to talk!"

And hand me a winning lottery ticket, I supposed. Nothing doing.

I burst out of the alley and onto a narrow little street—a dark, liquor store–studded canyon between tall walls of buildings. As the Feds rounded the corner behind me, I turned into a *botánica*, vaulted over the counter—lucky I was wearing slacks that day—and was out the back door while they were still knocking over saint-shaped candles and bottles of prosperity oil. The thought of the bad juju that would follow them made me smile.

Then my own luck ran out. The alley behind the *botánica* ended in a brick wall on one side. The other side was closed off by a chain link fence and secured with a sturdy padlock. I took a run at the fence. Didn't get halfway up before two sets of arms were pulling at my legs.

"Damn, you're strong," one of the Feds muttered.

He got a kick in the teeth for his troubles. I flailed, but he had me by the waist and seemed to be taking the pop in the kisser personally. He slammed me down on the pavement and put a knee on my sternum. I opened my eyes to daylight stars and the steely glint of a .38 Special half an inch from my nose.

"What happened to 'we just want to talk'?" I asked.

The Fed spat out a couple of teeth and swiped a sleeve across his mouth, leaving a long red streak across his cheek.

"You rejected that opthon when you chothe to athault a federal offither," he growled. His face hardened, and he cocked his gun. Fed Number Two put a hand on his shoulder.

"We're looking for Dr. Lorena Claw," said Number Two.

"Why?"

"We have reason to believe that she contacted you with an intent to sell military secrets."

"What? No," I stammered. I tried to sit up, but Number One leaned on his knee in a way that meant business. I let out a groan and shot a pleading look at the Fed who hadn't tasted my loafers.

"Come on, Edwards, don't kill the little lady," Number Two said.

"But—"

Number Two, who was clearly in charge, tightened his fingers around his partner's shoulder. Number One grudgingly leaned back and let me drag myself to a sit against a bank of garbage cans.

"You've got it all wrong," I explained. "It's Dr. Claw's project. She—"

"There's no one by that name employed by the military."

"But I saw her ID."

"Maybe you should have looked a little clother." Number One sneered and holstered his weapon as if he'd a grudge against it.

"We saw her enter your offices with a portfolio full of cash," said Number Two. "When she came out again, the portfolio appeared... substantially lighter." He narrowed his eyes. "Where are you banking these days, Miss Archer?"

Wouldn't take a Fed to figure out I did my business next door. Good thing I'd listened when that little voice had told me to wait to make the drop. That little voice had saved my skin more times than I could count.

"Doethn't matter," Number One said, dabbing at the side of his mouth. "Fifty agenth are crawling up your ath with a microthcope ath we thpeak."

"So that's what that burning sensation is," I said. "I'll cancel my proctologist's appointment. You boys can knock yourselves out. I've got nothing to hide. You, on the other hand, might want to do something about that lisp. It's not very becoming."

Have I mentioned how my wise ass sometimes gets me into trouble?

Before his better half could restrain him, Number One sprang across the refuse and landed on top of me, knocking us both into the garbage cans in an explosion of incense-scented rubbish. The crash of aluminum filled the alley as we rolled together through the trash, his hands like a steel band around my throat.

"...teach...you...a...lethon..."

Not far away, Number Two was tutting about professionalism, but he seemed remarkably unconcerned about his partner's unprovoked attack on a civilian. Something cut into my back, and stupidly I wondered what my dry cleaner would say. Then, suddenly, everything grew very still. A warning growl rumbled in the air behind the cans. Number One even stopped slugging me long enough to look up in wonder.

The dog was still scruffy and wild-looking when it stepped out from behind the trash cans. But it was a lot larger than I had remembered—or maybe it was just the angle. With one paw on either side of my head, nose-to-nose with Fed Number One, it looked damned impressive. Another growl rumbled in its throat.

"...the hell..."

That close, I could see the white hairs vibrating on the animal's chest. The brown hairs on its legs were tipped with black. The effect was surprisingly elegant, and I was overcome by the urge to run my fingers through it.

Still growling, the dog leaned in until its nose almost touched that of the now wide-eyed Number One. His hands slowly slid away from my neck.

"Your dog have its shots, Miss Archer?" Number Two asked quietly.

"Not my dog." When this was all over, though, I'd half a mind to change that. Slowly, quietly, Number One eased himself off me and backed away.

"Glad to hear it."

Number Two cocked his gun. The dog launched itself forward just as the weapon discharged. I heard a yelp and a thump, and I was on my feet.

The dog had gone down, but it sprang up immediately. I rubbed my eyes. Maybe Number One had bashed my melon on the pavement harder than I thought. Feds didn't muck around with pantywaist firearms. The .38 was a hand cannon. Should have blown the mutt's leg right off.

"Rabid beatht," Number One said.

I dove into him as he unholstered his weapon. The shot went wide. As the dog turned toward us, an ugly red stain on its left shoulder, I could have sworn it was enjoying itself. We watched as it loped toward the back wall of the alley, graceful and nonchalant, and then at the last moment, faded into the bricks. I turned to the men.

"Did you see—"

Number One clearly had not forgiven me enough to revel together in the weirdness. No sooner had I turned to face him than he brought the butt of his pistol cleanly down across my temple.

As I sank to the ground, darkness swallowing the alley, the son of a bitch finally looked satisfied.

❖

It was after eleven by the time I dragged myself home, had a bath and a stiff drink, and found her number. I sat on the kitchen table while I dialed, a French cigarette in my mouth and a filet mignon slapped over my right eye. There was another one in the freezer. I might have been dropping the case, but there was no way in hell Dr. Lorena Claw—or whatever her name was—was getting a penny of that sweet retainer back.

"Yeah, this is Amy Archer," I said when she picked up. "I'm through. Did you hear me? Finished. Finito. Done."

"I don't understand," she said.

My head was pounding. My body felt like it had been dragged across a mile of rough road. I took a long pull on the cigarette and leaned against the window.

"I don't know who you really are, or why you want this code broken. But a couple of hours ago, I nearly got my ticket punched by a pair of trigger-happy G-men who think you're trying to sell military secrets."

"If it's a question of money—"

"Sweetheart, ain't no amount of money in the world worth getting on the wrong side of J. Edgar Hoover. I'm sorry the boys are passing notes behind your back, but I should have listened to my head instead of my—-never you mind what. If you think I'm going to help you lose this war for us, sister, you've got another one coming."

There was a long silence on the other end, and then she said, "You're scared."

"You bet your sweet tushie I'm scared! My last case was a stolen Pekingese! I'm out of my league. And I don't traffic with the enemy."

"I'm not the enemy," she said.

"You're not working for Uncle Sam."

"I never said I was."

I slapped the steak back onto the plate, crushed out the cigarette, and took a swig of Scotch from the bottle. Beneath the bottle was the little codex. I'd been fiddling with it despite myself.

"You told me you were overseeing a secret military project," I said.

"But I didn't say it was *my* project. Please, Miss Archer. Amy. Mel. I can explain. Will you let me explain?"

I hesitated.

Every ounce of my common sense screamed no. But the Scotch was stronger—and smoother. Maybe I was loopy from having my noggin bashed around all afternoon. Or maybe it was because I'd seen my life flash before my eyes back in that alley, and realized how lonely it was. I was dropping the case; nothing could change that.

But she had called me Mel.

"I'll come get you," she said.

"Nothing doing, babe." I might have been lonely, but I wasn't stupid.

"Then take a taxi and meet me at the Gypsy Room."

I let out a low whistle. The Gypsy Room was a far cry from the beer-and-pool halls where I usually found myself of a Friday night. I wondered if they'd let me in with scuffed loafers and my face looking like it had been through a meat grinder.

"Put on your best suit and tie," she said. "I'll see you in an hour."

The line went dead.

❖

Right before Marlowe flew the coop, I had invested in a spiffy trousers-and-jacket combo in charcoal silk: made for a man, but hand-tailored for me. With a white blouse, red tie, and wingtips, it was sharp. I pulled my hair back into a bun, stuck it through with a pair of black lacquered chopsticks, and dashed on a bit of color from the age-cracked lipstick I kept in my disguise kit. Not exactly Beverly Shaw, but slick enough that if the Gypsy Room didn't let me in, there'd be any number of dolls happy to take off in my taxi to go watch the lights. I strapped on my sidearm, put the codex in my pocket, and went down to the street.

When the cab pulled onto the Sunset Strip, the Gypsy Room was bustling with dames in diamonds and dapper tuxedo-wearing daddies. I was outclassed and underdressed, but I got my share of once-overs, even with half my face swollen up like a purple balloon. One dishy blonde really took a shine to me. Wanted to drown my troubles in champagne and dance me into the sunrise. Any other time I'd have taken her up on it, but right then I only had eyes for one gal, and she was walking through the door.

Dr. Lorena Claw was dressed to kill in a red satin gown. Her hair was pulled up in some complicated knot, a few finger-curls dangling down her neck. Her jewelry was simple but expensive. Five tuxedoes leaped forward to light her cigarette, but she was looking at me like I was the only dame in the room. It was only when she got close enough to touch that I noticed the scarf over her left shoulder was actually a sling.

"Ouch," she said, reaching out with her good arm to touch the goose egg sitting above my eyebrow. Her fingers were cool and soft, and they met my skin with a tingle.

"What happened to your arm, babe?" I asked.

She smirked like she was waiting for me to catch up with the joke, elbow resting on my shoulder, fingers really working that goose-egg. It should have hurt, but it didn't. Felt more like she was rearranging something the Feds had knocked out of whack. It was good.

"There," she said. "All better."

She took my fingers in hers and led me onto the dance floor. There was a bit of awkwardness when we both tried to lead, but then the band slowed it down and we settled together nicely, my hand on her good shoulder and hers on my backside.

"You still haven't answered my question," I said.

She pulled me closer, rested her cheek against my hair.

"You smell like meat."

And here I'd thought I'd heard all the best pickup lines.

"Spent the evening with a steak on my face after your friends at the Bureau worked me over," I said. "Guess I don't clean up as well as I thought."

That knowing smile again. She was warm and brown and smelled like something I couldn't quite put my finger on: water, smoke and sand. It was nice, though, and after the day I'd had, I was happy to just stand there basking in it. The Gypsy Room wasn't my kind of joint, normally, but it sure was swell. A place where the troubles of the day faded into a haze of champagne, swirling skirts, and soft jazz. I might have drifted off right there on her shoulder when she suddenly said, "I gave them the language, you know."

"Who?" I asked muzzily. I nuzzled her neck, but her jaw had gone rigid with irritation.

"All of them. I gave each one a different language, and look how they're acting."

I sighed.

"Sweetheart, it's over. At least it is for me. Why don't we just enjoy what's left of the—"

"You wanted an explanation. Here it is. I gave the people different languages. Then there was bickering. And then there was war. And now when I try to help them, they twist my gift around and use it to shut me out while they destroy each other. I won't have it."

I stifled a groan, but I knew the signs. Storm on the horizon, and it was going to be a doozy. Already the dame had stopped making sense. The plate-throwing was next. I grazed my fingers along her nape, tried to take her mind off it.

"The Feds said you're not even with the army, doll. I know it hurts, but you've gotta let it go or someone's going to get killed."

Her dark eyes blazed back at me, and for a moment there was nothing else in the world but that black, burning, all-consuming gaze.

And then the shooting started.

At first I thought it was a raid. The cops didn't care about gals dancing together, and they usually left the fancy joints alone. But maybe someone had told them there was coke in the back. Or H. You could never tell with the rich. I grabbed her hand.

"Come on, doll, let's make a run for it," I said.

They say it's hesitation that gets you: that split second when your brain grabs the reins and instead of acting, you stop to give the matter some thought. But when I saw the barrel of the heater gleaming in the stage lights, I should have used my melon. I had a Smith and Wesson under my jacket, but when it all went down, I didn't have time to untangle myself from Lorena and pull it. Instead, I just tightened my arms around her and jitterbugged her out of the way.

Which meant that I was the one took a slug in the back.

"Definitely a .38," I gasped as I slumped against her chest. Left side, right below the shoulder blade. Cheese and rice, but that stung.

"Shh."

No use asking if there was a doctor in the house. Even the tuxedoes were rushing around like decapitated chickens. Lorena looked around. Then she leaned me over her injured shoulder and lifted me up.

"Your shoulder...hurt yourself..."

"Stop talking."

I don't know where she was thinking to take me, but when we got to the alley behind the club, we found ourselves up against a wall of pistols. The three were military, all right, from their identical buzz cuts to their shiny GI shoes. They were also stout, muscley, and red as clay. A grin cracked over my lips. Or maybe it was rigor. Either way, I'd been right about Uncle Sam and the Navajos.

Meanwhile, Lorena was working my back like it was a jigsaw puzzle. Her friends had let in the daylight, but she was trying to push it back out. Again, it should have hurt a lot more than it did, but I wasn't whining.

"Look what you've done," she hissed at them.

"Put the woman down. We have no quarrel with her," one of the men said.

"No, you only quarrel with each other. Take the good gifts I gave you and hammer them into tools of war."

Her fingers slipped and slid through the blood. The blood felt hot on my skin. It was hard to move, and I couldn't stop shivering.

"The world has changed, Little Brother," the man said. "There's a larger war going on, with an enemy that threatens all of us. Give us the codex and be on your way."

"Little Brother?" I gasped. The moon shone bright and harsh, setting Lorena's black, black hair alight with blue fire. "Who are you?"

She gently sat me against the doorjamb, wiping her fingers on her scarf, and began to go through my pockets. She didn't need the sling anymore; the gunshot wound on her shoulder was healed. Drawing the codex from my pocket, she touched her fingers to my cheek and stood. My shivering stopped. As hot wind swept through the alley, swirling papers and rubbish around our feet, Lorena Claw spoke.

"I am the one who brings forth magic from laughter." Her lips didn't move, but the words reverberated all around us, in the air, the walls, and the windowpanes. "I am the messenger. The medicine-bearer. I named the animals and stole fire from the mountain for my people. I named the tribes and gave them language. They think they've outgrown me, but when they're ready to receive me again, I shall return. I am the trickster. I am Little Brother. I am Coyote."

She held out the little codex toward the men. One of the men reached for it, and it burst into flame. My silk jacket was soaked. Everything was starting to spin. While I watched, Lorena's form quivered and shook. Then it melted like brown sugar in the rain, and came up again in the familiar canine form that had stolen my breakfast and saved my bacon.

The men opened fire, but Coyote just grinned as the bullets peppered the wall behind her. Then it all went dark.

❖

Some time later a rough hand shook me awake.

"Must have been some party, girly," the copper said as I blinked in the daylight.

Morning traffic whizzed by on Sunset. Someone was cooking bacon and eggs. A jackhammer thudded nearby. No, that was in my head.

"Am I dead?" I rasped.

"Dead drunk, more like. Come on."

"No."

The club was locked up tight, the alley swept clean of any trace of gunfire, Uncle Sam, or disappearing coyotes. And yet I couldn't shake the feeling that I hadn't seen the last of Lorena Claw. My body felt like it had been through a laundry wringer, and my shirt was stuck to my back. But aside from this, I seemed no worse for wear. As I wobbled to my feet, something tinkled to the ground behind me.

"Is that blood on your jacket?" the copper asked as I bent to pick it up.

"It's nothing."

The object was a .38 slug, flat as a pancake. Pretending to tighten my shoelace, I slipped it up my sleeve.

"Hey, I know you," the copper suddenly said. "You're that lady dick."

"At your service."

"Yeah, yeah, I've seen you down at the station." A grin spread across his face, he dropped the attitude, and for a minute, I thought my luck might be changing for the better. Then he patted my shoulder with a beefy mitt. "Tell Marlowe I said hi."

FOR ALL ETERNITY
VICTORIA OLDHAM

Water lapped gently at the side of the boat, the occasional sharp splash caused by a couple out for a romantic late-night ride under the full moon. Cara slept fitfully, the sheets stuck to her as she tossed and turned. Her dreams, as they had been for months, were haunted by the caress of a beautiful woman, short hair falling in wisps around her face, full lips kissing every hot inch of skin.

Cara cried out as the woman's hand slid between her legs. Her dream lover's eyes, the color of the Mediterranean sea, crinkled slightly at the edges with damnable amusement every time she made Cara come.

Cara woke abruptly at the sound of footsteps outside her cabin, her final cry echoing in the room. Untangling the sheets from her wet thighs, she moved cautiously to her door, peering through the early dawn light at the rest of the boat. It wasn't the first time she had woken from that particular dream thinking someone was in the room. And as usual, there was no one there, just that strange silky fog that filtered in off the canal. She never knew whether to be relieved or disappointed.

With a sigh she fell back into bed, letting the quiet lapping of water lull her back into a dreamless sleep.

❖

"Women of mythology have often been portrayed as banshees, as women with insatiable sexual hunger or the desire only to lead men to their deaths or eternal damnation. If this were really the case, we'd have population control well in hand."

The class tittered slightly at the vague reference to sex, as her freshman classes always did. Cara swept her blond hair off her shoulders, enjoying the way it fell heavy against her lower back. Teaching mythology in Italy was a daunting prospect, given that most of her students had grown up steeped in the stuff. But she worked hard on presenting old information in new ways—especially the way women were viewed as monsters or whores.

"But, Professor Grace, you have to admit women are the more sensual of the human species," one of her more argumentative male students said from the back of the room.

"No, that's the way women have been *portrayed*, which is my point. There are plenty of men who ooze sensuality too. And plenty of women who can't be bothered with sex at all. It's about perception, and changing those perceptions. Of course," she said with a wicked smile, "there's no question some of these mythological women were very, very sexy." She glanced at the clock at the back of the room. "Okay, that's it for today. For class next week, I'd like you to research a female figure from any myth and find a way to reinterpret the person she might have personified. Have a nice weekend."

The students filed out, more than one sending her a smitten smile. She smiled back, keeping it professional. The only woman she wanted was the one who made love to her every night on her boat. *Excellent. The only sex I want is with a fantasy. That's healthy.*

She shut her leather briefcase with a sigh and headed back to her houseboat to get ready for the faculty mixer she had been cajoled into attending. As one of the only American professors there, she was a popular novelty, and although it was flattering, she always left the mixers feeling like an animal with a reprieve from the zoo.

❖

Music drifted softly from the house as Cara made her way up the long walkway from the canal. She hadn't been to the house, damn near the size of a mansion, previously and she grinned wryly at the thought of her little houseboat. Obviously the faculty member who owned this place was tenured.

She handed her coat to a butler dressed in full uniform and took a glass of champagne from a tray. The room was tastefully decorated, modern without being cold, a look that was hard to get right. She wandered through the room, her fingers tracing the odd piece of beautiful antique furniture. Various other faculty members stopped her for a word, but a strange sense of anticipation niggled at her, and she didn't stop to talk to anyone for long.

She turned down a hallway with fewer people and stopped in front of a beautiful painting of Medusa. Not the Medusa of nightmares, with her head full of writhing snakes and her hateful glare, but a Medusa full of sensual curves, an inviting smile, her snakes secondary to her come-hither stare. Cara shivered and thought of her dream woman. Medusa wore such a similar expression of desire it made her panties damp.

"Do you like it, Professor? It was painted by a close friend of mine."

Cara choked on her sip of champagne. That voice. It was the voice of the woman in her dreams: soft, husky, deep, penetrating. The heavily accented Italian utterances held promises of screaming orgasms and mind-bending bliss. She didn't want to turn around. She needed the face to match the voice, but the possibility that the woman of her dreams actually existed in the flesh would be too much to handle.

Instead, she focused on the painting, willing herself not to faint. "It's stunning. I've never seen a rendering so beautiful, so full of passion instead of horror."

"It's the premise of what you teach, is it not, Professora?"

Taking a deep breath, Cara finally worked up the courage to look at the woman speaking to her.

And time, like her heart, stopped.

It's her.

Short wavy dark hair fell across her forehead, almost hiding her eyes. Full lips smirked as if with a private joke. And her eyes…

"Professora? Are you all right?"

"Have we met? I mean, at the university? Or somewhere else?" Cara blanched slightly at the abruptness of her question, because although the woman in flesh in front of her had haunted her bed for months, she was certain they had never met.

"No, Professor Grace, I do not believe so. But I've followed your work, as mythology is something close to my heart, as you can see. I am Nereza Fiametta. But friends call me Nera."

A female faculty member glided to Nera's side, and Cara noted the way the woman pressed her breasts against Nera's arm. Nera threw her an apologetic glance and Cara simply nodded as the woman led Nera away, a proprietary hand on her arm.

Cara looked back at the painting. Medusa seemed to be laughing at her.

❖

Cara thrashed in bed, the sheets tangled around her thighs, tight against her wet center, rubbing against her clit. Her breasts were swollen, heavy with desire, her nipples rock hard beneath the fingertips of her imaginary lover. She screamed through a final orgasm, staring into eyes that seemed to change color like the ocean depths. Full lips crushed her own, bruising in their passion, and a tiny feeling of panic blossomed in her soul. The kiss deepened, harder, longer, the woman's tongue plunging into her mouth as her fingers plunged inside her.

And she felt it. Her soul slipping away, drifting like a sexual river into the woman's mouth. She yanked her mouth away and ripped herself out of the fantasy.

Her pussy ached, the sheets were drenched, and the scent of sex rode the air. Trembling, she touched her lips and gasped when she found them swollen, a tiny bite stinging under her fingertip. That same heavy bluish fog misted through the cabin.

She leapt from bed and threw on the light in the bathroom. Looking in the mirror, she saw the reflection of a woman who had been thoroughly fucked, flushed from orgasm with a sexual afterglow. The faint outline of a bite mark showed on her left breast.

What the fuck? Since when does my fantasy woman leave marks?

Shivering, Cara threw on sweats, made coffee, and took it to the deck, where she sat and watched the boats getting under way for the day's ventures. She replayed the night before over and over again. Did the Italian professor really look so much like her fantasy lover? Or was her desire so strong she was convincing herself her fantasy was there in the flesh?

Watching the gondolas drift past in the early morning light, she closed her eyes and thought about the party. No matter who she had asked, no one else had seemed to know much about their hostess. Most weren't even sure what department she worked in. Every time she thought she caught a glimpse of Nera through the crowd, she lost her again. By the end of the night she was frustrated and convinced she had imagined the whole thing. In all likelihood, she had probably seen Nera around campus and subconsciously used her as a fantasy figure. Of course. Sure. And the bite mark was from her own nails, not someone's mouth.

Ignoring her overstimulated body, she went back inside to get ready for work. She stopped to pick up a slip of paper by the door.

Dear Professora,
  It was lovely to meet you last night. I'm sorry we did not get more time together. Would you meet me for dinner tonight? I would very much like to get to know you better.
    Sincerely,
    Nera

❖

Still bothered that she didn't know when the letter had come through her letterbox, Cara smoothed her black silk skirt down for the umpteenth time. Before she could knock, the butler opened the door and ushered her inside. His silence unnerved her, as did the emptiness of the enormous house.

She followed him into a room she hadn't seen the night before. It was far cozier, smaller and more inviting than the reception area had been. A fire illuminated the room, and half-full wineglasses sat in front of two enormous chairs.

The butler left the room and she filled the time perusing the paintings gracing the walls. The depth and array of mythological scenes was stunning. All of them included various women in states of undress, all sensual, all beautiful, all figures of myth. And they all had the same sultry stare that had unnerved her the night before.

"I'm glad you like my paintings. You remind me of these women."

Cara nearly spilled her wine all over the place when she felt Nera's breath against the back of her neck.

"I'm sorry. I didn't mean to startle you."

Cara turned. There was no question about it. Nera was the woman from her dreams.

"No, not at all. I was just fascinated by your paintings. They're so lifelike," Cara said, nervous beyond words. She had been coming under this woman for months, and now that she was with her in the flesh, she had no idea what to say that didn't include,"take your clothes off, right now."

"Please, sit. Is wine okay? It's from my own cellar."

"Thank you, yes. What department are you in? I'm sure we must have met before."

Nera waved a hand dismissively. "Oh, here and there, you know. Let's not talk about work. I wish to know more of you."

Cara's thighs tightened. She wanted Nera to know a hell of a lot more of her, but she continued with the small talk, aware she was doing most of the talking. Nera redirected any questions she asked back to her.

The butler announced dinner, and when they walked to the dining room, Nera placed a warm hand on Cara's back, sending chills down her spine and making her nipples harden instantly. Cara liked her sex on the dark side, and Nera's touch ran through her, promising exactly what she desired.

"You are very beautiful, Cara. I'm so glad you came to dinner," Nera whispered, her breath warm against Cara's neck.

Suddenly all Cara wanted to do was sink into Nera, rip their clothes off, and have a long night of rough and rampant sex. Hearing Nera's low chuckle, she snapped out of it and moved to her seat. What the hell was going on? Why couldn't she get her mind from between her legs?

"I'm really glad you invited me. I kept looking for you last night, but I guess I kept missing you."

Nera smiled, her gaze distant. "Yes, the faculty member who wanted my attention for the evening kept me busy. I didn't wish to be rude, but I would much rather have been with you. She was quite… unsatisfying."

The food arrived—a feast for the eyes and palate, although Cara was finding it harder and harder to concentrate the more turned on she became. Nera radiated sex, and Cara's panties were so wet she was worried her skirt would have a damp patch.

"I don't mean to be overly forward, Cara, but am I correct in assuming you like women?" Nera stroked each of Cara's fingers in a slow caress.

"Yes. Clearly. I mean, you do too, obviously?" Cara stared at Nera's fingers sliding slowly along each of her own, and the fog that filtered through her boat every morning suddenly clouded her mind. Oh God, she needed Nera inside her.

Nera continued eating, continuing to escalate Cara's desperation with subtle strokes, sexy smiles, and definite suggestions of sensual delights. Every bite she took made Cara wish it was her Nera was devouring, sucking on, kissing, and fucking.

After dinner, Nera led them, wineglasses in hand, through the living room onto a small balcony overlooking the river. Cara's knees were so weak she could barely stand. She trembled as Nera stood behind her and lightly nuzzled her ear.

"You're so very beautiful." Nera's lips grazed Cara's neck and if she hadn't been pressed against Cara's back, she would have sunk to her knees.

"I don't know why, but I think I know you," Cara whispered, about to dissolve into a puddle of need. Nera alternately bit and kissed the back of her neck, her hand buried in Cara's hair, pushing her head forward so she could get to more of her neck.

"Perhaps it is just that your soul recognizes something it wants, *caramia*." Nera pulled Cara against her body and kissed the side of her neck, making her way over her shoulder, moving the thin strap of her tank top away with her lips.

"Please." Cara's control shattered and her mind clouded. She couldn't think, all she could do was feel. Every brush of Nera's lips, the weight of Nera's hand in her hair, the small circles Nera traced on her hip, made her lose a bit more of herself. Everything came down to one thing—she needed Nera to make her come, just like she had for months in her dreams.

Nera gently moved away from her and Cara keened, desperate at the loss of contact, but the ache was quickly replaced by a sudden bit of clarity. The sexual fog enveloping her lifted enough for her to get her balance back. She steadied herself before turning to face Nera.

And the fog slammed back into her, making her panties drench and her nipples tent the fabric of her tank top. She grasped the railing behind her to keep from falling to her knees and begging Nera to take her.

"Cara, let me walk you home. It's a beautiful night, and I'd like to spend more time with you. Will you allow me?"

Cara nodded, confused. Why didn't Nera just take her to bed and fuck her senseless? Surely she felt whatever it was Cara felt?

"Yes, of course." Cara gathered her things in a daze and accepted Nera's hand as they strolled from the house out to the canal. The streets were empty, the night dark. It was the off-season, and the waterways and walkways were devoid of all but their own footsteps. They cut through a particularly tiny walkway to reach the canal where Cara kept her houseboat. Stopping abruptly, Nera pressed her against a wall, her hands sliding up Cara's skirt, over her thighs, pulling her hips tightly against her own. Her lips crushed Cara's, her tongue hot and insistent.

Cara groaned into Nera's mouth, pressed her hips hard against Nera's, desperate to feel Nera inside her. Nera stopped, placed her hands on top of Cara's skirt and rested her forehead against Cara's.

"I want you, Cara. I want to make love to you."

Cara's response, the only one she was capable of, was to kiss Nera as deeply as Nera had kissed her.

"Now. Hurry." Nera yanked away and roughly led her through the alley, and the next, until they got to Cara's boat. Cara quickly unlocked the door and glanced back to make sure Nera was actually there, that she wasn't having some kind of psychotic breakdown.

But she was there, her nipples straining against the black silk shirt, her hands clenched in fists. The blue fog Cara woke to all the time surrounded Nera, and suddenly Cara wasn't just inordinately aroused, she was also a bit nervous.

Nera stifled those nerves when she moved forward with almost supernatural speed and picked Cara up, pulled Cara's legs around her waist, and carried her through the cabin to the bed. Nera let her down and yanked Cara's skirt and top off. She stopped for only a moment, her gaze burning Cara's skin as she looked her over.

Meeting her gaze, Cara gasped. The colors of her eyes really *were* changing. The blues were melting into one another, shifting like water, just like…

Nera fell on her like a woman starving, sucking her nipples, twisting them between her fingers, biting her skin, her hands everywhere, and just as in her dreams, everywhere she touched, Cara burned.

"Say my name, Cara. Tell me you want me."

"Oh God, Nera. Please. Please fuck me. I need you."

"Again. Tell me what you want me to do." Nera sucked hard on a nipple.

Cara cried out, so close to orgasm. "I want you inside me, Nera. Please, take me. Take me like you do in my dreams. Please…"

Nera growled and roughly shoved Cara's legs apart. She pushed two fingers in, then a third, and pushed hard and deep, pumping into her, her eyes penetrating as she watched Cara's face.

"Come. Now, Cara. Scream for me, baby."

Nera twisted her fingers slightly and Cara came, screaming as her orgasm ripped through her. Better than her dreams, better than anything, ever.

She opened her eyes. Nera watched her. She looked…hungry. Like someone who had been starved for far too long. She cried out when Nera expertly flipped her onto her side without coming out of her and added a fourth finger inside her.

"You've been dreaming about me, haven't you, *bella*? You've been begging me for this every night, riding me, giving yourself to me. Give yourself to me now, Cara. Give everything to me."

Cara whimpered when Nera's thumb pushed into her ass and her hand thrust deep, hard, filling her completely. The pressure, the pleasure, was overwhelming, too much to take, but if Nera stopped she knew for certain she'd die. Nera's other hand slid beneath her head and cupped her cheek. She slid two fingers inside Cara's mouth.

"Suck, baby."

Cara did as she was told, sucking Nera's fingers in time to Nera's fingers thrusting so deep, so hard, inside her. She moaned around Nera's fingers when she added a third. Everything was full, every part of her belonged to her fantasy woman. She careened toward another orgasm, felt it building and building.

"Look at me, Cara. Look at me when you come, and say my name, one more time, baby. Scream for me," Nera whispered in Cara's ear, thrusting harder inside her as she took her fingers from Cara's mouth.

Cara managed to look at Nera as she had been asked. She screamed and her orgasm exploded. "My name! Say it, Cara. Now!"

She didn't want to. She didn't want to say Nera's name ever again. But it was too late.

"Nera! Oh my God. Oh my God, no."

Succubus.

Her gaze locked on Nera's and terror warred with orgasm. Nera's pupils had turned to flames, literal flames, washing out the blue till it became white. She opened her mouth and held it just over Cara's and Cara cried out as she watched the blue light of her soul leaving her mouth to dance on Nera's tongue before disappearing. Nera's eyes closed and she moaned as she drank Cara's soul, her hips thrusting hard against Cara's thigh.

Throwing her head back, Nera howled. As Nera climaxed, Cara watched her swallow the blue threads of her soul. She closed her eyes and moaned when Nera's hand thrust into her, again and again, harder and harder, until she came a final time, her back arching as she filled Nera's hand.

Unconsciousness closed in on her, but before the darkness claimed her, Nera whispered against her ear, "You're mine now, *caramia*. For all eternity."

SOLSTICE
KARIS WALSH

Ty stood at attention in the general's command tent, fighting to hold still and not fidget. She wished she had taken a few minutes to compose herself after she and her cadre arrived at the temporary HQ for the Lycan Resistance, but as usual she had rushed headlong into human form and human contact. Now she had to stand in front of the only person she would acknowledge as her alpha with twigs in her disheveled ponytail and her wolf barely under control. Her cadre had made the long trek from their home on the tundra to the command center in the dense forest near Varesska in wolf form and she was exhausted. Certain of her cadre's discipline and aware that survival depended on their wolves' heightened senses and faster speeds, Ty had allowed only minimal shifts back to human form. They had made it safely to HQ, but even she felt the edges of her humanity blur and fade. She needed all her strength to simply remain upright and keep her mouth closed when all she wanted to do was flop on the floor and pant until she recovered.

"You're the youngest alpha in the Resistance, yet your cadre is reputed to be one of the toughest fighting forces we have," the general said conversationally, standing close to Ty. He must be able to smell how close to the surface her wolf was and seemed to be gauging her self-control. He intruded on her personal space, his direct eye contact making her every exhale threaten to morph into a growl. She alternately fought and pleaded with her wolf, just managing to keep her eyes averted and her breathing quiet. She was relieved the general was a male. If she added any sexual attraction to her already shaky control she wouldn't be able to keep her wolf from breaking free.

"Although," he continued, "some say your pack is too hot-headed and dangerous." The general paused as if giving her a chance to defend herself and the Lycans under her command. Ty remained silent. If she spoke without being asked a direct question the general would take her down. Her strength might be a match for his wolf, but he had her beat in both experience and shifting agility. Even so, her wolf demanded a chance to fight, to challenge his dominance. Ty's struggle was only betrayed by a slight curl of her lip, the merest hint of a snarl.

The general smiled and pushed another inch into Ty's space before stepping away and sitting behind his desk. "Have a seat." He waved toward a chair. His aggressive tone and challenging stance disappeared, but Ty remained vigilant even as she sat and crossed her legs casually.

"The people of Varesska will be celebrating the Winter Solstice soon," the general said, shuffling through some papers on his desk until he found what he was looking for. "Ah, here it is. The queen's advisor, Leo, is calling it a Celebration of Progress in honor of the advances they've made in coal mining and processing. Whatever the name, it is our Winter Solstice. Have you ever gone to the festival?"

Ty was startled by the question and by the unexpected wave of sadness she felt as the memory resurfaced. "Only once. I was very young."

The general nodded with a compassionate look and for a moment he wasn't her leader but simply a member of her pack. No Lycan was untouched by pain or loss, and strong emotions always accompanied any reminder of the time before their Resistance had been necessary. "I need you to go back again. You will have three days before the solstice and then you will be able to avenge those you lost. It is a dangerous mission, but the fate of the Resistance—of the Lycans—depends on its success. If you accept?"

"We accept," Ty said, answering for her cadre without hesitation.

"Not your cadre. You. The mission is yours alone," the general said. "We have rescued the queen's son from his mountain stronghold and will return him to the city on the solstice. We need you to break into the palace and kill Leo before we arrive. It is vital that you are successful, but you will most likely be captured before you can escape. Are you willing to give your life for the Resistance?"

Ty allowed herself to briefly meet the general's eyes. "I am."

❖

Two nights later, Ty followed a group of off-duty sentries as they left their barracks at the Royal House and headed toward the edge of town, where the taverns and brothels had dominion. She had been observing the guards since her arrival in Varesska the day before and had quickly settled on her mark. The chosen guard's restlessness and youth made her a likely candidate for Ty's purposes—she ought to be easily seduced, easily convinced to sneak Ty into the palace. It was only a pleasant bonus that the sight of her made Ty's mouth water and her sharp canines pierce her lips.

Ty slipped through the shadows as she trailed behind the boisterous group of sentries. Her mark occasionally glanced behind, a frown creasing her delicate features, and Ty had a moment of doubt about her choice. The young woman was the only one who seemed to sense the group was being tailed, and Ty wondered if her own desire had led her to misjudge the guard's vulnerability. She briefly considered changing her focus to another female in the group, but that thought made her wolf howl with such force that Ty almost fell to her knees in the street. She staggered a few steps before she managed to calm her inner turmoil. She had made her decision and she would make it work.

The group of sentries seemed to have a specific destination in mind and passed several taverns before they finally entered one called the Broken Hart. The wooden placard hanging by its door showed a crude drawing of a wolf tearing into a deer carcass—a theme she'd seen repeated outside most of Varesska's shops and inns. The images were mostly of wolves engaging in various forms of violent behavior, designed by Leo no doubt to reinforce the citizens' idea of Lycans as uncivilized and brutal. Disgusted by the lies, Ty hated to patronize the bar, and only her sense of duty—and her growing desire to finally get close to her mark—made her push through the door and into the dimly lit tavern.

Ty leaned against the bar, ordered a drink, and tossed a few coins on the counter in exchange for a glass of vodka. She sipped the clear liquid and fought to keep her face from revealing her distaste. Everything was too warm, from the oily-tasting vodka to the room with its blazing fire and wall torches. She tried to shake off her memories of the day Leo's guards had reached her village. She had been in wolf form, on a routine patrol of the village's flocks and fields, when the shouts and smell of smoke had alerted her to danger. She arrived home too late to help, and several days later members of the newly formed Resistance found her sitting among the ashes of her family home. She'd been twelve then, and that was years ago. She was no longer a child. She would finally have a chance to avenge her family, her pack. She glanced at her sentry out of the corner of her eye, not making direct eye contact but still feeling the sensation every time the woman's gaze rested on her. She was about to head over to the guards' table when her mark made the move for her.

"Evening," Ty said casually when the sentry came over to the bar next to her and ordered a drink.

"Hello," the woman said after a slight hesitation. She picked up her glass and moved as if to head back to her table, but instead remained at the bar.

"I'm Tyvka." Ty held out her hand and waited a few seconds before the sentry reached over and shook it. She carefully pulled her hand away when she felt her claws start to emerge, fighting the sudden desire to yank the sentry closer. "Friends call me Ty."

"Mina," the guard said briefly. Ty had expected the sentry's eyes to be brown, matching her hair, and she was oddly pleased when she saw that they were flecked with greens and gold instead. She was even more pleased to realize that this woman was much too young to have been involved in the destruction of her village.

"Mina," she echoed, enjoying the feel of the name on her tongue. Her voice sounded rougher than it should and she tried to control it. "You look very warm."

"A little," the sentry admitted. Even with the fire and the heat from crowded bodies, Mina still wore a deerskin jacket and mink stole. Her boots were fur-lined, probably rabbit. The assault of different odors was distracting. Besides the conflicting smells of the furs, Mina wore a cloying perfume that was too potent for Ty's heightened senses. She couldn't understand why her wolf kept pushing her closer to these scents instead of pulling away as she would have expected.

"Let's go outside for a while," Ty offered, more for her own relief than as part of her plan. Mina simply nodded and followed her out the door. Ty walked without looking back until she came to a shadowed alley. She stepped off of the street and the second Mina followed, Ty crowded the young sentry against the side of a building. Mina was nearly her height, but Ty's added muscle and her wolf's desire made her seem larger.

"I shouldn't..." Mina raised her head and her gold-flecked eyes glittered with arousal.

Ty put her hands on the wall on either side of Mina's head, letting her claws elongate and dig into the wood. She hadn't doubted her ability to seduce a sentry on this mission, but she hadn't expected to be seduced herself. She felt a rumbling growl start deep inside and leaned forward to kiss Mina in an attempt to silence her wolf.

Their lips met in a gasping, drowning kiss made of nothing but passion. Ty felt her enlarging canines roughly brush against teeth and she moved her head to the side. She couldn't risk being exposed as a Lycan, but turning away from Mina's kiss only brought her in contact with a smooth neck that was even more tempting than Mina's mouth. Ty kept her lips protectively over her teeth and only allowed herself to lick the beating pulse, the soft skin below Mina's ear, the rigid tendons that supported Mina's flung-back head. She glanced at her hand to make sure there was only a hint of claw before she reached under Mina's deerskin shirt, dragging her nails over a taut nipple and nearly losing control of her wolf as Mina sighed and arched under her touch.

A few more minutes of this and she'd completely lose her ability to maintain total human form. Already thoughts of her mission, her duty to the Resistance, even her responsibilities for her cadre blurred under the force of her desire and Mina's need. She managed to check her instinct to rake her claws down Mina's torso, tasting her blood and marking her as a mate. Instead, she thrust her hand down the front of Mina's leather pants, careful only to graze Mina's clit firmly with her nails. Just one touch and Mina cried out, rubbing against her and making Ty stiffen with need. She pulled her claw away and replaced it with her softer palm, cupping Mina as she sagged against the wall, her breathing eventually evening out.

Ty tugged her hand free, stepping back into the shadows. She wanted to say something to console the sentry, who looked shocked at what they had done, to find some way to salvage her forgotten mission. She didn't trust herself to speak, though. To open her mouth and show her canines, or worse, have her voice come out as an unintelligible growl or snarl. So she simply turned away from Mina, running into the night until she was far enough from the bar that she could rip off her clothes and let the shift take her.

❖

The night before the solstice, Mina slipped out of the barracks and jogged through the shadows until she reached a small park on the outskirts of the city. It was never safe for her to shift, and now with the solstice approaching, it was more dangerous than usual. She had to take the chance. She couldn't contain her wolf any longer. The experience with that stranger from the bar had left her shaken, out of control. Her infrequent sexual encounters had always been with women who didn't excite her enough to call her wolf. If she felt a strong sexual attraction, she had learned to walk away and not risk her life, or her family, for mere personal satisfaction.

But Ty had been different. She had called Mina to her and there had been no question that she would answer. Mina could still picture Ty leaning against the bar, the muscles on her forearm sharply defined, her posture tense and prepared for flight. Mina hadn't been able to tell how much of the red glow in Ty's black hair and eyes had been due to the firelight, or to something shining from within, but she had been unable to resist the desire to approach her.

Mina shed her heavy furs and slipped naked into the icy fountain in the center of the park. She ducked under the frigid water, wetting her hair in an attempt to remove the stench of the perfume she wore to camouflage her Lycan scent, and to freeze out the memory of Ty's touch. Ignoring her strong emotions and walking over to the bar had been risky enough, but following Ty into the dark alley was suicidal. To let herself be touched and kissed when her wolf was revolting against constraint, to expose her neck and lean into the other woman's searching caresses. Insanity. Mina knew she should have fled the moment her growing canines had rasped against Ty's teeth, but instead she had opened herself up and risked exposure as a Lycan.

Mina's father had managed to spare his family by hiding them directly under the royal guard's watchful eyes. She was alive only because he had volunteered as a member of the sentry when the Civilization began and she owed it to him to keep their family secret. Yet she wondered how long they would have to live in hiding, not only denying their true natures but delivering fellow Lycans to their death for Leo's cause. Mina chafed under the necessity of sacrificing her connection to her wolf just to stay alive. What good was living half a life?

Relieved of the overpowering perfume and furs, Mina was able to detect traces of Lycan scent in the park. She found evidence on her infrequent nightly wanderings of other Lycans still living in Varesska, and she hoped there might be even more outside of the city. She had never revealed her knowledge of these illegal inhabitants, had never taken part in any of the hunts that Leo occasionally required. But she worried that trouble during the solstice might force her to choose between killing one of her own or facing certain death.

"You're Lycan." A shocked voice broke Mina out of her distressing musings. She'd been so caught up in her inner turmoil she hadn't noticed the increasing wolf scent until Ty was standing right next to the fountain. Mina glanced toward her weapons that lay under her furs, but Ty stood between the sentry and her silver sword. "Hiding among the guards themselves. Brilliant."

The absolute hatred in Ty's voice chilled Mina's already icy skin. With her weapons and her sentry training, Mina thought she stood a chance of defending herself against the powerful Lycan who stood before her. Without her sword, however, and with little experience in shifting, Mina knew Ty would rip out her throat before she could even grow a full set of claws. A shiver ran down her spine as she recalled Ty's mouth on her throat the night before. Her own desire had been so intense, her fear of being discovered as a Lycan so fierce, that she hadn't noticed that it was an enemy who had taken her in the alley. At least she now had an explanation for her foolhardy urge to get close to this stranger.

"So, coward," Ty continued, her voice rough and wild enough to make Mina flinch. "How many of your kind have you killed to save your own pelt?"

"None," Mina whispered, unsure why she was so determined to make Ty believe her. "I've never killed a Lycan."

"Nor have you made any effort to save one, I'm sure." Ty paced restlessly in the space between Mina and the weapon, her red-accented black eyes never wavering as Mina slowly climbed out of the water and sat on the cement edge of the fountain. Mina didn't try to deny the truth of Ty's statement, but she refused to cower in front of her. She sat erect even though she was naked and exposed, resisting the urge to cross her arms and hide the stiff peaks of her nipples.

"It is only temporary," she said. "While Leo is in power it's too dangerous for any Lycan…"

"Do you think I don't know that? I watched the royal guards burn my village, kill my family. And you try to lecture me about *safety*?"

Ty's last words came out as a snarl and Mina fought the instinctive reaction to lower her eyes or act submissive in any way. She had little experience with other Lycans except for her family and limited knowledge of pack life. Even so, her wolf recognized Ty's call as strongly dominant. Mina squared her shoulders and kept her head raised. She didn't belong to Ty's pack and would not recognize her as a superior.

"I wasn't even a sentry when the raids began," she said, not foolish enough to refer to the purging of Lycans by the customary term "Civilization." In desperation she repeated the words her father had often used to appease her guilty conscience. "It's important that Lycans survive, in any way necessary. Then, when the uprising comes…"

"It's coming now." Ty's voice transformed to a deep growl. She stepped closer and threaded rough fingers through Mina's hair, pulling her head back and again exposing her pale throat. "The Resistance has been fighting this battle while you've been living in royal luxury. *You* are the enemy and I should kill you right now."

Mina sensed Ty's brief hesitation and she slipped off the ledge and onto her knees, Ty's fingers still tangled in her hair.

"What would you have me do?" she asked, her voice quiet as she leaned her forehead against Ty's belly. She inhaled deeply, her breath catching as the scent of wolf—so close—made her body vibrate with need. "Should I announce that I'm a Lycan and be killed on the spot? What purpose would that serve?"

"If you truly want to serve, then leave this city and join the Resistance." Ty's snarling tone revealed her doubt that Mina would dare to be so brave. "Use your training and skills to save your people, not murder more of them."

Mina shook her head against the taut muscles of Ty's abdomen, a reluctant groan escaping her throat. "I've heard rumors of a Resistance, but nothing certain." She had assumed her father would tell her if there were facts instead of simply rumors, but hearing Ty's conviction fueled the doubts that had been growing in her mind lately. Doubts about her father's intentions and her own participation in his deception. It had been easier to pretend that there was nothing for her beyond Varesska's walls, beyond her duties as a royal guard.

To divert her mind from those uncomfortable thoughts, Mina instead focused on the tantalizing, overpowering scent of wolf. She pushed Ty's shirt up and skimmed her mouth over hard muscles and soft skin. She inhaled through her nose, her body growing tight with need as she licked the thin trickle of blood she inadvertently drew when her canines erupted more easily and swiftly than they ever had. Ty's hand remained fisted in her brown hair, but suddenly it felt more like a caress, less like a threat. Mina took that as a silent, if reluctant, acceptance of her touch and she opened the buttons on Ty's pants. Hastily, she pulled them down, spurred on by Ty's rapid breathing and her own desire as the potent Lycan scent hit her full force. She left slender trails of blood as her elongated claws raked down Ty's thighs, making Ty gasp and arch at the slight pain.

For the first time, Mina felt every part of her respond to another's nearness. Ty smelled of wildness, of country air and spruce trees, of wolf. Without hesitation Mina's mouth found Ty's wetness. Tears trickled down her cheeks, their saltiness mingling with the sweeter taste of Ty on her tongue. Grief and remorse and anger coursed through her as she faced her cowardly compliance with her father's deceptions, followed by a sense of loss over the wasted years spent in the city and far from her own kind. Most of all, however, an overpowering sense of returning home, of belonging, filled her. Her breathing deepened along with Ty's and her hips jolted when Ty's shook in orgasm.

❖

Ty released her hold on Mina's hair and staggered a few steps away before she turned her back and roughly pulled her clothing back in place. She grabbed Mina's cloak, unbuckled the scabbard, and threw the fur at Mina, who knelt shivering on the pebbled ground. "Get dressed."

Watching Mina dress, Ty stood silently, blood dripping from her palms where still-elongated claws dug into her clenched fists. Her mission was more successful than she had expected. She had planned to seduce a guard and had instead found a mate. Mina's compliance in her plans was certainly more assured than if she were simply a lover, but Ty felt no satisfaction in their joining.

"I had no idea..." Mina's voice faltered to a stop, but Ty could easily guess the feelings their mating had brought close to the surface. No idea there was an organized Lycan community just beyond her city's reach, no idea her wolf would respond so strongly to another of her kind, no idea how little depth of connection and emotion her life as a human—without a pack—truly had.

"I didn't know there was a Resistance, but now I do," Mina continued. "I'll leave the city with you, fight with you."

In a heartbeat Ty was standing close enough to ruffle Mina's hair with her breath. "It's too late now," she growled. "The fight is coming to the city, along with the true heir to the throne. Choose your side."

Mina's voice shook but she still refused to lower her eyes and submit to Ty's dominant posture. "You," she said quietly, but without hesitation. "I choose you."

"Then get me into the Royal House," Ty said, taking a step back as she resisted the urge to either push Mina back to her knees or drop to her own and reclaim her mate. Lessons in submission were pointless now. Ty had accepted that she had little chance of getting out of Varesska alive after she completed her mission. Her odds of survival were even lower with an unprepared and recognizable guard as her ally. She felt a flicker of pain at the thought of Mina's likely death, but she pushed it aside.

"Dawn will break soon and the celebrations will begin," she said. "Most of the guards will be outside watching the crowds. I need to get inside. To Leo."

Mina nodded and they started toward the palace, keeping to darkened alleys and back streets. Ty grasped Mina's hand as they jogged through the shadows. She told herself the gesture was meant merely to reinforce Mina's willingness to help, but she needed the contact as well. For some unknown reason, her wolf had chosen this unlikely mate and Ty felt the conflicting desire to protect her, even as she led her to a certain death.

After her initial shock at discovering Mina was Lycan eased, Ty's conviction that Mina was a traitor diminished as well. If Ty hadn't seen the purge herself, hadn't seen her family murdered, would she have been as willing to embrace deception? Would she have believed the comforting lies and promises of a vague future uprising? Ty burned with a desire to show Mina *her* world, where pack history, values, and traditions were honored and defended. She wanted to introduce Mina to her cadre, teach her Lycan ways, run with her across the barren tundra and sleep with her under the brilliant stars far from the city lights. Since the loss of her family, Ty had lived in solitary companionship with her cadre. In Mina she glimpsed a chance at a new family, short-lived as it was to be. She tightened her grip on Mina's hand and felt an answering scrape of claws along her wrist.

Getting inside the Royal House was easy with Mina's help. Mina distracted the guards at the side entrance while Ty slipped into the hall and crouched in a shadowed recess in the public courtroom. One more guard to lure away from his post and Ty was in the interior rooms of the palace. A breathless and pale Mina followed soon after, the strain of her actions evident on her face.

"Leo will be in his dressing room," Mina said quietly. "He'll only have one guard with him until he's ready to go outside. Then he'll be surrounded and it will be impossible for you to get to him."

"Then it must be done now," Ty said. She had returned Mina's silver sword when they reached the palace. At every step she worried Mina's resolve would falter and she would alert the other guards to Ty's presence, but her mate remained steadfast. Ty slipped her fingers through Mina's hair and pulled her close for one quick, hard kiss of gratitude and sorrow.

Mina led Ty through the winding corridors. They turned the last corner just as the door to Leo's room opened and three men came into the hall.

"No," Mina whispered. Ty recognized Leo and the guard with him, but the third, and unexpected, man was older and draped in heavy furs. Ty sniffed as she caught the scent of perfume. Mina's father.

Ty's decision was made so quickly she was barely aware of it. She could possibly fight them all, but if she failed then Mina would be killed as a traitor. Instead, she stepped in front of Mina and raised her arms in the air just as the men turned toward them. Her priorities shifted, her mission failed, as she willingly became Mina's prisoner.

Ty saw Mina's father react to her scent as his nose twitched and his eyes narrowed. "A Lycan! Excellent work, Mina. Now step away from her, my daughter," he said, his eyes never leaving Ty. He gestured at the male guard. "Detain her."

The guard slammed Ty against the stone wall and blood trailed from her temple as he started to bind her wrists. As if breaking free from a spell, Mina unsheathed her sword, her wolf howling in defense of her mate. She slit the guard's throat, but almost as quickly she stumbled, staring in stunned horror at the hilt of her father's dagger protruding from her belly. A slow stain of blood spread on her fur cloak.

Mina dropped to her knees, and Ty grabbed her sword as it fell from Mina's useless hand, screaming in rage as she plunged it into Mina's father's chest.

"I have to get Leo," Ty growled, hovering over Mina. "Shift and your wolf will heal. I'll be back, love."

"Can't…" Mina said weakly as she collapsed next to the two corpses.

"You can. You are Lycan." Ty shifted, her wolf calling Mina's. Calling her mate.

❖

Deep in the woods, a few miles outside of Varesska, Ty lay on a bed of pine boughs, cradling her dozing mate. After Mina had shifted, Ty had caught Leo and avenged her family. She'd found Mina and followed the limping brown wolf through the ancient maze of tunnels beneath the palace until they had resurfaced on the edge of the city. Once Ty had sealed the heavy wooden door, she'd shifted to join her mate and they'd raced out of Varesska and into the forest beyond.

Ty ran her hand lightly over the healing wound under Mina's rib cage. Mina stirred and trailed sleepy kisses over Ty's shoulder before she raised her head and captured Ty's mouth with her own. Ty rolled Mina onto her back, deepening the kiss, her canines and claws extending to claim her mate. Tomorrow they would rejoin the Resistance. Tonight they would celebrate the solstice together.

THE OTHER SIDE OF THE MIRROR
VALERIE BRONWEN

*D*on't be afraid.
 The words echoed through her mind as Meg sat up in bed with a gasp, her heart racing.

The entire room lit up again with an eerie white light.

The thunder followed almost the instant the light vanished, big glowing dots still in the center of her vision. She shivered, pulling the covers up around her. Rain was beating against the sliding glass doors leading to the balcony outside her bedroom, and she could make out whitecaps on the lake through the gloom. She took another deep, cleansing breath—the way her therapist had told her to. Her heart was racing, and she leaned back against the hard headboard, closing her eyes and trying to clear her mind of the dream she'd been having.

Deep, cleansing breaths. It was just a dream, that's all. Just a dream I can't even remember.

She slid out of bed, reaching for her robe where she'd left it on the floor beside the bed. She stood, pulling the silky robe over her bare shoulders. She ran a hand through her dark hair—grown out some from the butchering it got in the hospital, but still shorter than she would prefer. She walked over to the sliding glass doors and flipped on the balcony light with a flick of her fingers on the switch. The grass of the backyard glittered with water in the arc of light before it faded into blackness again. Rain was pelting the glass doors, which also vibrated slightly in the gusting wind. She stood there, looking out, feeling the cold air coming out of the vent in the ceiling just to her left. She shivered and pulled the robe tighter.

The lawn gradually sloped down to the shore of the lake. The light on the dock was dark—since it was always on, the bulb must have burned out.

Lightning lit up the sky again, followed by another loud crack of thunder that shook the house.

She turned away from the window, pulling the curtains shut. The house was cold—too cold, and she debated for a moment or two walking out into the hallway and adjusting the thermostat, but decided not to. She walked back over to the bed, yawning as she let the robe drop from her shoulders. She sat down on the edge of the bed and was about to swing her legs up when she noticed that the room was getting lighter.

Puzzled, she paused. Out of the corner of her eye, she noticed the source of the light.

She turned her head and inhaled sharply.

I must be dreaming, she thought, closing her eyes and opening them again quickly.

The enormous mirror on the wall was *glowing.*

She froze momentarily, and shook her head when she realized what it must be. *I thought I was getting better.* Sighing, she climbed back under the covers—yet kept her eyes on the massive, ornate antique mirror on the wall.

The hallucinations were easier to deal with when she went with them, rather than trying to resist. Resisting led to blurry vision, headaches, nausea—and as crazy as they were, as crazy as they made her feel, it was better to just go with the crazy rather than fight it and make herself really sick.

All a result of the accident—and she might get better.

Someday.

The doctors weren't really sure—which was frustrating.

She might not ever be *normal* again.

In one instant, her life changed forever.

She didn't remember the accident, or anything else, really, from that morning. Her last memory was from the night before, kissing Julia good night and getting under the covers. She was tired—it had been a long day, the construction guys had been in and out all day, and dealing with them always wore her out—and she just wanted to go to sleep, so she mumbled *I love you* as her head hit the pillow and she drifted away.

Had she only known…

Traumatic amnesia was what the doctors called it, and they doubted she would ever remember anything from the morning life pulled the rug out from under her. What she did know came from the police report, which she had read so many times she practically had it memorized. She and Julia had been leaving Tulane's campus in Meg's Toyota Camry when a student ran a stop sign, demolishing their car and killing Julia instantly.

The student had been texting while driving and escaped with a few cuts and bruises.

Meg lost the baby in the emergency room at Touro Infirmary while still unconscious—which left her feeling empty and sad when she finally woke up. She hadn't even known the insemination had taken—her follow-up appointment hadn't been for another week. Julia, at least, had died without knowing the pain of the loss—which was no comfort at all.

At first, she'd just been numb, in shock—unable to feel anything. This new world, of antiseptic smells and her hovering sister, of IV drips and medications, of loss so overwhelming was one she didn't want—a nightmare she couldn't seem to wake up from. Each passing day hammered her new reality into her mind. Her love was gone, their child lost. In one fell swoop, she'd lost everything that mattered most to her—all because of a stupid text message some stupid, spoiled college boy was sending to one of his buddies—something that could have waited until he was safely parked somewhere.

When at last she was able to feel again, she'd been overwhelmed with anger and rage—rage at the thoughtless, careless student; at God, life, everything. And the anger burned itself out, with depression rushing in to fill the emotional vacuum.

Her sister Anne had been there to take care of everything. To deal with the doctors, the lawyers, the funeral arrangements—brisk and ruthlessly efficient, Anne had always been good at that type of thing, which was why she was such a great personal assistant.

But Anne couldn't make the depression go away—nor could she do anything about the hallucinations.

The mirror became brighter, and she sat up in the bed, afraid to look but afraid not to. *It's just a hallucination*, she told herself over and over. The accident had damaged a part of her brain—they'd explained it to her, but it was too complicated for her to remember or understand—the bottom line was that every once in a while she might have a hallucination. *And face it, girl*, she told herself grimly, *a glowing mirror is better than seeing a tiger in your backyard, or a pterodactyl swooping down out of the sky to eat someone at the streetcar stop.*

She'd been sitting on the front balcony of the now empty-seeming house she'd shared with Julia on St. Charles Avenue when the last had happened. It had been unsettling, as all the hallucinations had been—but all she could do, as her doctor kept telling her, was relax and go with them.

Another part of her new reality that required adjustment.

She reached for her glasses on the nightstand, slipping them on and shivering a little as everything came into clear focus.

She'd never cared for the mirror, but it was one of the few possessions Julia loved—Julia who wouldn't notice (or care) if she was drinking out of Baccarat crystal or a Flintstones jelly jar. Julia simply never cared about things like that—her work was the most important thing to her. She never seemed to care whether her clothes matched, or if her hair was combed. It was part of her charm, Meg had realized, part of that intrinsic something that made up Dr. Julia Shelby, professor of European history at Tulane University.

When Meg had moved into the huge house on St. Charles Avenue, she'd taken charge—getting rid of junk, rearranging furniture so the big rooms with the high ceilings and hardwood floors became comfortable and livable. *You're just a natural nester—I love it and I love you*, Julia had said when it was all finished, sweeping Meg into her arms and kissing her. *I can't wait to see what you can do with the lake house.*

Meg recoiled the first time she saw the mirror—she thought it was hideous, with its enormous dark green metal frame with cherubs and roses surrounding the huge reflective glass. It predated her in Julia's life—with a pang she remembered they'd only had three years together—as had this house on the north shore of Lake Pontchartrain, near Eden Isles with the twin spans across the lake to New Orleans just visible in the distance. She'd considered taking the mirror down—its greenish metal frame was screwed into the wall, and it did take up a huge space that could have been better utilized, but she couldn't bring herself to do it. Julia had loved the mirror—she'd often found Julia staring into it, her hands touching the angels and cherubs shaped into the metal. "My grandmother bought it, in France just before the war," Julia explained once. "It may have belonged to Catherine de Medici. At least that's the story."

As an expert on the French royal house of Valois—particularly the period of Catherine de Medici—the mirror obviously meant a great deal to Julia.

And it was one more reminder that Julia had once lived, had once shared this room with her, that they'd made love in this very bed.

So she'd kept it hanging there, to help her remember.

This was the first hallucination since she'd fled the city a week earlier, hoping that being in a place that wasn't quite as haunted with memories would make the healing easier.

And of course the first hallucination I have here has to do with that fucking mirror, she thought grimly, gripping her coverlet with both hands.

The light coming out of the mirror began to dim a bit around the edges, and she thought she could make out trees, or foliage. She leaned forward, not willing to get out of bed and get closer.

The center of the glass seemed misty through the light, like headlights on a car piercing through a gray fog, but as she watched, the mist began to swirl and take shape.

The shape of a woman.

Involuntarily, she screamed.

And the light went out.

There was nothing there, just the mirror reflecting the room in its calm surface.

She heard footsteps coming down the hall in a hurry, and she leaned back against her pillows and the headboard, closing her eyes as her bedroom door opened and the room flooded with light.

"Are you okay?" her sister Anne asked, coming over and taking her hand, sitting on the edge of the bed. She was wearing her fuzzy pink robe, her hair sticking up around her head like Medusa's snakes. "Did you have another nightmare?"

Meg didn't answer at first, trying to decide what to say, and finally simply nodded in agreement. *Better a nightmare than a hallucination—a nightmare won't mean a trip to the doctor.*

"Do you want me to sit with you until you fall asleep?" Anne asked, her voice gentle. "I mean, with that storm out there"—she shivered—"it's no wonder you had a nightmare."

As if to emphasize her point, thunder cracked and the entire house shook again. Meg stole a glance over at the mirror, almost daring it to be glowing with light, but all she saw was the back of her sister and the wall opposite the glass. "No, that's okay," she murmured, closing her eyes again and sliding down into the bed. "I'll be okay, really."

Anne leaned over and kissed the top of her head before padding lightly out of the room, turning off the light and closing the door behind her.

Meg opened her eyes and watched the mirror, but the hallucination was over, and in a few more moments she fell asleep.

The next few days passed, and there were no more hallucinations. Meg went for walks in the morning along the road, picking wildflowers and waving at neighbors. She worked on the flower garden behind the back porch, read several books, and resisted the urge to take pills. She also worried about Anne. Her older sister was going through a rather nasty divorce, one that seemed to just get nastier with every passing day. Meg had never liked her brother-in-law Aaron—there was something smarmy about him just below the surface of the good-ole-boy façade he liked to project—and was relieved when Anne finally left him. Anne hadn't told her what had happened to finally drive her out of their house in Jackson, but Meg figured when she was ready to tell she would. The accident had been conveniently timed, if one wanted to think that way—it gave Anne the out she needed to leave Jackson. They didn't have any children—Sam and Sara were from his first marriage, and Meg wondered if Anne missed the children she had no claim on. Sometimes, when Anne thought she was alone, or Meg was out of the house, she would cry—muffled heartbroken sobs that pierced through to Meg's very soul. Whenever she would ask, though, Anne would simply dismiss her concerns with a "my problems are nothing compared to yours."

As though anyone can compare miseries, Meg always thought, but never tried to force the issue. When Anne was ready, she would talk about her failed marriage and the ugly divorce.

She was dreaming about Anne about a week after the mirror hallucination, a horrible nightmare with Aaron chasing them both, a foolish but frightening grin on his face, a bloody hatchet in his hands. Every time they thought they'd escaped him, gotten away, he popped up with that horrible grin.

She sat up, gasping for air, her heart racing. It seemed so real…

…and then she noticed the mirror was glowing again.

She felt her heartbeat increase, and a cold sweat broke across her brow. She swallowed because her throat had gone dry. There was a glass of water on her nightstand, as always, but she didn't move. It wasn't the moon's reflection—the curtains were closed. A quick flick of her eyes to her right verified that. She blinked a few times, shook her head—but the mirror kept glowing brighter until she had to avert her eyes. Dots changing color quickly danced in front of her eyes as they adjusted to the abrupt change.

I'm not dreaming. Dreams are never this vivid. And it's not a hallucination—I never have the same one twice. This is happening, this is real—or I've lost my mind.

But do crazy people question their sanity?

The light began to dim as her mind kept racing, desperate to find any answer that precluded years of therapy and drugs. She turned her head—yes, the mirror's glow *was* dimming, but this was because colors were appearing, swirling on the smooth surface, struggling to take shape, assume a form.

She released her breath in a loud gasp and reached for her glass. She took a sip of the tepid water—her mouth now as dry as her throat—and another before putting it back in its place. She slid down the satin sheets, the coverlets bunching around her, her glasses firmly planted on the bridge of her nose.

The colors were still fluid, becoming a little more formed. A lovely aquamarine square in the upper right hand corner of the enormous mirror began to spread, like wet paint slowly dripping and spreading down a slanted wall. Only the aquamarine was bleeding straight across to the other upper corner. The deep emerald green rectangle stretching from corner to corner at the bottom began undulating and running upward.

Her breath caught a bit as she realized the browns and blues in the center were forming the silhouette of a woman—a shape similar to the one she'd seen in the mirror the night of the storm.

It—it can't be, she insisted to herself, aware that her nipples had become hard against the soft flannel of the nightshirt.

But it was happening.

Curiosity was trumping fear—she was still afraid, she knew that from the gooseflesh on her arms—but she couldn't look away from the mirror any more than she could stop breathing.

One of the browns elongated, fading to a light tan as its borders became more solid and defined, textured until she knew it was a suede leather boot, well worn and wrinkled around the ankle, fitting closely to a shapely calf just as the other took form a few inches to the left. The aquamarine deepened, a splotch of bright yellow she hadn't noticed becoming bright and aglow like the sun. The undulating green became long blades of soft, damp grass.

Her figure, her shape was becoming clearer and clearer, and Meg caught her breath again as one of the graceful hands slowly rose to brush several locks of long chestnut-brown hair away from the face.

The woman was beautiful, with a heart-shaped face and slanted green eyes. Her thick lips were parted in a smile that deepened the dimples just below sharply cut cheekbones. The lustrous hair blew about her head as though caught in a breeze that Meg could *almost* smell and feel. The air in the bedroom felt cleaner, fresher, more pure somehow. Her white blouse was open at the throat, and a vest matching the boots was buttoned closed over a narrow waist just below her breasts.

She licked her lips, still smiling, and stepped back away, growing smaller the further away she moved. She stopped, no longer filling the frame of the glass, and beyond her Meg could see a forest, a stream, and a small bridge over the stream.

The woman raised her right hand and beckoned Meg forward.

Fascinated, Meg pushed the covers aside into a pile, and placed her feet on the carpet, pushing herself to her feet—

—but the moment she felt the carpet on the soles of her feet there was a large crash downstairs—

—and in a blink of her eye the mirror was just a mirror again, reflecting back her darkened bedroom.

She reached up and pulled the chain from the ceiling fan, flooding the room with light.

She knew she had to go see what had made the sound but she stopped for a moment at the mirror, staring at her reflection. She touched the fingertips of her right hand to it, before hearing a moan that sent her out into the hallway and to the stairs. She flipped the switch and hurried—the moaning was followed by loud swearing—in Anne's voice.

"Damn! Damn! Damn! Damn!"

She pushed through the swinging door into the kitchen, where Anne sat on the floor, rubbing her bare ankle with both hands. She looked up ruefully. "I tripped like the stupid bitch I am," she said, and Meg noticed her eyes were filled with water.

"Does it hurt?" She knelt down beside her sister. The ankle was swelling, and the skin turning a hideous shade of purple.

Anne bit her lower lip and nodded.

Without another word, Meg wrapped some ice in a towel and handed it to her sister. "Should we go to the emergency room?"

Anne shook her head. "No, it'll be fine."

"We'll go tomorrow if the swelling doesn't go down." Meg helped Anne to her feet and back to her room.

"I'm supposed to be taking care of you," Anne said as Meg turned off the light switch and headed back to her room.

She stared into the mirror for a good few minutes before climbing back into her bed again.

❖

Anne's ankle wasn't broken, just a mild sprain that didn't even require a cast—just crutches and rest for a few days.

Meg didn't mind taking care of things around the house, or even taking care of her sister. But each night when she went to bed, she found herself watching the mirror, watching and waiting to see if it happened again. As more time passed, first days and finally a week, she became more and more convinced she'd imagined it all.

So you had the same hallucination more than once, there's no rule that says that can't happen, she reminded herself as she folded towels in the laundry room one afternoon. Anne was able to walk on her own with just a slight limp, and she could hear her banging around in the kitchen. *I think the real problem here is you've become obsessed with the woman you saw in the mirror.*

Much as she hated to admit it to herself, she did spend a lot of time wondering about the woman she thought she'd seen.

Maybe I am losing my mind, she thought as she loaded the pile of towels into her laundry basket. She hefted it onto her hip and backed through the swinging door into the kitchen. Anne was sitting at the table, drinking coffee and working the crossword puzzle in the *Times-Picayune*. Anne didn't even look up as she walked across to the back stairs. She couldn't stop thinking about the woman in the mirror—the way the pants fit her muscular legs, the deep hollow at the base of her tanned throat, the hint of deep cleavage inside the blouse. She licked her lips as she stored the towels in the master bathroom, and caught sight of the photograph of Julia on her nightstand.

Julia.

A wave of sadness forced her to sit down on the side of the bed heavily, and she buried her face in her hands. She took several deep breaths, the way her therapist had taught her, and fought to get the grief under control. The pills were in the top drawer of the nightstand, but she resisted the panicked urge to shake one out and make everything, the sadness and the grief, go away for a few hours.

Will this ever stop hurting? Will it ever stop blindsiding me?

She glanced over at the mirror. *Maybe I am focusing on the mirror—my fantasy—so I don't have to deal with reality.*

She wiped at her eyes. *Now you sound like your therapist.*

The pain aching inside, she walked over to the mirror and pressed the fingertips of both hands to the smooth glass. She traced the carved angels and flowers entwined on the green metal frame. *What is this mirror? Where did it come from?*

She closed her eyes. Julia had loved the mirror—the first time Julia had brought her to the house on the north shore of the lake, Meg had been so enraptured by the house she really hadn't paid any attention as Julia showed her around and explained the provenance of some of the pieces.

She concentrated. *What had Julia said about the mirror? Oh, yes, it may have belonged to Catherine de Medici—who was reputed to have dabbled in black magic and communed with demons, perhaps even the devil himself.*

In her mind's eye, she could see Julia walking in front of her into the bedroom. Her graying long red hair pulled back into a ponytail, wearing a Tulane sweatshirt over her favorite worn pair of jeans. Julia had walked directly to the curtains and pulled them open, revealing the sun shining on the lake and the small balcony with some plastic patio furniture pushed over to one side. The view of the lake had taken her breath away, and she'd crossed the room and thrown her arms around Julia, kissing her on the tip of her nose. She was so excited to be there, couldn't believe someone like Dr. Julia Shelby would be interested in her, a nobody—but she was. And they were going to have a future together—

She swallowed hard to get rid of the lump in her throat.

"Meg?" Anne called from downstairs. "Is everything all right?"

Meg bit her lower lip and walked to the door. "Fine," she shouted back. "I'll be right down." She glanced back at the mirror, and for just a moment she thought she saw the figure of the woman on the glass again.

But she dismissed it with a slight shake of her head. Just her imagination.

It was nearly three in the morning when she woke up. The curtains were open, moonlight casting shadows to the other side of the room. As always, she reached for her glasses as she sat up in the bed, the alarm clock glowing 2:47 in green. She looked over to the mirror, but nothing—it was reflecting the room back. She sighed and took a deep breath. She took off her glasses again and was just about to put them down on the nightstand when she saw a pinpoint of light in the center of the mirror out of the corner of her eye.

Her hands shaking, she placed her glasses back on the bridge of her nose and waited.

The light grew, spreading across the surface of the glass until the entire thing was glowing. It wasn't particularly bright, and she thought for a brief moment if perhaps the moonlight was affecting it—and then the colors began swirling and trying to take shape.

But this time—this time she wasn't afraid.

She threw the covers back and stood up, walking over to the mirror.

She watched in wonder as the colors continued running and swirling, shapes forming and then breaking up, and nervously she placed the fingertips of her right hand on the glass.

And they went through it.

She pulled her hand back as though burned, taking a step backward.

She held the hand to her face and could smell sweet flowers—lilacs, maybe—as her mind tried to process what had just happened.

And almost against her will, she put her hand against the glass again.

This time her hand did not pass through *(that had to be my imagination, it just had to, my hand couldn't have passed through solid glass)* but rather rested lightly on the surface. It wasn't cool, though, as she would have thought, given how close it was to the vent on the upper wall blowing cold air at her. The mirror was warm to the touch, and seemed as though it were actually getting warmer.

Yet strangely she felt no fear.

The shapes and colors began to form the outline of a woman again, a woman standing on grass with a stream behind her, mountains in the far distance.

And she was smiling at Meg as she continued to take form.

She raised her right hand—

—and it came through the glass.

Come with me and be my love. The woman's mouth moved behind the glass, yet Meg could somehow understand what she was saying.

She swallowed as their eyes met.

The woman's eyes—there was something about them.

They looked—they looked like *Julia's* eyes.

This is crazy, this is crazy, this is crazy—

She reached out her own hand, and touched the woman's hand. It was solid, and warm, and as their hands came together there was a sighing sound, as though the mirror was somehow now content.

Join me. The woman's mouth formed the words. *All you have to do is step forward.*

Meg bit her lower lip, and pressed her foot against the mirror—

—and it went through.

She stood on the other side of the mirror, in the cool damp grass.

The air was fresh, pure, scented with lilacs.

"Who—who are you?" Meg managed to stammer out. It was almost too much for her, but she had to know.

The woman smiled. "My name is Melusine." Her voice was soft, with an almost musical lilt to it. She raised Meg's hand to her lips and kissed it. "You knew me in your time as Julia."

A tear ran down Meg's cheek, and her breath caught in her throat.

"Hush, no, my dearest," Melusine whispered as she brushed the tear away. "You will never suffer or be lonely again."

Hand in hand, they walked down the path to where a horse stood, his head down as he fed on the emerald grass.

"What is this place?" Meg asked, looking around, breathing in the soft, fresh air.

"A place where nothing can ever hurt you again," Melusine replied.

Meg looked back over her shoulder at the mirror.

"You don't ever have to go back," Melusine whispered. "Do you want to stay here with me?"

Meg turned back to her, and nodded. "Yes," she replied in a soft voice.

The mirror shattered.

"Welcome home," Melusine said, taking Meg into her arms.

Home, Meg thought as she gave herself to the embrace, *I am finally home.*

Skin Walkers

D. Jackson Leigh

Eden Thayer was a myth-buster.

She'd traveled the world, either disproving rumors or exposing the ordinary science behind a variety of so-called miracles and local legends.

After her book hit the *New York Times* bestsellers list, research money rolled in at the university where she taught. The school's administration swooned at her feet. But that was three years ago and the pressure to produce a second book was mounting.

The problem was that requests to investigate ghosts and pseudo-miracles were all sounding the same. She needed new material, something different, something powerful.

That's how she ended up on the Wyoming prairie, watching helicopter jockeys herd wild horses toward a life of captivity. The U.S. Bureau of Land Management's Wild Horse and Burro Roundup always attracted the usual animal rights protesters. The protesters were always irritating to the feds, but usually harmless. Until this year.

The key to herding with helicopters was the release of a domesticated horse into the wild herd before the chase. When the wild herd hesitated at the mouth of the holding pen, this "Judas" horse would lead them inside.

At least, that's how it was supposed to happen.

This year, a mysterious black horse kept showing up and turning the herds west onto private land instead. Spooked wranglers began to babble over their evening beers about a "Jesus" horse with unnatural blue eyes. Local Shoshone whispered stories about "skin walkers."

It didn't take long for the rumors to leak out and turn the town that was the roundup's base into a three-ring circus. Television crews and tourists filled the hotels. Enterprising Shoshone donned tribal clothing and set up a camp outside of town, where they offered trinkets and ancient tales to eager tourists.

Desperate to defuse the situation, BLM agent Bill Sanders promised Eden free access and publishing rights if she could punch holes in the growing mystery so the tourists would go home and leave the feds to deal with the bothersome Jesus horse.

That's why she was curled in a sleeping bag on a mountain ledge overlooking a Wyoming prairie and getting ready to ride a black mustang to her next bestseller.

The beginnings of first light woke the high prairie gently, softly illuminating the flat plain of waving grass and scrubby trees. Huge mountains stood sentry at its edges and the morning's breath carried their delicious scent of evergreen forest and water. She wasn't thirsty, but instinct told her she should drink now while nourishment was near.

She took a few steps toward the water smell and was startled at the clop of her feet against the hard ground. She looked down and froze. Hooves.

This hadn't happened since she was a child, these vivid dreamscapes in which she transformed into a horse. Not since, on the advice of a therapist, her parents sold her beloved pony, then gave away the pictures, books, and plastic models of horses that covered every surface in her bedroom. Not since they moved from their house that was a bike ride to the stables to an urban neighborhood where there were no horses.

She trembled, rooted by fear that her childhood malady had returned.

But as the wind whipped through her mane and tail, her fear evaporated with the morning's dew. She forgot her parents' disapproval and her therapist's cautions. She remembered only the primal joy.

She started out slow, adjusting to her unfamiliar binocular vision. Then she ran. Opening her nostrils wide and filling her great lungs, she relished the feel of her muscles sliding smoothly, her legs eating up the ground in long strides. She ran for the sheer pleasure of it, for the soul-

deep elation that filled her. Her ecstatic whinny rang out and echoed back from the mountains.

The answering call brought her sliding to a halt. She stood, blowing and scenting, her breath a cloud in the chill air. Black as midnight, racing across the flat with her tail raised like a flag in the wind, the newcomer circled several times, then came to a halt in front of her.

They eyed each other. She could feel the dark mare's dominance, see it in her posture. She breached etiquette by extending her nose first and the dark mare jerked her head to the side, her ears pulled tightly back in warning. Then she stepped forward to offer her nose, too.

They shared breath, learning of each other. Then the newcomer squealed and struck the ground with a sharp hoof, issuing an invitation as she wheeled and galloped away.

They ran, side by side, matching stride for stride as they weaved and circled in the tall grass, testing and measuring each other.

The pounding of hooves began to fade and the whup-whup of helicopter blades jolted Eden from her dreamscape. She rubbed her eyes and groaned. The sun had already cleared the mountain peaks and the day's roundup was under way.

"Damn it. Get your ass up, Thayer."

She scrambled out of her bedroll, already dressed, as the ground began to vibrate and grabbed her binoculars to focus on the approaching thunderhead of dust.

Eyes feral with fear, the wild horses fled from the sky predator that hovered low over their backs, pushing them relentlessly toward the government holding pens. She was glad now that she had wisely camped on a mountainside ledge, safely out of their path.

She followed the herd's flight until a foal, its young lungs and thin legs too weak to keep the pace, stumbled and fell out of the group while its panicked mother ran mindlessly on.

She knew the baby couldn't survive on its own and the wranglers wouldn't ride out to get it, so she swung her saddle onto the rented gelding's back and hurriedly cinched the girth. He snorted and shifted nervously at the scream of a natural sky predator, and Eden spun around to witness a surreal tableau unfold.

A gigantic eagle, clutching a lifeless chicken in its talons, shadowed the helicopter that dared invade its territory, then dipped toward a new player galloping in from the west. Eden's breath caught in her chest.

"It's her."

It was clear the black horse was on a trajectory to intercept, but the herd was nearly a hundred strong and Eden doubted it could turn them from their frantic flight. It would take something they feared more than the helicopter that dogged their heels...something big, like a...

"Ho-o-ly shit!"

A grizzly bear bound onto the plain some three hundred yards ahead of the herd and stopped. Just as the black mare joined the front-runners, the beast reared up to its full height, stretched its massive paws into the air, and roared.

The herd leaders hesitated, then followed the Black in a wide arc away from the new threat. The helicopter swung around to turn them north again, but the eagle swooped down from overhead and dropped its prey onto the main rotor, spraying blood and guts across the copter's bubbled windshield.

The mechanical bird wobbled, then abruptly turned north toward the remote airport that was its nest. The horses were safe for now... Except one.

Plaintive whinnies drew her back to the prairie. The Winchester strapped next to her leg wasn't made for bear hunting, but she wasn't about to leave the defenseless baby to be an easy meal if the wind shifted and the bruin headed that way.

The little mustang stood trembling and uncertain as Eden approached slowly. Her gelding nickered to the foal and Eden gambled on the baby's instinct to follow. Their progress would be slow with the exhausted filly trailing, so she resigned herself to another night of sleeping on the hard ground after they found the herd...if they found the herd.

❖

The herds' tracks led to a desert canyon, which led to another, then another until one appeared that was lush with grass and had a thin creek wandering through it.

The water was still muddy at its widest where the herd had

obviously paused to drink, so Eden moved upstream to fill her canteen. She soaked her bandanna to wash the dust from her face while the foal drank its fill. Finished, the little filly folded its long legs and collapsed to sleep on a bed of thick grass.

"Guess this is where we'll camp," Eden said to nobody.

Her voice sounded out of place among water tinkling over rocks and wind whispering through the grass, and she ached to be something other than human in this raw and natural world.

She sighed. This was no time for dreams and fanciful thoughts.

She hobbled the gelding and set him loose to graze, then collected an armful of deadwood from under the scrubby trees that lined the creek. The moon wouldn't rise for another hour or two, so she built a small campfire, more for light than heat. Dinner was a couple of granola bars.

The filly slept deeply and Eden fought the urge to rise and stand guard over her as a herd mate would. Instead, she pulled her bedroll around her shoulders and settled back against her saddle to sort through the swirling remnants of her day.

A series of incredible coincidences? She didn't think so.

Professional animal trainers with the skill and resources to orchestrate what she had seen today were a small group, so it shouldn't be hard to dig out the name of the rogue trainer doing this.

Eden smiled. Book number two was practically on its way to the editor.

The chapters were taking shape in her head when she was alerted by the gelding's rumbled greeting. A hulking shadow approached in the twilight and an overwhelming urge to run made Eden's skin itch. Instead, her hand found the cool barrel of her rifle and she slowly stood. A breeze feathered her hair back and she relaxed. Not the rank scent of grizzly.

An impatient snort broke the stillness and the Black stepped into ring of firelight.

Eden had seen plenty of horses with blue eyes, but they were always pintos, duns, or otherwise light-colored breeds. As far as she knew, it was genetically impossible or at least rare for a completely black horse. Still, this mare's eyes were swatches torn from the summer sky.

Eden looked down. Boots. She wasn't dreaming again.

They studied each other. Nostrils flared to suck in Eden's scent and the Black jerked her head slightly, noisily blowing out a breath as if surprised.

Eden held out her hand and the mare stepped forward to sniff it. Its eyes glowed like blue lasers and a warm tongue washed across her palm. This animal was not wild, confirming her theory that a human trainer was behind this "Jesus" horse.

"Hey, beautiful. You must smell the oats from my granola bar."

The Black shook its head and stepped closer to stretch her neck in graceful arch. Stiff whiskers tickled Eden's neck and a gentle mouth lipped at her skin. She shuddered as a flash of something familiar touched the edge of her consciousness. She cautiously brushed her fingers along satin-like hide and the mare affectionately rubbed her broad forehead against Eden's shoulder.

Then the Black withdrew and went to the sleeping foal to nudge it awake. The little filly rose and sidled close to the newcomer, opening and closing her mouth in a submissive gesture. The Black rumbled deep in her chest as she sniffed the foal thoroughly, then she gave Eden one last look and melted back into the darkness. A low, firm nicker summoned and the filly lifted her head in shrill answer before hurrying to follow.

Eden listened to their fading hoof beats. She should be happy that she'd been relieved of the foal and was close to busting this myth. Instead, she felt lonelier than she'd ever been in her entire, solitary life.

❖

The tavern that doubled as a bar and restaurant was crowded and the clatter of dishes, shouted orders and a hundred simultaneous conversations set Eden's teeth on edge. The scent of hot sauce, greasy fries, and thick slabs of grilled meat filled the air around her, but she could still smell the stench of stale tobacco on the man who dropped into the chair across from her.

"Like I said when I phoned you, Ms. Thayer, this ridiculous rumor has gotten out of hand. The Bureau had to bring wranglers in from out of state because the locals all quit. Unemployment is over fifteen percent around here, and the salary I'm paying for a few months' work is more than most of these people make in a year when they are employed. I don't understand it."

Agent Bill Sanders waved a frazzled waitress over.

"Hey, Bill. What can I get you tonight?" the waitress asked, pulling a pencil from behind her ear and an order pad from the back pocket of her jeans.

"Cheeseburger, fries, and a light draft."

"How 'bout you, hon?"

"Just coffee," Eden said.

The waitress hurried away, and Bill returned his attention to Eden.

"Bobby says he saw you out there yesterday when that damn Jesus horse showed up and turned another herd."

"Yes, I got lucky."

"So? What do you think?"

"What I saw out there, Mr. Sanders, was a well-coordinated ambush."

"We thought it was a fluke the first time it happened, then we cursed it as bad luck the second time. The third time, the local wranglers tucked their tails and headed back to town to get drunk and spread tales about a she-devil horse with blue eyes." Sanders glanced across the room and grimaced. "Speaking of blue-eyed devils—"

The woman striding toward them had eyes like jewels set in the sculpted angles of her long face, and her dark hair shone against her bronzed skin. A barrel-chested man with a hawkish nose and a shaggy mountain of a man trailed behind her, but a jerk of the woman's chin sent them to the bar to wait.

She stopped at their table and Eden could literally feel the soft brush of the woman's curious gaze before it moved to Sanders and turned laser sharp.

"Next time your helicopters buzz my land, Mr. Sanders, I'm going to shoot their rotors off." Her voice was low and smooth, like honeyed wine, and matter-of-fact rather than angry.

"Good evening, Ms. Walker. It's good to see you, too. Allow me to introduce Eden Thayer. Eden, this is Danielle Walker. She owns fifteen hundred acres that border the federal lands."

"You should be careful of the company you keep around here, Ms. Thayer," Danielle said, her eyes still on Sanders.

He shifted nervously and scowled. "You know damn well those horses may be on your land today, but they'll return to federal land tomorrow or the next day or next week. You don't own them."

They both moved back when Danielle put her hands on the table and leaned toward him, her expression fierce.

"The federal government doesn't own them either, Mr. Sanders. They're wild and I'll do everything in my power to see that they stay that way. The prairies belong to the wolves, the buffalo, and the wild horses. Not to the ranchers' cattle you let graze there instead. A day of judgment will come. And when nature rises up to reclaim what's hers, guns will not be needed to stop weak, selfish humans."

She was halfway across the room when Sanders, red-faced, scrambled to his feet and shouted at her back.

"You don't own the airspace, Ms. Walker, and shooting at those helicopters will only land you in a federal prison."

Danielle didn't acknowledge his threat. The hawk-nosed man scrambled after her, but the larger man cast a dark look at Sanders before he, too, followed.

"She's a nut case." he grumbled.

Eden let out the breath she was holding, and Sanders waved away the plate the waitress slid onto the table.

"Just put it in a bag for me. I've lost my appetite for now."

"Sure, I can do that. But you're gonna lose more than your appetite if you try to take on Dani Walker. She's the next thing to God around here."

"She's even crazier than I thought if she believes she can tell the federal government what to do. And who is that Neanderthal that acts like her bodyguard?"

The waitress broke into a wide smile, her eyes dreamy. "Henry? He's just a big ol' teddy bear. Surely you aren't scared of him."

"Just put my food in a bag, please?"

The waitress shrugged and took the plate of food back to the kitchen.

"You can see that we've got no support here among the locals," Sanders said. "I need you to crack this fast so we can arrest the people behind it. After yesterday's screw-up, I received authorization to also make a sizable donation in the form of a grant to your program at the university if you can help us."

Eden should be pleased at that news, but her mind was on the unexpected tingle that filled her when she looked into Danielle Walker's eyes.

❖

"The name suits you."

Eden stopped her slow stroll down the Main Street storefronts and Danielle Walker stepped out from a dark doorway, her eyes silver under the street lights.

"My name?"

"It means beautiful, doesn't it?"

All traces of the intimidating woman in the restaurant were gone. Her gaze locked with Eden's, eyes begging for something Eden couldn't quite grasp. Then the moment was gone and Danielle's expression dissolved into a half smile.

"You always did enjoy irony," she said.

"I beg your pardon?" Eden felt as though a conversation was going on, but she still hadn't caught up with it.

"Myth-buster. Isn't that what you call yourself?"

"You've read my book, Ms. Walker?"

"It's Dani. And no, I haven't read your book. I looked you up on the Internet. Interesting work."

"It's easier than you would think. Science or a good investigator can explain a lot that people can't or don't want to understand. In this case, I think the culprit is more likely an expert animal trainer than a shape-shifter. Surely you don't believe there are people who can transform their bodies into animal forms. I'm pretty sure it would be scientifically impossible."

Dani's eyes gleamed. "Skin walker. Not a shape-shifter. Come with me."

Eden wasn't sure if it was a request or a command. "Why should I? I don't know you, but apparently we're not exactly working on the same team."

She was startled when Dani's hands folded around hers and a warmth spread up her arms and into her chest.

"Because you need to understand the 'myth' you're trying to discredit. And because you know you can trust me."

They had just met, but Dani touched her with the casual ease of two people who were well acquainted. Even stranger, Eden felt as if she did know her, had known her.

And she knew with absolute certainty that she could trust her.

❖

Four Shoshone, dressed in ceremonial costume, sat in a semicircle around a blazing campfire. Their drumbeats, rattle shaking, and soft chanting were a muted backdrop for a fifth man, a shaman who stood and faced the crowd of thirty or forty tourists.

He waved a bundle of sage and sweet grass over the fire, then dropped it in the flames. Even though they sat some distance away on the lowered tailgate of Dani's truck, the fire's thick smoke found them, its acrid taste bitter on the back of Eden's tongue.

The shaman's musical baritone carried easily across the open field as he alternated between song and story, laying out for mesmerized listeners the legend of Shoshone skin walkers, warriors who were not shape-shifters, but could project their minds into animal familiars.

Eden swallowed against the sharp tang of the smoke. She felt dizzy. The sound of the drums seemed to swell around her.

Listen with your heart, Eden.

It was a whisper in her ear. She glanced at Dani, but her attention appeared riveted on the storyteller. She must have imagined the words.

A sixth Indian, draped in a bearskin complete with head and paws, began to prowl the outer edges of the firelight. Eden flashed back to the grizzly she had seen on the prairie. She thought of the shaggy-haired man she had seen at the restaurant.

Listen and remember.

The drums were now a thousand hoof beats thundering in her ears, and a wave of nausea washed over her. She gripped the metal tailgate under her hands to ground herself. Was there a branch of peyote hidden in the herbs the shaman burned?

Remember and come back to me.

She needed to get back to her hotel, away from the chanting and smoke, but she swayed when she tried to stand. "I don't feel very well," she mumbled as blackness closed in and her knees gave out.

❖

Colors swirled around her. She was tumbling, floating through a series of scenes, glimpses she couldn't hold on to long enough to make sense of them.

Terrified horses stampeded on all sides of her. She was running, too, wild with fear until a dark figure, strong and calm, shouldered through the herd to gallop beside her.

She groaned and tried to focus. Dani's face, etched with concern, hovered.

She closed her eyes and a serene plateau stretched before her. A female warrior, tall and lean in loincloth and little else, yanked an arrow from the chest of a fallen bison and turned to her. Dani's blue eyes, full of triumph, glinted above violent slashes of war paint. *Mukua dehee'ya.* Spirit horse.

Then the prairie turned to pavement and she was riding in Dani's truck. She drifted until strong arms lifted her.

The satin sheets were cool under her fevered skin. She felt them gathering around. Murmured, worried voices. Dani's friends.

"She's fighting it. I think you should get a shaman, Dani."

"You should have gone more slowly, my friend. I know you have longed for her, but she might not be ready."

"She *is* ready. She walks without understanding, but her heart seeks mine. I know it."

Eden opened her eyes. She saw them now. Humans, yes, but more. A grizzly, an eagle, a midnight black mare.

No, no. Impossible. The smoke. It had to be filled with hallucinogens. She gasped and her body jerked with bone-rattling, teeth-chattering chills. Gentle fingers combed through her hair.

"Dani—"

"No. Leave us. It'll be okay."

Cold, so cold. Quick hands pulled at her clothes. A down blanket covered her, then lifted and searing flesh pressed against her naked back. Hot, so hot.

The glare of the sun against the desert sand was blinding, so she watched the yearlings play from the cool of the tent. Warm hands slid under the light gauze of her shift to caress her breasts and teasing lips feathered along her neck. *Johara, my jewel.*

Sweet elation. *Asima, my protector. I had hoped you would find me as soon as you returned.*

Always, my sweet. But it was I who was lost until you found me.

The desert was gone and she was standing on a broad tree limb, watching a lone rider enter the forest. She grinned at the sight of the teen with startling blue eyes and ebony hair. She grabbed a vine and swung out. They tumbled together to the ground, rolling and wrestling to a stop.

Found you! Some Amazon warrior. You never saw me coming.

Ha. I let you capture me. I felt you, knew you were there. I will always know you.

The flesh under her hands was real now and arousal coursed through her. She was hungry, starving for the body naked under hers.

She savored the tongue dancing with hers, licked at the throbbing pulse point, nipped and sucked at the hard, puckered nipples. She slid lower to nuzzle into the familiar scent and dine on the swollen flesh she had surely tasted many times before. She held tightly to the narrow hips bucking under her attack. When the rock-hard thighs tensed and trembled with release, she drank of her.

At last, her fast was over.

Her heart was so full, so full of joy that it hurt. She sobbed against the lean belly under her cheek. She rolled on her back and Dani's long body, so soft, covered hers.

"Eden, my Eden. So beautiful. I have missed you more than words can describe."

Mouth and hands, sure and knowing, touched her in all the places that made her shudder and gasp. The sweet spot below her ear, the crest of her shoulder, the swell of her breast. Blunt nails scraped across her sensitive buttocks, teasing fingers danced along the inside of her thighs to cup her, then slide through her wetness.

"Please. I need you," she moaned. "I need you inside."

And she was filled, tight and deep. She whimpered as the fingers withdrew and filled her again. She tried to hold on to the sweet pleasure, rising to each thrust, opening to welcome the light that had been missing in her life, this lifetime. But it was too much to contain. She let go, knowing it would be hers again and again, and a burst of pleasure infused, penetrated her body soul deep.

"Dani, Dani. *Muka dehee'ya.* My Asima." She sobbed the names like a prayer.

Dani's blue eyes glistened with tears now. "When we began, you were my Philippis, lover of horses." Her fingers were gentle against Eden's cheek.

"And you were my Melanippe, the black mare."

It was clear, so clear to her now.

How could she have not recognized her on the prairie? How could she have not seen it when they met in the restaurant?

"We've spent many lifetimes together, Johara, my jewel, *Nea kwee*, my wife. Each time it seems an eternity until we find each other again."

"Have you been lonely, love? It seems cruel that one of us is always born knowing and must wait for the other."

"Yes, but it makes our reunion all the more joyful."

They held each other close, stroking and gentling away the years apart, until they at last felt assured their reuniting was real.

Eden chuckled. "I guess I need to find a new occupation."

"Not necessarily. Knowing now can make it even easier to spot the pretenders. But we can talk about that later."

Dani settled onto her back and Eden curled against her side, her cheek against Dani's breast, her ear against the comforting thud of her heart. She smiled, anticipating the invitation they both knew would complete their reunion.

"Will you walk with me now?"

"Always. Forever."

They closed their eyes and found their familiars on the prairie…a black mare with sky blue eyes and a shimmering chestnut of sun-kissed gold.

Then they were running, wild and free across the prairie, manes and tails whipping like banners. They were two hearts unfettered by time, death, or human skin.

Always. Forever.

Forget Me Not
Rebecca S. Buck

Ada Faithful staggered slightly on the uneven cobbles. It could have been a result of losing her footing on the smooth stones, or it could have been the copious amount of rough gin she'd taken. Her skirts dragged through a puddle, growing heavy. Inches of water, mud, and God knew what already soaked up from the hem of the dark green silk.

Now night had fallen, the sky a heavy, starless blue; the moonlight only thin, washed-out illumination. Ada was growing cold. She'd left the house without bonnet or shawl, not knowing where she intended to go, but knowing she had to get out into the air where she could breathe. She'd wandered aimlessly, keeping to the shadows, spurning enquiries as to her well-being, and trying to keep the tears from flowing. Her throat ached with the repressed sobs.

She'd wandered around the huge rock on which perched the castle, attempting not to think, just wanting to get away. But there were too many people, drinking at the inns around its base, so she turned towards the river. She'd only been on foot in this part of the city once or twice, and certainly never alone. Oblivious to the nature of the area into which she strayed, she hadn't noticed the eyes watching her from alleys, had barely noted the stench of rotten humanity filling the air. The houses began to huddle and squat close to each other, leaning as if in conspiracy to trap their residents in their poverty-stricken embrace. She didn't notice where she was until it grew suddenly darker. There were no gas lamps, only the vague flickering of lantern light from some of the windows.

Out of the shadows, a creature approached her. Staggering, eyes dark hollows in the night, the shape of a wide mouth just discernable.

"You're in my patch, love," came the voice, rough and ageless, but definitely female.

"I beg your pardon?" Ada blinked, shaken momentarily out of her stupor of confusion and distress.

The woman, who was taller than Ada, stepped towards her. Ada realised she should be intimidated, and though her heart beat a little faster, was surprised just how numb she felt. "I do business here, little Missy. Sling y' hook."

Realisation dawned on Ada and she drew her breath in sharply with the knowledge. "No, I'm not…I mean, you're mistaken."

"I don't care what you are or aren't. I won't have you 'ere taking my business. Sod off." The woman's breath was in her face, laced with alcohol.

"Gin," Ada said.

"What? You're not one of them temperance woman, are you?"

"No. Do you have any?" Ada felt reckless. If this woman could haunt the streets by night, lost in the shadows, why not lose herself and her troubles in a similar oblivion?

"What's it to you?"

"I'll buy it." Ada suddenly remembered she had no money. She thought quickly, then her hand went to her left wrist. "With this." Before the other woman's eyes, she held a diamond and ruby bracelet. She'd only been wearing it two days, a gift from her fiancé. It felt heavy, binding, and she hated the sanguine rubies.

The woman squinted, as if she did not completely believe what she was seeing in the darkness. Then she reached up a stubby-fingered hand and grasped it. Ada did not let go.

"My gin?"

"Pleasure, missy." The woman handed over a glass bottle. It was cold, and still over half-full, judging from the weight. Ada released the bracelet. The woman turned and hurried away, as if her luck might run out if she lingered for any longer.

Ada uncorked the bottle and lifted it to her lips tentatively. The sharp odour of the gin stung her nostrils, and she almost cast it aside. But she wanted to be numb. Not to think. If the whore could block out the misery of her life, why could it not work for Miss Ada Faithful? Gin need not be the comfort of the poor alone, surely? She tilted the bottle and let the gin pour into her mouth. It was bitter and strong. She swallowed and it was like trying to take down broken glass, with the taste of turpentine. But the fire warmed her chest and belly. The sheer recklessness comforted her. This was breaking the rules. She smiled and took another, longer, drink.

A little unsteady already, Ada looked about her, trying to establish in which part of the town she had found herself. To her left, the city climbed a slope, to spread along the top of the sandstone escarpment. She could make out the straight lines of the lace factory rooftops, the chimneys of the gaol and Shire Hall. Beyond that, she knew, were the respectable merchants' houses, the gas-lit streets. She did not want to return home, but it was an altogether safer place to be than the edges of the Narrow Marsh slums, where she now knew herself to be.

Ahead of her, a flight of steps led upwards. Though they were entirely in darkness, she walked towards them, determined to climb out of the stinking slums. Maybe, in a more respectable part of the city, she could find a doorway in which to seek shelter for a while.

The stone stairs were steep and worn uneven. Ada's footsteps sounded loud, echoing from the buildings crowding on either side of her. The gin sloshed in the bottle she carried in her left hand, and occasionally the glass clinked when she caught the brickwork at the side of the steps. The only other sounds were more distant. A whir and a clatter from the factories, where the machines never slumbered; a dog barking and a shout in the night from the slums below. She was about halfway up when she heard another sound, closer. A rhythm of footsteps in time with her own. Ada paused, listening hard. Nothing. Perhaps the gin was fooling her senses already.

She began climbing the stairs again, heart pounding with the exertion and desire to get out of the shadowy passageway and onto the wider, lit street above. She detected the footsteps behind her again and began to panic, sure now that she was being followed by some lowlife from the slums, convinced such a man could only intend to ravish her and slit her throat. She climbed faster, breathing hard.

Finally, she emerged onto the cobbles of the street above, the wide and respectable High Pavement, home to several fine dwellings as well as important public buildings. But still, her logic blurred by the gin, she ran. Her muddy skirts flapped heavily around her ankles as her eyes darted around for a place to hide from whoever was following her. To her left, high above the pale illumination of the gas-lit street, loomed

St. Mary's church, a medieval edifice, its tower the highest point in the city over which it had watched silently for centuries. A few steps under a wrought iron archway led into the dark churchyard. Ada glanced behind her quickly and, seeing no one watching her, fled up the steps.

She followed the flagstones to the back of the church, where it was remarkably close to the warehouse buildings just beyond the churchyard. A tall, pointed headstone, pale white in the limited light, drew her attention. Without another thought, she threw herself to the damp grass behind it, screening herself from the path and from anyone on the street beyond.

A few deep breaths steadied her slightly, but her hands were still shaking. She uncorked the gin once more and took a long drink, suppressing a cough as it tore at her throat. As the alcohol hit her stomach, she began to feel calmer. Perhaps she'd been mistaken. There didn't seem to be anyone following her now. Or maybe it had merely been someone innocent making their way up the steps behind her. It need not be anything sinister. She peered out from behind the headstone. A dark shadow moved in the street. Ada held her breath. But the shadow moved on, without seeming to acknowledge the existence of the church at all. There was no evidence whoever it was had been following her.

Drawing an unsteady breath, Ada sank back to the ground, her back against the marble headstone.

"You're like me."

Ada jumped, startled to hear a voice so close. A female voice, remarkably clear in tone. She swallowed hard and wondered if it was the gin, tricking her. Glancing around, she saw no one.

"You're like me."

The same words again, an identical echo. Ada turned to her left this time, and the mystery was solved. There was a girl with her in the churchyard. Though it was dark, Ada had the impression of youth. The girl wore a pale-coloured dress, and her skin was nearly as pale. Unlike Ada, she had remembered her head wear, and wore a simple pale-coloured cap. She was not finely dressed, but nor was she in rags. Ada took all of this in, while doubting her own eyes. Could gin cause hallucinations? Why would there be a girl in the churchyard?

"I'm Christabel Jessop. You're like me."

"What on earth are you talking about?" Ada was pleased her

words sounded to come out of her mouth coherently. It felt like more of an effort than it should have done.

"You needn't be rude. We're alike. What's your name?"

"Ada Faithful." A moment later, Ada wondered why she had revealed her name. "Why are you in a churchyard?"

"Why are you?"

"I asked you first." Ada's eyes were growing accustomed to the level of light in the churchyard. The girl was pretty. Even through the haze of the gin, Ada couldn't help be a little intrigued. It was oddly comforting not to be alone in her misery.

"I'm hiding."

"What from?"

"The same as you."

"In that case, have some gin." Ada offered the bottle, but Christabel refused it.

"I never touch it."

"Me either." Ada shrugged, and feeling a little pathetic, took another, shorter drink. She placed the bottle on the damp grass beside her. As she waited for the burning in her throat to calm, she looked at the girl. She had a vague perception that the gin was rendering this whole encounter less bizarre than it really was. "So how am I like you?" she said, hearing the challenge in her words.

"You've given your heart to a woman."

Ada drew in her breath sharply, the fog in her mind clearing quickly. Her heart pounded, and she felt almost fearful. She wasn't sure if she was more afraid that this strange girl knew her truth, or that there was such a truth to be known and spoken of. She had never spoken of it, barely acknowledged it before now.

"How…how…why…how…?" was all she could manage in response.

"I know. You're like me."

"You mean you have given your heart…well…"

"Yes. Lillian Fields. She's fair, tall, and so alive. So very much alive."

Ada felt wistful suddenly, hearing the love and desire in Christabel's clear tone. She sighed and felt keen eyes regarding her face.

"Her name? What's her name? The girl you love?"

Ada looked away, up at the square tower of the church, a tall shadow against the night sky. "Maud. Maud Hutton. She's the daughter of my father's business partner." Maud was beautiful. Her hair was raven and fell in long waves when loosed from its usual tight braids. Her face was strikingly angular, but graceful with it. And she was the most articulate woman Ada had ever encountered. She'd been enthralled on their first meeting and sure she was, unaccountably, in love by the end of their second. The greatest surprise of all had been when she had begun to recognise that Maud returned those secret feelings.

But Ada was engaged to Jim Collett, a man her parents approved of, and whom she did not hate but yet could not love. She'd agreed to marry him mostly out of pity, she thought, for he was a rather shy, awkward young man, who would smile rather than speak, and always seemed in fear he would let everyone else down. Besides, she was not sure if her love for Maud was even real love. How could it be? And yet, once she had given her consent to the marriage, she felt as though she had begun to drown, slowly, slipping further under the surface every day. Finally, tonight, her need to breathe had caused her to run from the house, just as dinner was about to be served. Maud was to be present at the dinner. To sit opposite her, to exchange glances that said more than impotent words, to be so close to her, and yet only have a heart full of questions and doubts, a knowledge of the impossibility of it all, was too much to bear. Just to see Maud in the soft candlelight of the dining room caused a pain in all of her body she seemed incapable of soothing.

"Is she beautiful?"

Ada was recalled to her present situation, in the cold churchyard with the strange girl by her side. "Yes…" she began dreamily, tempted to launch into a description of Maud. Then she stopped herself. This was too preposterous, even with half a bottle of gin in her belly. "But why do you care, and why am I telling you? Why are you even in this churchyard in the middle of the night?"

"I have more reason than you to be here."

"How's that then?"

"Would you like to hear a story?"

Ada was suspicious for a moment, of such an odd question. But the gin and her lack of desire to return home were enough to produce an affirmative response.

"Yes. I'm intrigued," she acknowledged.

"Oh good!" Christabel's excitement was almost childlike. She hunched across the grass to move closer to Ada, their skirts brushing. To Ada's surprise, Christabel took her hand between both of her own. Christabel must have been in the churchyard a long time, for her skin was very cool to the touch. Ada let her hand rest where Christabel grasped it lightly, the strangeness of the night making her more permissive than she would otherwise have been.

"There was once a young girl. They said she was pretty and would marry well, though she wasn't especially rich. A lace merchant's daughter was she. But she didn't wish to marry, and they began, eventually, to think her rather queer.

"There was another girl, a little older. Very tall, and with fair hair, but handsome more than pretty. She was a milliner, a very fine one at that. Her fingers were nimble and she had an eye for what suited every face. She made, for the lace merchant's daughter, the most beautiful bonnet she had ever seen. It was trimmed with lace and the most graceful feathers."

Christabel paused and sighed. She turned and appeared to be inspecting Ada's appearance. She moved one hand from Ada's and reached up to her face, running a cool fingertip lightly from her temple to her chin. Compelled by something in that touch, Ada allowed it, despite herself, and found she missed it when Christabel drew her hand away. "Beautiful it was. It would have suited you."

"Was it your bonnet?" Ada asked, beginning to see where the story was leading. Christabel placed a gentle but commanding finger onto Ada's lips. It tickled, pleasantly. "Hush, and I will tell you." Ada obeyed, as Christabel took her hand between her own again. This time her soft touch was welcome, and Ada was glad of it as she waited for the story to go on.

"The lace merchant's daughter loved her bonnet. But before long, she loved the milliner more. The whole world seemed to make sense to her then. And it barely seemed a surprise that the milliner loved her back."

Christabel leaned closer to Ada, who found her heart beat faster. She could feel Christabel's breath on her cheek. It sent a shiver through her whole body, made her skin prickle. "The love, between two women, it is a wonderful thing," Christabel said, her words charged with passion, though still soft. "But then you know that, do you not?" Her hand stroked over Ada's face again, turning her so they were looking into each other's eyes, but still not quite seeing, in the darkness. Ada knew she should move away and could no longer blame the gin for her reluctance to do so. So long now she had wanted this close proximity with a woman, to feel those soft lips against hers. Christabel was not Maud, but Ada had not kissed Maud, only imagined how it could feel. She could smell Maud, that trace of violet she always wore, and, closing her eyes, see those blue eyes looking into her own. She kept her eyes closed, and her lips tingled with a desire that seemed to be growing into an insatiable craving, as Christabel's own lips promised to brush hers, as she continued to speak, in what was now a throaty whisper.

"You know what it is to love a woman. You know what those two lovers felt...and they did love. In the dark hours of the night, they would lie together, knowing nothing could be more perfect, more pure, than the love they shared. Such passion, so deep it was almost a pain..." Christabel's hand slid over Ada's jaw, lower, onto her throat, where Ada felt her pulse throb against the slight pressure. Lower still, and her hand was caressing Ada's shoulder, the swell of her breast. Ada, eyes still closed, sighed. It was Maud's touch she felt, and she was captivated by it. She felt the burning pain of Christabel's words, the heat surging low in her abdomen. Everything that had seemed so wrong, that had caused her to accept Jim's proposal as some sort of act of contrition, felt suddenly pure and powerful and right, as Christabel caressed her body and their lips touched for the slightest of moments.

"They were very much in love, the lace merchant's daughter and the milliner. But they knew the world would scorn them. They swore very solemnly they would be together always, that this one brief, passing life was too small for such love. Little did they know how fleeting their moment would be."

Christabel ran a hand up Ada's spine to caress the back of her neck and twine in her unruly hair. Ada sighed. The other Christabel slid lower, pressing through skirts to reach the focus of Ada's need. Now Ada moaned with the building desire, the frustration she felt every time she looked at Maud. Maud filled her head. Though she knew it was another girl, Christabel, to whose words she listened, all she could think of was Maud. Maud's slim fingers touching her, working for her release, just as she had always dreamed. She reached desperately for Christabel, drew her to her with all of the force she longed to use with

Maud, and kissed her, a deep, exploratory kiss, as she drew Christabel close, needing to feel a woman's form close to her. She felt the swell of breasts against her own, felt the curve of Christabel's waist in her grasp. She smelled violets again. Maud.

"Oh yes, yes my love…this is how it should be." Christabel pulled back slightly, gasping for breath. There was pure joy in her tone. "You are like me, Ada Faithful." Ada pushed forward, compelled by an urge she couldn't understand but was powerless to resist, to kiss Christabel again, to taste those soft lips once more. She was hungry, she felt she wanted to consume the other woman. She wanted to kiss Maud until her lips were bruised. But Christabel drew her, irrevocably. Christabel held back, just allowed Ada the slightest brush of her lips. Ada was aware of hot tears streaming over her cheeks, but she could neither stop them nor explain them.

Christabel kissed her softly, then spoke again. "But, my love, do you not want to hear the end of the story?"

"Tell me." Ada was breathless and aching, full of a desire she had never known before.

"The lace merchant's daughter and the milliner swore they would spend their forever together. They declared that if one should die, the other would surely follow, consumed by grief. Christabel and Lillian would never be divided, for neither of them would be able to bear life or the cold eternity of death without the other."

"I understand," Ada breathed, thinking still of Maud. Her heart was singing at her final realisation of how much she loved Maud. She could not live without her. She would tell her so, the first chance she got. "I understand. Forever together."

"I knew you were like me…you understand forever…" There was something darker, a sadness in Christabel's tone. Ada felt it as a weight in her own heart. "A life is not long enough, however long it is lived. It is over so soon."

"But to make the most of each moment…"

"Yes, my love. To know what it is your heart desires and to follow it…to grasp a tight hold of it." Christabel grew restless, her hands moving more quickly, more roughly over Ada's body. Ada felt herself respond to her very apparent desire. She was approaching a crisis of her passions. The sensation pulsed through her veins in waves, molten hot.

"I know. I know what it is I want," Ada replied. Maud filled her mind.

"You can have it. I can give it to you, my love. Forever, with me."

Ada tensed, suddenly fully aware of Christabel. This was not Maud, and Christabel's voice had taken on a strange tone. "No. You are to spend your forever with Lillian. I have my Maud. And I'm going to find her tonight…"

"She will leave you. She will spurn you and leave you, to be alone." Christabel spat the words at Ada with real venom. Jolted out of her illusion, Ada was afraid.

"Is that what happened to you. With Lillian?" she enquired.

"You didn't hear the end of the story yet," Christabel said plaintively.

"Tell me."

"The lace merchant's daughter was taken ill. It was influenza and she was never strong. She died."

Ada gasped at the wave of sadness that overtook her. Her mind was racing to understand, and failing. "But I thought…"

"I was the lace merchant's daughter."

"Yes."

"I was."

"I don't…understand…" Was Christabel a madwoman after all? Ada backed away slightly, but could not quite break the spell. Something pulled her to Christabel.

Christabel seemed to be smiling. As Ada watched, she faded. The solid woman began to fade. Skin, pale in the darkness, became suddenly translucent, until Ada could see the outline of a headstone a few feet away through Christabel's body. Wide-eyed, her heart hammering, Ada did not scream. She stared. Christabel was still there, she could feel her, but now she could barely see her. She was a mist in the form of a woman, a wisp of white in the dark. A ghost.

Compelled by a logic she did not control, Ada turned to look at the headstone against which she had been leaning. White stone, with black engraved letters. Even in the night she could read the name. *Christabel Ann Jessop.* She couldn't make out the words below, but the dates stood out very clearly. *1861–1880.* Christabel Jessop had been dead for ten years.

"You're dead." She spoke the words to the white haze in front of her. Try as she might, she did not feel afraid. Indeed, she did not even doubt her sanity. How could she not accept what she saw with her own eyes? In moments, Christabel was solid again, looking at Ada with hollow eyes.

"I am lost in forever and I am alone." Christabel's voice was full of pain. "You're like me. You can be with me."

"Is that what you thought? That you could seduce me into eternity with you?"

"You wanted to be with me." Christabel sounded so plaintive that Ada could not help a swell of sympathy.

"What of Lillian?"

"She lived. She let me go into forever on my own. She visited my grave for a while. But then life's currents drew her away. When it is her turn to come to this side, she will never find me. I am lost. But you could share this with me."

"Surely I would have to die to do so?" The notion sparked real fear in Ada's stomach. Would Christabel attempt to keep her, by any means? Her life seemed suddenly so precious to her.

"Death is really nothing. Just a moment and it is over. It is what you must leave behind, and what you find on the other side you should fear. Not death."

"I don't want to die. I love Maud."

"She is human. She is fickle and will change her mind. If you should die, would she follow you into forever?"

"I would not expect it. This life is enough. Shared with her, whatever we face." A new joy surged in Ada's heart as she spoke of convictions she was only now aware of. She would not marry Jim. Even if they had to leave home, leave the city, she would find a way to share her life with Maud. She would not be Christabel. She would not be a ghost of herself while she was alive, and she would not spend eternity in sadness. She would live every moment well enough to die happy, knowing she had loved.

"This life is short. Do you not see? It is perilous. I can give you love, always." Christabel reached out a cold, pale hand. Ada let her grasp her own warmer fingers, but she shuddered.

"I am not your Lillian, and you can never be my Maud. I am sorry,

Christabel, but I will take my chance with life. I am like you. And I will live my life how you wanted to live yours."

Christabel's eyes widened and her grasp of Ada's hand tightened. "Death is cold, Ada. I am alone here."

Ada felt the sadness creeping up her arm, a chill spreading into her body. Tears sprang into her eyes. To slide into death with Christabel seemed a real possibility. She fought it, clung to her love for Maud, her new hope.

"Remember your life with joy. You knew love. In moments you have shown me how important that is. Rest, Christabel. Have faith in your Lillian. She will find you."

"What if she does not?"

Ada could not fight the tears. She pulled Christabel closer, brushed a gentle kiss on the cold lips. "She will find you. Rest."

"You will go to your Maud. You will love her, with every living breath?"

"I will, I promise."

Christabel reached for another kiss. Ada allowed it. She closed her eyes and prayed to anyone who would listen that love was as powerful as she craved it to be.

When she opened her eyes, Christabel was gone.

Ada lingered a while in the dark churchyard, her eyes filled with tears, but her heart surging with hope, determination, and joy. She would fight, if fight she must, but Maud had to know the extent of her love.

She took the walk home through the dark streets quickly, her head aching a little in the aftermath of the gin, the remainder of which she discarded. In the back of her mind there was a slight fear, a vague doubt, that Christabel had been a figment of a gin-and-distress-turned brain and she'd actually spent the past hours in the churchyard alone, drunkenly muttering to herself. A ghost? It seemed so ludicrous as she walked, more or less sober, back through the respectable residential streets to her home. And yet the doubts were so easy to push away. Christabel had seemed so real. The emotions were so real.

Even if it had all been a drunken delusion, Ada would not undo it. She saw now the path she wanted to take into the future. All traces of the distress that had caused her to run alone and frightened into the night, to want to lose herself in gin, had faded. Maud was her future, and she would seize every living, breathing moment.

❖

The next morning, after a few hours of sleep more peaceful than she thought possible, Ada, now respectably attired complete with bonnet, shawl, and gloves, walked to St Mary's churchyard. She skirted the slums rather than passing through them, and instead of gin from a whore, she bought blooms from a flower seller. She took sweet peas to bid farewell, and rosemary to remember. She climbed the stone steps into the churchyard, glancing briefly at the square tower, a honey-sweetened grey in the sunlight which glinted from the stained glass of the intricate windows and filtered down into the shadows of the churchyard.

Ada went straight to the pointed white headstone. There were Christabel's name and the dates of her short life. Tears pricked Ada's eyes again. But then something arrested her vision. Stars of blue in the grass. Ada smiled.

Forget-me-nots.

"She remembers you, Christabel. Sleep. Wait for her." She barely whispered the words. "And I will love my Maud. Because of you."

THE OTHERS
NELL STARK AND TRINITY TAM

Most people didn't update their last will and testament before leaving for a Saturday-night soiree. Then again, most people believed that vampires and wereshifters were creatures of myth and movie. Sometimes, Olivia missed the luxury of ignorance. She knew all too well what dangers walked the streets undetected. Had it not been for the intervention of providence on a night much like this not so long ago, she would have been one of them.

Not that she was a bigot. She had friends among the Others. She had even fallen in love with two of them. Technically, her romantic interest in Abby and Alexa had begun before they'd been turned, but there was no denying the fact that the grace and power they'd inherited as shifters made them even more attractive.

There was also no denying that were-women spelled trouble. Abby had walked away from their relationship after only a few months, and Alexa had never truly been attainable to begin with. Olivia needed to fall for a nice, human girl without any feline bones in her closet. Someone normal and dependable, someone who grew metaphorical claws once a month instead of literal ones.

Yeah. Right.

She pulled up the collar on her pea coat as a gust of cold air brought tears to her eyes. Even a Manhattan native never quite grew accustomed to the chill of a skyscraper-lined wind tunnel. The address her contact had provided was a few blocks east of the downtown financial district, and not for the first time, Olivia marveled at the ability of the Others to conduct even the most sordid of activities right under the nose of City Hall.

The Red Circuit party was by all accounts a barbaric affair, its time and location changed each weekend. Olivia's contact had refused to give her any information about who was in charge or the channels through which news was spread. Alexa had told her a little about what to expect: the deadly "dogfights" between wereshifters, the vampires' brutal "raffle" to drain a homeless human dry, the sadomasochistic "record" to see how many lashes a shifter could endure before their inner beast rebelled against the torment.

At once repulsed and morbidly curious, Olivia would probably have been drawn to the Circuit even if she hadn't had business there. But tonight, she needed to stay focused. Her sole purpose was to establish credibility in the underbelly of the shifter community by scoring a large order of drugs. If she played her cards right, this would be the first step on a long road toward apprehending and convicting Christopher Blaine, a front-running presidential candidate who secretly owed his allegiance to a powerful werewolf alpha bent on eradicating vampires and enslaving humanity.

Olivia didn't much care for vampires, but she had no intention of sitting idly by while Blaine siphoned illegal drug money into his campaign. Especially when a deadly virus transmitted by those drugs had nearly killed Abby last year. Physically, Abby had recovered. Emotionally, she had grown more and more distant before finally turning her back on their burgeoning relationship. Desperate to know why her tune had changed so quickly, Olivia had tailed her into the Poconos, where Abby had pulled over at a scenic overlook, walked into the woods, and transformed into a large cat.

Abby had never returned any of her calls. When Olivia had finally shown up on her doorstep, the building superintendent had informed her that Abby had moved out of state. She was gone, but Blaine's dirty work was still on the streets.

Olivia shook her head to dispel the memory as she paused before the address she'd committed to memory. The door opened into a dimly lit hallway that bent almost immediately at a ninety-degree angle. It was impossible to tell who—or what—lurked around the bend, and she swallowed hard around the unusual tightness in her throat. She was a cop after all—she didn't get nervous on an op. Except this wasn't just any op. She thumbed off the safety on her firearm as she moved forward. Every muscle in her body grew taut as she forced herself to step around the blind corner.

Twenty feet away a dark-haired woman stood before a large wooden door. Despite the chill of the corridor, she wore only a white tank top and jeans. Legs splayed, heavily tattooed arms crossed beneath her breasts, she was simultaneously sensual and menacing.

The gatekeeper smirked at Olivia's wary approach. "You're new."

Olivia bristled at her patronizing tone, forcing herself to remain silent. When she stopped a few feet away, the gatekeeper leaned forward and inhaled deeply.

"Only human." Her eyes narrowed. "But you've been palling around with a few of us recently." She cocked her head. "Tell me, what do you hope to find behind this door?"

Olivia knew she couldn't pass herself off as a party girl looking for a good time. "Business."

The gatekeeper stared hard at her for one fraught moment before moving aside to tap in a code at the keypad next to the door. "Pleasure is much more fun."

Olivia had no doubt what would happen to her if she misstepped. Death was only one option, and worse fates were easily imaginable. Without another word, she crossed the threshold into an atrium that ended in a downward-sloping staircase. The low pulse of a far-off beat set the walls to throbbing. To her left was a coat rack, to her right a small booth presided over by a muscle-bound man. He beckoned to her.

"Your sidearm."

With a sigh, Olivia unstrapped her weapon and turned it over to him in exchange for a small token. She had known this would happen, but that didn't mean she had to like it. Determined not to let the loss of the gun undermine her self-confidence, she squared her shoulders and began the descent. With each step, the thunder of the music grew louder, engulfing her like a riptide, sucking her down.

At the bottom of the stairs another corridor opened onto a large rectangular chamber, nearly filled to capacity and pungent with the scent of sweat-permeated air. The partiers writhed in time to the music, some emulating the professional—and naked—dancers who displayed themselves on a stage at the far end of the room. A makeshift bar had been set up along the right wall opposite an archway through which patrons came and went frequently.

As much as she wanted to explore, Olivia shouldered her way through the press of flesh to the bar as instructed and ordered a double brandy. Shivers arced up her spine. She was the prey in a room full of hunters.

Thankfully, she caught the bartender's attention right away. After placing her order, she tried to circumspectly take stock of her surroundings. To her left, a stocky, hirsute man drank deeply from a dark beer. As he raised his arm, his shirt sleeve slid up to reveal the tattoo of a bear on his forearm. Olivia doubted the tat was just for show.

To her right, a young couple was locked in a passionate embrace. At first, it was difficult not to stare at them, but as the woman kissed her way down the man's throat, Olivia's stomach lurched. She spun away at the first blossom of red against pale skin, the man's blissful groan echoing in her ears despite the pounding music.

"Brandy." The bartender slid the drink into her grasp and swept up the bills she'd thrown on the rough wooden surface.

"Hey, I ordered a double!"

He didn't turn, and when every light in the room went out save the strobe, she didn't press the issue. As she braced herself against the bar, a spotlight zeroed in on the pole in the center of the stage.

"It is time." The sibilant murmur bled from the speakers to echo around the hall. "Time to test the Record."

Olivia's neck prickled as the audience chanted *Test the Record. Test the Record.* The room seemed to ripple as the tide of humanity surged toward the front of the room. Olivia had no particular desire to see what was about to happen, but she could hardly leave now. Mentally, she tried to prepare herself for the sadomasochistic spectacle to come.

"Abigail was reborn only last year, but she believes that she can break the Record."

"Abigail." The crowd murmured her name as though she were some kind of religious icon, but the word struck Olivia like lightning beneath her skin. Abigail. Could it possibly be *her* Abby? New York was incomprehensibly populous, and surely there was more than one shifter with that particular name. Olivia scanned the stage frantically, desperate for reassurance that some other Abigail was about to be put on display.

A figure stepped out of the darkness dressed entirely in black leather and holding a long, cruel-looking cat-o'-nine-tails. Blond hair fell to her waist, but her face was hidden by a falcon's-head mask. She stepped to one side of the pole and cracked the whip dramatically. The crowd cheered.

Olivia sensed motion at the corner of the shadows, and she leaned forward, breathless with dread. In another moment, her chest seized as two men escorted a naked, flaxen-haired woman into the center of spotlight. Abby. Her Abby, on display for this roomful of bloodthirsty monsters.

As she finally gasped in a breath, Olivia's only consolation was that no one could hear her over the roar of the crowd. The men trussed Abby up to the pole so tightly she was standing on her toes, hands stretched high above her head. Her firm breasts rose and fell quickly, and Olivia could see a glimmer of moisture between her thighs. When an answering rush of arousal blindsided Olivia, her stomach rolled. How could she possibly be turned on? How could some small part of her want to be on her knees in front of Abby, shielding her nudity from the crowd even as she worked her toward climax with lips and tongue and teeth?

"What's happening to me?" she murmured, fingernails digging into the wood of the bar.

"The Record is fifty-seven lashes." Once again, the disembodied voice rolled through the hall.

The whip rose and fell. Once, twice, three times. The dom's hand was steady, her rhythm precise. The tails of the cat looked like they were caressing Abby's skin, but on the seventh lash, her mouth fell open and she winced. By the fifteenth lash, her teeth were gritted and her eyes squeezed shut.

By the twentieth lash, her blood began to drip onto the floor.

Torn between wanting to vault onto the stage to stop the torment and wanting Abby to triumph over the Record, Olivia remained frozen. A full-body shudder racked Abby's slim frame; her lips formed unreadable words. Was she talking to her inner beast? Was she close to capitulation?

Abby's head snapped up, her blue eyes dark and wild and pleading. She seemed to silently beseech the crowd to give her some sort of human connection to which she could cling. That look broke Olivia's heart all over again.

And then their eyes met.

Recognition flared in Abby's face and, for an instant, the chanting crowd disappeared. Helpless to turn away, Olivia watched as despair chased confusion from Abby's finely chiseled features. She convulsed, and the crowd gasped. As the seizures continued, Olivia bit her bottom lip so hard she tasted blood. Abby writhed in her chains, her lithe frame contorting so sharply Olivia feared her bones would snap. But instead, her body blurred and she collapsed in on herself, defying the laws of physics as a large, spotted feline materialized in her place.

Olivia's lips formed the word she couldn't find the voice to speak. Cheetah. Abby's other half was a cheetah, and she was beautiful. Teeth bared, poised to leap, she roared at her tormenter. Olivia's pulse raced as she realized the chains had broken during Abby's transformation. The dominatrix had a gun belted to her waist, but Olivia had no idea whether she could reach it before Abby sprang. Sweat flooded her palms as she realized someone was likely to die—right here, right now. Maybe even Abby.

The masked woman let the whip fall to the ground. She stared into the cheetah's eyes. Faster than Olivia could follow, Abby leapt—but the dominatrix was faster. She drew her sidearm, fired, and darted to the side before those long, curved teeth could close around her throat.

Olivia pushed into the crowd, wanting to scream, but her voice would never have been heard over the tumult of the crowd. She wanted to lash out, but everyone here was stronger. Abby had been shot. Possibly, probably even dying, yet no one else in the crowd was acting like anything was amiss. Some of them were even laughing. There was only a smattering of applause as the two men dragged the cheetah off the stage.

A rush of dizziness swept over Olivia. She swallowed hard and focused on taking deep, even breaths. This was no time to betray any kind of weakness.

"The cat is fine. She was tranquilized."

The words were spoken very close to Olivia's right ear, and she suddenly became aware of a presence at her back. She spun to face a tall, slender woman with cocoa-colored skin and long, dark hair whose sensuous smile jarred with the coldness of her eyes.

"Hello, Olivia. I'm Brandy."

Olivia blinked. Her brain felt slow, her thoughts disjointed. She stared at her untouched glass. "So that's why the bartender only gave me a single." Brandy's answering laughter pierced through the haze that had settled over her mind. "You're certain? About the tranquilizer?"

"She'll be back on two legs within an hour. Though she might not want to show her face—she didn't last very long."

Olivia suppressed the urge to defend Abby's honor, especially since she suspected she was partially to blame for Abby's shift. If it was true, what did it mean? Did Abby still have feelings for her? Or had she simply been so surprised to see her in this place that she had lost control at a critical moment?

"Let's find a place to talk," Brandy said.

Brandy led her to a cluster of tall, round tables. She had only to direct her cool stare at the small group of men gathered around the nearest in order to commandeer it. Once they were seated, Brandy folded her hands on the table, displaying elegantly manicured, crimson-tipped nails. Olivia couldn't get a good read on her. Most Others betrayed their nature in some small way if you knew what to look for, but Brandy could easily be either shifter or vampire. Or perhaps she too was "only human."

"Why don't you start by explaining why I should be taking a meeting with someone who used to be a state's prosecutor?" Brandy said.

Olivia relaxed at the accusation. She had expected it. Finally, she was on familiar ground. "If you know that, then you also know I was fired."

"Or perhaps that's just what the DA wants everyone to think."

Olivia bought herself a few seconds by taking a sip from her glass. "That would be a good theory if this were a crime show."

"I want your explanation."

"Fine." Olivia rolled the glass between her palms, its comforting weight anchoring her to reality. "I became obsessed with a case I couldn't solve. When I refused to let it go, I was dismissed. Only afterward did I discover the truth."

"The truth?"

"That vampires and wereshifters exist. That they walk among humans undetected."

Brandy's fingernails tapped against the table's lacquered surface as she regarded her shrewdly. "And now?"

That sort of vague, open-ended question was exactly what Olivia wanted to avoid. She cocked her head and remained silent.

"You were a formidable prosecutor. A crusader for 'justice.' What do you fight for now?"

"I'm done fighting." Olivia prayed that the bitterness she injected into the words was believable. "Look where it got me. Now that I know the truth, I'm not interested in surrounding myself with the ignorant. I've found a new employer. If you're watching me as closely as you seem to be, you know who that is."

Olivia focused on schooling her features into impassivity. That bluff could easily get her killed. By leaving the identity of her employer vague, she hoped Brandy would inadvertently help her. She wasn't working for anyone but herself, but she had recently been seen in the company of several powerful vampires and shifters. Whoever Brandy answered to would likely want to forge a business relationship with any one of them.

"I can get you what you want." Brandy grasped Olivia's hand firmly, fingertips stroking across Olivia's knuckles. "When you leave, walk three blocks east and one north. You'll see a black van parked in front of a warehouse on the south side of the street. Knock on the passenger-side door. Don't bring any company." Brandy's smile glittered brilliantly in the light of the strobe. "Do bring plenty of cash."

"I won't disappoint." Olivia was proud when the words remained steady. As soon as they were out of her mouth, she stood. "Are we finished?"

Brandy arched one razor-thin eyebrow. "So sure you don't want to hang around? Share a dance?"

"Maybe next time."

Ignoring Brandy's smirk and the stare she could feel on the back of her neck, Olivia strode away. Ignoring too the vampires' hungry eyes and the shifters' suspicious glances. She maintained her ramrod posture until she had retrieved her sidearm and secured it in her shoulder holster. When the front door closed behind her, she sucked in a deep breath of wintry air and sighed in relief despite the chill that knifed her lungs.

Mostly, she wanted to find a halfway-decent bar and calm her nerves with a drink before following Brandy's instructions. But Brandy had watched her leave, and whoever was in that van would be expecting her. Any delay might be misconstrued. Besides, she wanted to get this whole cloak-and-dagger business over with so she could go home and turn on late-night television and temporarily forget having seen things she shouldn't.

The walk took longer than anticipated, and by the time Olivia caught sight of the black van, her teeth were chattering. Steeling herself, she tapped on the tinted glass of the passenger window.

The door opened, and she leaned in to catch a glimpse of whoever was inside. The man seated in the driver's seat was blatantly unattractive, his angular face craggy and pockmarked, but it was impossible to look away from his nearly colorless eyes. He beckoned to her.

"Get in." His accent was foreign. Eastern European probably.

Adrenaline sluiced through her veins as she battled against her instinct to turn away. This move might turn out to be very unwise. She could easily wind up dead. Or turned. The thought made her cold, but she couldn't turn back now. The Others worked within the boundaries of human law only when it served their purposes. If she wanted to bring down Blaine, she would have to take risks that would have once been unthinkable.

The van's interior was shrouded in acrid smoke, and her eyes immediately began to water. The driver withdrew a cigarette from his shirt pocket and lit up. His fingers trembled and his right leg bounced restlessly against the seat. Olivia's heart pounded even faster. Was he on something? Sampling his own merchandise?

Suddenly, a pistol appeared in his free hand, pointed at her head. Her blood turned to ice, and she lunged for the door handle. The sound of the autolock sliding home was as loud as a gunshot. Desperate to mask her fear, she channeled it into rage and forced herself to look down the dark barrel of the weapon.

"What the hell is this!"

"I need reassurance." His rasping monotone grated on her frayed nerves. "My colleagues don't think you're setting us up. But I do."

"Wonderful." Olivia tried to sound annoyed instead of terrified. "Why don't you tell me what I can—"

A dark shape slammed into the driver's window, followed by the sound of shattering glass. The man shouted hoarsely as he was showered with the shards. Olivia fumbled for the lock even as she squinted through the haze for a glimpse of her rescuer. When she finally managed to focus on the woman who was now holding a gun to the dealer's head, all thoughts of escape fled.

"Drop your weapon, asshole." Abby's voice was low and menacing. Dressed in a long black coat and knit hat, face flushed and eyes bright, she was still the most beautiful woman Olivia had ever seen. But Olivia couldn't acknowledge her surprise or delight. She had to salvage this mission, and to do that, she had to act like Abby's intervention had been planned.

"Thanks for the backup, babe."

A flash of uncertainty crossed Abby's face, but she was smart enough not to voice it. "Anytime."

Olivia turned to the man who had threatened her. "As you can see, I didn't trust you either. Let's just forget this ever happened and make the goddamn deal already."

The driver glared at them until Abby cocked her sidearm. He muttered something indecipherable under his breath Olivia was sure she'd rather not hear anyway. Abby heard it, though, and shoved the gun into the man's temple.

"Watch your mouth."

"Fuck! Fine. Jesus." He raised his hands in a show of surrender, and when Abby put up her gun, he quickly bent down to rummage in a cooler resting between the front two seats. "What the fuck do you want, anyway?"

"Something that goes well with a party."

"How much?"

Olivia watched him closely to ensure he wasn't reaching for another weapon. She also didn't dare meet Abby's eyes. "Ten grand for tonight. If my employer is pleased, I'll need more next month."

When he finally held up a bulging plastic bag, Olivia pulled the thick envelope from her inner pocket and passed it to him. Exchange made, she glanced at Abby. "Hit the locks, baby?"

Abby punched the button with the butt of her gun and pushed open the door. "Let's go."

Olivia suppressed a sigh of relief as she climbed out of the van. Her senses were on overdrive, and she had to struggle not to look over her shoulder as they walked away. When Abby linked their arms together, she couldn't help but lean into the touch. The heat of Abby's body, the comfort of her presence was so familiar, so right, she had to remind herself Abby had been the one who walked away. Everything they were doing now was just for show.

After two full blocks, Olivia finally spoke. "Thank you."

"Thank you?" Abby's grip on her arm tightened. "That's what you have to say? What the fuck are you doing, Liv? You're going to get yourself killed!"

Olivia's head swirled. Abby wasn't pulling away. Abby smelled good. Abby had willingly played the role of her dark knight. She couldn't put the pieces together, and she wanted so badly to slow down. "Wait. What—"

"No." Abby tugged at Olivia's arm and looked over her shoulder. "Just keep walking, and keep your voice down."

Olivia worked to calm her riotous mind by counting the sidewalk cracks. "I'm undercover," she managed.

"Yeah, I got that part. Why?"

The panic receded gradually, like the tide before the moon. Olivia took a deep breath. "The bad drugs. I know where they came from, and I'm going to stop it."

Abby's fingernails dug into the skin of her forearm. "Wait a minute. Is this about me? About me getting sick?"

"Not just you." Olivia risked a glance at Abby. Her jaw was tight with…anger? Distress? She smoothed her palm across Abby's hand. "But it started with you. After…after you left, I followed you. Into the mountains. I saw you change."

Abby stiffened. "I had no idea. I'm sorry I hurt you—you must have been so confused. But what you're doing is crazy. You have to stop."

"I don't. And I won't." Realizing she sounded like a child, Olivia quickened their pace. "It's not just about you. Now that I know about this world, I can't pretend as though it doesn't exist. There's a war coming, and I have to do my part. I can't do what you do, but I can do something."

Abby stopped in the middle of the block and grasped Olivia by the shoulders. "I wanted to protect you from this."

Her eyes were wide and wild like they had been on the stage of the Red Circuit. How close was her cheetah to emerging?

"I know what you were trying to do," Olivia said. "But it didn't work out that way."

Abby's fingers pressed hard enough to leave bruises, but Olivia didn't mind. "If you do something like this again, you have to tell me. I'm not going to let you go unless you promise."

Despite everything she'd been through in the past two hours, Olivia's skin tightened with arousal. "That's not a very good threat."

Abby choked out a laugh. "Damn you, Liv."

She pulled away then, and Olivia felt the loss so acutely that she gave in. "I'll call."

"Good." Abby rocked back and forth on her heels. "Start when you get home tonight."

Olivia managed to rein in her smile, but only just. "All right."

Abby walked away, but Olivia had a gut feeling she would double back and shadow her until she was safely ensconced in a cab. She'd never asked for a guardian angel, but strangely, it didn't feel oppressive. She'd seen things tonight that most humans didn't even dare to imagine, but all of that paled in comparison to the sensation of Abby's fingertips digging into her skin. Abby was back in her life.

As she turned toward the nearest avenue, the smile broke free.

Emily
Ronica Black

Nothing else had been on her mind. Work was now nonexistent, food wouldn't stay down, and sleep...sleep had become a nightmarish hell from which she could barely escape.

The stereo started. She thumbed up the volume and Evanescence riffed through the house. The music kicked up her heart, making her realize she was excited for the first time in two days. Her ritual time was all she had left. And...Emily.

Everything was set and ready to go. Ouija board, candles, wine, drugs, razor blade, and soon, blood. Natalie settled on the cold bathroom floor and leaned back against the giant tub. Carefully, she ran her fingertips over the tiny white tiles of the floor, readying herself for the ceremony. The scent of rubbing alcohol and mouthwash lingered in the air. She scratched a match across the lighting strip on the matchbook and brought a thick flame to life. Sulfur and smoke assailed her senses and she smiled as she lit the three black candles. Though her hand shook a little, she felt confident and sure. This was what she wanted. What she needed.

Emily.

She shook out the match and poured the wine. It gurgled and looked bloodlike as it spilled into the glass. In the near distance she heard what sounded like a door crack open or closed. She paused, her heart racing as she waited for more. It slammed, and though she knew no one was physically in the house, she trembled, hoping nothing more would come. With a new sense of urgency she opened the pill bottle, poured out three Klonopin, and shoveled them into her mouth to chew. The wine followed; she finished the entire glass. The sensation would come soon, she had to hurry. With the razor blade in hand, she chanted the familiar words. She called upon the darkness, the powers that be, called upon them to listen to her pleas. She asked for permission to enter the other side, asked to see the one she loved, the one she'd lost, the one she longed for. She offered her blood, her self, her mind and soul. Anything to see Emily just one more time.

The blade shook in her hand as she pressed its biting edge into the scarred skin of her wrist. Blood surfaced stubbornly and she had to clench her jaw and press harder, tugging at her skin. A murmur of pain escaped her as a tear ran down her cheek. Dark red drops fell onto the Ouija board and she called out, crying for Emily as the blade fell from her hand. Hurriedly, she spelled out Emily's name on the board, streaking the blood as the stylus moved. Then she sat back, beginning to feel light-headed, and asked if she was permitted to see her.

A door cracked again, this time the bathroom door. She pressed her heel to it, forcing it closed. The distant music was muffled and the knob turned as she wedged her leg harder, keeping it closed. The knob twisted some more and then stopped suddenly. Pounding started, causing her to jerk. It shook the door.

It was here.

She closed her eyes and pleaded with the forces that be.

You can have anything you want. Just please. Let me see her once again.

"Can I see Emily?" she asked, desperate.

And then, as her vision began to fade and the blood slowed from her wrist, the stylus of the Ouija board moved and answered YES.

❖

Dr. Vicki Moreno filled the empty silence by stirring her already tepid hot chocolate. She'd filled it upon her patient's arrival and it was already cold, just like the mood of the session.

"You're still having the nightmares?" Vicki asked, concern coming through to taint her voice. She had to get Natalie talking. She looked like hell and sounded just as bad.

"Yes," Natalie responded, barely a whisper. She clenched her spindly hands and spun the wedding band on her finger. Her body was slumped in the chair and Vicki swore she could see her shoulder bones poking through the threadbare cardigan.

"How often?" she asked, disappointed but not surprised to hear it.

Natalie bit her upper lip in a gesture that Vicki knew well. It meant she was carefully considering how much to share.

"Every night."

Not good enough. "How many *times* a night?"

Again she sucked in on her top lip.

"Three? Four?"

Natalie didn't answer.

"What about the walls, Natalie? Do you still see the walls cracking upon awakening?"

Natalie looked away and Vicki fought a sigh. Natalie wasn't progressing. Wasn't progressing at all. In fact, she seemed to be getting worse.

"Yes," Natalie finally muttered. "They creep up the walls to the ceiling."

"Every morning?"

"I think. Yes. The only time it doesn't happen is when I wake from a nightmare. But—"

"But what?" she said softly, encouraging her to continue.

"Sometimes I don't know when I'm awake or when I'm dreaming. Sometimes the walls are cracking and I think I'm—awake."

"Are you awake?"

"I don't know. I don't want to talk about it."

"Why not?"

"Because I can't explain it."

There was a long silence and Vicki kept stirring her useless drink. She'd offered Natalie one upon arrival, but she'd refused despite looking terribly cold. Now Vicki was wishing hers was hot so she could sip it for the both of them.

"Let's talk about the shadow man. Last time you said he wasn't just in your dreams anymore."

"He's not a shadow. He's a black mass."

"But you know he's male?"

"Yes."

"How?"

Natalie skipped the question and answered the previous one. "He comes when I'm tired or almost asleep or when I'm least expecting it. It's a weird feeling. Like I'm falling. My stomach drops."

"What does he do?"

"He—" She swallowed with obvious nerves. "He rushes at me."

"He runs at you?"

She shook her head. "He rushes. He has no feet."

"I see."

"It's fast. He's fast. I can't ever move."

"What else happens?"

She turned her head as if the question had physically struck her. "He—he says something."

"What does he say?"

Natalie continued to stare at the floor. Her hands twisted into one another.

"Natalie?"

"He says it in this really deep voice. This scary, awful, non-human-sounding voice. Almost like a growl."

Vicki waited, stirring and stirring.

Then finally Natalie spoke. "He says—he says…'cunt.'"

"Cunt?" Vicki cleared her throat and sipped the tepid drink, dribbling some on her chin.

"He says it as he's rushing at me. Like he wants to kill me."

Jesus. Vicki wiped her chin and forced the shocked look from her face.

"Is that all he does?" she asked calmly.

Natalie blinked slowly. "To me physically, yes."

"He doesn't tell you to hurt yourself or others?"

Natalie seemed surprised. "No."

"Okay, then. So the shadow man is still a problem and now he's speaking. Let's talk about your medication." Their brief med check session was almost up and it was obvious some time needed to be spent discussing it. Natalie had been prescribed several drugs at an inpatient facility nearly a year before due to an attempt at suicide and Vicki, based on the recent info from the pharmacy, was beginning to wonder if Natalie took the antidepressant and antipsychotic at all. Vicki clicked the mouse over the order she'd sent two months ago to the pharmacy. Only the Klonopin had been picked up, and there'd been no request for a refill on the other two.

Natalie's dark hair hung in stray strings around her face, but her sparkling green eyes looked out seemingly oblivious to the obstruction.

Her pale lips were now lush and had more color than before thanks to the attention of her teeth. And for a moment, despite Natalie's dwindling care about her appearance, Vicki was struck by her raw beauty.

"I see here that you've only been taking the anxiety medication. Why haven't you been taking the others?" Vicki asked.

"I take them," Natalie finally said. "I must've forgotten."

"How can you take them when you don't even pick them up?"

"I said I must've forgotten."

"Surely they must've handed you all of them at the pharmacy."

Natalie didn't answer, just stuck out her chin.

"Natalie, have you ever taken them? Since you left Brookside, that is?"

She wrung her thin hands and Vicki noticed the redness in the pads of her fingers. It contrasted sharply with the milky white paleness of the rest of her.

"I've picked them up before."

"But have you taken them?"

Her green glass eyes focused on Vicki. "Sometimes."

The office grew quiet with only the distant ticking of Vicki's clock in the far corner. Outside the rain fell, fogging up the already gray, heavy day. Cars splashed through the passing street, hitting the same watery potholes again and again.

"It's very important for you to take your medicine, Natalie," she said softly. "Very important."

"I know."

"Can you promise me you'll try harder?" It would help with the shadow man and the nightmares and most obviously her depression. She really needed her to take them before she ended up back at Brookside, or worse.

Natalie nodded, childlike. Vicki was again struck not only by her beauty but by how much she'd changed since she'd first walked through the door. Gone was the healthy, somewhat vibrant, young professional. What remained was a skeleton of sorts. As if Natalie had been slowly withering away, piece by tiny piece, just blowing away in the passing wind.

Vicki knew the main reason why and she decided to touch on it again, to see where Natalie stood with it.

"Have you been thinking about Emily?"

Natalie looked up sternly. The shadows of her cheekbones sharpened as she clenched her jaw. "I think about Emily all the time."

"How often?"

"Every single second."

Emily had been Natalie's longtime partner, and when she'd been killed in a terrible car accident, Natalie had gone downhill and eventually tried suicide.

"The process hasn't changed at all?" Vicki kept her voice calm and soothing. Emily was still a very touchy subject.

"What process?"

"The process of grieving. Remember we've talked about that several times."

"I grieve. I grieve all the time. That's my process." The words were suddenly jarring out of her. Quick and sharp. "I'm tired of you people telling me to move on, to take one day at a time, to get past the shock and anger. I miss her! I want to be with her!"

Vicki sipped her cold drink again. She blinked a few times to get her bearings. "Are you still wanting to leave here to be with her, Natalie?"

Natalie bit her lip and looked upward. Then, "Yes."

"You want to die?"

"No."

Vicki cleared her throat. "You don't want to die?"

"No. I don't. I want to be with her. Here, there, wherever."

"But in order to be with her there, you would have to die."

Natalie sucked in a frustrated sounding breath. "No, Doctor." She stood.

"Natalie, please. I need to know if you're considering suicide again."

With a quick swing of her purse over her shoulder Natalie faced off with her at the desk. "I never tried to commit suicide, Doctor."

"But you—"

"I never tried to kill myself. I don't want to die. I told you idiots that at Brookside, but no one listened. And as for you, if you can't help me with these—these nightmares and hallucinations, then no one can." She dug in her purse and placed several old bottles of medicine on the blotter of the desk. "You can keep these. I won't be needing your services any longer."

The door slammed as she exited and Vicki sat examining the bottles of medication.

"Just as I thought."

The antidepressant and antipsychotic were all full. She hadn't been taking them. And God only knew for how long.

❖

Natalie ran home in the rain. She had to see Emily. Had to be with her again. Why couldn't anyone understand? A car splashed her as she struggled along, but she didn't care. Her hair was soaked and plastered to her head and the rain was freezing the instant it touched her skin. She hoped it made her sick, sick enough to go into a fever-induced coma. Maybe then she could see Emily without the dark man, without all the tricks he played on her.

But anything was worth seeing Emily. Anything. She could touch her, feel her, smell her. Hear her laugh and feel it vibrate her body. She could smell the sweetness of her breath, hear the moans of her pleasure, feel the tight slickness between her legs as they made love. Yes, she could have it all, just as if she were here.

Her breath was squeezing out of her as she slowed before her small house. The rain continued to pummel down, and despite there being no wind, the front rocking chair was moving. She stepped onto the covered porch, ignoring her overgrown lawn and neglected car. A note nailed to the door caught her eye as she shrugged off her raincoat and stepped out of her boots. She pried the paper from the nail and read quickly.

Dear Natalie,

You are destroying yourself and what you are messing with is downright dangerous. Natalie, it's evil.

Call me when you stop, and please make that soon. For your sake. You have changed so much these past two years.

Your concerned friend,

Viv

Natalie crumpled up the letter and tossed it aside. Viv had first refused to come to the house last week. She'd said all the doors opening and shutting gave her the creeps. She'd seen Natalie's wrists; she'd forced Natalie to tell her what she was doing. The news had devastated her even though Natalie hadn't shared every detail, and she'd begged Natalie to get help and to stop. But Natalie had refused, her Emily too important. And now the letter.

Viv was saying sayonara, she couldn't handle it.

Natalie pushed her way inside, tossed her boots and coat, and headed for the wine. The house was shadowed and quiet, a dank dusty smell to it. There were no pictures or anything that would invite memories. She refused to have such things staring at her day in and day out. The floor creaked underfoot as she opened the bottle and drank straight from it while making her way into the bathroom. Water poured from the bathtub facet as she turned the knob and steam began to fill the room. A nice hot soak would do her good, maybe a Klonopin or two. Maybe Emily would come without the dark man. Sometimes she did, but only for a brief moment. A smooth quick touch to the cheek, a slight brush of the hair from her face, or if she was lucky, a soft delicate kiss to her lips.

She longed for such an encounter despite how brief it might be. She stared into the foggy mirror and thought about Viv's letter. About how what she was messing with was evil. The word hung in her head as a rush of cold air drifted into the bathroom. She slammed the door and sucked in on her top lip. Then, on the mirror, she wrote the word EVIL.

If what she was doing was evil, she didn't care. Emily was worth it. And besides, it couldn't be evil. She wasn't asking for anything awful, only Emily. She wasn't worshipping anything, good or bad. So how could it be evil?

After stripping out of her clothes, she eased into the tub and killed the running water. Breathing deeply, she relaxed against the tub and allowed the water to saturate her skin and muscles. It seemed to massage her insides. She closed her eyes, reached for her Klonopin bottle, and chewed two down with what was left of the wine. She sighed, feeling really good. Emily was coming, she could feel her. How strong would the connection be?

Her fingers skimmed across the razor blade to the needle. Carefully she plucked it from the edge of the tub and stabbed two of her fleshy fingertips. She allowed the blood to drop into the water, mesmerized at how it sank and spread. A smile spread across her face and remained as she leaned her head back, listening to the blood drip twice more before it stopped. Her mind numbed, heated, and grew heavy, and then blissfully light.

She opened her eyes and looked up. The walls began to crack with vein-like splits, crawling upward to the ceiling where they ate away the plaster to reveal the heavy, gray cloud-filled sky. The rain poured down on her in teasing but steady drops. She laughed and held up her hands, welcoming it.

"Emily," she called. "Emily."

The clouds began to part and the sun squeezed through, shining down on her. It illuminated the bathroom just as the door opened, showing Emily standing in the frame wearing a red teddy and matching red lipstick. Her hair was blowing in a warm breeze coming from above.

"Natalie," she said, coming toward her.

Natalie grinned and held out her hand. "Emily."

"I've missed you," Emily said, sweeping in to kiss her long and hard.

Natalie groaned as Emily's hot, slick tongue slipped inside her. This was better than any time before. Better than the snowy mountain where they made love beneath the shelter of a large, low-hanging tree. Better than the beach, the bedroom, and the couch. This was Emily at her most erotic, most passionate.

The kiss deepened as Emily slid into the tub, writhing against Natalie, sucking on her lips. "I love you, baby," Emily said. "I love you like no other. You are my everything. You are my…" She held her face. Her eyes were a swirling beautiful brown. "Everything."

Natalie ran her hands up under the wet, sticking teddy. "And you are mine. You know you are. I can't get you out of my mind."

"I know," she purred as she gyrated her hips, straddling Natalie. The teddy came up and off and disappeared as it fell from the tub. Natalie stared at her dark nipples and her smeared lipstick. Emily was glistening wet and coming at her again, kissing her hard as she slipped her hand between Natalie's legs.

She felt so warm against her, so hot in the warm water. Her mouth was like molten velvet and her hand, her hand was magical, knowing exactly how and where to stroke her.

"Oh God," Natalie said, unable to control the intensifying pleasure. Emily threw her head back and laughed.

"Yes, Natalie. Say it again. Say it again and again." She dove back into her, biting playfully hard into her neck. Her hand continued and Natalie closed her eyes, overcome with ecstasy. Emily groaned and continued to devour her, pumping against Natalie's leg. She grabbed Natalie's hand and placed it on her breast.

"I want you to come, Natalie," she said. "I want you to come so hard."

Natalie cried out as Emily hurried her pace, stroking her clit expertly up and down and up and down.

"Oh God," Natalie said. "Oh God, oh God."

"Yes, Natalie." She leaned again. "Are you close?"

"Ye-es."

Emily laughed and nibbled on her ear. "Then, come, cunt."

The voice wasn't Emily. It was the dark man. Deep and demonic in her ear. And then there was laughter, his laughter.

Natalie's eyes flew open. Her stomach twisted in fright and horror. The man was on top of her, all black and slimy, licking her neck with a long, hideous tongue. His lips peeled back as he laughed, and his black, slime-crusted skin morphed into mist and then back into skin again.

Natalie struggled, pushing him away. But her hands couldn't seem to find him, slipping off his slimy skin one instant and then moving right through him the next.

She managed to push herself up as the form laughed and pulled at her body with grotesque hands. Desperate, she flailed, trying to jump from the tub. Screaming and shoving she slipped and fell, smacking her head on the edge of the tub as she tumbled out. Her body hit the floor bone-crackingly hard, slamming her cheek against the tile.

And as she lay there, unable to move, the dark man ran his hands up her legs to her buttocks, laughing.

In her mind she asked a single question.

Who are you?

The answer came on the mirror. The letter D formed in front of the word she'd written earlier, spelling…

DEVIL.

❖

Vicki pulled her car to a stop in front of Natalie's house. She'd been trying to reach her all day and had even left several messages. Finally, worry got the better of her. She'd never tracked down a patient this urgently, but Natalie seemed on the brink of doing something very harmful to herself. After she'd looked further into her background and made a few calls, her concern had led to near panic.

Climbing from her vehicle, she took in the neglected yard and the tiny house still glistening from the fresh rain. The storm clouds hung in the air, circling the sun as if waiting to gather and pounce once again. An older model car sat in the driveway, giving promise that someone might be home. Maybe Natalie was just avoiding her phone calls. It wouldn't be the first time a patient ignored her and her advice. It happened more than she'd like to think.

She trotted up the stairs and knocked on the door. A crinkled piece of paper blew a little toward her feet. She opened it and read, and her panic returned. She knocked on the door again and called out. There was no answer and she was about to knock again when the door suddenly clicked open. She pushed it further and shouted a hello. The house was dark and quiet.

Vicki made her way inside. "Natalie?"

No answer.

Her nerves began to get the better of her. What if something had happened? What if someone had broken in? Was Natalie okay? She decided to check the house quickly and leave. She didn't like the feel of it. It was cold, dark, and yet oddly smothering. Like something was pressing down on her and watching her closely.

"Natalie? It's Dr. Moreno. Are you okay?" She moved from room to room until finally she came upon the bathroom and edged the door open. She inhaled sharply as she saw Natalie lying nude on the floor, apparently unconscious. "Natalie!"

She ran toward her and skidded on her knees to her side. A quick check of her pulse confirmed life, and she tapped her cheek and called her name as she scanned her body for injuries. Other than the blood on her mouth and head there seemed to be none. The blood on the edge of the tub suggested she had fallen and hit her head. But wait. The bath water was pink too. What the hell had happened?

Quickly she dug out her cell phone, called 911, and reported the situation. She covered Natalie with a towel and gently squeezed her shoulder.

"Natalie, come on, come around."

The bathroom door slammed closed behind her and she jumped. Someone was in the house. Her heart leaped to her throat and she backed to the wall, phone in hand. A small whimper came from Natalie.

"Doctor?"

Vicki knelt, too afraid to put her back to the door. "Natalie, yes, it's me."

Her eye was open and she licked her dried lips to speak again. "You came here?"

"Yes. I was worried and—"

"You were worried? About me?"

"Yes."

"You—you shouldn't have come."

"Why? Natalie, is someone in the house? Did someone do this to you?"

She began to sob, but still seemed hesitant to move. "Ge-get out."

"What?" Vicki whispered.

"Get out!"

The door flew open and a rush of cold wind came at them, slamming Vicki against the wall, spinning Natalie around on the floor. Natalie cried harder and tried to fight against the unseen force. Vicki screamed, unable to move. Something whispered in her ear. Something demonic.

"Bitch," it said and she screamed again.

Suddenly Natalie was up on her feet, staggering around. She shouted at something, cussed at it. She yelped and jumped back as slash marks appeared on her abdomen. And then her face jerked as something seemed to slap her. Crying and yelling, Natalie scurried toward the tub and grabbed a razor blade.

"You want me?" she yelled. "You can have me." She started to slice at her wrist.

"Natalie, no!" Vicki grabbed at her hand. "No!"

Natalie froze and stared at her. "I have to, Doctor." Slobber ran down her chin from tears and fright. "I've let something in. I've let the devil in and now he won't let me go."

"Natalie, don't hurt yourself. Please don't."

"I have to! And then I can be with Emily forever."

Vicki struggled, still powerless to move. Hot, putrid breath wafted over her neck and a hand slid up her leg. She cringed as she tried to speak.

"Natalie, think about it. You won't be with Emily. You won't."

"Yes, I will!" She trembled. "I see her all the time. You—you don't understand. I see her. On the other side."

"Natalie, you won't. It's a trick. It's all…it's something evil."

"Which is why I'm leaving! All I want is Emily!" Natalie ground her teeth and shoved the blade into her wrist, tearing open her skin. She screamed and so did Vicki.

"Natalie!"

But it was too late. The wound was deep, and she collapsed on the floor as her dark crimson blood pulsed onto the tiles.

The force pinning Vicki down suddenly disappeared and she nearly fell from the wall. She pressed a towel to Natalie's wrist, pressed down hard, and prayed. Behind her voices called out.

Human voices.

❖

The morning was bright and seemingly cheery, despite the previous day's happenings. Vicki sipped her blissfully hot coffee as she made her way to the hospital ward. She hadn't slept the night before, unsure about many things. A late-night phone call to a priest finally eased the question of her sanity. It seemed that demons were real and what she'd experienced was indeed evil. But what worried her most was Natalie. The demon she'd let in seemed to be the least of her problems. Vicki had spent the rest of the night trying to decide how to best approach her.

She found Natalie behind the third curtain, wrist heavily bandaged, leather straps wrapped around her arms so she couldn't harm herself. Nearby a patient moaned in subdued mental agony.

Natalie was already awake when she entered.

"Good morning," Vicki said.

Natalie turned to face her. Her cheeks and eyes looked heavy from the sedative they'd given her, the dark bruising already turning yellow.

"Morning."

"How are you feeling?"

"Numb."

"That's probably good at this point."

Natalie blinked slowly. "You came. Yesterday."

"Yes."

"Because you cared."

"Yes."

A tear slipped down her cheek.

"I do care, Natalie. I care very much. In fact, that's the reason I'm here. I have something I need to tell you."

"What is it?" Her eyes were large and liquid with darkness shadowed beneath. Her face looked sallow and pale around the bruising.

Vicki took a big breath. "Natalie, Emily isn't dead." Natalie blinked but said nothing.

"She's a woman you were obsessed with two years ago. She filed charges against you and—"

"I see her on the other side." Natalie seemed strangely calm and almost completely lucid.

"What you saw wasn't real. It was a dream or a hallucination or a trick of evil."

"I saw Emily. She was mine. And I was her everything."

"Are you hearing me, Natalie? Emily isn't dead. She's alive. She's healthy. And she's never been with you."

"Yes, she has. Many, many times."

Vicki placed her coffee on the nearby counter and ran her hands through her hair.

"I don't think you're hearing me, Natalie."

"I am."

"Then what did I say?"

"That Emily is alive."

"Yes. And how does that make you feel?"

She smiled, her eyes feverishly bright. "Fine."

"Fine?"

"Yes."

"Why?"

"Because I no longer need Emily. Now I have you. You are my everything and soon I will be yours."

Study Break
Rebekah Weatherspoon

I keep my eyes on my translation as Cleo watches me. My breasts are exposed, but she's watching my eyes as I look back and forth between the pages of my book and my notes. The assignment is easy. Translate the first page of your favorite book from English to German. It's no challenge, the homework, but keeping still under Cleo's focus takes all of my effort.

I want her. I always do, and she knows this. I picked her the first day of Rush. I saw her across the quad that afternoon and as I approached their designated table, Cleo saw me. Through my awful scraggly hair and my zits—and my weight—she saw my potential. My skin is clear now and my hair tamed, but she still sees past my size eighteen jeans. It's my eyes, she tells me, and my boobs and my lips, but my eyes that she loves. I think it's my focus. And my obedience.

Daddy told me I would be a member of Alpha Beta Omega Sorority the day I graduated from middle school. I only assumed I would be placed in the Alpha Chapter at Maryland University because it's the closest to Mama and Daddy's house in D.C.

The sorority is a front. An organization that Demon-Class A.6, as the government refers to him, created. My father, Dalhem, though not by birth, is the only pure demon-bourne left in this part of the world. His vampire children need to feed and the humans they drink from need to be trained from an early age. We must learn to share our lives with our demons, our vampires, and appreciate the need for our services. Away from our parents for the first time, the select few of us pulled from the student body to join the local chapter where our Sister-Queens wait for us.

Daddy's assigned me to his most powerful demon, his favorite.

My Sister-Queen, Camila, is beautiful, but young by vampire standards. She loves me and respects that I refuse to have a sexual relationship with her. My sorority sisters jump at the chance to sleep with their demons. I do not. Though at this point Camila doesn't mind. She's taken a human of her own to see on a monogamous basis. They are happy and probably making love at this very moment. But they are far from my mind.

Cleo is still watching me.

I adjust the black and red blanket over my shoulders. Every room in the house has security cameras. We aren't monitored constantly, but just in case one of our demons happens to check the feeds, I sit with my back to the mount in the top left corner of Cleo's room. I expected several things to happen during orientation—like forcing myself to socialize—but I never expected what I found with Cleo.

Our relationship is a secret. It's my choice. The favorite pastime for the teenage girl is gossiping. Say what you like about the way I look or my shy, reserved nature, but my relationships won't be offered up for spectator speculation. Cleo likes this idea, and a month ago she agreed to my other terms. Now she is my mistress. She directs me and I obey her. We are both happy.

The other girls just think I'm shy and I've latched on to Cleo because she is bold and loud. A drop-dead gorgeous African goddess, and she has taken a shine to me, but the truth is I saw her strength and I chose her. She's a favorite in Alpha Beta Omega, a junior where I'm a freshman. And I'm sure the other girls do talk about the time Cleo and I spend alone or the fact that neither of us participate in the weekly orgies, but as far as I am concerned, it is just talk. Nowhere near the truth.

Cleo looks back down at her own anthropology notes for a moment. Soon she watches me again.

"Lick your finger," she says. My dorm room across campus is the only place we play full out. Here in the Alpha Beta Omega house, as Cleo likes to say, we pre-game.

I do as she tells me and lick the tip of my middle finger. I know what she has in mind, but I wait for her instructions.

"Good, Bunny." That is our joke. "Now rub your nipple." I do as she tells me. My hand drifts to my breast. I cup it and spread the moisture from my mouth around. Cleo knows how it makes me feel. I am already wet. I'm always aroused when we're together, often when we're apart. My breasts are especially sensitive. I rub the tip and hold back a shudder. My eyes give me away, though. They flutter closed.

"Look at me while you do it." Her voice is calm and distant, but I can tell that she's hot and ready. I watch her brown eyes, the same shade as her soft brown skin, as she watches me. She licks her lips, not casually. Her mind is racing, I can tell. She's thinking the same things as me. She wishes there were no camera. She wishes there were no chance of a nosy sorority sister bursting in. She wishes that studying in my cramped dorm room made more sense than stretching out in her spacious suite. The bathroom is camera free, but it's shared with Danni, the junior girl in the adjoining bedroom. We'll both have to wait for more.

Almost as if to curb our arousal, the phone rings. It's Camila. Only our demons use the landlines. I drop my hand as she turns for the phone, but I don't cover myself.

"Ahoy hoy," she sings into the phone. Cleo and Camila are friends. They were lovers once, but there's a genuine respect and they enjoy each other's company. Camila is nearly sixty years older, but they click very well.

"Just studying with B," she says. Cleo flips her notebook closed and leans against her pillows. She stares at my breasts as she speaks again. "No, that's cool. Okay. See you in a sec." I watch her as she hangs up the phone.

"It's my turn to feed," Cleo tells me. "Camila's on her way up."

"Oh," I say as I close my book. Then I tuck my E cups back into my bra. "I'll go down to the study lounge." I pull my shirt back into place and drop the blanket.

It's another rule we have. I don't offer my feedings with an audience and neither does Cleo. We orgasm when our demons feed. There is no way to avoid it. The pleasure is unparalleled and instant. After, you are sex crazed. You want more, and usually our Sister-Queens are more than willing to take us in other ways. Our sorority sisters too. Casual sex is a constant thing in the Alpha Beta Omega house and something I'm just not comfortable with.

I enjoy my feedings with Camila, even though I don't talk about it like the other girls do. Immediately after, I want Cleo's hands on me, and when it comes to Cleo, I don't want to see Camila take her neck.

I'm jealous, but it goes both ways. I also don't like the idea of Cleo watching someone put their mouth or their hands on my body.

"Wait," Cleo says. She puts her hand on my knee. I freeze. She bites at the corner of her mouth. "I want you to stay."

"I should go." This is me speaking, Benny, not her submissive Bunny-pet. "You're already worked up. I should go and Camila can take care of you."

"I know she'll take care of me, but…" Her voice changes. She is stern now and I know my place. It's what I asked for. "I want my Bunny to stay. I want you to watch," she says.

My first instinct is to argue. We've discussed this before, but then she is watching me again. I live to please her. Her joy is mine. My body and my heart are hers. We are on my terms, but I've never been able to deny her.

"Why?" I ask.

"Because I want to look at you while I come."

My pussy clenches at the thought, but I am still wary. For me, several things could go wrong. Camila needs this feeding to sustain her sanity and her vampire flesh. She needs our blood in controlled amounts, at set times to guarantee our safety. It wouldn't help any of us if my hangups were to interrupt their interaction, but that is not the real reason I should leave. The last thing I need is a visual reminder of the one thing I want, but cannot have, the only thing Cleo refuses to give me: the exchange of her human life for the powerful existence of a vampire. I'd happily service Camila for the rest of my natural mortal life, but she's not the demon I want. It's Cleo.

Cleo would transform the act of feeding for me from a duty to an act of giving, offered fully from my heart. If she would change, not only could I serve her, but I could sustain her. She could live off my life blood and I could feel a certain security of knowing that the demon I'm bound to is also my mistress. That would be the ultimate act of submission for me. I trust her in ways I have never trusted anyone before. And she loves me as much as any human can love another. That love is the foundation for our arrangement. She wouldn't take these demands from any other girl. But this part of her life—her vulnerability, her human nature, her family, and her faith—are things she's not willing to part with.

From the way she describes him, I think her father might be

indifferent, but her mother will never accept the fact that Cleo is gay. As a Baptist preacher, her mother would never accept us as a couple, forget what we really are to each other, that I am her pet. She would never take her only daughter as a demon and she would never give herself as a feeder to become part of the larger family Cleo and I will have one day. Though Cleo knows the reality of our universe, her beliefs remain intact.

It's the possibility of damnation she fears along with the loss of her mortal family. When you know the Divine exists, you fear its counterpart, but I've explained to her many times that she has nothing to fear. Only those vampires who cross Dalhem risk true damnation, and I know she won't break any of his rules. I won't let her. If she changes, she will be one of Dalhem's children. Nothing can touch her. Her heart is too pure. She is shrouded in good. She doesn't believe me. It doesn't change the way I feel. I want her.

I look at her hand, now on my thigh. I should go.

"Trust me," she says. "I'll take care of you too. Just stay."

I want to argue, but I don't. "Okay."

Cleo leans over to whisper in my ear. On camera this looks normal. We are best friends, and girls whisper. "I want you to watch and think about all the things I'm going to do to you tomorrow," Cleo says. She licks me before she pulls away. "Do you want me to remind you?"

We have somewhat of a routine, but Cleo always has her surprises. "Yes, please."

She sighs and leans back against her headboard. "You'll be in your room at three."

"Yes."

"If you're good tonight, I'll kiss you." Another joke. She always kisses me. "I'd tell you the rest, but Camila doesn't walk that slow." If she bothers to walk at all. "Is the kiss a good enough reason?" Her finger strokes my ankle through my sock.

"Yes."

"Good. Stay."

I don't say the words very often, but I say them now so she knows I trust her.

"I love you," I say plainly. No bitten bottom lip or sentiment.

Cleo grins.

There's a knock on the door and a moment later Camila enters.

She is strikingly beautiful. Three-quarters Mexican, a quarter Scots, with full lips and wide hazel eyes that shimmer when she laughs and glow when she feeds. Her hair is cut short, nearly shaved in the back, spiked up elegantly in the front. She's in jeans and one of her usual black tank tops. All curves and perfect proportions, she is shorter than Cleo and I both, but her power is a physical thing.

You feel it in her presence once you commit to the bond. I can't explain this connection. I love Cleo. I *will* marry her when she's ready, whether she's mortal or not, but for now we are both bound to Camila. It is a blood bond, one of the strongest in Heaven and on Earth, and even when Camila is close, it makes me crave the touch of our vampire queen. This is the bond I want with Cleo.

Camila has pure demon blood in her veins, and Daddy tells me that makes our bond even stronger. Not a drop diluted by human weakness, but she is gentle and so kind. I am eager for our next feeding, though I would never admit it.

"Hey. Am I interrupting?" Camila asks with a smile that shows the sharp points of her canines. Her voice is lovely too. Rich and smooth. Ginger, her human girlfriend, is very lucky.

"No," Cleo says.

"Not at all," I add.

Camila approaches the bed, and almost as if she commands it so, we both crawl to the edge of the mattress on our knees to meet her. She kisses us both, me softly on the corner of my mouth as she gently cups my cheek. I would only let my demon touch me this way. My demon and Cleo.

"How are you?" she asks with a sweet smile that makes my heart stutter. It's the bond. I can't help it.

"I'm good." She draws a smile out of me.

"Good." She turns then, butts heads with Cleo and lightly kisses her lips. It's a friendly kiss, but I wouldn't mind if they'd skip it.

"Hey, shithead," Camila says.

"'Sup, bitchface. Cool if B stays?" Cleo asks.

Camila blinks in surprise. She knows how I am. "Of course. Are you okay with that?" She can read our minds, but she doesn't unless it's completely necessary. This isn't one of those times.

"Yeah. I don't feel like going back to the dorm," I say. "It's cold out."

Camila laughs. "It is." She turns her focus back to Cleo. "Let's do this so I can get out of your hair. Should we lie down or would you like to sit?"

I take my feeding sitting with Camila behind me. The drawing blood from the wrist takes much longer and there's a risk of eye contact. And I feel less comfortable offering a feeding face-to-face. It's harder to control the movement of my hips.

Cleo glances over her shoulder. "Hmm, let's lie down.—Come on, Benny." She nods for me to follow. The three of us climb up on the bed. I sit up while Cleo lies down, Camila between us. I know exactly what will happen next. There are plenty of ways to get creative during a feeding, to add to the sensations, which is actually redundant if you're attending to the real purpose of the transaction, but there are certain things Camila must do.

Cleo watches me again, but my eyes are on our Queen. Camila props herself on one elbow and leans over my mistress. Her other hand slides deep into Cleo's thick afro and grips the back of her head. She'll move regardless. At some point it's likely she'll try to jerk from Camila's grasp. Though she'd be quick to heal her, Camila won't risk tearing the artery. She holds my head steady the same way when we are together. Usually my eyes are shut and I think of being somewhere else, with someone else.

I dream of Cleo setting me at the foot of her bed. A real bed with sturdy posts in a house far from this one with no cameras and no prying eyes. She'll bind me naked at the foot of the bed with my hands behind my back and my knees on the floor. I'll have to watch her undress slowly. She'll talk to me the whole time as she pulls her shirt over her head and unclasps the bra that holds her heavy breasts with their dark tips. She'll tell what she has done during the night while I am sleeping. She'll tell me of the other human blood she tastes so she doesn't drain me. I'll be jealous, but now she'll know. It makes me desperate to please her. She'll tell me how much she wants me.

She'll approach me and waste no time bringing my head between her legs. I'll lick her, suck her off until she is growling, and then when she can't take anymore, she'll feed. She'll lift me from the floor, but my hands will stay bound. She'll kick my feet apart and fuck me with her fingers while she drinks from me. And I'll come over and over again. It's all I think of when Camila and I are together.

Cleo takes a deep breath and closes her eyes, then she is watching me again. I meet her gaze and for once I'm afraid of what she is thinking. She slides her arm under Camila's body. I tense for the embrace that will bring their bodies even closer, but Cleo touches my fingertips. I think of what this feeding would be like if I wasn't in the room and I consider how far things would go if Cleo and I weren't together, and suddenly I want to leave. I start to shiver instead. To hide the goose bumps on my skin I pull the red and black blanket back up to my chin. My shuffling has Camila looking over her shoulder at me.

"Sorry, it's cold," I lie to her with a hint of a smile. The heat is on full blast. She rolls in my direction, uncertain.

"Are you sure? We don't have to do this." *But I do*, I tell myself. Cleo's made a demand of me. I can't let her down.

"Yeah. I'm fine."

"Okay. You stop me if you need to."

I appreciate the suggestion, but if I interrupt we'll only be here longer. "I will."

Camila scoots back into Cleo's arms, closer this time. I imagine their breasts are pressed together. They are careful to keep their legs apart.

"Are you ready?" Camila asks softly as she grips Cleo's thick curls again. I flinch as she licks my mistress's neck, searching for the perfect spot to pierce. She asks for herself; once the blood hits her tongue she is more demon than queen, much more animal than human. She has the strength and the practice to control herself, the internal cues to keep from killing us, but for a moment she must let go. It's in her nature. She licks Cleo's skin some more, then settles her movements. She is ready. Her shoulders are tense and a low growling purr emanates from her chest.

Cleo's reply is strained. "Yeah. Do it." But she keeps her eyes on me.

"Next time, wash your neck. You smell," Camila jokes. Cleo smells amazing, like cherry blossoms and vanilla. It's the lotion I gave her.

She laughs, then reaches for my hand again. Her eyes focus on my lips. "You're smelling your own breath, asshole. Just do it."

Camila chuckles lightly, then strikes without warning. Cleo's eyes squeeze closed and her grunt is loud. The mechanics of the bite are simple. Camila's teeth penetrate deep to create the puncture, then recede slightly, holding the feeder in place, but allowing a small amount of room for the blood to escape. The feeling is pure ecstasy. The icy slice of our Queen's fangs through your skin cools the incision, but the rest of you becomes fire. You orgasm instantly, no building up with a slow burn or thrusting charge barreling toward a finish. You come, instantly, almost painfully. Your clit twitches violently and your pussy convulses—at first. You feel her tongue as she encourages the flow faster to the surface and then you come, again.

Cleo orgasms once more, cursing this time under her breath as she grips my hand tighter. Her eyes are still closed. I imagine how she is feeling. I imagine her wet pussy and I think of all the things standing in our way. I want Cleo to know how I taste. I want my blood to sustain her.

We all have a unique flavor. I imagine Cleo's is rich and dark like the rest of her. I don't have to imagine that Camila enjoys it. Their bodies are even closer now. Though layers of denim and cotton separate them, their legs have become intertwined. Cleo is forceful. I imagine Camila used to love being fucked by her before our freshman class came through and changed things.

Cleo moans. The sound tears through my heart. If she did talk, I'm suddenly worried about whose name she would say. Still my body responds. Dry heat threatens to close up my throat, but saliva pools in my mouth. My breasts ache now. I hold still so my nipples don't rub along the fabric of my shirt. I'll come a little if they do, but not enough. My thighs press together, though my clit needs more than Cleo's promises for attention some hours in the future. It's torture, but I stay and continue to home in on things that I shouldn't, like the sounds Camila is making. She echoes Cleo's whimpers and pants with shudders and growls. She makes the same noises when we're together, but then again, I pretend she's someone else.

The feeding goes on for a while, probably only a few minutes or so, but it feels like hours. Their bodies move together eventually, following the pumping rhythm of Cleo's hips. She can't help the reaction she's having, and I can't look away. Cleo holds my hand even tighter. Her nails will leave marks on my palm. I don't mind because the small pain is the only proof that she hasn't forgotten that I'm in the room.

Eventually Cleo's heavy sigh lets me know Camila is finished.

She will seal the wounds with a few drops of her own blood that she'll harvest with her fangs from the side of her tongue. Then Camila will leave. If they were still lovers, she would stay. Cleo would go down on her, maybe. Or maybe they would kiss.

I am off the bed before Camila completes the ritual. "I have to pee," I offer as a pathetic excuse before I slam the bathroom door behind me. I hate to consider what Camila must think of me now, almost as much as I regret sticking around in the first place.

I'll need a few minutes to myself, even after Camila is gone, but Cleo doesn't care. She is through the door a few moments later, closing us in. She's breathing heavy. I stay calm.

"I'm sorry. I can't do that again," I tell her.

"It's my bad. We *won't* do that again. I swear. Camila's going to delete the tape. She doesn't care," Cleo adds before I can react. But I do care.

She locks the door leading to Danni's bedroom.

"Wait—"

"Danni's not here."

"We can't—"

Her body crushing mine against the sink stops my words. "Yes, we can." She kisses my cheeks and my eyes. She grinds her thigh between my legs. She's so close I feel the heat come off her skin.

"Do I have to remind you who's in charge, Bunny B?" she whispers to me.

"No," I say when *yes* is what I mean. Gently, I nudge her back a step. "You didn't watch me."

"But I felt you." She gently traces the skin on my neck. "I think about it, B. What it would be like to have you here."

"No, you don't." I jerk my head away before she can kiss me. She pulls me back. Her brown eyes are dark.

"Listen to me. I do."

Her arms surround my waist and she draws me to her. I don't resist this time. I kiss her back, even though I'm breaking my own rules. We promised to be honest with each other, to admit when we are in pain or when our limits have been pushed too far, and Camila has shredded my limits tonight. I can't think clearly. I can't find my resistance.

Cleo's hand is busy between us. My jeans are undone and my underwear invaded, but when I close my eyes all I see is Camila with her lips on what is mine, her fangs coming between me and my mistress in a way I wish wasn't necessary.

I start to pull back, but Cleo kisses me deeper, urges me to let go. Her fingers flex inside me, searching for something I am too stubborn to give. I hold out as long as I can. I fight, praying that one day Cleo will give me what I really need.

I shiver helplessly as her lips move to the slope of my neck. I don't want to give in, but when she bites, I come.

AWAY WITH THE FAIRIES
LESLEY DAVIS

Rhyannon stifled a yawn behind her hand for the second time in as many minutes. *For heaven's sake, who knew vampires were* so *boring,* she thought as she was forced to listen to the handsome vampiress, Zofia, extol the virtues of life as an immortal. *Again. Blah blah, ancient lineage, yadda yadda live forever.* Rhyannon only just managed not to roll her eyes as Zofia started up again on all that could be gained from just one bite. She had long since stopped really listening as the woman started in on the sacred blood rituals. Just the mention of them, quite truthfully, made Rhyannon's stomach roll. She resisted the urge to pull her hood further over her face to block out her companions. She was grateful for its concealment and the deceptive lightness of the fabric in the cloying heat of the tavern. For a moment she let herself soak in the atmosphere, reaching out to the timbers and pitch that moulded the tavern's walls. The tavern was old, very old, with a history all its own. It stood as the centre point on a patch of land that marked a neutral ground between three local factions—all very different cultures and creatures, all preternatural, and all existing uneasily with their neighbours. Rhyannon knew that out of the three, the vampires and the werewolves were the ones most prone to violence. She had long heard tales of their bloody histories as they tested their strengths against each other. Though observing the women opposite her now, all she saw was arrogance and indifference. She couldn't help but wonder if time had mellowed their need for war and dominance. She hoped so.

"I could offer you endless nights of passion. Undead lust is very powerful." Zofia leaned across the table, her voice rumbling seductively.

Rhyannon wondered if that tone was supposed to draw her into the vampire's thrall. She saw Zofia's face register surprise when she wasn't moved in the slightest. Thrall or not, Rhyannon balked at the whole idea of being with anyone not entirely living. She admitted Zofia was attractive, in an unusually pale kind of way, and her face bore a regal austerity that was oddly appealing. She obviously dressed for seduction. Her pale chest was flagrantly on display through her shirt. Rhyannon had been hard-pressed not to laugh, though, every time Zofia let her fangs show. The flash of the pointed canines had captured her attention, but probably not in the way Zofia hoped for. All Rhyannon could wonder was how she stopped from piercing her bottom lip every time she let those fangs drop.

Obviously realising she was losing her audience's attention, Zofia changed her track. "Of course, should the thought of living for eternity not be what you desire, you could always try Fuzzy here." She flipped a thumb in the direction of her drinking companion. Rhyannon recalled she was named Wallace. They'd only been introduced briefly before Zofia had dominated the conversation. This woman was larger, broader, and seemed constantly on alert. The slightest noise in the tavern made Wallace's head shoot up and her keen eyes sought out the cause.

"Admittedly," Zofia drawled, "you'll probably spend most of your time trying to rid yourself of all the hair she sheds."

Wallace shot the vampire a sour look, then turned her attention back to Rhyannon. "I can't offer you eternal damnation like you'd get if you got stuck with my friend here," she said, "but I'm a great hunter. You'd never want for food."

"And what if she's a vegetarian?" Zofia asked smartly. "Look at her. She's incredibly slender and delicate. Your kind of meals would make her a butter ball in no time."

"I…I…I could always order in, I guess." Wallace looked decidedly nonplussed as she blustered.

Though the werewolf female wasn't in full pelt and looked human enough, Rhyannon could still see the pathetic hang-dog expression clearly written on her face. She marvelled at how she had managed to get stuck in this tavern with two of the worst nightmares for conversation she could possibly have come across. She hadn't been vying for attention and yet she had these two trying desperately to outdo the other in their seduction techniques. So much for a quiet night out getting to experience the nightlife and its colourful inhabitants, she sighed. She had hoped to go unnoticed so she could get a feel of the mood among these people. Instead, the drink she had paid for was bitter and unsatisfying, and the company was wearing on her soul. She lifted her hand to brush back a lock of hair that escaped from her hood.

"You have beautiful hair," Zofia remarked immediately, her dark eyes raking over Rhyannon and falling to rest on her slight cleavage on show. "It's like moonlight, so pale and shiny."

"I like shiny," Wallace commented guilelessly. In an instant, Zofia whipped out a coin and flipped it into the air. Wallace caught it immediately in her large hand, grinning at the game.

"Go buy yourself another drink, furball, and leave me and the pretty lady to talk."

Wallace's head instantly bowed. She was being dismissed from the table and was not happy about it. She began rumbling under her breath. The bell from the door chimed and, distracted from her own pitiful whining, Wallace's eyes trained on the entrance. Zofia sighed at her antics but looked up too.

"My oh my, now, there's something you don't often see walking into a place like this. We have new blood in the house tonight." Zofia cut a look at Rhyannon. "Must be the waning moon bringing everyone out."

Rhyannon spared a look over her shoulder. Standing at the bar was a woman with a short crop of hair, the colouring very similar to Rhyannon's own. She wore some kind of uniform with a heavy cape and looked very starched and proper. *Handsome too*, Rhyannon noted. She caught the fire in Zofia's eyes ignite as she studied the woman.

"Look at her ears," Zofia spoke almost to herself. "She's a fairy."

Wallace snorted. "She's not a fairy, she doesn't have wings. You have to have wings if you're a fairy."

"She's got pointed ears," Zofia argued.

"So do I when I've got my wolf on," Wallace retorted.

"Yeah, but you're all furry and smell of dog, this woman doesn't." Zofia inhaled deeply and a small smile curved her lips. "She smells of the outdoors."

"I…"

Zofia stopped Wallace's comment with a raised hand. "You bring most of the outdoors in on your bloody great paws. This woman is a fairy and I bet she would reek of magic if I got closer and more… intimate."

Rhyannon sat back in her seat and regarded the vampire. "You can smell magic on the preternatural?"

"I have many skills. It comes from living for hundreds of years," Zofia said with a smug smile.

"Oh dear heavens, save me," Rhyannon muttered under her breath, hoping that the vampire wasn't going to start in again. She felt the presence behind her before a voice even spoke.

"You called for me?"

"Oh slick move, very slick," Zofia said, eyeing the newcomer intently.

Rhyannon looked over her shoulder. "Can I help you?"

The woman smiled at her, though it never reached her eyes. "I think, maybe, *I* can help *you*. What is one so fair doing out consorting with," she spared a glance around the room, then stared down the two women at the table, "new friends?"

Rhyannon felt the woman crowd in just a little closer behind her. The heat from her body warmed Rhyannon through her sheer cloak and summer dress.

"What's your name, Fairy?" Wallace asked, sniffing at the air, probably searching for magic but sneezing loudly when she snorted up some tavern dust instead.

"I am Odelina, but you can call me Odel."

"You're very big for a fairy. You're our size. I thought fairies were only this big." Wallace held a meaty thumb and finger an inch apart. "Itty-bitty things, like bugs."

Odel bristled visibly. "Fairies are not bugs, and you would be surprised by how many forms we can take."

"So you're what? The Queen of the Fairies because of your size?"

Sighing, Odel shook her head. "No, that is someone else's job. Someone much more qualified. I'm merely a soldier."

"Where are your wings?" Wallace was on a roll.

"We don't reveal our wings to just anyone, Wolf."

"But what if you needed to make a fast escape from here? You could, couldn't you? You could bust your wings out and fly away if threatened?" To emphasise her point, Wallace deliberately bared her teeth and an ominous growl escaped from her chest. In an instant it was stifled and Wallace squeaked out a startled yelp. Her eyes widened in fear at the sudden appearance of a long sword's point pressed menacingly at her throat.

"Are you threatening me, whelp?" Odel asked stonily, her sword pushing in fractionally and piercing Wallace's neck. Zofia looked torn between distancing herself from her foolish friend and wanting to check out the blood now trickling from Wallace's wound.

"No, no, not at all." Wallace purposely kept her gaze away from Odel, suitably cowed.

Rhyannon coughed quietly and the sword was instantly sheathed.

"Wise move, mutt." Odel stared the contrite wolf down.

Wallace rubbed at her neck with a grimace. "Fairies carry swords?"

"It's a harsh world out there for the preternatural community. You can never be too careful." Odel looked about the tavern. Everyone's attention was suddenly somewhere else. "We're not even safe among our own. It's a fool who goes out unprepared these dark days." She drew in a sharp breath as the sharp point of a knife made its presence known at her stomach. She looked down to see Rhyannon's hand holding the weapon. "Not so helpless after all, my lady." She bowed her head in acknowledgement and the knife was duly removed.

"Why are *you* here?" Rhyannon asked. "You're a long way from home."

"My people are hearing stories, rumours of an army threatening to test the borders of the fairy kingdom."

"With what intention?" Surreptitiously, Rhyannon looked around her. Now the others in the tavern were all ears and listening intently to the fairy speak.

"To invade and take our lands, lands that have been rightfully ours since time began."

"And if these rumours prove to be true?" Zofia asked, a small smile playing on her lips.

"Then I'm going to serve as warning to those who wish to go into battle with us. We have more magic than you bloodsuckers and tick carriers can imagine."

Zofia and Wallace both bristled at the derogatory comments. Zofia sat up straighter in her seat. "Your people send in one fairy soldier against a whole tavern full of vampires and werewolves. Either you're all-powerful or your people are running scared and you were the only one woman enough to stand up to us." She looked Odel up and down. "But you don't look that big to me, Fairy."

"Size matters nothing when I possess the one thing our nation was founded on."

"And what's that?" Wallace asked, still worrying at her throat.

Odel leaned forward over the table and the nervous werewolf shrank back. "A magic more powerful than you can possibly imagine."

Zofia snorted inelegantly. "Magic has no hold in our world now. It's outdated. What are you going to do, sprite? Turn my hair blue with a few choice words or de-fuzz Wallace here?"

Wallace gasped out loud at the thought. "I don't want to lose my fur," she whimpered.

The people in the tavern started to crowd in a little closer with a swell of angry whispers. Some of the men looked like they were preparing to take action. Odel slowly removed her sword from its sheath again. This time when she spoke, she spoke to the whole room.

"I have it on good authority that tonight this tavern welcomes the rulers of the vampire court and the werewolf pack. And not just them, but also the leaders of their armies are assembled." She cast an eye around the room. "It's so nice that you could all join me for this occasion. I bring you word from the Queen of the fairy folk herself. You will *not* cross our borders." Odel paused, then added in a voice of steel, "For if you do, you will suffer the consequences."

"And a bunch of little fairies are going to do what exactly?" A deep male voice rang out. Rhyannon spied him lounging at the bar, his military bearing revealing him to be one of the vampire soldiers.

"We shall show our true might." Odel shrugged off her cape and her large wings burst forth. Not fragile things, but wings imbued with muscle and might. They shone with a burnished bronze as if forged from the finest metal and were tipped with lethal barbs. She opened them fully, forcing the people behind her to step back or risk getting hurt. "I warn you for the last time, neighbours, never judge someone's power by their mere size. You cross our borders, we will take a step back onto yours." With a flourish of her hand, Odel let loose a shimmering rainbow of dust that covered her from head to toe.

"Fairy dust, ooh, I'm so scared," Zofia muttered sarcastically.

Rhyannon was satisfied to see the vampire's face suddenly pale even more as Odel began to shift and grow before all their eyes. The fairy first began to slowly gain height over the occupants of the tavern and then she grew taller still. There were some startled screams and frightened yells as Odel grew at an almighty rate. Everyone pushed back and away from the transformation happening right before them. Terrified, they huddled together at the other side of the room as Odel's size increased. Some tried to escape out of the door but found it sealed. No amount of pulling or banging on it worked the door free of its frame.

"There's no escape." Odel's voice boomed off the tavern's walls as she all but pressed into the ceiling. She rested one hand on the thatched roof and peered down at the frightened occupants of the tavern. Her sword had grown too and its lethal blade shone in the tavern's lights. She lifted it carefully over the heads of the nervous vampires and werewolves. "This is but a fraction of the size I can grow to. Imagine an army like me with this impressive might. We could fly into your lands on silent wings and wipe out each and every one of you."

Zofia hastened to her feet. "You dare come into this tavern and threaten us all? We have done your people no harm."

"Not as yet, but we have seen the plans you have worked up between your military men. Not all your clan wish to fight against us. They prefer to continue living in the peace that exists between us all." Odel twisted her sword so it caught the light. Wicked glints shone along its impressive length. "Your own plans were leaked to us by ones who could only have been in your war rooms. Think about it. You're not as safe in your own lands as you believe."

Zofia looked around the room and caught the eye lines of certain vampires and werewolves alike. Rhyannon watched the silent communications with interest. Zofia then turned back to the giant in the room.

"I think it's safe to say you've made your point, Odel. Tell your Queen we meant no disrespect in considering expanding our lands. It was an idle thought that should never have been made public knowledge by loose tongues. We regret that it brought fear to your esteemed people." She bowed nervously, her dark eyes flicking toward the lethal sword that hung high above everyone's heads. "Tell your Queen she has nothing to fear from either house." She looked around the room again and a large male werewolf nodded.

Rhyannon recognised him as the current Alpha of the werewolves. She'd already identified Zofia as the vampire next in line to reign once the current King tired of leading his immortals. She recognised the familial arrogance and the ornamental ring bearing the family crest Zofia wore. Now she knew the key players, it was Rhyannon's turn to speak.

"I thank you for that reassurance, Zofia." Rhyannon removed her hood and let her hair flow free. The pale blond tresses lit up the room with an unnatural glow. Standing, she appeared before them all, radiant and shimmering. She looked around the room, satisfied to see the apprehension in many an eye. "Be assured, my power is even stronger than this soldier's. Fear us and leave our lands untouched. You'll only get one warning from me, so heed it well."

Everyone nodded swiftly, looking to Rhyannon and Odel in undisguised terror.

At a nod from Rhyannon, Odel shrank back down in size.

"I think our business is concluded here, Your Highness. May I escort you back to your kingdom?" Odel's sword was still in her fighting hand but she held out her other arm gallantly.

Rhyannon rested her hand lightly on Odel's forearm. She turned to Zofia and Wallace. "Thank you for the scintillating conversation, ladies. I learned so much about your people tonight thanks to your... attentions." She tossed a few coins on the table. "Buy everyone a drink on me, as a thank you for their kind hospitality to a stranger in a very strange land." She let Odel lead her through the tavern, amused by how everyone stepped back in fear. Odel unlatched the door that opened easily for them and closed it quietly behind them as they left.

"How long before the spell wears off?" Odel asked, risking a swift look over her shoulder back toward the tavern as they hastened away.

"Just a few more minutes, but I resealed the door for a while so that no one could attempt to follow us."

"Then I suggest we waste no more time. Let's take to the air and put this place behind us." Odel sheathed her sword and flexed her wings. A soft steady thrumming sounded in the air as she vibrated her wings, preparing for flight. She helped Rhyannon push her cloak aside. Underneath, the Queen of the Fairies possessed a magnificent set of wings resembling the purest gold filigree.

"I won't be sorry to shake the dust of this place from my wings," Rhyannon admitted. "Let's get out of here and not tempt our staying any longer." Taking to the air with a graceful manoeuvre, Rhyannon rose above the ground and looked down at where they'd been. The tavern looked so small from the air, the three roads that led to each faction's territory stood out starkly on the ground. Rising higher, Rhyannon looked north. The vampires' lands were a dark and dismal vista. The ornate castles built high on imposing hillsides were fashioned with cruel spires, their bricks a sullen grey to match the landscape. The whole land looked empty and devoid of life. Rhyannon thought how fitting that was for such a race. To the west lay the werewolf territories. In marked contrast this was a veritable forest, trees of every variation tangled tightly together to hide the ground from prying eyes. Rhyannon had a fondness for the wolves. They were creatures of a transforming magic like the fairies could empower. But like the vampires, they were bound forever to the cycle of the moon above. Fairies had no such limitations. Rhyannon looked east and found her home.

"Your Highness, if you're done sightseeing, we need to go." Odel was already flying away, looking eager to be on safer soil.

Rhyannon's wings carried her after her mate. "You did well in there, Odel. I love the uniform, where did you get it?" As the Princess Consort to the Queen, Odel had long since handed in her soldier's garb for a ruler's cloak and crown. Rhyannon had gotten a special kind of thrill seeing her lover in the clothing she had wooed her in so many years before.

"I borrowed it from Alfre."

"You look mighty fine in it, my dear. It brings back sweet memories."

Odel turned around to hover until Rhyannon drew up beside her. "Flattery will get you everywhere, my Queen. Do you think we suitably put the wind up the vamps and wolves?"

"I hope so. Every generation we have to prove ourselves again to these people. It's a good job all of us are long lived, so we can make sure we don't pull the same tricks every time."

"I think we did well this time."

"Yes, showing our might in size was a marvellous inspiration from you, my dear." Rhyannon flew past her, then called over her shoulder, "Well, don't you want to get home?"

Odel put a spurt on and raced after her wife. "Don't think I didn't notice that damn vampire all but had her beady eyes wedged between your cleavage," she grumbled.

"I'm surprised she could even see mine with the glare of paleness from her own chest she boldly had on display."

"Vampires know little shame." Odel flew at Rhyannon's side, tempering her wings to match their speed. "What did you make of the werewolves? This was *our* first time meeting our neighbours, and I wondered what you had learned."

Rhyannon reached out and they flew together hand in hand. "I found the vampires a haughty and selfish breed. They appear to look out only for themselves. All those years of immortality have worn away their manners. As for the werewolves, I rather pity them. They are obviously in league with the vampires but held in such disdain they are nothing more than lap dogs."

"I found the smell offensive in the tavern." Odel made a face.

"That's because you, my love, are used to the fresh air and bright meadows we live in. We are blessed to be surrounded by the perfume of flowers and not the rank odours of people and badly fermenting ale."

"The sun seems to shine more on our territory too."

"I'm sure the Fairy Goddess had a hand in that for us." Rhyannon relaxed and felt the warmth from the swiftly setting sun caress her face. They flew over their lands, hailed by the fairies on guard at the borders and at various strategic points. She caught sight of a trail of fireflies taking to the air, their bodies tiny beacons to light up the night when it fell.

Odel tugged on her hand and drew Rhyannon down with her. Together they landed on the huge brown centre of a sunflower. She held her close and reverently kissed Rhyannon on her forehead. "You are a fabulous Queen. I was never in more awe of you than when you revealed yourself and shone in your glory."

Rhyannon smiled. The shimmering effect was something only royalty could manifest. It was a warning to predators that here stood a powerful creature, stay away or be harmed. "Do you truly believe they will abandon their plans now?"

Odel looked up at the sky, pointing as she spotted something heading their way. "Let's find out."

A ladybug landed beside them on the flower and dutifully told them all they needed to know. Rhyannon patted his shell gently and bid him safe journey home. Odel chuckled as his message sank in.

"So, word is the vampires and werewolves are now arguing over whose stupid idea it was to even think of engaging the fairy folk!" She rubbed her hands together gleefully. "We'll keep our spies in their camps as always, but I think we did what was necessary this day."

Rhyannon agreed. "Our literal *fly on the wall* eyes and ears never have been rumbled by ones who never think to look further than their own nose." She kissed Odel sweetly. "I almost feel sorry for them. We have everything in peace here while they have to wage war to fill their empty lives."

"That's because they don't understand real magic." Odel rested a hand on her wife's stomach. "The life we can create is where the true magic lies. The Goddess blesses us with same-sex pairings, with the ability for us to mate and produce offspring. That's a great deal of power she entrusted for ones so small." She nuzzled into Rhyannon's neck and kissed her pulse point. "You carry our next King or Queen. I can't think of anything more magical than that expression of our love."

Rhyannon agreed wholeheartedly. She smiled into the eyes of her beloved. "Do you think they'll ever realise that the magic we performed today wasn't quite what they realised?"

Odel shook her head. "I don't think they'd ever suspect you'd shrunk them all down to fairy size before you even set foot into the tavern. Or would know that the magic I performed meant I merely doubled in size and was not really the giant I appeared to be to their tiny eyes!"

Laughing at the trick they'd pulled, Rhyannon drew Odel down to lie upon the flower. "Would you care to watch the night fall from atop a flower throne, my sweet? On this flower we are perched high above the field and can watch the fireflies dance."

Odel cuddled in close. "I can think of no better place to be,

Rhyannon. We can count the stars before we head home. I can already see our favourite shining through, heralding the night's fall."

"The second star, there on the right? The one that you told me you wished upon and which guided you on your journey to my side?"

"The one that always guides me home to my fairy Queen and my heart." Odel ran her tongue sensuously along Rhyannon's full bottom lip. Rhyannon's mouth opened to permit her entrance and they kissed languidly. Odel's hands pushed aside the thin cloak so she could reach inside and run her hands over Rhyannon's slim body. Her hand rested for a moment on the slight bump that was just beginning to show, then moved lower with purpose. She tugged at Rhyannon's dress and slipped her hand under it, smoothing her palm up a soft, firm thigh. Rhyannon gasped softly as Odel's fingers reached higher still and found her wet and wanting.

"Here's where the magic truly begins," Odel whispered as she pushed aside the flimsy panties covering Rhyannon's sex and swirled her fingers in the rich moisture waiting for her. She lifted her hand up and licked at her fingers greedily. "Sweet nectar," she crooned and returned her fingers to the source, teasing Rhyannon with soft touches and a well-positioned thumb.

Rhyannon bucked beneath her lover, her breath escaping in soft pants as she strained to push her body closer to Odel's tantalising fingers. She heard the unmistakable sound of wings beating as Odel's own passion rose and her wings began to flutter in arousal.

"Sweetheart, what are those barbs on your wings?" Rhyannon had to ask before passion clouded her mind completely.

"Rose thorns. I had my brothers help me attach them with honey so that I looked suitably threatening."

Rhyannon smiled as she looked up into the face of her mate. No one looking at her now, her face suffused with love and passion, would ever think of her as threatening. But Rhyannon knew that Odel would protect her to her last breath, which was why she alone had accompanied her to the tavern.

"My fearless warrior," Rhyannon sighed, then gasped as Odel entered her. Odel's fingers knew exactly where to touch. So in tune with her lover's body Odel coaxed endless shivers and bolts of pleasure through Rhyannon's small frame. Rhyannon clutched at Odel's shoulders, clinging on tight to the only stability she knew. The petals she lay upon rocked with her in tandem to the motion Odel commanded. Odel whispered soft words against her lips, encouraging her, delighting in Rhyannon's beauty and professing her love for eternity. Rhyannon's hips bucked as Odel took her. Slowly the pleasure built until Odel placed a thumb firmly on Rhyannon's clit and rubbed. The added stimulus made Rhyannon cry out into the night sky and she saw more than the stars above as she climaxed in her lover's arms. Protectively, Odel covered them both with her wings, shielding them from the night sky and enveloping them in an intimate embrace.

Sated, Rhyannon tugged Odel closer, kissing her with a lazy passion. "I pity our neighbours not knowing this joy, making love under the stars with the flowers as their mattress." Her own hands began a gentle foray down Odel's uniform, her nimble fingers finding places to slip inside to touch and tease her eager mate.

Odel nodded absently, already surrendering to her lover. When she spoke her voice was husky, roughened by her need. "There's really nowhere more perfect than being away with the fairies."

IN THE BELL TOWER
MJ WILLIAMZ

Jackson Square is a carnival ride for the senses. The sights and sounds of the street merchants, the smells of delicious Cajun food wafting from one restaurant or another, and the feel of the heavy, humid air pressing on the crowds. It was summer, and there was no place I'd have rather been than New Orleans.

I woke just past sunset that June evening and climbed out of my custom-made, extra-wide coffin to peer down on the square. From my vantage point of the old bell tower in St. Louis Cathedral, I watched the comings and goings of the scantily clad tourists and the carefully practiced choreography of the local pickup artists.

One group in particular caught my attention. There were five women in their early twenties. They were laughing and talking as they emerged from Pirate Alley onto Jackson Square.

Two women led the group, walking arm in arm. Two of the others giggled as they looked around, but the fifth woman looked scared, like she was trying to climb into herself to keep others from noticing her.

She was the beauty of the group, her insecurity incongruous with her wavy blond hair, deep blue eyes, and tight tan body covered only by a pink spaghetti strap top and short white denim shorts.

I watched as a man in cutoffs and a blue T-shirt approached her, gaping holes showing in his smile. He slicked back his greasy hair as he attempted to strike up a conversation with her. Her friends kept walking, and suddenly, she was alone with this man in the middle of the crowd. No one paid any attention to them as he grabbed her arm.

The jump to the ground seemed to take an eternity, and I was moving as soon as my feet hit the grass. Unseen to the humans, I sped to the man and woman and tore his hand from her arm. I twisted his arm behind his back.

"Get the fuck out of here. Now!" I shoved him.

I heard him mumble something about "dyke" as he stumbled off, nursing his sore limb.

"Thank you." Her voice was soft, with an accent from the North.

"No problem. I've seen his type around here many times. Why didn't you scream or something?"

"He told me if I caused a scene, he'd kill me. He said he had a knife in his pocket."

I fought a smile and motioned to the crowd. "Sunshine, he wasn't about to stab you here in front of a million people."

"I guess I feel stupid now."

"No need for that. Fear makes it hard to think clearly. Just be more careful, okay?"

She nodded.

"Now weren't you with a group earlier?"

"I was, but they're feeling no pain and probably didn't even notice I'm not with them."

"Well, this isn't a safe area for a young lady to wander around by herself. Can I walk you back to your hotel? Or maybe you'd like to grab a drink?"

She favored me with a bright smile, and my crotch clenched. This woman was beautiful, and I imagined she tasted as good as she looked. I decided then and there to find out for myself. I smiled back at her, flashing my dimples.

"I'd love a drink. I think I need a hurricane."

I steered her toward my favorite watering hole in Pirate Alley. The bartender Antoine saw us and called out, "Hey, Dawson! What can I do you for?"

There was a decent crowd, but we pushed through to the bar with ease. "I'll have a Turbo Dog, and the lady would like a hurricane."

"Oh, little sister," Antoine cautioned in his singsong voice. "Those can be dangerous. You think you'll be able to trust Dawson here after a couple of those?"

"Will I care?" my new friend shot back.

"I like this one." Antoine handed us our drinks.

"Me too." I winked at him and followed the girl to an empty booth by the pool table.

I extended my hand across the table to my date. "As you may have guessed, my name's Dawson."

"Is that a first or last name?"

"It's what I answer to."

She laughed, a magical sound that embraced me in warmth. "My name's Amanda."

"Amanda," I repeated. "I like that. It's nice to meet you, Amanda."

"Likewise."

"You seem to be more relaxed now. I'm happy to see that."

"I'm sorry, but all those people creeped me out. I don't usually like crowds."

"You're in the wrong part of the city, then."

"Yeah. I get that."

"Will your friends be worried?"

"Oh, yeah. I should probably text them."

She slid a thin phone out of her shorts pocket, and I watched her fingers dance along the keypad. I imagined them dancing across me. The night was young. But patience was not my strong suit.

"Tell me about yourself, Amanda."

"I grew up in Seattle and now live in Portland. I'm here with my friends on vacation. We've always heard about how cool this place is. We finally decided to check it out."

"I'm sorry you're less than impressed."

"My impression's improving." She smiled again, and I melted. I didn't even know this mortal, but she had me wrapped around her little finger.

"Do you shoot pool?" I asked.

"Doesn't everyone?"

"I'll break." I stood and walked to the table and tried to focus on the balls rather than the beauty watching me.

I didn't knock in a single ball but couldn't have cared less as I watched her bend forward, her top falling to afford me a view of her small, firm breasts. My slacks were wet. I had it bad for this one.

I shot again, and when it was her turn, she leaned over further.

After her shot, I walked up to her and stood a hair's breadth away. "You are a tease, Amanda from Portland."

"Are you complaining?"

"I am not."

She beat me easily, and we sat as Antoine brought us each another drink.

"So, Dawson, how long have you lived in New Orleans?"

"I was born and raised here," I lied easily. I had actually been born three hundred years earlier in Ireland, but she didn't need to know that. Yet.

"You have the most beautiful green eyes," she said.

"I declare, you just might make me blush."

"No need to blush. It's true, though. They're a piercing color."

"I wonder what I could pierce with them."

"Probably anything you'd like. They're accented so well by your jet black hair." She reached out and ran her fingers through the sides of my short hair.

Before I could respond, the volume in the bar increased tremendously as a group of tourists walked in behind a man dressed in gothic boots, black jeans, a white shirt, and a cape.

"Vampire tour," I said.

"What?"

"The vampire tour must have just ended. They end here so everyone can drink."

"Do people really believe in vampires?"

"Sure. This is New Orleans, sweetheart. People believe in all sorts of things."

"Do you believe in vampires?"

"Of course I do. I'll even show you one, if you'd like."

She sat up straighter. "Are you serious?"

"Dead. Come on. Grab your drink and let's get out of here."

I took her hand and led her back into the noisy night. She seemed more at ease. Whether it was me or the hurricanes, I couldn't be sure, but I opted to believe it was me.

I led her past the street merchants and past the façade of the cathedral. We turned down the side of it, and I pressed her into the wall. "You sure you want to see this?"

She reached her free hand behind my head and pulled my mouth to hers. The kiss was brief, but it was enough to make my clit and nipples hard.

"I want to see whatever you want to show me."

"Sunshine, you just made my night." I kissed her hard, slipping my tongue between her lips. Our tongues moved over each other, fanning a fire that threatened to consume us. I cupped her breast and squeezed lightly, running my thumb over her erect nipple.

"God, yes," she murmured against my lips. She pressed her pelvis into mine. I moved my hand lower and stroked between her legs, feeling the moist seam of her shorts as I pressed it into her.

"Come on." I pulled her with me down the side of the building.

"Where are we going?"

"To see the vampire."

"But I was having fun!"

"Oh, trust me. There's plenty more where that came from."

Looking around to be sure no one was watching, I pulled her behind an overgrown bush. We kissed again, and this time, she set her drink down and ran her hands along the front of my body. My nipples strained against my shirt, and she bent and ran her tongue over them. She started to lift my shirt, but I stopped her.

I reached behind her and opened a hidden door. We walked through it and into the church. Inside, I pinned her against the closed door and picked up where we left off. I lifted my shirt over my head and stood bare-chested for her enjoyment.

"Dawson! We're in a church," she whispered.

"So? God's seen me naked before."

"I can't do this here. I'm sorry."

"No problem, come on." I took her hand and led her up the old wooden stairwell that led to the bell tower. When we finally reached it, I said, "Are you ready?"

She nodded, and I led her into the open area where I lived. There was a table and chairs, several old crates with candles atop them, and, of course, my coffin.

"What is this place?"

"A vampire's lair."

I lit some candles and took a bottle of wine and two glasses from a crate. I opened the wine, filled both glasses, and handed one to Amanda.

"Is that real?" She motioned to the coffin before taking a sip of wine.

"It is. And this is a real lair. But you have nothing to fear."

I took her in my arms and kissed her, hoping to get her back to where she had been. She kissed me back finally, urgently. I took her wine from her and set it on the table. Together we got her shirt off and stood bare skin against bare skin.

"You're beautiful," I whispered against her neck, my fangs briefly escaping their protective sheaths as I kissed her jugular, which throbbed with her arousal.

"What if the vampire comes back and finds us?"

"You needn't worry about that." I knelt in front of her, kissing her taut belly as I unbuttoned her shorts.

"How do you know?"

I sighed. I wasn't in the mood for talk, but I liked Amanda and wanted to be honest with her. I sat her at the table and pulled the other chair around to sit in front of her. I took her hands in mine and stared into her eyes.

"Amanda, I'm going to tell you something, but first, do you like me?"

"Of course."

"Do you want me?"

"Very much."

"This is where I live."

"What?"

"I live here. I'm the vampire."

She laughed and leaned forward to kiss me. "You're funny."

I pulled away and bared my fangs for her. The color drained from her face.

"Amanda," I said calmly. "You mustn't be afraid of me. I mean you no harm. I just needed to be honest with you."

She shook her head and finally said, "You're going to kill me."

"I'm not. I could have done that by now."

"Surely you mean to feed off me." She moved her hands to her neck.

"Sunshine, I obtain strength from any bodily fluid. So I don't need your blood. I don't need to kill you. Or even harm you. I promise."

The reality of what I said appeared to finally dawn on her and she smiled. "Any bodily fluid?"

"Any."

"Even...you know?"

"That happens to be my favorite."

"I'd be crazy to trust you."

"Believe what you will, but I assure you, no harm will come to you on my watch."

"You seem so sincere."

"I am, my dear." I stroked her cheek and brushed a strand of hair off her face.

She placed her hand over mine and leaned forward to kiss me gently, tentatively. I kissed her back and pulled her to me, needing to feel her bare skin against mine again.

She moved my hand to her breast as her tongue slid into my mouth. The skin was so soft and smooth, the nipple so hard. I pinched it and tugged on it, and she pressed her hips to mine again.

I helped her step out of her shorts and continued to kiss her, even as she sat back down. I broke the kiss to see her fingers between her legs. The sight furthered my arousal as I watched her fingers slide past her engorged clit and inside her wet cunt. She moved them in and out and I thought I'd go crazy if I didn't taste her.

She must have read my mind as she drew her coated fingers over her nipples before tracing my lips with them. I opened my mouth and sucked on them, her juices the elixir of the gods.

"Do you feel stronger?" she asked.

"I do, but hunger is not the only need I wish to feed." I dropped to my knees and licked her clit. I placed her legs over my shoulders as I buried my tongue inside her. I greedily sucked her lips and licked her satin walls. She tasted divine, as I knew she would. I pulled her hood back and took her swollen clit in my mouth. I pulled it between my teeth and flicked the tip with my tongue. Her hands on the back of my head pressed me into her. Her hips thrust as she rode my face.

I probed her pussy with three fingers. She groaned in pleasure when I added another. I moved my hand in and out of her, forcing it deeper with each plunge. Her breathing became ragged, and I felt her body freeze as her cunt closed around my fingers, convulsing over and over.

When she finally relieved the death grip she had on my head, I let go of her clit and kissed her mouth, sharing her flavor with her. She kissed all over my face, cleaning every drop of come.

Amanda stood and unbuttoned my cargo shorts, easily slipping them off me. Her fingers were immediately on my clit, and I grabbed her by the wrist.

"My sensitivity is heightened right after I feed. I must warn you it won't take much."

She smiled a devilish grin and moved her fingers against me anew. The world was already going black as everything faded save the feelings in my nerve center. I fell to my knees, unable to maintain my balance. Rocking against her fingers, the world exploded from within me, and I saw bursts of colors behind my eyelids as what felt like molten lava shot through my veins.

"You're easy." She laughed.

"That was only round one, sunshine. I'll make you work for it now."

I stood and took her by the hand, leading her to my coffin.

We climbed in and picked up where we left off until we were satiated. We fell asleep in each other's arms just as the sun came up over Jackson Square.

BLOODSTONE
SHERI LEWIS WOHL

May 1, 1687
New Haven, CT

Death wasn't the end. She knew it to be true even as she dug, the sound of the shovel hitting the earth loud in the quiet night. The earth, already soft from Sarah's burial the day before, made her work easier. The smell of dirt and decay wafted up through the air as she worked and a breeze picked up, ruffling the leaves of the nearby trees. She continued to dig, careful not to disturb Sarah's final resting place. When the hole was at last large enough, she laid the shovel aside.

With effort, she dragged his body to the edge of the hole and rolled him in. The shroud she'd made from fine linen, her stitches precise and equal, hid his familiar face. Lifting her skirts, she crawled into the hole to make certain he was positioned as comfortably as possible. His wait could be as little as a few months or as long as several centuries. She simply didn't know how long he'd have to lie beneath the cold soil.

Once satisfied, she reached up, took the dagger, and laid it across his body. Her fingers stroked the firm leather of the sheath. If only they'd found the missing stones, none of this would have been necessary. But they'd failed to find them. and now he was dead. Or rather, somewhere between life and death.

While he waited here, the stones would be located. When they were, they'd be restored to the dagger and power would once more be his.

She crawled out of the hole and silently shoveled dirt over his body, patting it down to obscure any trace of disturbance. When the sun rose in the morning, she'd be gone. She stepped back and held the lantern up. No one would ever know the grave of Sarah Trowbridge held anything except her body. She smiled, blew out the flame, and walked into the darkness.

Present Day
New Haven, CT

Chapter One

Adriana James hiked up the strap of her messenger bag and groaned. The weight made her shoulder ache. The trip had taken way too long and was none too comfortable. That she was finally here wasn't a relief.

Not for the first time, she wondered how in the world she'd allowed herself to be talked into this. There was a good reason she'd moved away from here, and "never coming back" had been her mantra since she'd caught a one-way flight out seventeen years ago.

Bright and beautiful this morning when she'd left Spokane, now at a little past ten in New Haven the night was deep and dark. The tiny airport was all but deserted save for her and the handful of other passengers who'd made the short connecting flight from Boston. Within minutes, she was the last one standing, so speak. Standing in the deserted parking lot, that is. She'd just about given up hope when a taxi came around the corner.

She gave the man directions and was grateful when he turned out to be uninterested in small talk. Tired and depressed, the last thing she wanted to do was chitchat. She also didn't bother to call home. Not yet anyway. She didn't want her conversation with Riah to be anything except private. The driver might not be chatty, but that didn't mean he didn't have big ears.

New Haven was quiet this time of night. Just like she remembered it. She shut her eyes and tried to relax for the half hour it took to get from the airport to the house.

The house was dark, the lawn overgrown, and the gate squeaked when she pushed it open. Shifting the bag on her shoulder again and hauling her rolling suitcase up the three steps to the porch, she dug the key out of her pocket. Unlike the gate, the front door swung open without a sound.

The air inside was stale and musty, as if no one had been here in years. In a way it was true. Other than her mother, no one probably had been in this house since she left nearly two decades ago. Friends and neighbors had drifted away years before she'd left. She'd tried to stay and then even for her, it became impossible.

Now she was back, and as she stood in the entryway, a chill ran up her spine. She didn't care what Riah said, coming here was fucked up and all she really wanted to do was grab her stuff and catch the first flight back to the West Coast. That was her home, not this place where misery had made its mark.

But she was here and she might as well make the best of it. If everything went well, she'd have all the loose ends tied up within a couple days and she could go home. It wouldn't be a minute too soon.

Leaving her suitcase where she dropped it, Adriana went to the living room and turned on a lamp. Warm light spilled over the room. Chills raced up her arms. Everything seemed to be exactly as it had been when she'd walked out the front door all those years ago. Even down to the glass sitting on an end table. She'd been drinking iced tea that night.

"What the fuck, Mama? What the fuck," she whispered.

Unexpectedly, tears welled up in her eyes. It surprised her as much as the time capsule state of the room. Bitterness had sustained her estrangement with her mother for so long she didn't think she had anything left. Apparently, she was wrong.

"She loved you."

Adriana screamed and whirled to find herself face-to-face with a woman she didn't know but who looked like her mother. She was a little taller than Adriana's five feet one, with dark skin and blue eyes. The same blue eyes of her mother.

"Who are you?" Her heart was still wildly beating and she wished Riah was here with her. Where was her favorite vampire when she needed her?

"My name is Vespera and I'm your aunt."

"Bullshit." Her mother was an only child, as was her father. Their entire family consisted of the three of them. Now it consisted of only Adriana. "You need to leave before I call the police."

"Please," the woman said calmly. "It's important I talk to you. Your life is in danger."

Adriana rolled her eyes. If this chick only knew. She'd gone up against vampires, werewolves, and all sorts of preternatural creatures. Even without Riah, her vampire lover extraordinaire, she was pretty capable of taking care of herself. "I hardly think so."

"Give me ten minutes and if you still don't believe me, I'll go."

"Ten minutes?" She really wasn't liking any of this but she'd also prefer to forgo police involvement if possible.

Vespera nodded. "Ten minutes."

"Okay, you're on the clock."

Chapter Two

From the shadows, Elizabeth peered in the window of the old home. For almost two decades she'd been waiting for this night, and now that it was finally here, her heart raced. The ground vibrated with the surge of energy her presence brought.

She frowned as she thought about the old woman. She'd been cagey, powerful, and no matter what Elizabeth tried, unbreakable. Her sole victory: destroying Michael despite Sabira's protection. Unfortunately, just not before he'd managed to hide the stone.

It had taken years to realize the key to finding the last stone lay with the daughter. By the time she did, the daughter had dropped out of sight, never to return...until now. The death of Sabira brought her back along with a bonus Elizabeth hadn't expected, the elusive Vespera.

How she hated the sisters. Sabira and Vespera had been nothing but trouble. She particularly hated Sabira, *the patient one.* She'd been everything Elizabeth wasn't. Petite with flawless dark skin, silky black hair, and eyes the color of a cloudless blue sky. Men were fascinated with her exotic beauty while women admired her. Only her daughter seemed to be able to stay away.

Vespera, like her twin sister, was lovely, yet she didn't have the same magnetic personality Sabira had possessed. Vespera had never married while Sabira had enjoyed fifteen years with the handsome wizard, Michael. Fifteen years too long in Elizabeth's book. Sabira's spells of protection had been hard to break and when she did, she'd only been able to reach Michael. His death was a mild satisfaction, for she'd failed to touch Sabira and her child, and she'd also failed to find the bloodstone.

For seventeen years she'd waited for another chance at that stone. She wouldn't fail again.

Too bad she couldn't hear the conversation now. She wanted to know what the two women talked about. For tonight, she'd have to content herself with the reality that they were here. Tomorrow, while they attended to the details of death, she'd take back the stone.

Now she could only do one thing. Calling the darkness, Elizabeth began to chant, power flowing out like the ocean tide until it wafted across the yard and over the house.

Chapter Three

"Wait." Vespera held her hand up. Her face grew troubled.

"Hey." Adriana shrugged. "It's your ten minutes."

Seriously, what was up with this woman? If she wasn't so tired, she'd kick her ass out. It probably was because she was exhausted that she'd even allowed herself to be drawn in. Well, that and because she was curious. She wanted to know why Vespera claimed to be her mother's sister. Okay, so maybe she looked like Mom, but still, wouldn't she know if her mother had a sister? As much as it pained her to admit it, perhaps not.

Her parents hadn't exactly been verbose when it came to talking about their families or their pasts. Their conversations were always firmly grounded in the here and now. Looking back wasn't something she ever remembered either of them doing. The absence of family tales had been such a normal part of her upbringing that she'd never thought it odd…until now.

"She's here," Vespera said.

She? "I'm tired, and your cloak-and-dagger crap is getting on my nerves." Might as well be honest. Weird as her parents might have been, she was too exhausted to give a damn right now.

"Please, allow me a moment."

"No. I'm tired and I'm done with this shit."

Vespera didn't appear to hear Adriana. Her blue eyes were narrowed and her breathing quickened. "Goddess protect us," she began, her arms outstretched. "By the power of the moon, I call on you to guard this house, this woman, the stone."

The floorboards shuddered beneath Adriana's feet; the whole house seeming to shiver. Something she couldn't quite describe wafted over her skin, bringing the hair up on the back of her neck.

"What the hell…" Blackness began to tinge the edges of her vision.

Adriana came to on the sofa, her eyes blinking from the assault of bright lamplight. Vespera had pulled a chair next to her and held a cool, damp cloth to her forehead.

"How are you feeling?"

"What the fuck just happened?" She still felt the quiver of something very odd in the air, as if the house was filled with a strange presence.

"I cast a protection spell on the house so that she can't get in."

She again. "Who can't get in? Who would even want to? I don't think I know many people in New Haven anymore."

"She's not a friend."

Wearying didn't even begin to describe this woman. "Can you just spit it out?"

Vespera's blue eyes seemed to grow sad. "I'm sorry. This is all very confusing for you, I know. It is well past time for the truth. So, let me tell you a story about a man, a woman, and a bloodstone."

Chapter Four

The bloody bitch! How dare she cast a spell over the house? Like that would even stop her? They hadn't faced each other for many years, but even Vespera had to remember who the better warrior was. Elizabeth was a Keeper, and from all accounts, one of the most powerful. Few had ever measured up to her, and none would ever have to again.

The Keepers had waited over three hundred years to get this close, and she was the one who would finally set him free. Then and only then would they return to Tigeran. With the victory, the throne would be theirs and she would sit at his side.

But first, she needed to stop Vespera. Though Vespera's presence was unexpected, it did not mean she was unprepared. On the contrary, in this uninteresting world where people scuttled about like insects, she'd had years to hone her skills. True, Vespera was a powerful Sorceress, but she was stronger. A little time was all she needed to break through the protection spell to retrieve the stone.

Elizabeth turned and faded into the shadows, making her way to the green. Like the Keepers before her, she took a key from her pocket to let herself into Center Church. The building, indeed the land itself, had changed over the years. What once had been the open land was now hidden from view beneath the latest incarnation of the church. In the crypt, headstones rose from between the brick cobbled floor in a macabre landscape.

For the Keepers, the evolution proved advantageous. It served to keep *him* safe century after century. Even with the steady stream of visitors who came to view the old cemetery beneath the floors of the church, he was protected as he lay concealed within the oldest known grave.

She dropped to her knees and carefully removed the bricks from around the headstone of Sarah Trowbridge. Once she had the earth exposed, she started to dig with the small shovel she'd taken from a storage closet at the back of the church.

She dug for a full half hour before she reached it. Beneath the soil, still sheathed in tooled leather, the dagger looked as beautiful as the day it had been buried. Its magic remained strong even after all the years. She wrapped her fingers around the hilt and pulled it from the sheath. The metal of the blade gleamed and it vibrated gently in her palm. The feeling of holding it in her hand was indescribable. So many others before her had wished for this honor, and yet it had fallen to her.

Rightly so.

She was the chosen one. She'd known it since the day of her induction into the Order of the Keepers. Even then she'd realized how special she was. Her destiny was intertwined with his and the power that would belong to them soon.

The only flaw was the empty depression on the hilt of the dagger.

Five stones gave the weapon its true power. He had been poised to rule both worlds when the intact dagger had been used to part the veil between the worlds on that long ago Beltane night. What happened next was the tragedy the Keepers had been trying to right for centuries. Four of the five stones had been restored to the dagger. Only one remained, and now she was about to seize it.

Chapter Five

"So spit it out already. I've had a long day and what I'd really like to do is have a drink and go to sleep."

Vespera nodded. "Did you ever know what your mother's name means?"

Great, a history lesson. That's exactly what she needed tonight. "Yeah, patience or something like that. Dad told me when I was a kid."

"The patient one."

"Whatever, get to the point."

"Your parents really were the perfect match, you know. He was the strongest warrior in Tigeran, and Sabira was both brilliant and patient. They brought out the best in each other."

Patient…her mother? She wondered if they were talking about the same person. The one she remembered had been sullen and angry. She'd thought for years that her mother's scorn was because she blamed Adriana for the death of her father. At least that's what she'd thought until tonight. Walking into the house had been a huge surprise.

"My mother was volatile."

Vespera shook her head. "No, she wasn't, but she wanted you to think that."

"Bullshit."

"No, not at all. She acted the way she did to protect you."

"Again, I call bullshit. My mother looked me in the eye and told me that she wouldn't have me in her house because I was…I am…a lesbian."

Vespera put a hand on her arm. "I know what she said to you and I can tell you it was a lie. She loved you until the day she died."

In her heart, Adriana desperately wanted to believe that was true.

But the look on her mother's face that last night lingered in her memory. That look of scorn had broken her heart. She'd wanted to believe in the unconditional love of a parent, and it had turned out to be a fairy tale—at least where her mother was concerned. Her father had been a different story. He'd been a huge support as she'd struggled with her sexuality and finding her place in the world. The only time she'd ever felt like he'd let her down was the day he'd died. Her heart still hurt.

Outside the night grew darker but the house held a stillness that hadn't been there before. She wasn't sure if the spell Vespera put on the place was responsible or if it was something else. Didn't matter. She just wanted her to finish her fiction and leave her alone. Bad enough she had to return here. All this bizarre talk about her mother's love and a dangerous woman stalking her was a bit much.

"You hold a secret that could destroy two worlds. The only way to keep both worlds safe was to send you away. As long as you didn't know the secret, you couldn't expose it. If your mother didn't know where you were, neither could she. You were safe and both this world and Tigeran were safe."

"Tigeran? What is that?"

Vespera smiled as if just the thought of it warmed her heart. "It's the place where you were born."

"I was born in New Haven."

"No, you grew up in New Haven, but you were born in Tigeran. It's a beautiful place and you, my dear, are responsible for keeping it safe."

No, none of this was true. Adriana had seen her birth certificate and she'd been born right here in the Yale–New Haven Hospital. "That's not right."

Vespera gave her a small smile. Vespera looked so much like her mother that despite wanting to believe she was some crazy woman who'd wandered in to terrorize her, she found herself listening.

"You and I come from a beautiful world called Tigeran. Your mother is of magical blood, as am I, and as are you. Your father, as I told you, was a great warrior who fell in love with Sabira and took her as his wife. You were but a tiny infant when the call came. You see, we are from a long line of Sorcerers, all with great power and all charged with keeping the worlds safe. When this town was very young, Bernael, a bitter and evil warlock, used a magical dagger to part the veil between the worlds. He came through intending to destroy the barrier so he could rule both worlds. He would kill any and all who refused to serve him and enslave all others. To give the dagger full power, the hilt held five stones: a peridot for rebirth and growth, an onyx for vigor and strength, a fire opal for dynamic energy, an amethyst for nobility, and a bloodstone for purification."

A bloodstone? Adriana's hand went reflexively to the stone that lay between her breasts. Her father had given it to her only days before his death and she'd worn it ever since.

Vespera nodded as her gaze followed Adriana's hand. "Yes, that bloodstone. Without the final stone in the hilt, the power of the dagger waits. Our ancestors followed him through the veil and, after removing the stones, placed a spell on Bernael that has kept him captive for centuries."

"Why not kill him?"

"To kill him, we needed the dagger lost during the initial struggle. Though we've looked over the years, we've never been able to locate it. He had help, you see. They call themselves Keepers and over the years they've found four of the stones. All they need to restore Bernael to full power is the bloodstone. A Keeper was outside this house tonight. I believe they've suspected all along what your parents did to keep the stone safe and have been waiting for your return."

"Me?"

"You and the stone you carry around your neck."

"So let's just kick her ass and be done with it."

Vespera laughed. "You are so like your mother. Do you understand why she sent you away now? She couldn't risk you coming back, couldn't risk knowing where you were. She didn't care that you were a lesbian. Not at all. She loved you deeply and simply wanted to keep you safe and prevent Bernael from coming back."

Even after all the years of feeling bitter and angry, she did believe. And why not? Considering she was in love with a vampire and belonged to a group tasked with fighting rogue preternatural creatures, finding out she was from another world really wasn't so shocking. She could hardly wait to tell Riah and the others.

As if everything she'd ever struggled with suddenly clicked into place, Adriana felt the weariness swept away. "So what do we do now?"

Chapter Six

The first day of May dawned bright and lovely in Adriana's hometown. Or rather, what she'd always thought was her hometown. How did a person get to be her age and not realize she wasn't from this world? She'd always felt different but figured it was because she was gay. To live in a society where being anything but straight was often frowned on seemed to pretty much explain her feelings.

After talking most of the night with her *aunt* Vespera, her life seemed to make a lot more sense now. The most amazing part of the whole story was that in Tigeran, the world where she was born, being in love with another woman wasn't unusual. The way Vespera described it, Tigeran sounded like a heaven. People were free to love who they wanted with equal rights and protections. Heaven.

The only problem? She would be a hunted soul in Tigeran. Even more hunted than she found herself right now. It seemed power struggles were not relegated to this world alone. In Tigeran, the right to rule was just as bloody as here, and had been forever. As the daughter of a warrior and a Sorceress, she'd have a target smack in the middle of her back. At least here, there appeared to be only one gunning for her. In Tigeran, according to Vespera, there were many to be wary of.

Of course, with Riah at her side, who would dare to touch her? Her beautiful, sexy Riah could make confetti out of anyone, man or woman, so she figured she'd be pretty safe no matter where she lived as long as they were together.

The thought stopped her. Would Riah look at her differently once she found out Adriana wasn't even from this world? Riah loved her unconditionally…right?

No, she wouldn't even go there. They were together. Forever. She refused to think any differently.

On the sofa, Vespera slept while Adriana stared out the window at the landscape of her childhood. Little had changed in this neighborhood during the years of her absence. She remembered the trees, the cemetery just down the street where so many notables made their final resting place. Yale University sprawled nearby with its beautiful Gothic buildings and interesting history. It felt as though she'd never left.

Except everything was different. Even beyond the absence of her parents. Everything in her life was different—her past and her present. As shocked as she was about her heritage, in a way learning the truth felt great. She'd been the odd man out, so to speak, in the Spiritus Group. The only one without a paranormal background. She wasn't a vampire like Riah and Ivy, or a vampire hunter like Colin, or a werewolf like Cam. Neither was she a witch as Kara had so recently discovered. No, though an integral part of the Spiritus Group, until last night she'd believed she was the only straight-up human. Not any longer.

If her aunt was right, she'd better darned well get some rest. A war was about to begin and she was marshal of that parade. Clutching the bloodstone, she headed upstairs to her old room. Maybe she could get a few hours of sleep before the funeral.

Chapter Seven

Elizabeth sat in the back of the church listening as the minister droned on about Sabira's virtues. Bah. If they only knew. She'd been a fraud, as had her man and the child who now sat in the front pew with Vespera. She watched the backs of their heads, knowing they'd feel her eyes on them.

The dagger waited inside her bag, its power radiating through the leather and into her skin. Beneath her feet, *he* waited, his days of slumber nearly at an end. The way Vespera shifted in her seat, Elizabeth could tell she felt it too. The magic the Sorceress had called upon to cloak the church wouldn't last long. Already she could feel the power of the dagger eroding the spell. By the time darkness fully engulfed the church, the only magic surrounding the place would be hers. Vespera and the daughter they called Adriana would be dead.

Finally, the service came to an end and the family began to greet the mourners at the back of the church. Elizabeth waited until they were all gone and the minister had retreated to his office to shrug out of his funeral finery and be on his way. Since she was the church caretaker, he would leave it to her to lock up.

Dusk was beginning to settle, a rosy moon just starting its ascent into the night sky. Energy from below seeped through the floorboards, sending a buzz of excitement through her whole body.

At the door, Vespera turned and their eyes met. A flash of recognition made Vespera's back stiffen. Her hand went to the other woman's arm. Elizabeth smiled before turning and fleeing to the crypt doors. At the top of the stairs, she paused, listening until she heard the soft sound of footsteps quickly coming her way. At that moment, she sent her magic out, wiping away the last traces of Vespera's protective spell. As she did so, she heard the sound she'd been waiting decades to hear. He was rising.

Chapter Eight

Adriana stopped in her tracks as the floor literally rolled beneath her feet. "Sweet mother of God, what the fuck is that?"

Vespera's face paled, a pretty good trick considering the darkness of her skin. It wasn't comforting.

"He's here," she whispered and Adriana didn't miss the note of fear in her voice.

She was about to ask who and then the lightbulb came on. "Bernael?"

"Yes."

Not good. "What do we do?"

"We stop him, and no matter what happens, do not let go of the bloodstone."

Adriana's fingers curled around the pendant. Damn straight she'd hold on to it and kick some wizard ass while she was at it. She'd been around Riah and the Spiritus Group long enough to learn a thing or two. Squaring her shoulders, she steadied herself for battle.

"Any suggestions?"

"You've got to call the power. I know your parents never clued you in, but you've got it. You're of the blood, and now's the time, training or not, to use it. This world may very well be destroyed if you don't."

The floor heaved and rolled once more beneath their feet. This time, it nearly knocked Adriana off her feet. Vespera didn't need to tell her they were running out of time. She wished Riah was with her. Damn, she wished the entire Spiritus Group was here. If she'd have even an inkling of what was happening here, she'd have blown the whistle. Now there wasn't time.

The bloodstone, nestled between her breasts, grew hot against her chest. It had never done that before. That it was doing it now made the hair on the back of her neck stand up.

We are trav'ling in the footsteps of those who've gone before/and we'll all be reunited, on a new and sunlit shore. Oh, when the saints go marching in/oh, when the saints go marching in/Lord, how I want to be in that number/when the saints go marching in.

"Mama?" Adriana stopped halfway down the steps leading to the crypt. The voice she heard was as clear as if her mother was standing at her door softly singing just as she'd done before...before she'd sent Adriana away.

And when the moon turns red with blood/and when the moon turns red with blood/Lord, how I want to be in that number/when the moon turns red with blood...

Tears began to course down her cheeks. "Thank you, Mama."

She understood—everything.

Chapter Nine

The scream she heard was a voice she now recognized. Vespera. Adriana ran the rest of the way down the stairs. Her aunt lay in a crumpled heap near a pile of earth and bricks. She couldn't tell if she was still breathing. Another woman stood, a wicked smile on her face, her long hair tangled, a silver dagger held in her hands.

At her side, he rose, skin pale, eyes narrow, power throbbing in the air that circulated in the enclosed crypt. Once he might have been handsome. Now he was dirty and smelled of rot and something she didn't even want to put a name to. Their eyes met and ice slipped down her spine.

The woman was muttering, a curse, probably. The air grew thicker. *No time.* Adriana frantically searched. So many headstones.

She felt it more than saw it, and moved sideways toward a headstone, dark and leaning. The other woman screamed, the sound like something from the bowels of hell. She ran straight for Adriana, the dagger pointed at her chest. Adriana's movement was automatic. Her foot came out and she swiped it across the bricks just as the woman got close. The attacker went down on her back, the dagger flying out of her hands. Adriana caught it and just as quickly plunged it into the woman's chest.

Adriana looked up from the dying woman to see the man shaking off dirt. He almost seemed to shimmer. That couldn't be good. She pulled the dagger out of the woman's chest and turned once more to the headstone. There!

JOHN SAINT III

Above his name was a depression eerily similar in shape to the bloodstone pendant she wore. She wrenched it from her neck and knelt in front of the headstone. The song her mother used to sing to her all the time now made sense. Here was the saint with a number. And there was also the other little thing…a moon turning red with blood.

She'd wanted to be home with Riah tonight, not just because she didn't like to be anywhere but by her side—no, she'd wanted to share the rare occurrence of a blood moon. That moon combined with the other pieces of the seemingly innocent folk song told her what to do to stop this monster.

She fit the bloodstone into the depression on the headstone. The rush of power was immediate. Across the crypt, Berneal screamed. The brick floor shifted and heaved as though some giant moved beneath the stones. Headstones tilted and shuddered. She kept the dagger in her hands, and when Berneal rushed her, everything happened as if in slow motion.

His dead, cold hands wrapped around her neck. She couldn't breathe while his words seemed to come from inside her head.

"Die, bitch. You can't stop me."

As he picked her up and her feet left the soil of John Saint's grave, her feeling of power faded. Black began to tinge her vision. As her breath was cut off, the blackness continued until all that remained was a pinpoint of light. Her fingers ached as she held on to the dagger.

Call on your power. You can stop him.

Her mother's voice again. She thrashed, fighting him until once more her feet touched the earth of the grave. At that instant, a hand gripped her ankle and she didn't care that it had risen from beneath the soil. All that mattered was that the moment those fingers wrapped around her flesh, power roared through her and before the blackness obliterated her vision, she plunged the dagger into Bernael's chest.

Adriana came to lying on the brick floor next to the undisturbed soil of John Saint's grave, with Vespera holding her head and wiping dirt from her cheeks.

"What happened?"

Vespera smiled broadly. "You stopped him."

Adriana pushed up and looked around. It didn't make sense. They were alone. No Bernael. No screaming crazy woman. No disturbed graves. The only thing that let her know it wasn't a dream was the dagger in her hand and the bloodstone still stuck in the headstone. She reached out and took it back.

"That's it?"

Vespera nodded. "Once you pierced his heart, it's as if he and his keeper were never here. You destroyed him forever and will be given a hero's welcome back in Tigeran."

Yeah, Tigeran. The mysterious place of her birth. As she and Vespera left the crypt and walked outside, Adriana peered up at the moon, glowing big and red in the sky. She suddenly smiled and shook her head.

"No, Vespera, no Tigeran for me. I've got to go home." She put the dagger and the bloodstone in her aunt's hand. "My place is here."

"You're certain?"

"One hundred percent."

Vespera touched Adriana's face. "I can't protect you if you stay here."

"I can protect myself, and I have the Spiritus Group to watch my back."

"I hope they are strong, for others will come looking for you."

Adriana smiled, thinking of Riah and the others. "The strongest."

"They will come and you must be ready. We've won this battle, but the war is far from over."

Adriana covered Vespera's hand with her own. "I'll be ready."

Vespera nodded. "I believe you will."

Turning her attention to the dagger, Vespera returned the stone to the hilt and then quietly called her power. Dagger in her hand, she seemed to part the air. Then she was gone.

Alone, Adriana stared at the spot where a moment before her aunt had stood. *They will come.* The three simple words echoed in her mind. The implication scared her, but only a little. Bring it on, demons, fallen angels or whatever else Tigeran wanted to send her way. She had her own power now and she'd be ready. More importantly, she had Riah and the Spiritus Group. It didn't matter what world she was in—with that kind of backup, how could she lose?

Smiling, she slipped her hand into her pocket and pulled out her cell phone. "Hey," she said when Riah picked up after one ring. She could picture her standing in their bedroom, long hair flowing down her back, dressed in a pair of jeans and a T-shirt. She'd look incredibly sexy. "Have I told you lately that I love you?"

PLAGUED BY DARKNESS
L.T. MARIE

Malakai stood looking out over the dark city, her long leather jacket whipping at her sleek, muscular body. She stood there many nights, gazing out over the lights, watching people stroll the streets as a hawk would its next meal. Tonight, though, she had a particular human in mind that she wanted to observe. She'd been watching her for weeks—had memorized her nightly routine. The woman's raw beauty captivated her the moment she'd laid eyes on her, yet the woman had no idea Malakai even existed. It had to be this way.

"Misae." She whispered the name, liking the way it rolled off her tongue. She'd learned the name from the woman's answering machine the night she had secretly visited her apartment. Malakai didn't require lights to see; her keen eyesight allowed her to search the room as if she were standing in broad daylight. *Daylight.* Now there's a phenomenon she hadn't experienced in centuries.

Misae's apartment had been stripped of any personal items. No photos. No books of any kind that might give Malakai a glimpse into the young woman's past. Only a message from a man asking Misae to dinner alerted Malakai that she had acquaintances of any type. A flare of jealousy shot through her at the memory of the phone call, and she bared her fangs. Power personified, Malakai was untouchable in this world. But what she craved was something she could not have. The touch of another. One person who wouldn't shrink from her in fear when they found what fate had been bestowed on her.

She silently moved through the city, climbing to the top of the stone building with ease. Perching on top of the sturdy balustrade, hidden by darkness, she watched the Native American beauty move about her orderly apartment. The first time she'd visited Misae's dwelling, she'd taken her time moving around the spacious enclosure, wondering about the organization of the furniture. Placement of certain pieces seemed to be staged rather than used for function. At first, she thought maybe the woman had OCD. It made sense. Nothing was out of place. The chains to turn on two table lamps were both facing inward so that they would be easily accessible from the couch. The handle to the teakettle sitting on the stove always faced to the right. Then there was the way Misae moved. Her steps were even, but not bold. They were perfect. Too perfect. Five steps to the fireplace from the couch. Eight steps to the left to the kitchen. As the gravity of Misae's situation hit her, she realized the woman she had been lusting after was not obsessive, but blind.

Malakai silently jumped onto the balcony and peered through the window, her heart rate increasing with each breath. Misae turned as if sensing her presence, but that was absurd. The woman, after all, was without sight. Remaining motionless, she waited until Misae's attentions were elsewhere before moving around the balcony. Seeing Misae in her knee-length silk robe, Malakai felt like a voyeur. Her stomach was tied up in knots and she tried not to gasp when the woman released the ties on her robe and allowed it to fall to the floor to reveal a sheer white negligee. Misae was breathtaking and Malakai wondered if she knew of the splendor she possessed. But then how could Misae know of her own beauty when she couldn't even see Malakai standing a few feet away?

The wind picked up and a steady rain began. The seasons were changing and soon the rains would be constant. Malakai didn't feel the cold because she *was* the cold—one of the many who lived among the shadows. She'd lived this way for over three hundred years, and it was only now that she felt alone in this world. For centuries, she had walked the planet—moved from town to town, city to city. She'd lived through revolutions, famine, and world wars. She'd seen things that would make mortals shriek in terror. She'd taken thousands of lives, most of them deserved. She never killed for sport, or for pleasure. Those that died by her hand shouldn't have been born in the first place. They were the rapists, child molesters, and scourge of the earth. She did the world a favor by taking these people's lives, or so she rationalized in an attempt to believe she wasn't a soulless monster.

The lights went out in Misae's apartment as Malakai turned to leave. These were the times when she felt the most alone. She was used to the darkness, but never got used to the silence. She placed her hand on the railing, planning to disappear into the night. But just as she turned her back a gentle voice called out to her.

"I know you're there," Misae said, stepping out onto the balcony. Her shirt clung to her breasts, her nipples hardening under the thin material. She was most likely unaware of her appearance, but her body betrayed her ignorance of the cold. Malakai stood motionless, transfixed by the exquisite sight before her. "I can hear your breathing. Please, don't be afraid."

Afraid? Shouldn't Misae be afraid of her, a stranger she could not see, hiding in the dark of night?

Misae extended her hand into the darkness. "Give me your hand."

Malakai couldn't believe Misae's boldness. How did she know of her presence? And even if Malakai was an ordinary human, would Misae invite a total stranger into her home—a stranger who had been stalking her for weeks?

"I know you're still there. Still watching."

"How?"

Misae looked to her left, her hand following the deep voice. "I feel you."

"That is not possible," Malakai snarled, her emotions getting the best of her. How could this blind woman see her when a person with perfect sight could not? She was confused, and her uncertainty was making her uncomfortable. She nervously scanned the immediate area to see if anyone else was close by.

"It is possible. Please, come closer and I'll explain."

Moving from a crouched position, Malakai jumped and landed silently in front of Misae. She looked into the dark eyes that couldn't see her but somehow understood that wasn't entirely true. Maybe it was because of the way Misae was looking at her now—as if she couldn't just see her, but through her. "How did you know?"

Misae placed her hand on Malakai's cheek. "I've sensed your presence for weeks. The air moves differently when you're near. No matter the temperature, your aura is colder, darker. But I do not sense danger, only uncertainty."

"It still does not make sense. How can you sense my existence?"

"Your unique scent. It is what alerted me to your presence the first time."

"As I said, impossible."

"Is it?"

"Yes."

"You smell woodsy. A musky scent I can't quite place—earth on a warm summer's day. Now do you believe me?"

Malakai took a step back. Could it be Misae smelled the ground where she slept off the daylight hours? Impossible. "And you say you've known of my presence for weeks?"

"Yes. When I walked home a few nights ago, I could hear you above me walking along the balconies. I sensed you first. As I told you, it's your scent. Will you tell me your name?"

Malakai hesitated. If she revealed herself, she could no longer be one with the darkness. Her decision would not only alter her existence but most likely change Misae's life forever. Misae seemed so innocent, and what would happen if she exposed Misae to the horrors of her life? She couldn't risk this woman feeling disdain for her, so she remained silent.

"I promise your secret is safe with me."

"But what if my secret frightens you?"

"It won't."

Malakai leaned into Misae's touch, the hand against her cheek warm where her skin was cool. "Malakai."

"Malakai," Misae whispered softly. "Do you know its meaning?"

"Yes. My mother explained it to me many years ago." How many years ago now failed her. "It means 'my messenger.'"

"That is correct. Do you have a message for me, Malakai?"

Malakai took a deep breath and carefully brought their bodies close. She had to touch her. Caressing the side of Misae's face, she could feel the blood racing below her skin—see the pulse point pounding rapidly in her throat. She turned away. Being this close to Misae was too dangerous. "Aren't you afraid?"

Misae smiled. "No. But I am curious."

"Of?"

"Why do you hide?"

Malakai slowly moved away. The moment their connection was broken, she nearly stumbled and leaned against the balustrade for support. "You said it yourself. Cold. Dark. You sense what I am. Yet you ask."

"I want to hear it from you."

Malakai sighed and turned to stare out over the city. She'd never had this conversation with a mortal before. Vampires were to remain hidden from the population. If humans ever discovered their existence, they'd be hunted during the daylight hours when they were the most vulnerable. Outing herself would be dangerous, but instinctively she trusted Misae and couldn't deny her simple request. "Vampire."

Misae moved closer and wrapped her arms around Malakai's waist. "That's not what I asked." She rubbed small calming circles over Malakai's stomach.

Malakai groaned when Misae accidentally brushed one of her nipples with her fingertips. Or was it an accident? Misae didn't seem the type to do anything unintentional. Malakai's legs grew weak and she was slowly losing her composure. "I do not understand. I told you, I am a vampire. A cold, lifeless entity who walks the earth with no purpose. I have no soul. I am a monster. Is that what you wanted to hear?"

The low guttural sound that escaped Malakai's lips would have scared most people, but Misae didn't even flinch. She captured Malakai's arm and slid her hand into Malakai's. "Look at me. Do you know I can see you?"

Malakai stiffened. "Impossible. I know you are without sight."

"You like that word, don't you, Malakai? Not everything is impossible. I don't need eyes to see. As I said, I've sensed you for weeks. Could feel when you watched me. My skin tingles when you're near. I could feel you just now responding to my touch. *You* are anything *but* a monster."

Could this be true? After all these years, could Malakai have found the one person who could truly see past her disease? "How?"

"The answer is simple. Because I want to. I want to know you—who you are and everything about you. How did you become vampire? What are your secrets? Your desires? You see, Malakai, you may have been watching me, but I have also been watching you."

Malakai took Misae into her arms and held her fiercely. Her need for this woman was growing by the second. "I want you. But I'm...scared." She bared her teeth, this time not out of anger, but from desire.

Misae cradled Malakai's face and stroked the two incisors with her thumbs. "Scared? Of who you are or of what you could do?"

"Both. I have never *been* with a mortal before. I am very strong. I could…hurt you." The thought made Malakai sick to her stomach.

"The only way you could hurt me would be to walk away. I trust you. You could never hurt me. Ever!"

Malakai wanted to believe Misae, but her fear was too great. She'd never be able to face the untold centuries stretching before her if she were to seriously hurt—or worse—kill Misae during her time of passion. She loved her, but she was presented with a decision she didn't want to make. "I know you believe that. But I don't trust myself. I'm sorry. I must go."

Malakai ran as fast as she could, disappearing into the night. She wiped at the blood that stained her cheeks—tears of the vampire. She'd never shed them in all the years since she had been turned. Tonight was the first time she'd ever had a reason to feel sorrow.

❖

Misae stood on the balcony blinking back tears of her own. How could one so wild, so free, be so restrained in her hunger? For the first time in her life, she cursed her blindness. She never questioned being born without sight—only accepted it as part of her existence. But not being able to reach Malakai, to see the desperation she heard in her voice, to stroke that pain away, brought her to her knees. She cried out Malakai's name, but her words were lost on the wind.

"Come back," she whispered, but Malakai did not answer her call. She shivered as the rain soaked the thin material of her nightshirt, but it wasn't the cold that left her a shaking mess. She had a firm picture of Malakai in her mind's eye. Short black hair, dark eyes. An angular jaw and a bold nose that wouldn't be considered beautiful, but sexy on what she imagined was a handsome face. Misae had never seen colors or patterns—had never seen an actual human face. But the moment she sensed Malakai's presence, the picture formed instantly. Touching her tonight, it was as though she were an artist, sketching the final details of a picture that had eluded her for years. She'd felt complete in Malakai's arms, and now for the first time in her life, she felt less than whole.

The first night Malakai visited her apartment, Misae had

recognized the scent instantly. She breathed it in, tried to firmly plant it in her memory bank. She'd been worried that the stranger would disappear without ever saying a word to her. She should have been scared, but instead accepted Malakai's presence instantly into her life. What frightened her now was that even though they had only spent a few precious moments together, she didn't know how to go on without her. Less than an hour of knowing Malakai made Misae want to know her for a lifetime.

"You need to go inside," the deep voice instructed from somewhere in the distance.

"Malakai? You came back."

"Yes." Malakai's voice was rough but not aggressive.

"I was frightened when you left."

"Frightened? Of me?"

Misae looked into the darkness, feeling Malakai move to her left. She could hear the pain in her raspy voice. "No! No, love. Not of you. Of your leaving me."

A cry broke from Malakai's lips as she gathered Misae up into her arms. Misae wrapped her arms around Malakai's neck, holding on as though they had all of eternity to love.

"I tried but I couldn't do it. Please, don't cry."

Misae buried her head into Malakai's shoulder. She took in the sweet scent, basked in the joy of having Malakai in her arms. "Then don't leave me."

"I must. The sun will rise in an hour."

Misae gently tugged on Malakai's head, her lips carefully brushing over the tall vampire's. Malakai's incisors cut Misae's lip, and when she winced, Malakai abruptly pulled away.

"See what I have done," she growled. "I cannot cause you pain. I cannot bear it."

"No! Malakai, come here." She pulled Malakai close and moved back into her arms. "Taste me on your lips. Let my blood sustain you. Feed from me. Let me be your light in your dark world."

Malakai swiped her tongue along Misae's lips, her growl turning to a purr. "Do you know what you are asking?"

"I am aware."

"Misae," Malakai asked, tenderly licking the small puncture she had just made on Misae's shoulder, "what does your name mean?"

"Funny you should ask. It means 'white sun.' So you see, if you allow me to be your sunlight, you will never have to spend your nights in the dark, alone again."

"And if I should say yes?"

Misae brushed her palm over Malakai's chest, smiling as Malakai's breathing increased. She ached for Malakai, but the darkness was running out. "Then meet me tomorrow when the sun sets beyond the mountains and I will prove to you with everything in me that the darkness will no longer rule either of our lives."

RECYCLABLES
JOEY BASS

Toni smiled as she closed the classroom door quietly behind her. The silver-haired lecturer at the front of the theater hadn't looked up and showed no sign of seeing her come in. Toni liked it that way. It would give her a chance to watch Professor Shannon Flugle at work. Even though she had collaborated with Shannon on a number of cases, Toni had never studied her in the classroom.

"Certainly, many of the classic horror films are laughably over-the-top, but anyone who would romanticize vampires is doing society a disservice. Their parasitic lives are at best a tragic waste of potential." Shannon's voice carried to the back of the room without apparent effort.

The tragic waste is all those times I had you alone and never tasted you. Toni had worked with the professor on five major cases over the last two years and consulted her on a dozen others, but Shannon still seemed a mystery to her. Shannon had never shown an interest beyond the intrigue of the cases—enjoying the puzzles, deciphering clues, and untangling the criminal mind to solve crimes. Toni chastised herself for her unrequited attraction and sophomoric crush. *Next thing you know, you'll be writing her name with loops and hearts all over your notebook.* She frowned. She wasn't the type to chase women. She never had to go looking. They usually knocked at her door before she ever even noticed them.

Shannon stood in the front of the room, hip cocked to one side, elbow tucked into her body and resting in the palm of her other hand. "It is the same with any historical event. They soften the blow—blur its meaning. Which robs us of understanding it—truly appreciating its importance."

Toni settled back to listen. The lilt of Shannon's voice brought memories of when they first met. Toni had mispronounced Shannon's last name and the professor cheerfully corrected her, "It's an 'oo' not an 'uh,' Officer, like bugle. Flugle. Just think of a sick seabird." The police chief asked Shannon to help Toni with a missing-person case and they spent nearly twenty-four hours chasing down clues and then a final six searching the rough terrain of Devil's Gulch.

Toni stifled a growl as the image surfaced—Shannon slick with sweat taking a long pull from her canteen. Toni's nostrils flared, summoning the essence of Shannon—the light musk of her sweat mingled with the earth, sage, and fennel as it rode the heat waves of the baking canyon and tangled Toni's brain with cravings. She recalled watching a drop of water run down the professor's chin and neck, leaving a glistening trail on her dusty skin. Oh, how she'd wanted to be that drop.

"What about the *Titanic*?" a female student asked.

"Same thing." Shannon turned toward the whiteboard and added *Titanic* to the numerous words already there. "Hollywood made a mawkish love story, thus perverting the actual event—taking the focus off the *tragedy* itself and *minimizing* the horror. In a way, they made it not real. They wouldn't make a love story with nine-eleven as a backdrop. That was a horrible tragedy and America wants to use the loss, the hurt, and the *outrage*." She wrote the words her tone had emphasized. "Our government wants us to really feel that."

The skin on the back of Toni's neck tingled. She wondered if Shannon could feel her attraction as she moved the pen across the board. A wand tracing symbols as the magic moved through the wizard in waves.

Toni studied Shannon's round buttocks, imagining they shook with each letter. She could almost see the faint tremors from across the room. *Tits and ass, and a brain too!* Toni felt herself getting wet. She couldn't continue or she would lose herself in those daydreams of desire. She willed herself to focus on the task before her. She wasn't there for a date, no matter how much she wished she were. She had to show Shannon the photos of the crime scene. She was there to work a case, a disturbingly calculated and gruesome case.

Shannon faced her audience again. "They take tragedies and make them into romances—disguising the reality—dressing it up, like a pig in lipstick."

"Bloodsucking monsters made into love interests." Toni heard her own words escape and dance before the woman who entranced her.

Shannon's face rose toward where Toni leaned against the back wall. Their eyes met briefly. "Yes. Thank you." Although she was apparently speaking to Toni, Shannon's dark eyes seemed to look through her. Toni was disappointed when Shannon quickly turned back to her students. Pointing her fat pen at them, she said, "Vampires."

Shannon's tone was matter-of-fact and her face impassive. *Damn woman, I thought at least you'd be glad to see me.* Toni crossed her arms and shifted her feet. *Perhaps I have waited too long to make my move.*

Closing her eyes, Toni recalled the image of Shannon soaked to the skin by an unexpected rainstorm. The outlines of Shannon's chilled nipples had nearly sent Toni over the edge of the ravine they were traversing. The case had involved five juvenile delinquents who fancied themselves Satan worshipers, a number of pet disappearances, and one missing toddler, who thankfully was found alive.

"But they're only myths anyway. Why does it matter?" A male voice snapped Toni back to the room.

Shannon assaulted the board, which was now covered with words. "Because movies still *glamorize* them, warping the truth and the *myths*, *butchering* the *reality* of that myth." Her tone changed periodically as she wrote or circled words. "Behaviors made *taboo* by the myth are embraced by certain groups and those behaviors are..." Rotating on her heel, she recapped her pen and pointed it at her theater of students. "Those behaviors could be potentially harmful."

"But, that isn't Hollywood's fault," a girl in the front row said. "It's like 'guns don't kill people, people do.' I don't see how the *Titanic* or even vampires being used for a romance hurts anyone. It's the movies. It's all fiction anyway. How can it hurt reality?"

"Perfect segue." Shannon nodded. "That is what I want you to think about. Your next essay will discuss how the media affects popular culture."

A collective moan rose and Toni couldn't help but chuckle.

"Now keep in mind what's important here: crime, harmful

attitudes, and behaviors of the deviant mind, not Gucci handbags and hairstyles." Shannon waved a stack of papers at her students. Her eyes shimmered with mirth. "Here's your chance to tell me what you think. It's not a research paper. No brainiacs putting words in your mouth. This is all you. No heavy reading required."

I'd like to put you in my mouth, Toni thought. *Heavy breathing, unavoidable.*

Shannon handed out the stack. "I want your opinion—supported, of course, with examples." Each student silently took one sheet before quietly packing up. "E-mail me any questions. Have a good Easter break."

Students stood to leave, blocking Toni's view as they made their way toward the door. Toni was surprised no one stayed to ask questions. *If she were my teacher, I'd be hanging around all evening just to watch those lips move. Those lips and those hips.* Whatever those lips and hips were doing, Toni would savor it. Every time they worked together, she experienced a bittersweet reward. The case would be solved, but then she wouldn't see Shannon until the trial or the next case.

While the last few students exited, Shannon began packing her supplies, her back to the room. Toni slunk toward her, imagining what it would feel like to embrace Shannon from behind. A naked embrace. She'd rub up and down slowly, exciting herself and the professor with soft tickles along Shannon's back and buttocks.

"So, Professor," Toni said as she carefully leaned over Shannon and whispered in her ear, "care to join me for a bite?" Toni heard the professor's sharp intake of breath. She knew she had startled her when Shannon grabbed the edge of the podium, but Toni remained close beside her. *You are evil. Just plain evil.* Toni smiled to herself. She resisted the urge to kiss Shannon's neck. Instead she moved away, giving Shannon a bit of space, and asked, "Do you believe in vampires?"

"That, Lieutenant Nomikos, is a loaded question." Shannon heaved her pack onto one shoulder. "I know you're probably here on time-sensitive business."

Toni held up the envelope. "Crime scene photos, a consult, and we see where it leads us. You, me, and some stale coffee." Waggling her eyebrows, she was pleased to see a smile forming on Shannon's lips. She was glad that Shannon understood the cop humor that often horrified ordinary people. They both cared about the victims and empathized with the survivors and their families, but seeing the horrors they faced so frequently required some kind of distancing and coping mechanism or they couldn't do their jobs as effectively as they did.

"Always willing to help the boys in blue."

"Or the girls," Toni added, her heart swelling as Shannon's smile grew into a broad toothy attraction.

"Yes, Antonia, all the kids clad in blue," she said, emphasizing Toni's full first name with what Shannon called a Greek accent. The first time she'd used it, Toni almost shot beer from her nose and nearly toppled her bar stool, because Shannon sounded more like Rocky Balboa or a Brooklyn Italian than a Greek. "You know I try to be available, whenever I can. But..."

Damn and I thought I'd always like your butt.

"...I have a departmental meeting I can't get out of." Shannon moved away to erase the board.

"Maybe tomorrow, then? Are you free in the morning?" Toni felt a stab of disappointment. Not merely because the professor didn't seem eager to help her, but Shannon wasn't really looking at her either. She tried not to let her worry show as she continued, "The case is an odd one. You know I've grown to depend on your insights and expertise." *...as well as the refreshing scent of your skin and groin-tingling swell of your breast.*

Shannon was silent for a moment while she wiped away the evidence of her lecture. "It is always a pleasure to see you, Toni, and I know your work is important albeit unpleasant."

Did she just say it was a pleasure to see me? Always a pleasure to see me! Toni cleared her throat, allowing her voice to take on a low, calm and controlled tone. "Ah, well, I enjoy working with you too. Unfortunately unpleasant events come with the territory. We're lucky to have you." Inside, Toni was singing and running in circles. Her chest and shoulders filled with electricity and excitement. *But she's still not looking at you, Nomikos.*

Finishing the board, Shannon sighed. "Sometimes I feel like I've never left the Bureau."

"Twice the gore and crazies for half the price." Toni laughed with an ease that denied the anxious feeling growing in the pit of her stomach. It unnerved her that Shannon was avoiding her eyes. She loved the professor's chocolate gaze. She wondered if it was her imagination or if Shannon was trying to keep a physical distance from her. Whenever Toni thought they might be becoming more than just work colleagues, Shannon would turn to ice, leaving Toni to trail after her like an unwanted puppy.

Shannon nodded toward the door. "I'm sorry. I really have to dash." She paused, looking at her watch. "But..."

More of your butt. Toni tried to bolster her courage and deny her growing apprehension.

"...would you be able to come over to my place later tonight? Say nine o'clock?"

Toni tried not to act as if she'd just been Tasered. They were so close she could feel the heat radiating from Shannon's body. She swallowed. "Yes. Of course. Thank you, Miss Flugle."

"That's Dr. Flugle." Shannon's voice was suddenly husky. Silence filled the empty room. The air swirled thick with energy. After a moment, Shannon moved away. The door clicked closed behind her.

❖

The clock on the mantel chimed softly. Shannon buzzed Toni in at the garden gate and crossed to the mirror by the front door. She eyed the beige camisole beneath her black blouse. Even though the camisole had the come-touch-me-I'm-silky-soft sheen to it, it wasn't remotely transparent. Plus she was wearing a sensible beige bra her mother would be proud of. Blouse on? Blouse off? Deciding to leave it unbuttoned, Shannon flipped the blouse back onto her shoulders. She wanted a casual, relaxed look. It wasn't sexy and it wouldn't complicate matters any more than the inane risk of inviting Toni over again.

What were you thinking? The invitation had popped out before she could stop it. *Who are you trying to fool? You barely restrained yourself from running up the aisle and screaming her name with glee.* Shannon scolded herself and her weakness for short, thick black hair and moss-colored eyes. They weren't simply green eyes, but layers of feathery swirls with amber specks. She swore that sometimes those specks enveloped the green and Toni's eyes turned to gold—glittering glass of the Sahara.

Three quick raps on the door preceded it swinging open. Toni swept into the room. Her black leather pants and leather jacket meant that she had used the two hours to switch from her police sedan to her personal motorcycle. Shannon clenched her teeth to keep from whimpering. The officer haunted her dreams with promises of flying—the wind whipping by, tangling her hair and tickling her skin. *Damn helmet laws.*

Shrugging off her backpack as she knocked the door closed with her boot, Toni cheered, "Greetings, weary scholar." She held up a bottle and a brown bag, waving them. "I come bearing gifts!"

"Whatever it is, I fear Greeks even when they bring gifts."

"Excuse me?" Toni stopped midway to the kitchen.

"I'm misquoting Virgil." *Where'd that assitude come from, Dr. Flugle?* Shannon's heartbeat faltered. Did she fear Antonia Nomikos? Toni was adorable and delectable, but she also represented a danger to Shannon's way of life—maybe even her life itself.

"Have you given up wine for Lent?" Toni's confusion was evident in her tone.

"Ha, Lent? Hardly. Just a scholarly joke. Not even a good one. I'll eat whatever you have in that bag. Oh, and thank you for being so thoughtful." *Good, Shannon, remember your manners. Follow the rules of civility, proper etiquette.*

"No worries. I'll set it out," Toni said, her tone clipped as she turned away. "Take a look at the photos. They're in my pack."

She stared at Toni's back. *Is she trying to freeze me out?* Then Shannon's inner voice fired back, *You're one to talk, Miss Yesno Touchme Goaway*! It was as if she had two voices in her—one was her heart and the other, her mind. Her heart was drawn to Toni, felt safe with her, and wanted to be held by her. Her mind warned her of the dangers that accompanied stepping beyond a work relationship. Ever since their first meeting, she'd been drawn to the officer but instead of giving in to her attraction and admitting her feelings, she constantly struggled to keep Toni at arm's length.

Shannon found the envelope and laid some of the pictures on the coffee table.

Toni appeared from the kitchen carrying two plates piled high with roast beef on rye. "We got a double homicide. Very clean. Based on the wounds it should have been messy, but it wasn't. Checked out their home address. Place looks to be in order."

Sight of the dill pickle wedge made Shannon's mouth water, but her main urge was to toss aside the sandwich and bite Toni instead. *Stay on track, Shannon. Work. No ties. No slips. No troubles.* "So, the killer is a neat freak. You expecting more bodies?"

Toni sighed. "I don't know, Shannon. But, this was too bizarre not to call you. Given the bites and the fact that it was so clean." She poured two glasses of wine and joined Shannon on the sofa.

"Bites?" Shannon could feel Toni's weight as Toni settled into the cushions beside her. *Damn. Stay focused, Flugle.* "What kind of bites? Human teeth or do you mean maybe dogs were used?"

"A couple of puncture marks on the neck of one and what looks like an animal bite on the other—a messy wound, but very little blood."

While Shannon munched silently on her sandwich, a piece of onion took an Olympic dive to the carpet. She bent over, shifting on the couch to reach it, and when she returned to her seat she inadvertently bumped her ass against Toni's knee and almost straddled it. She quickly shifted over and sat with a thud, thigh to thigh.

She froze. So did Toni. Shannon caught her breath. Her brain blanked and her heart stopped in that moment. A moment that literally hurt her insides. She felt the heat of Toni's thigh, like a flame scorching through the layers of material and searing her skin. She thought she heard a growl deep in Toni's chest.

You feel it too, Detective? Shannon tried to appear unaffected by the encounter. "Uh, sorry, my back-up-cams are in the shop." She refocused on the photo to cover her disarray. "Well, a jealous lover perhaps, but it isn't a vampire. They normally don't kill their victims. Werewolves bite, but don't just puncture. Wolves don't usually clean up, either. And contrary to popular belief, they rarely attack humans."

"Okay…okay. I know I don't have as many degrees as you, but I can't tell if you're yanking my chain."

Chain? Baby, I'll yank your chain until your great-grandchildren feel it. "In what way?"

"The werewolves and vampires stuff." Toni picked up one of the photos. It was a close-up of the puncture marks.

"You didn't say there were any symbols that would reflect a religious cult. Nor was there anything to hint at a group orchestration, like a coven or cult. So I figured the scene you described suggests you're thinking vampires or werewolves. They don't usually stand on ceremony, but they can be either a group or solo practitioners, like

Wiccans. Of course, Wiccans are white witches and usually don't use human sacrifices."

"I'm a police officer, not a ghostbuster. I wasn't thinking a real vampire or werewolf. I don't believe in them, or zombies for that matter. Maybe psychotic Children of the Corn types who think blood gives them power, like those Wiccan weirdoes."

"Hey, I know a couple of Wiccans and they're perfectly nice and even sane people. They don't play with blood, well, except dragon's blood, which has nothing to do with dragons or real blood."

Toni laughed and took another bite of her sandwich, clearly passing the subject off as a joke. "Look, I was thinking ritual cult killing."

"Worshippers of Kali might focus on blood-letting, but you can't ignore the vampiric overtones here."

"I thought you were a Satanic cult expert, grounded in the reality of mankind's evils. I didn't know you worked on the X-files." Toni's tone was teasing.

She's not criticizing you. She just doesn't understand. Shannon reminded herself that Toni's naïveté, her ignorance, was yet another reason to keep her at a distance. How could she follow her feelings when she knew Toni lived in a completely different world?

Shannon flipped through the pictures, turning some sideways and upside down. "There's still a lot about me you don't know, Toni."

"I'm always willing to learn."

Are you really? Shannon batted the question aside and picked up a photo. *We're working on a case. Focus on these poor victims, bloodless bodies.* "Why drain them of blood? Why clean them up and set them out in the woods? If they weren't in their skivvies, it would look like they're just having a pleasant conversation after a picnic. Why the white underwear? Is it theirs or did the killer supply it?"

Toni pointed at the picture. "It reminds me of those paintings of little angels with their tighty-whities."

Shannon stifled a laugh. "Those aren't tighty-whities, but you're right. Cherubs." *Do you wear tighty-whities or boxers, my little butch cop?* Shannon wondered if she'd ever find out.

Toni continued to lean into Shannon. "Okay, so they're supposed to be innocents. Two clean little babies. Or like Christ. Maybe we missed some followers of Jade."

"That was two years ago." *Two freaking years and not one kiss from you. But I can feel your fire. Your desire.*

Toni continued, "I know she's in jail, but maybe…"

"That poser? Not a chance." Shannon shook her head. "Looking at the scene, I'd say completely different from Jade. No symbols. No weapon."

"Hmmm, we have the purity image and the blood…or the lack of it," Toni said.

After a thoughtful moment, Shannon replied, "Puncture marks and teeth point to vampire. Drained of blood…solid vampire, but they usually don't take a chunk, nor do they kill. Still looks like a vampire."

"Obviously, they took the blood, either for consumption or for external use. You think it's someone playing at being a vampire?"

The more cases they worked together, the more Shannon found herself enthralled by Toni's mind, her thinking process. Discussing ideas and theories with her was exhilarating. Shannon wanted to rip her clothes off and tackle the tough little Greek. She turned away from Toni, feigning interest in the scraps of sandwich left on her plate rather than giving in to her desire to wrap the policewoman in her arms. "It's no game."

"Very true. Two dead, and we have nothing to go on."

Even if Toni had missed the point, she was right. Shannon had a job to do. All thoughts of their naked warm bodies pressed together evaporated. People were dead and she had to get her head out from between Toni's legs, no matter how muscular and curved those thighs and calves might be.

Toni ran her finger around the rim of her wineglass. "It could be a Christ thing, and that reeks of Jade." The glass emitted a soft hum that slowly became a ringing.

"I'd have to be there to see if it reeks." Shannon watched Toni's finger go round and round. "There wasn't anything in the pictures. They were just dumped…set out there with no signs of ceremony."

"Like trash," Toni stated.

"But cleaned." Shannon's gaze followed Toni's finger still circling. *How can such a sexy finger be so annoying?* Shannon wanted that finger tracing circles on her skin, not wasting time on a glass.

"Like recyclables."

"What?" Shannon had heard Toni's comment, but her brain surged, and she needed to hear that word again.

"Recyclables. You know how little old ladies always rinse their cans and bottles? Last week one called to complain her recycling had been stolen."

"Shit. Toni…" Shannon grabbed Toni's hand and, without realizing what she was doing, clasped it to her chest. "Shit." *It can't be! Could someone be taunting a vampire?*

"What? Recycling. Does that mean something? How do two bloodless, clean bodies lead to recycling? It's not like you could reuse a dead body. Well, unless you were Dr. Frankenstein."

"Yeah…I don't know why I didn't see it." Shannon's mind was reeling with the thought of it. *Bastards! Killing just to send a damn message.*

"What the fuck?"

Shannon hardly heard Toni's voice. It seemed in a distant fog. "What, Toni?" Shannon realized she hadn't been listening.

"Last year we had a Satanic cult and a Christ-crucifying coven. Now a Frankenstein enthusiast is killing people to re-animate them?"

"No, what? Frankenstein. Where'd you get Frankenstein?"

"But you said—"

"Never mind, Toni." She took a deep breath to calm herself and gather the words she wanted to use. "Maybe the killer left them there to taunt someone."

"Taunt? You mean, like 'you can't catch me, I'm too smart'?"

"No, more like 'neener neener, look at this yummy lunch.'" Shannon looked down. Her cheeks warmed as she realized she was holding Toni's hand to her chest. She slowly moved her hand to her thigh, but didn't release it.

"Lunch? So we're talking cannibalism here. Someone's breakfast ruined because the kids interrupted?"

"They're empty of blood, Toni. Empty. Nice clean and shiny, like they're ready to be reused, but they can't be reused. They're clean but empty. Empty and dead."

"Wait. So someone killed them, drained them, and left them there to taunt someone who wants them?"

"Wants their blood."

"Like a vampire."

"Right, like a vampire." Shannon linked arms with Toni and leaned into her. Not for the joy and happiness that usually followed her discoveries, but for support. With this new realization, she was shaken to the core. Someone out there was taunting a vampire. She took a deep breath, willing herself to remain calm. Toni's warmth comforted her. "But the vampire wouldn't want them dead. Which means the killer is taunting the vampire. For what reason, I don't know."

"Does the killer think he's making new vampires? Does he think these two will become vampires?" Toni's voice rose, edging near incredulous agitation.

Shannon patted Toni's thigh, hoping to calm her. "That is something else entirely. They wouldn't have been left like that. See, vampires don't kill. They may even reuse the same person over and over. Killing someone or draining a vessel is a waste. This killer is—"

"Litterbug!" Toni's face lit up like she had just answered the million-dollar question. "Just tossing out perfectly good vessels, so wasteful."

How can you be so cute and sexy and yet such a dorkberry? "Toni, please, this killer really believes a vampire lives somewhere around here." *But do they know or is it a guess?* "We have to figure out why. Why they think a vampire is out here and why they want to taunt or tease them. What is either of these people going to do next?"

Toni took a deep breath, held it for a few seconds, before releasing it. "Okay. Let's play."

"Thank you. Now, I've killed a couple. Drained their blood."

"For what? To drink? To bathe in?"

I don't know. Neither or both? Does it matter? Shannon finally responded, "Doesn't matter. They aren't for me. I'm leaving them here to show you my trash, but it doesn't look like trash. It looks like recyclables, like it might be worth a pretty penny. But it's not. It's worthless, like wax fruit."

"Okay, why would you do that?" Toni tapped her fingers on Shannon's knee.

"It looks like it's good, but it's not." Shannon swirled the last bit of wine in her glass. "I want you to think they're reusable—but they aren't."

Toni nodded toward the kitchen. "Let me get the bottle." She jumped up and moved away.

Shannon immediately missed Toni's warmth and struggled not to show it. "But why them? Why display them that way?"

Before reaching the kitchen, Toni stopped and snapped her fingers. "Hey! You just said it." She paced between the sofa and the kitchen, as if reading the words from the floor at her feet. "You want me to think they're good, but they aren't. They look alive, but they're dead. What if the bodies were displayed to make someone hungry or thirsty? Make me want some? I mean if I were the vampire."

"Maybe you're on a diet or trying to quit…"

Toni closed the distance between them and sat back down. Beaming with excitement, she took Shannon's hands and exclaimed, "Maybe they're my last brownie!"

"Last brownie? Like you were saving them for later?"

Toni nodded, bouncing Shannon's hands as she said, "Yes. Right."

"Ah! Saving them for later, but the killer took them?" Shannon's heart was thrumming in her chest, partially because of Toni's forest eyes streaked with gold, and partially because of the fear of opening up and revealing too much. She had never seen the victims before, but the killer was taunting someone in her territory. Regardless of whether it was a personal affront to her or meant for another, it was serious business and she'd have to get to the bottom of it. *Tomorrow*, Shannon reasoned, *Toni tonight.*

"Exactly. This was personal." Pulling Shannon to her feet, Toni continued, "We have to see if there are any old bite marks on the victims. Then at least we'll know why these two were chosen."

"Good thinking." Shannon let Toni pull her away from the coffee table. She half expected Toni to suggest that they run right down to the morgue and check the victims. Despite her anxiety, she would follow Toni anywhere. Her desire to be with Toni had escaped from its bindings, and now Shannon couldn't rein it in. She was afraid to say anything for fear of destroying the moment.

"We find their vampire, get a list of his enemies, and then we find the killer. Brilliant!" Toni pulled her into a hug before playfully pushing her away. "Shit, now you have me acting like a real vampire is out there."

Shannon hesitated. Someone was taunting a vampire. Her gut clenched. One way or another, the game was over. "There is."

"Are you saying you actually believe that vampires and werewolves exist?"

"Vampire myths exist in almost every culture."

"Bogeymen?" Toni teased, whispering into her ear. "Ghosts and aliens, Shannon. Do you really believe all that hocus pocus, woo-hoo-hooey shit?"

"It's not all woo-hoo-hooey shit, Toni. One of my great-great-aunts even wrote about it back in 1881."

"Oh, I see. So belief in vampires runs in the family?"

"There have been vampires and werewolves throughout history. In myth certainly. Now, I know it sounds crazy, but there is more in this world than you and I can even imagine."

"Ah, 'there are more things in Heaven and Earth than you can dream of.' *Hamlet*?"

Shannon stared into Toni's eyes, begging for understanding. "Some things are beautiful, like hidden waterfalls or rediscovering animals we thought were extinct. And some things are scary ugly, and I'm not going there." Shannon's heart raced. She cared for Toni and didn't want to lose her. Desire warred with prudence.

"Demons and angels?" Toni asked, her gaze unwavering.

"I don't want to talk about any of them. Some things are just plain mysterious. That is all I'm going to say. Those are my personal beliefs. You're here for my professional opinion. My knowledge and training, nothing else."

"That's not quite true." Toni's eyes were locked with hers. "I'm hoping, if I'm lucky, that I might get something more."

Shannon's nostrils flared. She could smell Toni's heat. Toni's blood pumping through her veins and settling between her legs. She imagined the tip of her tongue touching the soft skin just below Toni's ear. Sweet, but salty too.

She reached up and held Toni's ear for a moment before letting her finger trail down Toni's neck to her shirt collar. "Well, Toni, you never know." She could smell Toni's essence, like the day they lay under a trailer reading the rantings a suspect had written on the bottom of his boat. Mingling with the smell of cloves and ginger, Toni's desire radiated from her in waves. Shannon wanted to rub that smell all over herself.

Her eyes met Toni's. Her breath stilled. The room hummed with their silence. The time for pretending was over. No point in holding back now.

❖

Slowly, Shannon turned, sashaying toward her bedroom. The mesmerizing movement drew Toni along. Part of her wanted to run down to the morgue and question the coroner about his findings, but her feet propelled her toward Shannon.

A phone rang from the kitchen.

Watching the professor's fluid motion as her ass swayed filled Toni with joy and longing. Shannon hadn't said anything, but Toni knew there was an invitation in those moves. She wasn't retreating to her bedroom. She was beckoning Toni to follow—inviting Toni to her bed, her body and all its lovely curves and flavors.

As Toni reached for those hips, Shannon stopped and turned. "Is that you?"

Toni was confused by the sudden halt and the question. "Of course it's me. Who else would it be?"

Shannon chuckled, motioning toward the kitchen. "Not you. The phone."

Toni's brain hadn't registered the ringing, but when Shannon mentioned the phone, it was as if Toni's ears remembered the sound. It was an echo of memory in her head, but now the apartment was silent. "Was a phone ringing?"

"It only just stopped. I don't think it was mine," Shannon said as she brushed past. "I'll start the coffee."

Toni felt herself deflate. The excitement that had filled her seeped out as Shannon moved toward the kitchen. She obediently followed, knowing she'd have to check the call.

As she pulled the phone from her jacket, Shannon planted a quick kiss just below her ear and then moved away as the phone on the wall began to ring. Toni froze, surprised and unsure of what to do next. It happened too fast. She wanted to recapture the feeling of those lips. Had it really happened? She heard Shannon's calm voice behind her.

"Dr. Flugle's residence."

Toni's phone buzzed in her hand, forcing her eyes and brain into action. The readout told her it was dispatch. "Nomikos."

A gruff voice filled Toni's ear. "Damn, we got another body, Nomikos. Annie's Glenn, just past the ball fields, eastside."

After giving her ETA, she disconnected and looked at Shannon. "You too?"

"Yes." Shannon smiled ruefully. "Save that conversation for another time?"

Toni's mood lifted. At least there'd be another time. She held out here hand. "Come on then, Dr. Flugle. Let's go hunting vampires."

THE ORIENT EXPRESS
SHELLEY THRASHER

Angelique sat in the first-class dining car of the Orient Express and fingered the petals of the deep-red rose that adorned her table. The sun, setting an intense crimson, blinded her for a minute as it penetrated the window across the aisle.

One of the three men in black business suits who sat there lowered the shade. Their voices were low, almost whispers, only an occasional word of their Oxford English drifting her way. Their heads almost touched, and she basked in the excitement shimmering from them. A beautiful young woman, perhaps their secretary, sat with them—rather old-fashioned looking in her long-sleeved, high-necked creamy lace blouse and mid-calf straight skirt.

The men reminded her of the Englishmen in Bram Stoker's *Dracula*, which she'd read ages ago, who were chasing Dracula across Europe to the Black Sea in hopes of destroying him. The book had introduced her to the Orient Express, and since then she had associated it with adventure and intrigue.

Cradling her globed glass of reddish-brown wine, she stared into it, wishing it were a crystal ball in which she could discover an exciting future. So far this dinner had met her expectations.

Her Tokay perfectly accompanied the nutty-tasting pâté de foie gras served as the first course. As she swirled the splash of wine the waiter handed her, its bouquet of fresh strawberries and vanilla almost overpowered her. Usually she preferred dry French wines, but this sweet Hungarian red seduced her as she rolled it over her tongue and softly chewed. She spread the delicate ochre pâté, sprinkled with mustard seeds, onto brioche, and alternated bites of it with sips of wine.

She was beginning her second glass when a pale, black-haired young woman with almond-shaped dark eyes fringed with long black lashes glided toward her. Her white satin blouse set off her scarlet pantsuit, just as her pale skin and lily-white teeth seemed even lighter compared to the bright red lipstick covering her full, pouting lips. Angelique's breath came more rapidly as she took in the open neck of her shiny blouse. The woman held the arm of a large, older man who seemed to want nothing more than to pamper her. Her blood-red nails shone as she grasped the man's forearm and steadied herself when the train abruptly rounded a bend.

Angelique gasped. Was this Countess Elena Andrenyi and her husband the count, reincarnated to accompany her? In her mid-teens, when Angelique read Agatha Christie's *Murder on the Orient Express*, she'd imagined herself as this very woman, a beautiful young American married to a Hungarian count. Part of the group who avenged the murder of her sister and her two children, she never bloodied her hands. She appeared fragile yet was stronger than anyone realized. She and her twelve co-conspirators literally got away with murder.

The woman paused at the table in front of Angelique and let the man pull out her chair. As he rounded the table to sit with his back to Angelique, the woman stared at her with an expression that made her sweat. It promised lusty sex between white satin sheets, with the woman's nails raking Angelique's back to produce beads of blood as red as her nail polish. Angelique stared back, and the woman transformed into a demure, harmless creature more likely to be Count Dracula's victim than his consort.

Angelique took a large swallow of wine and shook her head. This Hungarian red was potent. Usually she held her liquor well. Despite her dizziness she forced herself to refocus on *Murder on the Orient Express*. She'd read the novel so many times she finally promised herself that someday she'd travel on the famous train, but not as the wife of a stodgy man like the count. She'd escort someone as beautiful as the countess. That was her first clue that she was different.

The large man sat down and blocked her view of the temptress, so her mind jumped tracks as she spied another familiar-looking woman sitting alone three tables away on the opposite aisle.

Mabel Warren, the first lesbian Angelique had encountered in print, had appeared in another novel set on the Orient Express—Graham

THE ORIENT EXPRESS

Greene's *Stamboul Train*. The woman Angelique had just spotted sat sipping from a tumbler filled with a brownish drink Angelique immediately imagined as whiskey, for Mabel Warren was an aging alcoholic in her fifties. This woman emptied her drink and signaled the waiter for another one, clearly demanding that he waste no time.

While the present-day Mabel waited, she lit a cigarette and glanced at her wristwatch, then half turned to look over her shoulder. Finally, an attractive blonde in her late twenties sauntered in. The woman with the drink, her cropped hair mussed, jumped up and signaled the blonde, obviously trying to show her off to the rest of the passengers. The young woman looked at her companion as if she was acting ridiculous and sat down as if she would rather be anywhere else. She was probably wondering if her brown roots were beginning to show.

As a teenager, Angelique had admired Mabel Warren, primarily because she was a successful journalist unafraid to compete with men in the world of politics and high-pressure deadlines. Mabel Warren had helped Angelique realize she was definitely different from the other girls at school. However, she didn't want to compete with men or look like Mabel, with her short graying hair and worldly manner.

Angelique looked back at the other passengers in the dining car, especially those she'd already noticed, and finished her second glass of wine. To help pass the time, she might as well indulge in some more fantasies.

❖

The three men to her left were British diplomats, she fancied, traveling to Budapest. After she disembarked in Vienna, they would continue across Austria into Hungary. There they'd spend the night near the train station in a famous old hotel.

At dinner, the men would remark that it looked like the Hungarian Revolution had ended last month, instead of fifteen years ago. Buildings still lay in ruins in some sections of the city, which increased their feeling of superiority over the Russians. The Soviets clearly hadn't managed to help their satellite countries rebuild as successfully as the countries of Western Europe had, because East Germany, Poland, Czechoslovakia, and Yugoslavia didn't look much better.

Enjoying her fictitious scenario, Angelique decided one of the men

• 243 •

would be a spy, though she didn't know which one. And their secretary would be having an affair with one of them, the one with wavy hair.

Angelique cut a spear of asparagus into small bites and tried it. Delicious. Firm with just enough crunch.

Just then the large man seated with his back to her dropped his napkin and bent toward the aisle to retrieve it. The eyes of the dark-haired young woman blazed at her like a forest fire. The man wasn't actually her husband. Angelique quickly revised her story. He was her mother's young husband, escorting her back to Vienna. She'd run away from home when her mother married him. Obviously a philanderer who'd wed the rich older woman only for her money, he'd blinded her so completely she even trusted him to track down her rebellious daughter and return her to the family mansion.

The man had located the daughter in Paris and soon made a pass at her. But the fiery young woman slapped him and declared she was a lesbian and would inform her mother and everyone she knew in Vienna of that fact if he insisted on taking her back. He did insist, believing he could win her over during the lengthy train ride, but obviously he wasn't having much luck. The woman would slip out of her private berth tonight and knock on Angelique's door, having watched for her after dinner and located her compartment then.

She wouldn't say much, but their eyes would catch fire and their bodies would follow.

Angelique sighed and tried a potato. Ah, so fresh, and with more taste than its American counterpart, though perhaps she was simply hungry. And the sauce was a masterpiece of cream and flour and butter and some unknown ingredient. Perfect. The pepper steak was rare, exactly as she requested, and required almost no chewing. She stared at the blood that oozed from it and ribboned the white cream sauce.

Why was she feeling stoned? Had someone laced her pâté with Acapulco gold? She drank more wine.

Her new plane of awareness shot her into a fantasy about the older woman and her companion. She was actually a famous German novelist who enjoyed the leisure of train travel to think through the plot of her next book. Definitely a lesbian, a Gertrude Stein type, she liked to hire attractive secretaries more to inspire her than to do her typing and filing. She herself enjoyed those menial tasks, because they gave her the time and the opportunity to polish her work. She wasn't a wildly popular novelist, but a serious literary type who intended for her books to eventually be classics. However, her secretaries kept her in touch with the more superficial world she tended to overlook and craved occasionally.

Which of these women would notice her tonight and later knock on her door? Perhaps all of them?

Dessert consisted of a strawberry tart—a flaky delicacy full of vanilla pastry cream and topped with fresh strawberries coated with a red apricot glaze. Angelique savored the tang of the fruit blended with the sweetness of the cream and the glaze.

Hopefully her night aboard the Orient Express would be even a fraction as busy as she imagined it might be, but she decided to have one more glass of wine in case it wasn't. She emptied the bottle while the other diners drifted away.

Finally deciding to stand, she wavered and nearly tripped over her chair as she lurched into the corridor, reeling from table to table to steady herself. She'd expected the Orient Express to move more smoothly.

❖

Angelique careened down the narrow corridor of the first-class coach to her private compartment after prowling through several cars and exploring the fabulous train. During her tour of the first-class sleeper, she noticed two of the three men in business suits lounging in a two-berth compartment at the opposite end of the car. She giggled, amused at how serious they looked. The third one was entering an adjacent room with his arm around the large man who had sat with the woman with blazing eyes. Hmm. What was going on here?

Through her veiled awareness she glimpsed the gorgeous young countess in another compartment with the prim-and-proper woman who'd eaten with the three men. Her face grew even warmer when she realized the temptress would be sleeping only a wall away. The older lesbian and her companion were staying on the other side of Angelique and seemed very cozy. Now she was totally confused.

She sank into the red velvet armchair in her spacious room and tipped her spinning head back. The rhythmic noise of the iron wheels, combined with the wine, lulled her almost to sleep, but then she heard a thud and a loud whisper. "You crazy fool. You better be careful."

Shaking her head, she tried to determine where the sounds came from, but couldn't say for sure. By the time she jumped up and opened her door, the corridor was empty and quiet.

She must have been dreaming, she thought, so she stripped off her clothes, managed to pull on a filmy red gown she'd bought in Paris, and slid into bed. She was gliding across northern France, she mused dreamily as the slight vibration of the Orient Express rocked her to sleep.

A small hand on her shoulder shook her awake.

"What the—"

The small, surprisingly strong hand clamped her mouth shut. "Shhh. You'll wake the others. I thought you wanted me here."

As Angelique's eyes adjusted in the dusky light streaming under the door to her compartment, she discerned the dark brown eyes of the young woman she'd admired at dinner. Her eyes glowed almost red as she bent closer, her heavy perfume intoxicating.

"What are you talking about?" Angelique whispered.

"I saw the way you stared at me during dinner. Do you think I can't tell when a woman wants me?" She threw off her dark robe and stood there as white as a marble statue, then slipped under the sheet next to Angelique. "I'm Scarlet, and I'm all yours."

Angelique was sure she was dreaming this time, but the flesh under her hesitant fingers felt warm and smooth. She slid her hand down Scarlet's side to her small waist and up the swell of her hip. Scarlet snuggled closer and rubbed her full breasts against Angelique's arm, then caught the hem of Angelique's gown and eased it over her head.

She didn't care if this was a dream. Angelique settled back into the comfortable bed as Scarlet rolled on top of her and smoothed her hands over Angelique's face.

"You're very beautiful, you know," Scarlet murmured, then bit Angelique's lower lip as gently as if she were tasting a strawberry. Angelique countered Scarlet's teeth with her tongue, rolled her over, and nipped her cheek.

"Ah, you're as feisty as you are lovely," Scarlet murmured as she sank her teeth into Angelique's neck.

Angelique bucked, but Scarlet held on, and soon Angelique was wandering in a huge field of wildflowers, their colors and smells surrounding her until Scarlet slowly released her and she dropped onto her pillow.

She slept for a while, until the train slowed and she became aware of someone sitting on the bed next to her. The person had evidently opened the shades and the full moon glittered on long blond hair. "Who are you and—"

Again, someone hushed her, but by merely placing a finger over Angelique's lips. "I'm Ruby."

Gradually Angelique could make out the green eyes of the blonde who had sat with the older woman at dinner last night, though a thin red ring circled each iris. "What's going on? Are you two playing a trick on me? How did you get in here? I thought I locked my door."

"Ha. You couldn't have kept us out, even if we'd had to bribe the conductor, which we didn't. You were easy, and Scarlet said you're delicious."

Angelique had to be in one of the lucid dream states Carlos Castenada described in his *Teachings of Don Juan*. Why was this happening? She'd close her eyes and go back to sleep, and when she woke up it'd be morning and she'd be in Germany with her feet planted firmly on the ground.

As she squeezed her eyes shut, a hot hand caressed her leg, then slid up toward her stomach. Fingertips brushed her mound, then circled her navel, massaging her belly. "Ah, my little potato," Ruby muttered. "You smell so fresh. How I'd love to eat you, then lap your warm sauce. You'd melt in my mouth like tender beef."

Angelique was growing tired of this ridiculous dream, so she reached down to grab the imaginary woman, only to encounter a handful of silk-like hair.

"Let me love you," Ruby whispered as she followed Angelique's hand upward and bit the other side of Angelique's neck.

Energy rushed through Angelique with the power of a locomotive or a flash flood. She was caught in the whirlpool torrent, as if a hurricane, a tornado, a tidal wave surged through her, breaking every internal barrier she'd ever built. Finally exhausted, she collapsed against her pillow again, the smell of incense coiling through her like a snake.

The third time Angelique awoke, she sat up in bed and stared at the figure in the red velvet chair across from her bed. The window shade was closed again, but Angelique could make out faintly glowing red eyes.

"I didn't want to wake you," a soft voice said. "I would have sat here and watched you sleep."

"Who are you?" Angelique asked, though this had to be the young woman who sat with the three men last night.

"I'm Coral." She rose hesitantly and approached Angelique.

"I suppose you want to start to make love to me then bite my neck too." Angelique was past disgusted with this nonsense, but something kept her from dismissing this phantom she'd somehow conjured to her room. She needed to find out why she was having these visions and why her breasts and clitoris were pulsating like the throat of a warbler in full song.

"I want to love you, but you have to let me."

Coral sounded so apologetic Angelique lay back and patted the bed beside her. "Come here. You can't do any more damage than your two friends have." How could this beautiful dream woman possibly hurt her? In her long, high-collared gown, Coral looked like a schoolgirl playing boarding-school games.

But as Coral stroked Angelique's arm, her hand felt like it belonged to a grown woman. The pulsations in Angelique's clitoris grew from bird song to kettledrum, spreading outward as Coral's gentle, rhythmic touch ignited an explosion from the depths of her body. It inched upward, seeming to seek the light, lava moving uphill, Etna and Vesuvius and Krakatoa combined as the glowing red substance rushed through her and finally seemed to blaze through the top of her head.

When Angelique exploded, Coral cupped her face and kissed her eyes, her cheeks, her mouth. Angelique's shoulders dropped, and she melted into the mattress as Coral kissed her way down her body and thrust amazingly long fingers into her with what sounded like a scream of triumph. Angelique smiled in surrender. If only a real woman, an available one, could ignite such passion in her.

❖

The shrill train whistle woke Angelique with a start to the sun shining around the edges of the room-darkening window shade. Then a loud boom sounded and the train shook as if about to jump the tracks. It gradually slowed to a full stop.

She jumped up, ripped off her red gown, and threw on navy slacks and a pullover, accented with a red scarf. She'd had some weird dreams last night, probably from the wine, but what had just happened was definitely real. Strangely, she wasn't hung over, as she should be after drinking an entire bottle of Tokay. She felt energized, as powerful as the engine of the Orient Express.

She yanked her door open and rushed out into the corridor just as everyone else did. Two of the men still wore pajamas, as did the older woman whom Angelique had imagined as a writer. The three women who'd visited her dreams were dressed, as were the two other men. The women stood in a small circle, and when Angelique glanced at them she could have sworn their eyes momentarily flashed red. To her embarrassment, her entire body began to throb like it had last night.

"Did you hear that sound? What happened?" the writer asked. "Why have we stopped in the middle of nowhere?"

"How do you know we're in the middle of nowhere?" one of the men asked.

"Because I looked out the window, silly."

The writer evidently knew the man, who seemed as if he wanted to choke her.

"Where's the conductor? He should be able to tell us what's occurring," said the woman who'd called herself Scarlet last night, sounding exactly the way she had in Angelique's dream. She must have overheard her at dinner.

The conductor rushed into their coach. "Ladies and gentlemen. We've had an explosion in the first-class dining car. We're not sure what happened, but it's nothing to worry about. We're in Germany now, and as soon as the local authorities straighten things out and we replace the dining car, we'll be under way. In the meanwhile, you'll have your breakfast in the other dining facility. The staff will do everything possible to ensure it meets the same standards as the one you paid for."

Grumbling, everyone glanced at each other and started to return to their rooms. Angelique studied Scarlet, Ruby, and Coral, tempted to chuckle as she recalled her marathon dream. But as she straightened the collar of her pullover she felt one small scab, then another. Stunned, she fingered the other side of her neck and found the same marks.

She caught Scarlet's attention and glared at her, but the woman didn't indicate that she even remembered her from dinner, much less from any late-night intimacy. After she received the same reaction from Ruby and Coral, she decided to lay off the wine for a while.

Still puzzled, Angelique returned to her room to put on her makeup and dress for breakfast. But as she examined the twin holes on each side of her neck in the mirror, her energy began to leak like air out of a punctured tire.

What caused these marks? Had she scratched herself in her sleep? But they were so symmetrical. It was difficult for a dream to leave holes such as these and the soreness she felt when she relieved herself. She began to topple from the magical high she'd enjoyed until now. Maybe she needed to eat.

❖

As Angelique bit into her mushroom-and-cheese omelet, the dining car hummed with anxious, excited voices in several languages, just as her body still hummed from last night.

"Someone planted a bomb, intended for the first-class passengers at breakfast, but it exploded early."

Someone tried to joke. "Perhaps the terrorists forgot about the time change."

"Probably one of those never-ending protests against the war in Vietnam."

"I thought the students had given up all that nonsense."

Angelique had never paid any attention to politics, but as the swirl of rumors surrounded her, she decided to at least start reading the newspaper. People obviously did strange and dangerous things to promote their cause.

As she ate, the older woman, the one she'd pegged as a novelist, paused at her table and said, with a British accent, "May I join you?"

"Of course." Perhaps Angelique could discover these people's identity and reason for being on the train.

"Horrid way to wake up this morning." The woman caught a busy waiter's attention and immediately ordered black coffee and toast. "Have you traveled on the Express before?"

"No. And I'll always remember my experience."

The woman smiled. "Yes, riding this train is like being in a time warp. That's why I insist on taking it every chance I get. So much romance and intrigue embedded in the very fabric of the accommodations."

Angelique warmed to her. "That's exactly how I feel."

"And I try to convince all the actors I direct to travel this way too. Of course, the big-name stars insist on flying. Time is money for them. I prefer making B movies because the actors are usually impressionable nobodies who'll do exactly what I ask. We're all traveling together this time, except for the extras we'll pick up in Budapest."

"You're shooting a movie in Budapest?"

The woman buttered a piece of toast. "Yes, still another version of Dracula called *Dracula's Daughters*. Audiences never seem to tire of vampires."

Angelique almost choked on a piece of omelet. "I suppose you're right. Why do you suppose that is?"

The woman frowned and drank some coffee. "Hmm. It's almost impossible to untangle the interwoven fabric of sex, violence, love, and healing. The vampire speaks to that complex aspect of life."

Angelique didn't know how to respond. She wanted to believe her experience last night would keep her feeling as great as she did earlier this morning, but the magic was already evaporating like water from a vase of cut flowers. Maybe she could press the flowers of the three mysterious women's visits between the pages of a book and leaf back to them occasionally.

The woman finished her coffee and gazed at Angelique. "Thanks for the company. By the way, did you hear the news? A leftist group has claimed responsibility for the bombing."

"No. What group was it?"

"A German communist organization called the Red Army Faction. They've been responsible for a lot of violence in Germany lately. Their leaders were arrested a few months ago, but evidently a new crop has sprung up. It's becoming dangerous to travel, but that will never stop me."

❖

After a five-hour delay, the Orient Express sped through Munich and on to Salzburg. Angelique took a nap during the afternoon and dreamed of two groups of men in helicopters shooting at each other. Blood-splattered dead bodies lay everywhere, and one of the choppers exploded. Waking with a start, she vowed not to drink any more wine for a very long while.

After they crossed Germany and had almost reached Austria, once again, Angelique sat alone in the dining car. But she drank only mineral water and didn't fantasize about the other first-class passengers.

Instead, she gazed out the window at the distant mountains, dotted with onion-domed churches and villages clustered at their feet. The mountains seemed so rooted, so strong, so sure.

Her body still fizzed like her freshly opened bottle of water, but the longer she sat engrossed in the passing scenery, the more she could control the fizz and not fear it would build up in her and erupt like it had last night. That would embarrass her. She even hesitated to pick up her fork because when she'd touched anything metal today, static electricity had made her jump.

Every station they passed thronged with people, each with his or her own story. What was it like to live in the shadow of the Alps, to be sure of one's identity and allegiance?

As darkness closed in, she could gradually see nothing but her own reflection in the window. She'd pulled on a lightweight turtleneck to cover her scars, which were disappearing. What had happened to her last night? Would her memory of it fade along with the scars?

As she studied herself in the train window she thought about how self-absorbed she'd always been. Maybe her life resembled this window. She couldn't see out of it now, but when the sun shone or they passed a lighted station, she could. God knows she hadn't had much light around her so far. Was that why she couldn't see outside herself?

Her strange dreams mystified her. Last night she'd obviously hallucinated from too much wine, but the bloody bodies she saw this afternoon seemed even more real, and more unexplainable—like a vision—a gory one she could do without. And everything seemed red lately, ever since she'd bought her red scarf in Paris.

Her mother loved red, and she'd such a lightning, and lightening, effect when she visited every year at Christmas. She blew in like the north wind and made Angelique's world so bright she wanted to go out and play with the other children in her south Louisiana neighborhood. She loved everyone for the few days her mother stayed in town.

Her mother's excitement at seeing her on Christmas Eve, her lavish hugs and kisses and gifts, her tales of life in Vegas raised Angelique so high she felt like she could fly. But her mother always left after only two days, and Angelique always crashed to earth and everything turned black and unfriendly.

She'd spent her childhood looking forward to and dreaming of those two days. When Angelique was sixteen, she finally rebelled against her mother's behavior, so she staged the quarrel that kept her mother completely away and left herself in the dark.

Her recent stay in Paris had illuminated her world so totally that a bit of the brightness still lingered. At times now she could almost see in the dark, and the women who'd visited her last night, whether real or imagined, vampires or angels, had left their mark and helped her see even more clearly. They'd penetrated her darkness, and now she longed to connect with a woman on a deeper level than she'd ever known possible.

But she wanted someone gentler, more dependable than the women she usually picked up or the illusory women from last night.

Did she have the courage to follow these vague longings into unknown territory, or was she supposed to always stay in single rooms and eat solitary meals? Wouldn't it be more enjoyable to travel with someone? To have someone to look at instead of always staring at herself?

She finished her main course of roast chicken, potatoes, turnips, and carrots. Maybe she'd find such a woman in Vienna.

ERIS
WINTER PENNINGTON

*P*lease, please, please." Khloe chanted the words like a mantra, her voice wrought with the urgency of her need. Her hips pressed forward in a vain effort to try to grind her lower body against the post to which she was bound. Zaphara stood just inside the dungeon. Her long black hair was pulled back tight, revealing the high cheekbones and narrow chin that marked her as one of the Daione Maithe, a faerie woman of the Sidhe.

"How long do you intend to keep this up? Until her voice is raw from pleading?" The amethyst eyes beneath her darkly arched brows contained what appeared to be a well of disinterest and boredom.

"As long as it takes," I replied, finishing the task of working the saddle-soap paste into a leather bullwhip. I rose, draping the whip in a loose coil to dry on a nearby hook and rinsing my hands in a basin. "If it takes so long that her voice and groin grow raw from the begging, so be it."

I had taken Khloe as a patron some weeks ago, for very good reason. She was an escapist and lacking in a great many things, such as the ability to think before acting, but most of all, she lacked patience and discipline. Khloe was rash and self-absorbed, a hedonist who sought pleasure by any means. Careful observation had taught me that more often than not, she used drugs and alcohol to find that pleasure. She had sought me out at the Countess's little establishment for one reason alone: sexual gratification.

She'd stalked and begged and pleaded with me to play with her. Little did she know, as I bid her kneel on the rough stone floor of my dungeon, she would never come to my bed.

Lenorre, Countess vampire of Oklahoma, had forbidden it. Though I am a Prime and a force to be reckoned with, Lenorre is my Countess, and as a Domina employed by her, her word is my law.

It did not trouble me. The rules were in place for a reason. One of those reasons was to protect my patrons.

I do not sleep with them. Ever. Though my particular abilities lie in the heat of desire, both projecting and receiving, they do not come to my bed. I am an Eros vampire. I crave sex like blood.

If, for some reason, a scene was to get out of hand, Zaphara played not only the dark and gorgeous threat, but guardswoman. She would step in if I needed her assistance, either with a patron or by giving me space to regain my own bearings.

Khloe was eating out of the palm of my hand. Not so difficult to do, considering it was merely a matter of recognizing her desire and impatience and turning it against her.

Zaphara did not understand, not truly. She found great pleasure in being present during a scene, but it was the pain and defiance she relished.

I found my pleasure in their longing, their craving, the kiss of lust and desire, in finding the terrible secrets and shadowy places within their hearts and in turning them inward to face it.

I did not teach them to submit. I taught them to conquer their own inner demons, to rise like the phoenix from the flames of their own perdition.

I bent them, drove them, rode them, until they were slack and weak but whole, until every facet shone, the diamond pulled from the rough.

My diamonds, some more deeply hidden than others.

I had not yet stripped Khloe of the armor of her ego, of her childish self, but I would.

Consider me a therapist of sorts…one that wields a different set of skills and tools.

Khloe had followed my orders, remaining abstinent and free of intoxicants for nearly two weeks. I had ridden her hard that first week, harder than I've ridden most patrons in the beginning. But Khloe had not come to me for a gentle swing; the beast of self-destruction propelled her more fiercely than that.

Deep within her, she craved to be remade beneath the lash, baptized in desire.

I buried a hand in her brown hair, jerking her head back, exposing the long line of her pale neck. Her arms stretched high above her head, pulling tight on the small hook secured at the top of the wooden post. The drum beneath her skin tempted me with its sweet honeyed promise.

I would not be lured.

"Shall I allow you to destroy yourself or shall I destroy you, Khloe?"

Khloe, lost in sub-space, whimpered her response. The marks on her back from the whip earlier were still red like angry mouths. I kissed the milky skin of her neck and she flinched, then whispered, "Please," again.

I laughed, her body responding as if I'd touched her more intimately, though I had not. The energy between us crackled, though she was human and would not understand it. My belly grew warm. The blood in my veins began singing a soft tune.

"Not yet," I whispered, releasing the clutch of her hair. "You're too rash, darling."

"Please," she said, "I want you to bite me."

I traced the line of her naked spine, trailing the tips of my fingers to the edge of the creamy lace undergarments she wore.

"I'm very aware of your desires, Khloe."

"I've been coming here for two weeks. I'm clean. I haven't touched anything, not a drink, not a drug, not a person. Please!"

I pressed the line of my body against hers, letting her feel the vinyl of my attire against her naked backside. I bent close, whispering into the curve of her shoulder, "You've yet to learn a measure of patience, my dear. The simple fact that you're still begging me signals as much."

Khloe shuddered again, the heat from her skin leaping a notch, the scent of her arousal permeating my senses. My lips did not touch her, but even so, I could taste her, sweet and salty on my tongue.

I stepped away, ignoring her whimper of protest. Zaphara stood statuesque, watching the scene while feigning her boredom.

I went to the toy chest, retrieving a metal-tipped flogger. Khloe had, at long last, fallen silent.

Blindfolded, she did not see me. Mortal or no, I knew she could feel my presence behind her. She turned her head as much as her bound position would allow. The muscles in her back jumped with anticipation.

I waited, waited until the tension no longer strung her body tight, waited until she rested her cheek against the wooden post.

And then I whipped her, until her throat was raw from the screaming, until her skin broke under my lash, crying crimson tears.

I went to her when I was done, thirty lashes, no more, no less. I did not think she could handle any more. Tears stained her cheeks, soaking into the material of the blindfold, smelling of salt water and the perfume of her flesh.

My groin throbbed with need. The double-edged sword of my power cut us both. I discarded the flogger and knelt. Khloe was petite and her stature made it no trouble sliding my hands up the sides of her body. I kissed the backs of her thighs, shuddering, clawing her lightly.

Khloe groaned, arching her rear in an offering I would not take.

I pressed my mouth against her skin, catching the droplet of her blood on my tongue, shutting my eyes and salving her wounds.

I cleaned the blood from her back and rose, that vermillion gift coating my mouth like velvet.

"Zaphara, take her down and escort her out."

Before I stepped into the room in the back, a quiet place for me to regain my bearings, I witnessed Khloe's body go slack when Zaphara took her down. Khloe's head swung forward, too weak to protest.

❖

The door to the small sitting room opened quietly. "You need to feed," Zaphara said. I reclined on the couch, watching as she shut the door behind her.

Fortunately, Lenorre had seen to it that nearly all of the rooms within the club were soundproof, most especially the dungeon. It was not solely a measure to keep from alarming guests if I had a screaming patron, but to give the younger vampires a place where they could regain their bearings if the smell of sex, sweat, and pumping blood became too overwhelming.

The last place a hungry young vampire needed to be was in the middle of hot grinding bodies, thrusting and thrumming with life.

"I'll be well in a moment, Zaphara."

"You pushed yourself too far, Eris."

"I decide when and when I have not pushed myself too far, Zaphara."

"Why don't you just enchant her to stop and obey?"

I could have, of course. I could have reached into her mind and bent her to my will, but Zaphara did not understand my process.

"Enchanting Khloe would be no better than drugging her, Zaphara. She has to do this on her own. I'm merely helping her to find the tools within herself to do it."

Zaphara's expression turned disbelieving. "And you hope to accomplish that by driving her mad with desire?"

"I hope to accomplish that by teaching her to resist her desire."

The Daione Maithe tilted her head like a crow. "Still," she said, "your energy is low. Why did you not feed off her lust?"

"She is too weak, still. Surely," I said, "if you can read my energy so well, you can read that of the humans. She's abused her body with years of drug use and promiscuity. I'll tear greater holes in her auric field."

"Then," she said, "I'll fetch Davina."

I shook my head. "No, Zaphara. Davina is working the counter," I said, remembering the bandage she'd nigh been flaunting behind the collar of her shirt when I'd come in for the night. "She's a junkie, I've no interest to add my marks to the ones she's already collecting."

Zaphara considered me. "I was not aware that you were not feeding from one of the employee donors."

"Not unless I must. I am a *prime*, Zaphara. Most of us do not sully ourselves with the likes of bite-junkies."

"You're being stubborn, Eris."

I smiled, knowing it was not entirely friendly. "A Domina's prerogative."

Zaphara stepped forward, and the threat in her body language encouraged me to raise my brows.

"Tread lightly, Zaphara. Just because you are the Countess's pet does not mean you have any sway over me."

"And if I told you, you have sway over me?"

I was slightly surprised by her words. My heart slowed to a murmur in reaction before quieting completely. I hadn't meant to trigger such a response, but at times, it was uncontrollable. Every vampire has the ability to stop the beating of their heart, to stop the need for breath, it is a predatory instinct, but in that moment, it was a reaction bred from years of serving a Countess who perceived any emotional response as weakness.

I drew in a breath, forcing my heart to beat again.

I was little better than Khloe when Lenorre and I had met, but it was not drugs that I had been addicted to—it was power, the sharp-tipped steel of an Eros's power. For years, I lived blindly, believing that Anastasia, my maker, was the only one who could slake my hunger. To this day, I do not know how Lenorre managed to sweet-talk Anastasia into releasing me. Lenorre brought me with her when she came to claim territory in Oklahoma City. I had always had great control, something Anastasia liked about me. It made it all the sweeter for her to break me and force me to lose control.

Though an Eros vampire is a creature of lust and desire, Ana had taught me the darker shades of my abilities.

Leaving her was like waking from a long nightmare. Given my sins of the past, one might my think chosen profession strange. Silly as it may sound, using my talents for the better has become a repentance of sorts. When I approached Lenorre and explained my predicament to her, that I must feed off sexual energy and that this was the way I wanted to do it, she had not questioned, only told me to prove myself and she would allow it.

I am no fool now; as I sought to aid my clients, so Lenorre had sought to aid me, to give me a better existence.

"Eris?"

"Yes, Zaphara?"

"You haven't been listening to me, have you?"

I met her amethyst gaze, finding a dark amusement in it. "No. I stopped listening when you mocked me."

"I am not mocking you, lady."

"Zaphara, please, I know mockery when I hear it."

"Stop listening with your ears and looking with your eyes, vampire."

"What is that supposed to mean?"

"Look at me." She spread her arms out away from her body. "Listen to me. If you don't, I swear by the Gods, I'll never make this offer again."

"What exactly are you offering?"

She unbuttoned her trench, letting it fall neglected to the floor. "To give you what you need."

I didn't reach out to her with power, I flung it at her like a lash, sharp, pricking, stinging...

I knew intimately how it felt to be on the receiving end of that lash. Anastasia had also been an Eros.

Zaphara flinched, but gave no further indication that she had felt it.

"You've been playing too long with your toys, Eris," she said, her voice dark and sultry. "When was the last time you truly bedded someone? When was the last time you felt skin and sex through more than a lash?"

I laughed. "If you're trying to seduce me, Zaphara, it takes more than honeyed words and the promise of your sweet faerie flesh."

She reached out, catching my wrists. "Stop taunting me with your power and look through its lens."

The moment her skin touched mine, I felt *her*, sensed her, her desires mingling with mine like waves turning together, nearly overwhelming in their immensity. It took a great effort to break their hold, to separate her *wants* from mine.

My voice was breathy. "How long have you been celibate, Zaphara?"

"Years," she said.

"Lenorre," I said, trying to articulate my thoughts past the metaphysical weight of her unspoken yearning.

"I am loyal to Lenorre," she said, "but I am not her lover. Besides, you know as well as I she has her sights on another."

"The preternatural investigator," I said, remembering. Zaphara had been spying on the wolf-woman for weeks. Even those of us close to Lenorre were not certain what she wanted with her. "I suspect she'll request her aid in finding Rosalin's brother, if she hasn't staged the entire thing as a ploy to get close to...?" For the death of me, I couldn't remember the young woman's name.

"Kassandra," Zaphara said. "The werewolf's name is Kassandra. It is an opportunity, not a ploy. Lenorre seems to see something in her, aside from the mark she bears."

"Mmm, either that or she has something in mind that she wants to put in her," I mused.

"Lenorre is not as shallow as that."

"Too true," I said. "What about you, Zaphara? Why choose me to break your fast? I'd pegged you as a dominant, not a submissive, and you know I don't bed full-blown dominants."

"I like the challenge," she said, lowering her head as if to kiss me. "You thrill me."

"You'll not dominate me, Zaphara."

She released me. "I am relying on that."

I rose and she moved with me, like night and shadow. I pushed her back against the wall and pinned her with the line of my body.

"You'd be a positive feast, my dear, having fasted so long," I whispered against her neck, finding myself surprised by my own desire. She was warm, so warm, more full of life than any human I'd ever met. Her energy was like a well, so deep. How long would it take for the stone of my power to hit the bottom?

"Is that a yes, Eris?"

Never in a thousand years would I have ever expected this to be happening, for Zaphara to be offering herself to me. Though I had known desire played in her, I'd never realized in which direction that desire had been directed during a scene.

"It's not just pain and defiance for you," I murmured, moving back to the couch. "I knew you enjoyed yourself, Zaphara, but you're harder to read than most. I thought you envied my position."

"No," she said, "I envy your victims."

I wasn't sure what she wanted. Zaphara kept her shields tight, tight enough that it would have taken brute force and a battle of wills just to read her.

"What do you want, Zaphara?"

She smiled, and this time, it was purely predatory. "I want you to be strong enough to handle me."

I sat down, watching her. After a moment, I said, "Take off your shirt. I want to see that moon-kissed faerie skin in the light."

"Take off yours," she said.

"So, this is an arrangement of 'I'll show you mine if you show me yours'?"

"I come to you as an equal. Take it or leave it, Eris."

"If you get what you want, Zaphara, then it is only fair that I receive what I desire in turn."

"What do you desire?"

"When I make a request, don't argue with me."

She considered me for a long moment, and then nodded once, sharply. "Done."

I raised the curls of my hair, turning at the hips. "Unzip my bodice, Zaphara."

She obliged without arguing, freeing my torso of the vinyl bodice, dragging it down my arms and tossing it aside. I had to bite my tongue on a word of praise, knowing full well she would not have taken kindly to it.

I reclined, catching her hands in mine and guiding her long pale fingers to my breasts.

Zaphara touched me for the first time with a look of something close to hurt in her, not at all like she was enjoying herself.

I cupped her face in my hand, feeling the sharp slant of her cheekbone. "What is wrong, Zaphara? Why are you shutting me out?"

"I'm afraid."

"Of what?"

"Myself."

"Oh, Zaphara," I brought our faces close, "then let me show you that there is nothing for you to be afraid of."

"Are you so certain of that, Eris?" Her expression was menacing, but it wasn't the first time I'd seen anger and arrogance as a mask.

"Remove your clothes," I said, "and I will show you."

As she had agreed, she did not argue. She rose on her long legs and stood like a queen, cold, regal, untouchable...

But I would touch her. I would break the shell encasing her.

Sometimes, the harder the armor, the more tender one must make one's touch to peel it away.

I went to her and we were close enough in height that the kiss was not awkward. Zaphara's mouth tasted of warm pomegranates and wine.

Her nipples stiffened against my breasts, the metal of her piercings nearly as cold as my own skin.

I lowered my gaze. "Well, well, well," I said, "obviously, you like a bit of pain."

"Some," she replied, her eyes bright like gems.

I ran a hand down her lean body, reaching between her legs. "Mortals would weep for you, my dear."

She gasped when I touched her, placing a hand on my shoulder. I explored her slowly, tracing the folds of her with nothing more than a fingertip.

I whispered against her mouth, "What do you want?"

"You."

I took her hand, guiding her to the couch. Zaphara sat, allowing me to press her shoulders back until she reclined at ease. I raised my black skirt, gathering it in fistfuls and arranging the billowing material to pool outward like a flower around my legs. I knelt, pushing her legs open wide until every glorious silken fold of her was exposed.

Gently, I pressed my lips against the apex of her mound, sucking lightly where the most sensitive skin of her gathered and knotted. The muscles in her thighs tightened in response and I raised my eyes.

That awful wounded expression had vanished, replaced by a familiar dark hunger and fervent need. Her eyes shone like amethysts in moonlight.

Zaphara licked her full lips. "I beg of you," she whispered.

"Mmm," I murmured, bowing my head again, "since you're begging."

I scored her with my tongue, piercing the well of her with it, lapping at the honeyed dew that glistened there. Zaphara began to writhe, ever so slightly. I drew her clitoris into my mouth, grazing her skin with my fangs. Her hips jerked upward and a cry fell from her.

Yes, that was what she wanted.

Anastasia had taught me how to be cruel, how to break the heart, mind, and body simultaneously. For so long a time, too long a time, I'd walked beneath the cloak of her nightmare. I had lost myself, once, lost myself in power, in Anastasia's touch.

It made me all the more careful with my patrons, knowing intimately what my power could do to them.

Zaphara's hips bucked against my face and I surrendered my mouth to her, coaxing Eros cries from her lips.

"Eris," she moaned, "Eris, let go."

Equals. Were we, really? If I released complete control, would Zaphara make it unscathed? Would I?

"Eris," her voice was drawn tight, indicating she was close to release, "now, curse you! Let go!"

I did as asked, throwing my hands off the reins of power, releasing every wall and bar that had held it locked tight within me.

Zaphara came, thrusting her power and energy into me so fast and hard that I clawed at the cushions to keep myself upright, to keep my mouth against her.

The heat of her filled me like a soft sunset. I could taste warm honey and pomegranates upon my tongue. Our powers met like the crashing of firestorms. It knocked the breath from me, made me tear my mouth from her mound and cry out in ecstasy. Then it seized us both. Zaphara gripped my hair, bringing my mouth to hers. We became heat, flesh, passion, and senses, spilling back on the couch in a mess of limbs and fingers. Every touch, every brush, every stroke made my skin burn with a heat that was nearly painful.

My body screamed for more, for a thousand hands, a thousand mouths, a thousand greedy fingers. My darkness, a void of unquenchable yearning, a beast never satisfied.

Zaphara stripped me of my skirt, flashes of reality breaking through. Her fingers found me, pierced me, filling me to the core.

More.

Instinct drove me as I opened my mouth, sinking fangs into whatever bit of flesh was closest to my face.

Her blood spilled into my mouth like divine ambrosia. I sealed my lips over the wound, unsheathing fangs and drinking her sweet, sweet faerie wine.

The orgasm rushed through me. When it was done, Zaphara collapsed on top of me. Her body nestled between my thighs; her long hair with its purple highlights glistened like a veil of dark water over my skin.

Somewhere in the midst of our chaotic lovemaking, I must've torn loose the binding that had held it.

I buried my hands in all that silk, bringing her mouth to mine and kissing her lightly.

"How do you feel?" I murmured.

"Spent," she said.

I raised my brows, dragging my nails lightly across the slope of her rear until she shivered. "Is that a compliment coming from one of the Daione Maithe or are my ears playing tricks on me?"

Zaphara offered simply, "It was," and then stood to pull on her clothes. I watched her in silence. She pulled her long-sleeved black shirt down, tucking it into her dark jeans.

"You are a mystery, Zaphara."

She smiled, a dark curling of lips, and said, "My prerogative."

I laughed and rose, stretching, feeling the aftermath of the energy crackling in my limbs. "As you wish," I said, setting about retrieving my discarded attire and dressing.

If I had thought I'd glean more from Zaphara by bedding her, I'd been mistaken. The Daione Maithe was careful, too expertly guarded.

Perhaps, in time, she would come to trust me, to reveal more of herself to me.

I caught her gaze while she held the door open, waiting to escort me out.

Then again, perhaps she did trust me. Perhaps she had revealed as much of herself as she ever would.

We made it to the hallway that led to the main ballroom area of the club. Zaphara halted before diving into the throng of dancers. Her eyes lifted toward the second floor lining the dance room.

Lenorre stood at the top of the stairs, the train of her dress draped loosely over one arm. Her attention was fixed on some happening near the double doors that spilled into the club's lobby. The curls of her ebony hair were secured by a clasp of diamonds and amethysts, catching and reflecting the throbbing light, making the jewels glitter like stars. Lenorre glided down the steps, disappearing effortlessly into the throng.

Zaphara nodded lightly toward the doors, her attention pinned on a petite woman huddling against the wall.

"The wolf Lenorre has been watching," Zaphara said, her voice reaching my ears despite the pounding music.

I focused my senses, trying to tune in to that part of the club. They exchanged words that were washed away by the flood of music.

I managed to catch Lenorre saying, "*Kassandra Lyall*," before the music drowned them both out again. We may not have known what exactly Lenorre wanted with the woman, but I knew desire when I saw it. Lenorre was proficient at guarding her facial expressions and body language. I needed neither as an indicator. The one thing Lenorre could not hide was the intensity in her gaze when she locked eyes with the woman. And though the woman fought both her beast and herself, there too was a responding intensity in her.

The length of white in the woman's black hair stood out starkly. No doubt the humans believed it to be the by-product of something intentional, but Zaphara and I, like Lenorre, knew what it meant.

It was the mark of the woman's beast, the snowy fur of the wolf hidden within. Even across the distance, I could sense the energy of her beast like a heavy magnet.

"And so their dance begins," I said.

"Lenorre will seek her aid tonight," Zaphara responded almost idly.

"You've really no idea what has happened to Rosalin's brother?"

"None," she said. "Though Lenorre has her suspicions."

"Ah," I said, realizing, "but matters of the wolves stay with the wolves."

Lenorre, being Countess, presided over the preternatural community as a whole, but her reach only extended so far. Who better to infiltrate the Blackthorne Pack that Beta werewolf Rosalin Walker belonged to than another wolf? Lenorre's spies within the city could only penetrate and gain so much.

"Clever," I said, smiling in amusement. "But there's definitely more to it than that."

"What Lenorre does is her business," she said, finding a break in the crowd and leading us through to the rear exit.

So it was. Regardless, I found myself curious to know what exactly Lenorre was about.

"Eris," Zaphara prompted me.

"Yes, Zaphara?"

"What happened earlier," she said when we stepped out into the cool night.

"Worry not, Zaphara. I've no trouble keeping secrets if that's what you're requesting."

"I don't want things to become complicated."

"Oh, my dear," I said with a smile, "I assure you, they're not."

Blood Moon
Yolanda Wallace

My name is Alexandra Whitney. My friends call me Alex. My enemies call me much worse. Unfortunately, my enemies outnumber my friends. I'm a vampire hunter. If you think vampires are limited to the confines of cable TV shows, thick YA novels, and old black-and-white movies starring Bela Lugosi or Christopher Lee, think again. They walk among us. And there are more of them than you think.

Before I go any further, I need to get a few things off my chest.

First of all, those of us who do what I do get a little annoyed when people mention the B words. The Bs, in this case, being Bella and Buffy. I'm not even going to discuss Bella Swan or her (lack of) taste in men—I *so* would have picked Jacob over Edward, and I don't like werewolves any more than I do vampires. Both have control issues I'd prefer not to deal with. As for Buffy Summers, she was just a character on a TV show. Okay, a less than memorable movie first, then a TV show. A surprisingly good TV show, but a TV show nevertheless. In other words, Buffy wasn't real. I am.

I wouldn't put a stake in Sarah Michelle Gellar's heart for eating crackers in bed, but the diminutive actress isn't the first person I think of when I'm searching my brain pan for someone to have my back in a fight. And when I'm kicking vampire ass, I don't take time to compose cutesy nicknames for the villain o' the week. Glory? The Master? The Trio? Please. That's what writers are for.

Second, I am a hunter, not a slayer. A slayer sounds like someone who lies in wait. I don't like waiting. I'm a woman of action. I don't sit around twiddling my thumbs until the undead return to their lair, toss their keys on the counter, pour a warm glass of type O, put their feet on the coffee table, and say, "Here I am. Come and get me." My approach is completely different. I track them down and eradicate them by any means necessary. If that means leaving the environs of fictional Sunnydale or, in my case, a very real, a very hot, and a very humid Savannah, so be it.

And finally, fictional characters or not, I could never do what Bella and Buffy did. There is no way I would ever allow myself to fall in love with a vampire, no matter how brightly she glitters in the sunshine or how much product she uses on her hair. (Two things. Point one: For the last time, vampires *don't* glitter. They're not freaking pixies covered in sparkle dust. They're cold-blooded killers. Killers do *not* glitter. Point two: For me, the whole Angel or Spike debate is easy to solve. I'd stake them both.) When it comes to vampires, I think of the bloodsucking leeches as prey, not potential bedmates. I'm not here to suck face with them. I'm here to send them to hell. I'm not simply good at what I do. I'm the best. This is not a game for me. It's a way of life. And death.

Tonight is Halloween. I've been invited to a get-together at a friend's house, but I'm not going to be able to make it. Mia's going to love hearing that. She already complains that I don't get out often enough. "Your twat's going to dry up, turn to sawdust, and blow away if you don't use it once in a while, Alex," she tells me every other day.

It's kind of hard to get laid when I'm patrolling the streets from dusk to dawn seven days a week, but that's not the kind of information I can share with friends. Not if I want them to stay alive—or if I want to keep them as friends.

Being a hunter is a lonely existence. Like vampires, we're solitary creatures. My fellow hunters and I are each other's family. As dysfunctional as we are, though, we can't be counted on to remember birthdays or holidays. Oh, yeah. Just like a family.

My latest refusal to get in touch with my inner party animal will surely add fuel to Mia's fire. Not that she needs much kindling. She's enough of a firecracker as it is. She's the life of every party, whether she's throwing it (like this one) or arriving fashionably late (like all the others). I'm not much of a social butterfly, so I will readily admit that some of my other reasons for turning down her invitations were frivolous at best. But not this time. Aside from St. Patrick's Day, the annual three-day bacchanalia that takes place in town each spring, Halloween is my busiest night of the year, when it's even harder to tell the good guys from the bad ones.

The full moon isn't going to help. Humans are bad enough on most days. When the moon is full, their quirks are magnified tenfold. What do you think happens to preternatural creatures? It definitely doesn't make them any more of a pleasure to deal with, let me tell you. Now you see what I'm in for. On the other hand, tonight's blood moon—the first full moon after the harvest moon—is also known as the hunter's moon. Is this the day my kind takes back the night once and for all? Time will tell.

But that's later. Right now, it's still early. I should be resting for tonight—preparing my mind and body for what's to come—but, unlike vampires, I have a hard time sleeping when the sun's up. I have a hard time sleeping when the sun's down, too, but that's a story for another day.

I wrap a scarf around my neck to ward off the slight chill in the air. Cold weather won't take hold here in the Deep South for a couple of months yet, but I can tell summer is long gone.

My shoes crunch on fallen oak leaves as I walk through Johnson Square. Downtown Savannah is built around dozens of squares— Johnson, Ellis, Reynolds, Madison, Franklin, Wright, and Chippewa, to name a few. Tourists love them for both their moss-laden beauty and their historical significance. Locals hate them because, thanks to all the one-way streets, it takes us twice as long to get where we want to go. When I'm on foot, though, as I am now, I don't mind as much. Walking around, I have more time to enjoy the architectural wonders of this nearly three-hundred-year-old city than I do when I'm dodging drunks and shutterbugs in my car.

I head to my favorite park bench. No matter how long or how bad my Friday is, I spend every Saturday morning downtown. I come for two reasons: the people-watching and the free concert. The first reason is self-explanatory. The second requires a bit of background.

Franklin Helms plays his saxophone in the park five days a week. On Mondays, Wednesdays, and Fridays, he entertains the lunch crowd from the nearby office buildings. On the weekends, it's the tourists' turn. He doesn't ask for money or take requests, but if you happen to drop a bill or two into the open case next to his Stacy Adams–clad feet, he won't chase you down to shove it back into your pocket, either.

At first glance, he looks like a retired corporate executive. Instead, he's the best-dressed homeless man in America. His coarse salt-and-pepper hair is combed straight back, his beard is impeccably trimmed, his shoes are shined so bright they could blind you, and his tie is always knotted in a perfect Windsor. Every time I see him, he's decked out in a blazer, a crisp white cotton shirt, a corduroy vest, and cream-colored linen dress pants.

It took me a month of Saturdays (and a couple of Mondays) to realize that Franklin didn't wear a suit every day but the same suit. On closer inspection, I could see how thin the soles of his shoes were and how the nap of his tweed blazer had worn through in some places.

One day after he finished playing a medley of Johnny Mercer tunes, I asked him his story. He told me over a cup of coffee.

Instead of a retired corporate exec, he's a former life insurance salesman. The kind that peddled policies door-to-door and returned to collect the premiums each month. He and his wife (the former Helen Beasley from Alpharetta) were married for thirty-six years before she died suddenly. He was lost without her. He very quickly lost everything else. His car was first to go, the house he and Helen had lived in was last. In two short years, all that remained were his memories—and his dreams.

As a child, he wanted to become a musician when he grew up, but his father had refused to hear it, pushing him toward a career with less uncertainty. After Helen died, he used his last $20.00 to buy a dented saxophone, an unsteady music stand, and a sheaf of sheet music from a local pawnshop. With nothing but time on his hands and no one to share his time with, he painstakingly honed the talent he had let lie dormant for forty years.

His house on West Thirty-Eighth Street is now a distant memory. After changing hands a couple of times and doing a brief stint as a crack house, it currently belongs to a developer who plans to convert it into a Civil War–themed B&B. Ah, gentrification. Got to love it.

Franklin presently calls a much different place home. He lives in one of the dozens of tunnels burrowed under picturesque Forsyth Park.

It's a well-kept secret, but most of the historic district rests atop a series of subterranean passageways stretching from the northeast corner of Forsyth Park to Drayton Street. Unlike the crowded subway tunnels underneath New York City, however, few people are brave enough to live in an area once known as the Dead House. Franklin is one of the courageous few.

I found his "home" by accident. It wasn't like he invited me to his place for dinner. I was tracking a wily vamp who was trying to give me the slip when I suddenly found myself in Franklin's living room.

"I would offer you a drink," he said drolly just before I turned the vamp into a pile of ash, "but you seem to be a little busy right now."

Thanks to that unexpected encounter, Franklin's the only person who knows my secret. A secret he has sworn to take to the grave. Hopefully neither of us will be heading to our final resting places anytime soon.

I toss a ten-dollar bill into his sax case and place a large cup of French roast at his feet. He nods his thanks for both contributions. A large crowd has gathered to watch him play. Ever vigilant, I scan their faces for signs of trouble. No one seems squirrelly or out of place. I tell myself to relax, but downtime is a luxury I can't afford. Franklin sits next to me after he finishes his set.

"Sienna Jones is in town," he says under his breath.

I nearly choke on my triple espresso. "Are you sure?"

He nods. "I've seen her."

"How does she look?"

He looks at me strangely but doesn't ask why I want to know. My query makes me sound as if I'm asking about an old friend. Sienna's anything but. "Does she look like I described her to you or has she changed her appearance to throw me off her trail?"

Franklin blows on the steam rising from his coffee cup. "She looks like any other bloodsucker: dangerous."

Sienna Jones could best be called the one who got away. She's the oldest and most powerful vampire I've ever tracked. The only one I've had in my sights who has managed to survive the encounter.

I'm six foot one with the agility of a gymnast and the leg and upper body strength of a weightlifter. I've mastered every martial art from aikido to zipota. Even I wouldn't want to meet me in a dark alley.

The last time Sienna and I crossed paths, however, I was lucky to come away in one piece.

She was born five hundred years ago in a small village on what is now the Welsh coast. My records indicate she was turned shortly after her thirty-fifth birthday, when the bloom of youth had blossomed into full-fledged beauty. She immigrated to the New World four hundred years ago. She has lived in the Caribbean for most of that time. Her family owns sugar cane plantations in Cuba, Haiti, and the Dominican Republic, the bounty of which has made her a very rich woman.

She relocates every twenty years or so whenever the whole lack of aging thing raises a red flag or two for suspicious humans, but she always resurfaces—usually masquerading as some other member of her extended family. How many long-lost Joneses can there be? On second thought, don't answer that.

"If Sienna's in Savannah, she's out of her territory. What is she doing here?"

My grip tightens around the recycled paper cup in my hands. "Looking for me."

The last time we met was on her stomping grounds. Now she has made her way to mine.

"How does it feel?" she asked me on that fateful day. "How does it feel being the hunted instead of the hunter?"

I didn't have an answer for her then, but I'd better come up with one soon or my days above ground could be numbered.

❖

As night falls, I dress for battle. I pull my shoulder-length hair away from my face and tie it into a sleek ponytail. I pair my form-fitting black pants with a charcoal gray tank top. I strap a sharpened stake to each thigh, a silver dirk to each ankle. The supple leather of my calf-high boots matches my jacket. More sharp objects line the jacket's modified interior.

As a final touch, I drape a crucifix around my neck. The cross, a graduation present of sorts from the hunter who mentored me to be her replacement before she retired ten years ago, is for show. The weapons most definitely are not.

The holiday makes it possible for me to hide in plain sight. I leave my loft and join the hordes of people clogging Bay Street, the main thoroughfare through downtown. The sidewalks are overflowing. So are the bars.

My first stop is Churchill's, the English-style pub favored by local Anglophiles and British expats. I spot more Guy Fawkeses and Margaret Thatchers than I can shake a Pimm's at, but I don't see Sienna.

On River Street, where buskers, art galleries, and seafood restaurants compete for tourist dollars, I bump shoulders with a man wearing high heels, fishnet stockings, a curly black wig, black bikini briefs, and a silk teddy.

"Sorry," he says, wobbling precariously on the ancient cobblestones.

Why do straight guys always feel the need to dress in drag on Halloween? Some things should be left to the experts. "Nice outfit."

"Thanks." He runs a hand over his waxed chest and gym-toned pecs. "Going my way?"

"Not even close." The way I'm dressed, I must look like I'm on my way to a costume party instead of a confrontation. Mr. Rocky Horror probably thinks I'm trying to look like Lara Croft or a distaff Indiana Jones. If only he knew.

I walk into Kevin Barry's Irish Pub and order a Killian's. The bartender hands it to me in a plastic to-go cup. I sip the red-tinted lager as I walk the length of River Street. When I double back, my to-go cup is as empty as my search.

"If I were a vampire," I ask myself as I watch a breakdancing troupe defy the laws of gravity, "where would I go for an early evening snack?"

Then it hits me. I would go where the living and the dead rub elbows as if they were old friends. I take the elevator up to Bay Street, locate my car in the parking garage on Whitaker, and drive out to Bonaventure, the centuries-old cemetery that morphed into a tourist attraction after John Berendt mentioned it in *Midnight in the Garden of Good and Evil*, the true-crime novel that spawned a cottage industry. Even though Bonaventure's gates close to the public at five each afternoon, the place is going to be so busy tonight hungry vamps will have to line up for admission like the lunch crowd outside the Lady and Sons.

I park my car next to a tricked-out hearse from a local ghost tour and, like the many after-hours visitors that arrived before me, climb the jagged wrought iron fence. Once safely on the ground, I begin my patrol of the cemetery's 160 acres. Flickering candles spotlight couples having romantic picnics, rebellious teenagers competing to see how much trouble they can get into, and adventure seekers hoping to make contact with someone from the other side.

Savannah is widely considered to be one of the most haunted cities in America. Most of the ghost stories are romantic but harmless—tales of lost loves and mischievous spirits. The other yarns have a harder edge. Stories of drunken revelers kidnapped and forced into years of servitude at sea. Tales of the series of catacombs under Forsyth Park stacked top to bottom with skeletons. Rumors of vampires turning both the willing and the unsuspecting into human pincushions. Contrary to popular opinion, the rumors are true.

I head deeper into the cemetery, leaving the picnickers and the tourists behind. Concrete and marble monuments erected to honor the lives of the famous and the unknown surround me. I walk with my hands on my stakes. They offer me both safety and reassurance. This part of the cemetery is quiet. Too quiet. The lack of noise puts me on edge. Then a muffled scream shatters the silence.

Crouching low to make myself as small a target as possible, I move toward the sound. Two figures—one male, one female—are locked in hand-to-hand combat on an elaborately carved monument. The figure on top lifts his head and lunges toward the neck of the other. His sharp, pointed teeth practically glow in the dark.

The woman screams again. The man cries out.

Gripping a stake with both hands, I prepare to strike.

"God, Stanley," she gasps, gathering the scattered components of her Bride of Frankenstein costume, "it's never been this good before."

"I know." He spits out a pair of plastic vampire teeth as he fights to catch his breath. "We should play dress-up more often."

Shaking my head at the close call, I shrink back into the shadows and allow the lovers to continue their whispered conversation.

"Mia's right. If I mistake two people making love for a life-and-death struggle, I do need to get laid."

As soon as I let my guard down, Sienna comes hurtling out of the darkness. She's on me before I can react. I lose my grip on both stakes as we tumble through the dry leaves. My hands scrabble for the knives strapped to my boots. She reaches them first and tosses them aside. Then she tears off my leather jacket, leaving me defenseless.

Her lean body, as smooth and as cold as marble, presses mine into the dirt. She leans forward, the tendrils of her wavy black hair stroking my cheek. Her full lips curve into a smile. Her elongated canines glisten in the moonlight. Her dark eyes issue a challenge as they stare into mine.

"Are you looking for me?"

❖

The last time we met, I found myself in a similar position: at her mercy.

I'd tracked her in Punta Cana, the resort-heavy town on the Dominican Republic's east coast, after the hunter there called me for help.

"I have a vampire who walks in the daylight," Novius said, fear dripping from his voice.

He had reason to be afraid. A day walker is a rarity among creatures of the night—and a sign of how powerful Sienna had become. A vampire's greatest weakness had become her strength. How was that possible? And were there others like her?

"She has been living amongst us for years without incident," Novius said after I traveled to a land filled with white sand beaches and sunburned tourists. "A few months ago, bodies began to turn up. Dozens of people began to go missing."

"She has to be stopped," I said. "If she creates an army of vamps like her, they could take over the world. Every human in it would immediately be added to the endangered species list."

Novius volunteered to use himself as bait, giving me the honor of making the kill. We lured Sienna to a bustling free market in Bavaro.

"*Escúchame, señora*, please come into my shop for just one minute. I have T-shirts, photo albums. You would like some Cuban cigars? How about some Mama Juana?"

Ignoring the pleas of Dominican- and Haitian-accented merchants imploring me to buy some of their overpriced tchotchkes or a bottle of the local cure-all, I followed Novius and Sienna at a safe remove. Not safe enough. I lost sight of both after an especially aggressive shopkeeper pulled me aside to demonstrate how I could pull a gaudy oil painting off the frame and roll it up to fit in my luggage during the flight home.

"Real oil painting, not water. What's your best price?"

"Free."

Eschewing stealth, I ran through the curtained stalls like a bull in a china shop. I returned to the center of the market with no sign of Sienna or Novius. Then, like tonight, she was on me.

Moving faster than the human eye could see, she dragged me into an alley redolent of fresh urine and stale cigarettes. Like now, my weapons were useless against her. Instead of by force, she held me by will. I stood slack-jawed, hypnotized by her power—and her undeniable beauty.

"Where's Novius?" I asked when I finally found my voice.

Her left hand gripped my throat. Her right quickly disarmed me. "He is sleeping," she said with a cruel smile.

"As you should be. Isn't it past your bedtime? I could tuck you in if you like."

Her smile turned playful. But there was nothing mirthful about the pain her fingers inflicted as they dug into my throat. "How does it feel, Alexandra?" She lifted me off the ground with no effort whatsoever. I wrapped my legs around her waist in a futile attempt to ease the pressure on my neck. "How does it feel being the hunted instead of the hunter?"

"How do you know my name?" I rasped, expecting at any moment to hear the sound of my hyoid bone snapping in two. I clawed at her arm. The muscles felt like banded steel.

She slowly lowered me to the ground. "Because I have been tracking you much more successfully than you've been tracking me." Her accent was an intriguing blend of Welsh and Spanish. She leaned so close I could smell the almond-scented lotion on her porcelain skin. Even in the warm sunlight, her flesh was cool to the touch. Yet my body was on fire. "Leave me in peace, hunter. I am not the one you seek."

"Then tell me who is."

"Like you, I also count vampires among my enemies. But only a select few, not the entire race. Surely you don't expect me to betray one of my own. Rest assured justice will be served in this matter, but it will be served by my kind, not yours."

I shrugged. "It was worth a shot."

She studied my face as if she were committing it to memory. "You have proven yourself to be quite a worthy adversary, hunter." Her eyes flickered with an emotion I couldn't read. Her bright pink tongue licked the side of my neck. Her fangs grazed my skin. Gently pierced it. She leaned back to show me the red rubies of my blood resting on the tip of her tongue. Her tongue slowly receded into her mouth. Her eyes rolled back in their sockets as she tasted my essence. *"Deliciosa. Fresca. Caliente."*

Her words were a mockery of the hand-painted advertisement that adorned the adjacent wall. Instead of delicious, fresh, and cold like the Presidente beer being sold in the corner bar, my blood was delicious, fresh, and hot.

She released me. My hands flew to my neck. My throat felt raw inside and out. I took a deep breath of the thick, fetid air.

"Go now, hunter," she said, launching herself into the cloudless sky. Her voice lingered in my head long after she disappeared from view. "You are much too sexy to kill."

❖

She rends my shirt with a razor-sharp nail. She licks the valley between my breasts. Then she presses her face to my chest and inhales deeply.

"I can smell your fear, hunter. Are you afraid of me or how I make you feel?"

When she moves against me, I have to fight to keep my hips from returning the pressure. I counter her question with one of my own.

"What are you doing here?"

"I came for you. Try as I might, I can't deny the heat that passed between us when last we met." She licks her full lips. "I haven't felt such desire in centuries."

I offer a weak protest. "You...enthralled me."

She takes offense to my comment. Baring her fangs, she hisses her displeasure. "I did nothing of the kind. Such parlor tricks are limited to callow novitiates and lazy elders. I am neither callow nor lazy." Her voice softens. "What you felt...What *I* felt was real. I have searched for hundreds of years for someone like you."

"Someone sworn to kill you?"

She loosens her grip on my wrists. I flex my fingers as circulation slowly returns.

"Someone I can treat as my equal. Who knew I would find what I sought in a human?"

"Lucky me."

I free one of my hands. Grab a fistful of her lustrous black hair. Using the added leverage, I pull her off me and roll her onto her back. I drag my battered body to my knees and straddle her. Her eyes widen in surprise but she doesn't resist. She fixes her gaze on the cross around my neck. Contrary to the old wives' tale, the talisman of the faithful has no effect on her, adverse or otherwise. I slide a hand down her firm flank until I find her center. She undulates against my palm. Her nails dig into my thighs. A groan issues from her parted lips.

"You came for me?" I ask rhetorically. "What took you so long?"

Her fingers untie the leather cord around my ponytail and snake into my hair. She pulls me to her. Our mouths meet in a bruising kiss. Her teeth nip at my lower lip. Her tongue flicks at the twin drops of blood that form. I bare my neck. She puts her mouth on me but doesn't break the skin.

"Feed from me, vampire," I urge her. I can't remember ever wanting something—some*one*—so much. Who knew I would find what I sought in a vampire? "Make me yours."

She bites down. I gasp at the twin darts of pain. Pain quickly turns to pleasure. Spasms rack my body as her throat works. She swallows hungrily. Greedily. She soon withdraws, careful not to take too much. She holds me until my quivering muscles eventually relax and go limp. Then she regards me through eyes heavy-lidded with desire. *"Deliciosa."* She slowly, delicately licks the punctures on my neck. I can feel the wounds already starting to close. "You are exquisite, hunter."

"You're not so bad yourself." I draw a pale pink nipple into my mouth. Scrape it with my teeth. She hisses again. This time in approval.

She arches her back, offering herself to me. I want to take her. I want to feel her submit to me. But not here. Not like this. I cover her exposed flesh—so pallid it's almost luminous—and help her to her feet. "Let's go back to my place. I want to claim my prize in private."

"That's the best offer I've heard in four hundred years."

She lifts me into her arms. The full moon lights the way as we fly through the night sky. She locates my loft without asking me for directions.

"How did you know where I lived?"

"As I said, I have been tracking you for quite some time."

She lingers outside my door, waiting for me to invite her inside. I don't extend the invitation right away. First I toss my ruined tank top on the floor. Then I kick off my boots and shrug off my pants. I stand before her in nothing but my bra and boy-cut briefs.

"Do you like what you see?"

She murmurs in assent. "Very much." Her nostrils flare as if she's on the verge of losing control. "I'd love to see more."

I extend my hand. "Join me."

She takes my hand and steps across the threshold. In the living room, she lingers in front of my cache of weapons. Her long fingers caress a wood-handled mace with steel spikes. She lifts a cat-o'-nine-tails. When she flicks her wrist, the crack of the whip sounds like a rifle shot. "Someone's been a naughty girl."

"You haven't seen anything yet." I lead her to the bedroom, where I intend to show her just how naughty I can be.

I undress her with deliberate slowness. Why rush when we have all of eternity to be together?

Her body is amazing. Free of wrinkles or imperfections. She lies on the bed. Her hair fans across the pillow. The ebony tresses provide a stark contrast to the crisp white sheets. I kiss my way from her feet to her lips. Then I slowly lower myself onto her.

She holds my hair away from my face. *"Tan hermosa,"* she says in Spanish. "So beautiful. So beautiful and yet so deadly." She traces a finger over the battle scars that decorate my body like badges of honor. "I would much rather have you as a lover than an opponent."

"I could say the same."

I lower my head. Kiss the lips that whisper my name. I slip my hand under the pillow her head is resting on and wrap my fingers around the stake I keep hidden there. She stiffens when she sees it. Her hand covers mine, seeking to impede its steady progress.

"What's the matter, vampire?" I ask, continuing to slide the point of the stake across her skin. "Don't you trust me?"

Her eyes meet mine. Her hand falls away. "I trust you with my life."

I toss the stake across the room. It imbeds itself in the heart of the mannequin I use for target practice.

Sienna smiles. "Beautiful, deadly, and accurate."

I press my lips to her chest. How strange it is not to feel a heartbeat skip at my touch. I move lower. Her hips rise to meet my mouth. Her legs spread to accommodate my shoulders. I part her lips with my tongue.

"Yes, hunter," she sighs, her head lolling on the pillow. "Drink from me."

Her wish is my command.

When she comes, color infuses her skin. She looks almost human. The illusion is only temporary. The rosy blush in her cheeks soon fades, but my desire for her grows stronger.

She rolls me over. Her fingers slip inside me, penetrating all the way to my soul. It's my turn to submit.

"Abide with me, hunter. Be my consort."

"Yes, my queen."

Remember my earlier rant about not allowing myself to fall in love with a vampire? Let me amend that. I could never allow myself to fall in love with any vampire except Sienna Jones. She drove a stake through my heart the first time I laid eyes on her. Now she wants me to rule at her side.

Most of my fellow hunters won't approve of or support my decision to become her mate—after she turns me, some might pursue me as diligently as they would any other child of the night—but my mind was made up the day we confronted each other in that piss-stained alley in the Dominican Republic. All she had to do was ask the appropriate question. All she had to do was come for me. In more ways than one.

I'm not going to stop doing what I do after I become a vampire myself, but I will become more selective. Instead of staking every vampire I come across, I will seal the fates of only the unrepentant. Those who seek to kill for sport, not feed to survive.

Just as vampires cannot change their natures, I cannot change mine.

My name is Alex Whitney. I'm a vampire hunter. I always get my woman. This time, I get to keep her. Forever.

CONTRITION
MEL BOSSA

When she calls my name, I know who I am.

"Berenice," she says, and kisses the cleft of my throat.

But that's not my name.

Why can't I bring myself to correct her? Somehow, I know she's never been wrong about anything in her life. It's in her hands—the way they touch me.

She doesn't need to get my name right. I don't mind her calling me Magdalene, Athena, Isis…

"How much longer?" she asks me.

I don't know. I don't know when yesterday was, and tomorrow is only a gaping hole. I can't remember how I let her in—how did we get so deeply intertwined?

I always want to ask her name. Then she is with me, as she is now, and I realize she told me days ago.

I just can't remember what it is.

"How much longer?" she says again and again.

Why is she here? I should be with Aimee.

Where is Aimee? My Aimee.

I am thinking of her now.

Yes, Aimee, I am thinking of your eyes—the July sun cutting diamonds inside them.

I am thinking of when we met. I loved you before you even spoke. You looked at me from across the tables—it was a crowded restaurant, an awful steakhouse smelling of charred meat, Thursday morning, closing time, thirsty, hungry, elated from a night of dancing—and you stared at me without blinking, without playing. You stared until I looked away.

I'd never even thought of looking away, but you made me. You owned me from the start.

Did we know how to fall in love? We never really jumped, now did we? No, we were shoved in, both of us together. We thought we were holding hands on the way down, but they were bound, Aimee.

We couldn't have let go if we'd tried.

We walked out of the restaurant and the sun was rising.

It was like walking out of a dungeon.

Where did we go that night? My place? Yours? Does it really matter? I knew we'd make love wherever our bodies landed from this fall. Your bed or mine. It was a fantastic feeling, wasn't it? To know for certain, yes without a doubt, that the body, face, lips, skin you crave to touch are yours. There will be no resistance, no games. I walked side by side with you and I knew you'd let me burn all night. You wouldn't put me out with stories of old spiteful lovers or broken childhood dreams.

There was no need for conversation, Aimee. No, that's not it: There was *no way* for conversation. We'd been hit in the throat by love's five knuckles. Recognition. Intuition. Physical Impulse. Scent.

What is the last knuckle of love?

I don't know, Aimee. I can't remember.

It comes and goes, your face.

"Sophia," the other woman calls me now.

What does she want? I wait, but she never answers me. Who is she? How did I end up in her arms? This is the longest night of all nights. I don't know how to tell her I need to leave. But when morning comes, I'll know what to do about her. I'll get rid of her, Aimee, I promise. And I'll find you—we'll fix this. We'll put the thing back together. Our thing.

The thing that feeds the world.

"Murderer," she whispers close to my ear without breath.

This word seems to excite her. She is slipping her hand between my thighs and I swell under the touch.

"Killer," she moans.

This is her game? Have we played it before? What does she expect of me?

Aimee, we never needed to role-play in bed, did we? No, we watched TV, turned out the light, and all you ever needed to do to kick-start my heart was kiss my mouth and pull my hand into your worn-out panties.

It could have been like that for eighty-five years between us and it would have been all right. You didn't care if we never tried anything. You didn't care if we never used our imaginations.

We didn't need to. We always came. And with every day we loved each other, we came harder.

It's true, don't tell me it isn't. You'd be lying if you did.

"Berenice," she pesters me now. I feel her face—hand?—brushing my inner thigh. Why doesn't she just go down on me already?

"Taker of life," she says, softly. And I raise my hips to her mouth.

She moves away from me. Where is she going? I can't see anything tonight. Not even my window. I'm sealed into the black—part of it. I wait for her to come back, my body pulsing under the cover of darkness. I want to touch myself while she's gone, just a little—I need to relieve this ache, but I am fighting off sleep, or maybe I am already touching myself and numb.

Or…I've already come and I am sleeping.

When you got that job at the market, that's when it all went to the pits, no? Why did you have to fall into that net? Those girls—those pallid girls in their overalls smelling of compost—they wanted to be around you, but they never understood you. They lured you into their inner circle, offering you up to their Vegan Gods, celebrating your beauty, but all the while, they diminished it day by day. You stopped wearing perfume. You didn't want to dye your hair that lovely gold anymore. You didn't flush the toilet unless you shat.

You were so eager to be part of something, and it didn't matter what it was. So I let you. I let you set up your castle of cards knowing the hurricane was coming.

All weekend, you left me. And you went to stand behind a table of vegetables. No one ever sold so many beets, corn, sweet peas, before you. It's your smile, Aimee; it convinces us cynics to believe in beauty again.

I'd call you every hour, but you never answered your phone, now did you? You *couldn't*, you said. You had to be available and approachable. Do you know how much that angered me? How much

I suffered all those weekend days? Pretending to work on my thesis, drinking six cups of coffee a day, barely eating, jumping when the phone rang, but it was never you. Never you. And you had the audacity to leave the market with those cucumber witches to go get drunk every Saturday night?

Fuck you, Aimee. And fuck them too.

I'm here tonight because I want to be. I want this woman. You're not here. You're not here and I don't care.

"Come with me." She's back now. She's close to me again.

I want to ask where she went, but I'm sure she's already told me.

"You come with me now," she says again. And her voice is raw. What time is it? How long have we been playing this game? I can't break free from her. Not tonight.

You slept with all of them, didn't you? Yes, Aimee, you did. I talked too much and I read too much philosophy. You didn't need John Dewey's Pragmatism—you needed passion!

You screamed out all of your dissatisfaction to me one afternoon. I didn't see it coming. I stood there with the wooden spoon in my hand, the sauce dripping from it, and looked at you. You hated me looking at you. You hid your face inside your hands and I thought of the elephant man—just like him, you were diseased and these growing deformities on your soul were not your fault.

You threw things at me. You spat and cried. I thought you were ashamed of neglecting me and I played to your remorse like a child plays to his mother's tears after he's been whipped by her hand.

I held you and told you you were perfect. I believed it.

What did it feel like? To lie to me? To betray me? To snuggle up against me, red-nosed, bleary-eyed, pitiful, *loved*, knowing you were sneaking behind my back, making a fool of me? That night, that very night we had our final confrontation, you kissed me and fled out the door. You wanted to take a bike ride along the water to clear your head.

Things felt right. Things felt so right.

I sat back, leaned my head against the couch, and pulled my T-shirt up to my nose. It smelled like you. Your new earthy smell, and I thought of soil—what can come of it. I smiled for the first time in two months. We were going to be all right again. We'd reached another level. You'd matured. You'd understood I was the only sane thing left for you.

Yes, Aimee, I felt satisfied and vindicated. Your tears had soothed my worries.

And while I walked around the apartment—our apartment, our home—seeing every object with new eyes, feeling grounded, capable, efficient, you'd been in the arms of another woman.

As I lifted the newspaper in search of my eyeglasses, the truth of you hit me like a bullet through the cerebral cortex. You were out cheating! Oh, at first I dispelled the thought as one dispels the first drop of rain on the last day of vacation.

No, no, I told myself, you were out riding your bike along the water, and I clung to that idea. I clung to my sanity.

But I knew then. It was only that, an *idea*.

And ideas are hardly ever true.

"Come," she beckons me now, reminding me of her presence, reminding me that she never leaves. And I want to come, leave or stay. Her hands move along my body and I want to reach out, but I can't—or she won't let me. She is rolling onto me, pressing the length of her along my legs, womb, heart. I'm bathed in darkness, but her face is near mine, and if I want to, only if I want to, she'll flash her face for me to see.

But I don't want to see it. Oh God no. Don't let me see her face. I think I know what it looks like. I think I've seen it as a child. She was in my room once.

"Do you feel the hate in me?" she moans into my neck. There is a putrid scent to her breath and I want to recoil. I want to go back to where this started, but how can I bend back to a place that is out of reach?

Do you know the rage I felt that night? My body hardened like old clay around my soul. I clutched the newspaper inside my hand, hoping to strangle the malevolent passion that threatened to overcome my mind.

Then, as if all of the ocean's currents had come to a stop under the moon—as if they now refused to obey her command, I felt my own blood turn quiet and my pulse decelerate. I would find you.

I knew where you were. You were with Cass. That little tomboy heartthrob—Ms. Youth, Swagger, and Jest. She'd always left the room when I entered. She'd always turned her eyes from me.

I grabbed my keys and quietly left our home. Outside, it was twilight and I looked up to the blue stars, the fat sister moon, and drove through our neighbourhood, slowly, without angst or emotion. When I found you, I'd say, "You lied, bitch." And then I would leave, drive under the blue stars again, the sister moon, without angst or emotion.

It would be so.

I would have my vengeance through the look on your face.

I climbed Cass's stairs, knocked on the front door, waited, and turned the knob. The door swung open, showing me a darkly lit hallway and a light in the kitchen. I didn't skip a breath. I didn't skip a thought.

"Come now," she whispers, caressing my left breast. Under her touch, my heart is silent. How can it be silent? "You've chosen your path," she says. And there is a threat in her voice.

Where am I, Aimee? Where are you?

I walked into Cass's apartment, following the sound of your whispers. I came to the bedroom doorway and looked into the dim room. A candle lit your body. You were beautiful.

"Aimee?"

You didn't try to cover yourself.

Cass jumped out of bed, her small breasts heaving.

"Easy now," she breathed, looking not at me, but at my hand. "You don't have to do this."

What did I do, Aimee? What did I do? I hadn't noticed I'd picked it up. I hadn't known it had been near me, on the passenger seat—I hadn't felt its weight in my hand, walking up the stairs to you.

I hadn't minded the cold steel feel of it under my fingers.

"You come with us, now." She is still with me. She will never let me forget that night. No, I don't want to go. I don't want to go there with her. She has the face of Midnight Tales.

No, I can't go with her.

I want you, Aimee. I want to go back to you.

"You cannot go back to what you've torn apart."

Who is speaking to me? Aimee? Who is here with me?

"You blew her head off."

I open my eyes but there is nothing. There is nothing to see and nothing to hear, but her face, her voice. I can't be here. I can't leave like this.

I didn't know it was in my hand, Aimee. I'd been studying too hard.

Not eating enough. I didn't know what day it was anymore. Believe me, Aimee, please, oh God, please. Don't let her take me. Not like this.

"Think of her eyes—how they questioned everything she'd ever believed—as the bullet tore through her frontal lobe. Think of her last experience and you will know where you are."

I scream, but hear nothing.

I can't move, but I am moving. I am sliding across the sheets. No, no, they can't be sheets. The surface under my skin is smooth—polished. Aimee, please, tell her to stop.

"She is not here."

I am slipping now. There is nothing under me.

"But I am here."

Voices shout to the ends of the world.

"And I am Legion."

Oh God, oh please. Not like this. I beg you.

There are so many of her now.

I am burning.

Yes, but I alone, I am that burn.

Aimee, I know now.

Oh, Aimee, I know.

DEADLY GLAMOUR
L.L. RAAND

I'm a tracker. I spend most of my time chasing down renegade Sidhe who manage to seduce, bribe, or cajole the gatekeepers into letting them pass out of Faerie into the terra plane. My typical quarry isn't very bright or they wouldn't risk the Queen's wrath if caught—and I always catch them. Corralling them usually doesn't take long. I spend as little time as possible here, where I have to conceal my true self, even from the Others. Like most Sidhe, I don't support the Praetern exodus from the shadows that has made us all visible—and vulnerable. Besides, Weres, Vampires, and any of the human variations aren't nearly as satisfying as the Sidhe, or Fae as most of the world calls us, when it comes to matters of the flesh. I'd already been here longer than I wanted, but unfortunately, this mission was the most important in my long life, and if I wanted that life to continue, I needed to be successful. And quickly.

Just after midnight, I stood in a run-down parking lot that resembled an automotive junkyard, staring at a dilapidated one-story building with boarded-up windows, an unmarked door, and a roof that looked as if it might take flight with the next wind. Underneath my combat boots, the concrete surface was cracked and heaving, veined with clumps of scraggly weeds and crabgrass. If I didn't know this was Nocturne, one of the city's busiest and most notorious Vampire clubs, and if I hadn't tracked my quarry across worlds and through the back alleys of the seedier parts of Albany to this waterfront dive, I would have sworn the place was abandoned.

But I knew she was here. Jaelynn de Erinn, Crown Princess of the Seelie court and next in line to follow Queen Cecelia as ruler of all Faerie. Jael was the Queen's niece, the daughter of the Queen's brother

Karn, and as the matriarchal court was always ruled by a Queen and her consort, Jael was heir until Queen Cecelia had a daughter. I needed to return Jael to safety before anyone outside the Court realized she was missing—not only would her absence prove lethal to her Royal Guardians, led by my twin sister, but Jael was a virgin and would remain so by law until she ascended to the Throne of Thrones. If she was violated here on this plane, there would be war.

Wrapping my glamour around me, I changed my outward appearance to resemble a Were. My ability to control my outward appearance was something shared with all the Sidhe, but the speed with which I could assume a different shape and the duration I could maintain the illusion was part of my Changeling heritage and what made me so successful as a tracker. I could go anywhere and even another Sidhe would not be able to read through my glamour. The Princess would be glamoured, too, but whereas I could see through her illusion, she would not be able to see through mine.

Inside, the club was larger than most Vampire blood spots, and subtly more elegant. The ceiling lights, recessed behind exposed beams, reflected off the battered tin ceiling and provided just enough illumination for the predators to find their prey. Leather couches and sofas were scattered around the cavernous space in loose arrangements designed for group activity. Scaffolds and slings with nearby racks of whips and restraints were tucked into corners for those who wanted a physical warmup before their meal. A long, highly polished bar encompassed the far wall, fronted by leather-topped stools filled with humans and Weres waiting to host for the Vampire clientele.

The Vampire enforcers at the door studied me for a few seconds, recognizing I was a stranger. Unlike most Fae glamour, mine was more than an illusion projected to confound the observer. Mine was an actual physical change—I became what I envisioned, including sexually. Without glamour, I was female—with glamour, I could be either male or female. Tonight, I chose a female Were form, knowing Were females exercised total control over who they accepted as partners. I wasn't looking for sex. The Princess would undoubtedly be in Were form also, and she most definitely would be looking for sex—in any form. The enforcers let me pass and I made my way through the milling bodies toward the bar, taking advantage of the accepted voyeurism that was part of the club atmosphere to search for Jael. Although still early in the night, the feeding had already begun. I passed a female Were leaning against a column, a male Vampire kneeling between her legs. Her claw-tipped fingers, highlighted by a shaft of light from above, twisted convulsively in the long hair at the back of his neck in time with the orgasm that rippled along the surface of her naked thighs. Ahead of me, a partially nude human female curled in the lap of a female Vampire, her head thrown back, a tiny trickle of blood streaming down her throat as the Vampire fed. The human's eyes were open, but glazed as if sightless, her lips parted in a rictus of ecstasy, her hips undulating, rising and falling to the thrust of the elegant wrist between her legs.

I concentrated on the hosts serving two or three Vampires. Only the Weres, or a Fae masquerading as one, had the stamina to feed more than one host, although here and there a daring human lay stretched out like a sacrifice, Vampires feeding from neck and breast and groin. Jael would want to maximize her moments of freedom. Rumor had it she did not want the Crown, and her escape might be designed to destroy her acceptability as heir. The air was thick with the scent of blood and sex and vibrated with the sounds of pleasure.

I headed deeper into the room, scanning right and left for the Princess as I walked. Two bartenders worked behind the crowded bar, a large human male, clearly a blood servant as evidenced by the bite marks peppering his thick neck and bare torso, and a svelte brunette Vampire who moved like a song on the wind. I angled toward the Vampire and stopped abruptly when a body blocked my way.

"I haven't seen you here before," a female Vampire said softly, her eyes drifting down over my body, then slowly climbing back to my face.

"I haven't been here before," I said, having learned the truth is always the best disguise. "I'm not from around here."

She was young—at least she had been when she was turned—in her early twenties, cinnamon skinned with mahogany hair and deep green eyes. Those eyes sparked now with the red embers of a fully Risen Vampire, but her face retained a sweetness that made me think she hadn't been risen long. Her white silk shirt was open between her full breasts, her leather skirt short, accentuating the curve of her hips and ass. She was attractive. More than attractive. Compelling, made more so by her surprising air of delicacy. I was resistant to thrall, as were most Sidhe. The Fae and the terran Praetern lines had diverged when our ancestors took us to the Faerie lands, and we had never been primary prey for the Vampires. When we hosted for them it was always voluntary, and always for pleasure.

She moved closer, undoubtedly expecting her thrall to have an effect on me since she perceived me as Were. If I resisted, my disguise would be questioned. Her palm against my chest was cool and her lips were silvery pale. The crimson in her eyes spread, a fire raging on the verge of explosion. She was hungry, and her need quivered through me. I covered her hand with mine. "Just you."

Her breath was coming fast. Surprise flickered over her face and was quickly gone. "Are you new to this? Most Weres want multiple—"

"Not new. Selective."

She smiled. "Then I'm lucky."

She took my hand and I let her lead me along the bar and into the shadows. I searched as we walked. I still didn't see the Princess.

When we stopped, I leaned against the curved corner of the bar and spread my legs, pulling her in between my thighs. She was trembling. This wouldn't take long. I unbuttoned my shirt and slid her hand inside, molding her fingers to my breast. She gasped and, with a low groan, took my neck. The jolt of pleasure was not unexpected, but still shocking. She was young, but she was powerful. Someone very strong had turned her. I groaned as her full, firm breasts pressed against my chest and lightning shot through my blood. My head snapped back, my body jerked into orgasm, and I felt her writhing against me as her own release pulsed with the rhythm of her feeding. I didn't lose myself in her lust the way Weres and human hosts do, but I let the pleasure consume me until she pulled away. Shaking, tendrils of silken passion still curling through my core, I stroked her hair as she rested her forehead against my shoulder. When she finally stepped back, she studied me, a tiny frown between her arched brows. I could change my form, but I could not change my essence.

"Your blood has a flavor I've never tasted," she murmured. "Like the smell of springtime."

I stroked the arch of her cheek with my thumb. "And your bite is sweeter than any I've ever known."

She smiled. "What is your name?"

"Torren," I answered truthfully, and for some reason, I added, "and yours?"

"Daniela."

"Daniela," I murmured. "Beautiful."

She traced the line of my jaw with her fingertips. "I hope you come back again."

"If I do, I'll look for you," I said, kissing her palm. I wouldn't be back, and an unexpected wave of sadness coursed through me.

I released her hand and she drifted away. I moved back into the feeding throng, working my way toward the hallway at the opposite corner of the room. I found her halfway down, sandwiched between a male and a female Vampire, her eyes glittering with excitement and lust. Through her glamour I saw the flush of her skin and the racing pulse in her throat. They hadn't fed from her, but they would soon. The male's hand was inside her open shirt and she stroked the ridge of his cock through his pants. The female who knelt before her had pushed her diaphanous skirt up and was alternately licking and sucking her sex. I needed to stop them before one or both bit her, but I couldn't draw attention to her. The last thing I wanted was for her to drop her glamour and announce to everyone that the Fae Crown Princess was here unprotected.

I leaned against the opposite wall, letting them think I was only watching while I waited for an opening. Those around us were engaged in their own pursuit of pleasure, and paid us no attention. The Princess stared into my eyes, her full lips curving into an inviting smile. I smiled back, a fleeting image of the Vampire who had just fed from me racing through my mind. Another Vampire appeared out of the shadows, a gaunt, dark-haired male who said something to those with the Princess. They drew back rapidly and disappeared. Something about him alerted all my senses. He exuded power, and he was ancient. And for some reason, he sensed what the others could not—that this Were was something else. I let my glamour fall for an instant, and the Princess recognized me, her eyes widening. Then I moved to her, angling my body between her and this new figure.

"It's time to leave, mate," I said to the Princess.

"It's early," the Vampire said.

"And I intend to take advantage of the rest of the night with my mate," I said pleasantly, taking the Princess's hand. "I've had enough foreplay."

He gripped my wrist. "Not yet."

Ignoring his hold on me, I pulled the Princess behind me and faced him. "She's not available."

He snarled, his incisors glistening. "She's not what she appears, either. Who are you?"

"No one you want to challenge."

He laughed. "I believe I'll have a taste." He was fast, faster than I anticipated, and the blow came out of nowhere. My back struck the opposite wall, my head ringing from the strike on my jaw. He had the Princess by the arm and was pulling her toward a door at the far end of the hallway. I couldn't let him take her. He left me little choice. I unsheathed the sword strapped to the center of my back, and with a move I'd made a thousand times before, jumped up the wall and raced toward them just below the ceiling. I dropped down beside him with an arcing sweep of my arms, the sword singing. His body vaporized as his head struck the floor. Sword in hand, I grasped the Princess's arm and we raced toward the rear exit. A squadron of Vampires appeared out of nowhere and surrounded us.

"Drop your glamour," I said, releasing mine. Pulling the Princess to my side, I straightened. "I am Torren de Brinna, tracker of the Seelie court, and we claim protection under the treaty between Cecelia, Queen of Faerie and the Vampire High Council."

From behind me, a sultry voice said, "Unfortunately, you have just killed the *senechal* of one of the six Vampire Clan rulers in protected territory."

I turned to face the female, a breathtaking seductress with crimson curls, milk white breasts, and a mouth that promised untold pleasures. Tipping my head, I said, "Greetings, Viceregal. I apologize for this infraction, but the Princess was in danger."

"Understood," she said. "And you must understand, I cannot allow this affront to go unpunished."

"I do."

Francesca, Viceregal of the Eastern territories, surveyed the Princess, shaking her head in amusement. "You are far from home, Jaelynn. If you had asked for an invitation, I would have been happy to accommodate."

"Perhaps another time," the Princess said.

"Oh, most definitely." Francesca motioned to her guards. "Take them to my quarters."

We were escorted through a series of security doors, down a long hallway, and into an opulent sitting room. A few moments later, Francesca appeared and sat down across from us on a maroon brocade settee. She stretched out her arms and crossed her legs, her black silk dress sliding up her thighs with a faint sigh.

"I've just had a discussion with your Queen."

I waited. My fate was about to be decided.

"The Princess will return home, of course. Cecilia is sending the royal guards to escort her." Francesca's eyes met mine. "And you will remain here with me."

"In what capacity, Viceregal?"

"In any capacity I desire—and I do find the Fae so very enjoyable."

A blood slave. Ice trickled down my spine. "For how long?"

"A century—a very short punishment, considering the eternity you stole from the Vampire you beheaded."

I could not fight back while the Princess was vulnerable. I nodded my assent. "As my Queen commands."

Francesca smiled. "For the next one hundred years, as I command."

The door opened and a Vampire entered. A Vampire I recognized.

"Daniela will show you to your quarters," Francesca said.

"As the Regent wills," I murmured, following Daniela to the door. Perhaps the next century would not be as bleak as I had anticipated.

Fresh Meat
Clara Nipper

So how did you injure your knee, Miss Morgan?" I sat, my hands poised over the keyboard, as I regarded the young woman sitting on the examining table. Her head was shaved and she had tattoos covering every inch of her skin.

"Just Josie. Um…car, I mean bicycle wreck?"

I studied her. "Bicycle wreck, really?" Josie had a black eye and multiple contusions on both arms, visible even through the vivid colors of her tattoos, and her legs looked as if she had been kicked repeatedly.

Josie bit her lip. "Bicycle, yeah."

Turning my back to the computer, I said, "Listen, I didn't just fall off the new nurse's wagon. If you're going to lie about domestic abuse, that's your business, but at least come up with a more plausible story, okay? And…" I rolled over to the cabinet, rummaged in a drawer and handed her a business card. "Call this number. They can help you."

Josie clenched her jaw, tore up the card, and let the pieces flutter to the floor. "You don't understand."

I rolled my eyes. "I know. You love him. You've got kids and no money and no place to go. He only does it when he's drunk. He really loves you. *Please.*"

Josie snarled, "You gonna help me or not?"

"Sure." I returned to the keyboard and began entering information into the computer. "Under cause of injury, should I put natural-born idiot?"

Josie grinned maliciously. "Put anything you want. Just give me a brace and some meds and let me outta here. I have somewhere to be."

"He's downstairs in the car with his beer waiting for you so you can cook his dinner?" I was known as an outspoken and difficult nurse. It had gotten me in trouble. Reading from top to bottom, my name was Madeline Howard. I was thirty-two years old, single, stubborn, brown eyes, deep dimples, long brown hair that my last girlfriend described as sable, and a body that she called sinuous. I had to look up the word and liked it.

"Enough with this shit, okay? Stop with your self-righteous savior routine. You think if I really were a battered woman that making me feel worse would help? Where's the doc?"

Abashed, I said, "On her way."

Josie stared out the window. Silently, I took her blood pressure, pulse, and temperature. "So what did happen?"

"I'm sworn to secrecy, but it's not abuse."

"I'm sorry, but that's exactly what a victim would say!"

"Roller derby!" Josie exploded. "Roller derby, all right? Consenting adult women bashing the hell out of each other on skates. Roller derby."

I looked at her with new respect. "Why is that a secret?"

"Because everyone who finds out wants to join and we're not accepting new members, so it's usually easier to lie than to explain."

"Derby, huh? My parents watched that on television in the seventies. All the tripping and fistfights, totally brutal. Fake, right?"

Josie rolled her eyes. "Oh, my God, you're one of *those*. I'm so sick of hearing that, I could puke. We're real athletes and the bouts are legit. It's nothing like the television shows. We have fifty pages of rules to follow and we train hard."

"So no elbows? No fishhooks? No brawls?"

"Nope." Josie flexed her swollen knee and grimaced when it popped. "Is the doctor running behind?"

"Yes. You're her last appointment of the day."

Josie flopped back on the table, her paper gown rustling. "I've got to get to the rink. We're having a meeting before practice."

"Practice? With that knee, I'd say you're off skates for at least a month."

Josie shot upright, her eyes flashing with fury. "What the fuck? No way!"

I shrugged. "Sorry."

"Where did you get your medical degree?"

"Fine. Get a second opinion from the doctor, but I've seen a lot of knees and I know you need a rest."

"Shit. They're gonna kill me." Josie lay back again, staring despondently at the ceiling.

"Surely not."

"We have a bout coming up." Josie brushed her hand across the velvet nap of her head.

"So...I used to skate when I was a kid."

"That's a sweet story."

"I was pretty good," I continued as I typed "skater" into the patient's information.

"How nice for you," Josie replied woodenly.

"Actually, I miss skating. Could I try out?"

"I told you, we're not recruiting and we're not accepting fresh meat."

"Why?"

Josie's mouth twitched. "Just a rule. Very strictly enforced. Sorry." She shrugged.

"Can I come watch a practice?"

"Nope, they're closed."

"Can I just come skate?"

Josie grinned. "Yes, you can skate session any time. Visit the website to get the deets."

Indignant, I said, "Well, how did *you* get on the team?"

Josie laughed. "Just lucky, I guess."

I burned with rejection.

"Hello, how are you today?" Dr. Mendez entered, smiling.

After work, I looked up *The Dustbowl Devils* on the web. Their rink was downtown and public skating session was tonight. I put on jeans and a tee and drove to the rink. I paid at the window and went inside.

"Can I help you?" a pale, thin, wasted young man behind the counter asked me.

"A pair of skates, please. Size seven."

"Men's size seven?" the man asked.

"No...women's."

"Then you'd take a five in skates...let's see..." The man found a pair and handed them to me. I noticed his arm was speckled with track marks. He saw my gaze and crossed his arms over his chest. "Have fun."

"Um...do you know...Beelzebabe?" I had seen the photograph of the captain and I was as full of frenzied lust as a teenage boy. I tried carefully to appear casual but authoritative. I played with the skate laces.

His eyes sharpened. "Yeah, why?"

"She told me to meet her here tonight, that's all."

The guy snorted. "Not likely."

"Why not?"

"Because she doesn't interview fresh meat on Tuesdays. And the team is not accepting any newbies anyway." He moved to take the skates back but I clasped them close.

"She *did* tell me to meet her. Don't you have a number to reach her?"

"Don't you?"

My mouth twisted. I saw derby girls start to file in and drop their big duffel bags on the tables.

"Listen, session is almost over. Don't waste your money." The man tugged on the skates and this time, I released them.

"I really want to try out," I muttered.

"I hear ya. But they get lots of girls coming in, using every trick in the book to get on the team. It just won't happen."

"Why not?" I asked while watching the derby girls suit up. They were a small group and they laughed easily with each other. The thumping music drowned out any possibility of eavesdropping. The session skaters wobbled by in endless circles.

The roller girls all wore black and had hard bodies. Some were slim, some were curvy, but they all had a luminous beauty that was frightening in its intensity. Like walking into a viper's nest of supermodels.

"Listen," the man said, "there's another team in town. They're always accepting girls. You can head over there and still make practice." He tried to hand me a flyer. I waved it away.

Just then, Josie came in swinging gracefully on crutches. She saw me and turned white. I raised a hand in greeting. She said something to the girl she was with and came over to me.

"What the fuck? I tell you not to do this and you goddamn do it anyway?"

"You're supposed to rest that knee," I said.

"Seriously, get the fuck out." Jose began tapping my ankles with one of her crutch tips. "Go on. Now."

"Stop it!" I cried, stumbling and hobbling toward the exit. Josie followed, hopping on one foot, poking, prodding, and hitting me the whole way. "Stop!"

"This is not a joke. You have to leave." At the door, Josie put her hand on my chest and shoved me backward outside.

I stood on the sidewalk, my face flaming, my fists clenched. The derby girls appearing in twos and threes never even glanced at me as they entered the building. I crept to my car and sat with my bruised ego, watching the skaters arrive.

Gradually, session skaters began leaving in familial groups. The rink's thumping music stopped abruptly. A few derby girls skated out to the sidewalk for a last-minute tobacco fix. I watched them, my teeth clenched and my chest hurting. They smoked and laughed and gestured wildly. I didn't smoke, but suddenly remembered my ex leaving a partial pack in the glove box. I reached for them and awkwardly lit one, not inhaling. I leaned back in the seat, trying for as much cool as a nursing nerd could achieve. The girls never even looked at me. Some shadowy movement down the sidewalk caught their eyes and they startled like a herd of deer. They dropped their butts and rolled skate wheels over them all in a synchronized flurry and skated quickly back inside.

I looked in the direction the skaters had stared. From the darkness, a figure emerged and strode purposefully toward the rink doors. She was medium height with very short platinum curls tousled tight to her scalp with sexy wisps trailing down the nape of her neck. She wore black thigh-high platform boots, black booty shorts with the words "nom nom nom" emblazoned across her ass, and a tight black tank top. I could almost see her muscles rippling like a leopard's. Her face was a Botticelli sculpture of classic beauty. At the door, the woman stopped. She turned. She looked right at me. I trembled and my bladder quivered under her powerful gaze. She pointed to the exit driveway. I started my car and drove home.

The next day, I hated going to work as if everyone could see my embarrassment and shame over the foolish thing I had tried to do.

"Hey, what's with you?" Dr. Mendez asked me. "You're so quiet. Not yourself." Worry lines creased her forehead.

"Huh?" I was jolted out of my reverie of self-pity.

"Qué pasa, eh?" Dr. Mendez elbowed me.

"Nothing." I sighed, then covered it with a smile. "I just had a rough night, that's all."

"What's her name?" Dr. Mendez laughed.

"Oh, I wish."

"'Fess up. Now that I'm pregnant, I have to live wildly through someone." Dr. Mendez rubbed her swollen belly.

"It's too pathetic." I groaned, covering my face with a patient's folder.

"You joined an online dating service?"

"Don't make me say it," I cried.

"You started a second job with Amway?"

I rolled my eyes, the memory of my badgering Josie Morgan the same way in this very room turning my face scarlet. "Roller derby," I shouted.

"What?" Dr. Mendez stopped caressing her stomach. "Did you say roller derby?"

"Yes," I whispered.

"Did you join a team?" Dr. Mendez crowed. "That's great! I had no idea you were so cool and edgy! Oh, my God, I know a derby girl! When is your first game? I'm bringing everyone from the office."

"No, you can't," I croaked, my throat dry, my eyes swollen with the effort of fighting irrational tears.

"Why?" Dr. Mendez put her hand on my shoulder.

"Doctor, your eight thirty is ready." The voice crackled over the intercom.

"Because they wouldn't take me," I answered, my voice thick.

"Why not?"

"I don't know. They aren't accepting new skaters. Non-negotiable. I showed up for practice and they kicked me out." I finally wept softly, not realizing until this moment how badly I wanted derby and how deeply it hurt.

"Who are these women? You want me to make a call? I'm going to make a call. Don't you fret," Dr. Mendez said. "This is not how things are done in Puerto Rico."

"No, no, that's okay." I laughed with relief. Dr. Mendez claimed that in her native Puerto Rico, all it took to get what you wanted was a well-placed call to the proper connection.

"You don't want me to make a call? I'm ready to make the call, chica."

"No call."

"No call?"

"No. Thanks, though."

Dr. Mendez shrugged and rose. "If you change your mind, let me know because I see you in roller derby. It's so right. Stay here and take a minute." She closed the door as she left.

❖

The Dust Devils' rejection just strengthened my resolve. I would get on that goddamn team or die trying. First, I laced up my junior high school skates and went to the running trail to see how they felt. The skates pinched multiple blisters onto my feet. My lower back ached like I'd been heavy lifting and my legs burned and quivered with the effort to keep my momentum going. I thought skating would be like effortless gliding. It wasn't. By the end of an hour, my entire lower body was either throbbing or shaking. I staggered to a bench and sat down with a groan. Maybe I shouldn't join derby after all. Maybe I couldn't do it. They didn't want me and I wasn't fit enough, let it go already, I told myself, wiping sweat from my forehead. Just forget about it, my agonized feet advised.

Just then, a skater wearing a black Dust Devils tank top blew by without a glance at me. I ground my teeth. Oh, I wanted this. No matter what. I took off my skates and limped back to the car. I drove to the rink across town that was home to the Other derby team.

I walked in and went to the pro shop. A woman with choppy, multicolored hair and tattoo sleeves looked up from a bearing press. "Help you?"

"Can I join your derby team?"

The woman's face lit up and she leaped over the counter. "Sure! We'd love to have you! When can you start? Practice is tonight. Do you need skates? Here's a waiver for you to sign."

I took the sheet of paper. "Thanks. I'll think about it." I left, sulking all the way home. Apparently, I didn't *want* to join any team that would have me as a member. I showered and headed for the rink I wanted to call home.

I sat in my car and again watched the session skaters leave and the derby girls arrive. I waited for the one I really wanted to see. Maybe this was enough. Just sitting in a roller rink parking lot, filled with longing and watching the roller girls come and go would be all I'd get. I fumbled with another cigarette.

Finally, She arrived. I watched her stride toward the door with feline grace. A shining silver curl covered one eye. I longed to tuck it into back into her hair and run my hands through her smooth, short curls. But her biceps and deltoids were carved like a bodybuilder's. She terrified and aroused me simultaneously. I wanted to hide from her scorching gaze and be fucked by it. Again she stopped at the door and raised her nose as if sniffing the air. My heart thudded heavily in my chest like a stone in a drum. I flicked my butt out the window so she wouldn't see me so easily. The woman turned, her sculpted face taking my breath away. She walked to the curb, pointed at me, and again directed me out of the lot.

My sweaty hands had difficulty with my keys and the stick shift, but I finally left. Her poisonous green eyes almost glowed in the dark. She watched, still as a statue, until I turned the corner.

This went on for three weeks. I decided I had nothing to lose, and the frightening thrill I got from her staring at me was the hottest action I had had in years. Each night, I parked a space closer. Each night, she walked closer to my car before banishing me.

Her gaze became a drug. On the nights without derby practice, I couldn't settle in to sleep. I fought the covers, snarled at my pillow, and kicked my sheets. On nights when I had her dangerous gaze on me, I slept deeply as if dead. I forgot about skating. I didn't care about derby, I just wanted to do anything to have That Woman look at me. During the day, I was too afraid to have my fantasies go further, but at night, in my dreams, she showed me everything. More mornings than not, I woke up twitchy and blushing and could not calm down until I parked at the rink again.

Dr. Mendez offered me Valium and then Xanax, but I liked being upset and unsettled. I could feel my blood in my veins, plumping my skin toward her, my fluids turning my body and pushing me to her, like tides to the moon. I could feel my heartbeat in my cunt. It was agony and I loved it. I was ready for derby.

I skated early one evening before derby practice. I knew I would finally be invited in. I just knew it and I wanted to be ready. As I pushed myself, gasping, along the outdoor trail, I expected to be exhilarated and I felt nothing but cramps and aches in my whole body. My neck, my lower back, my hips, my knees, my ankles, and especially, my feet were clenched into throbbing knots. I tried to breathe and enjoy the sunset but I just wanted a hot bath and pain meds applied directly to my muscles.

I collapsed onto a bench and gulped water. The liquid sloshed over my face and splashed my shirt and I didn't care. I tried to remember Those Eyes and those close-cropped curls, but my closed, dry cunt had no memory. As I poked numbers on my cell phone, my chin dripped water and I didn't wipe it off.

"Hey, Lauren, come get me at the highway and the river. You're right. This is too hard. I can't do it." I snapped the phone closed and bent over to undo the laces of my skates. Water dropped onto the pavement, but it was from my eyes. I sank into an exhausted stupor while I waited for my ride.

When she finally arrived, I limped to her car and fell into the seat with a gusty sigh. We rode in silence for several minutes. Lauren drove past the parking lot where I had left my car.

"Hey! I have to pick up my car! Turn around!" Then Lauren drove past the turn to my house. "Okay, bitch, where are you taking me?"

"Derby."

"I'm not showered!"

"Showered *for* derby? What's going on?"

"I don't have the right clothes."

"Huh?" Lauren gave me the stink eye.

"I'm tired!"

"You're going. You want this."

"Like hell. I'll claw your eyes out first."

"Well, okay, but then we're going to the rink. Listen, you have bored all of us for the last month about how important this is to you, so it's time to shut up and skate."

"You don't get it…" I moaned, imagining the humiliating rejection, the embarrassed explanation to Lauren about the treatment I had not only been enduring but also enjoying. I withdrew in a furious pout.

"We're here!" Lauren steered her car into a space with such casual negligence that I cringed. When I came alone, it took me full minutes to select a space, position the car, and park perfectly. Sometimes I agonized over my choice and ended up moving my car two or three times. I looked around and noted the lot was full. Jealousy soured my belly like poison.

"Looks like a party! Come on!" Lauren grinned and jabbed me. She was out of the car and at the rink door before I could unbuckle my seat belt. I tried to yell at her to stop, but my voice had dried to a crust in my throat. My tongue was limp with panic. I moaned as I stood and hobbled after her, walking very slowly because I expected Lauren to be dismissed and come hurtling out any second. My eyes dilated as I put my hand on the door and waited. Nothing. I pulled the door open. Women's voices like harmonies swirled out. Suddenly, I was filled with a ferocious curiosity and possessiveness. How dare Lauren still be in there! This rink was mine. I had been shamed; I had put in the time; I had faced off against the captain night after night; I owned her in my heart by day and claimed her body at night; I was here first! I charged inside.

"You're late." Josie was at a table and handed me a booklet without looking up. "Sign this waiver, get skates and pads from Annie, and you have to run ten laps for being tardy."

I stood, shocked into paralysis. Josie was busily scribbling in a notebook. She sensed my immobility and, still staring at her paper, she spoke harshly while continuing to write. "Look, what are you waiting for? You've got one shot. Move." She glanced at me, her sentence unfinished. "Well, look who finally made it to Fight Club." She smiled coldly and gestured to the rink. "Go. Hurry."

I dashed to the counter where a tall, willowy redhead was passing out skates and pads to throngs of clamoring women. There was a happy babble and nervous laughter. I shouldered my way into the crowd and found Lauren, flushed and excited, trying on helmets.

"What the fuck?" I demanded, ready to punch Lauren, blaming her for not being thrown out.

"It's newbie night!" Lauren cried, as wiggly and gleeful as a Jell-o salad with colored marshmallows. "They only have them once a year! So what the hell, right?" She scooped up an armload of pads and a pair of skates and scurried to a bench.

I looked at the rink, as if that would explain everything. The core team of skaters was out there, including Beelzebabe, skating with impossible speed, ease, and grace. I felt nauseated. I would never be able to do that. They looked like they were flying, dancing, soaring.

I only knew their feet touched the ground because of the smooth whisper of their wheels whirring on the warm maple floor.

"Is that her?" Lauren whispered, staring with her mouth open.

"Yes." My heart was full of razors.

"God, is she a movie star?"

"Of course not!" I snorted.

"You know who she looks like?" Lauren said excitedly. "Linda Evangelista circa 1991."

I glared at her. "You are such a queen. You and your model mania. I don't see it."

Lauren punched me playfully. "Admit it! She does!"

"No. I don't see it. You're wrong."

I sat next to Lauren and tried to untangle all the Velcro straps. "Phew!" I held the convoluted knot of pads away from me where they lazily turned in the air like a robot cocoon.

"I know. Old sweat, isn't it great?" Lauren giggled. "Limburger."

I sniffed and winced. The evidence of all the derby girls who had been here before me. I wondered if Beelzebabe had looked at any of them, had kissed them? I yanked the pads apart and secured them to my wrists, elbows, and knees quickly, as if my speed could obliterate all those other women. Those whores who knew Her before me. Those ring-tailed bitchsluts who were welcomed and not rejected. I tied my skate laces with such a fury that one of them snapped.

Someone blew a whistle and skaters moved on to the floor. I limped with one skate on and one off to the counter. Josie was there talking to Annie, the redhead. I placed the skate on the carpeted countertop.

"Oopsy, someone needs therapy," Annie cooed, rolling another skate toward me.

"Don't put those on!" Josie barked. "Have you done your ten laps?"

I rolled my eyes, walked away, and sat on the bench again, stripping off the pads and one skate while constantly taking my temperature. How interested was I, really? Already this was such a hassle. Was it worth it? Did I even have a shot in hell with that woman? I looked at her, commanding the attention of all the women in the rink, and I snorted. No way. Just say no. I clenched my jaws and stood up in my street shoes and began my thudding jog around the rink.

"Welcome, everyone!" Beelzebabe announced. "So nice to see such a good turnout for newbie night." The veteran team all laughed in a way to freeze my blood. "Most of you won't be accepted, and just be adult about it." Some grumbling. "Those of you who make it," Beelzebabe continued, "better be fucking sure because you're in it forever." More sinister laughter from the team. I rounded the rink in time to see Beelzebabe grin like a death's head. "You have no idea what you're in for. And the level of commitment demanded of you is… inhuman." Another frightening laugh from the veterans. I was panting… halfway finished. "Okay, now for your own safety, I must advise any girl on her period not wearing a fresh tampon to either go home or go to the bathroom and change right now. If you're wearing a pad, go change into a tampon. No questions."

Puzzled looks and murmuring in the crowd.

"Do it!" Beelzebabe bellowed. There was a collective jump and a few girls skated to the bathroom.

Another woman, a beautiful, cool blonde, skated amongst the jittery newbies, wrinkling her nose. "You to the lav." She tapped one. "And you."

"What are you trying to do?" Beelzebabe thundered. "If I say go change, do it *now!*" A few more skaters stumbled to the bathroom. I was just finishing my laps, and even though my cycle had ended a few days ago, I was tempted to put in a tampon just to please them. I stood, gasping and sweating.

"You!" Blonde Ice pointed at me. "Get your skates on!"

I fled back to the bench where I fumbled with the equipment. "You have right and left mixed up and that strap goes on top, not on the bottom. Are you sure you want to try this? You realize it's *roller derby*, right? Not chess club?" A small brunette veteran, Poison, bent over me in concern.

"Hell no, I'm not sure of anything. But I want this and I can't let it go," I answered plaintively.

"You'll be fine, then." She smiled and patted my shoulder. Her cold hand felt good on my overheated skin.

"Okay, let's divide into four groups," Beelzebabe continued. There was a general shuffling. "We're going to go over basic skills, and while we are doing this, my veterans are going to be assessing your abilities. If we tap you, you're out. Just leave graciously. I'm going to call out what you're supposed to do and at my whistle, do your best. Ready?"

Lauren was next to me, giggling and biting her nails. "I'm so nervous," she whispered. "And I didn't even want this." Lauren fidgeted and grinned at me. "But oh my God, I want it now!" A fiery gleam blazed in her eyes.

I felt a dull, heavy hatred for my dearest friend. She was another body I had to climb over to get into Beelzebabe's arms. I looked at Beelzebabe: that perfectly chiseled face, the scalp-hugging, platinum-blond curls that cried out for my fingers to twirl into them, her body bursting with voluptuous curves, her ease on skates fluid and fierce like an eagle poised for killing flight.

"Right knee fall!" Beelzebabe called and blew the whistle. A great clattering as women all dropped to one knee. The rink resounded with loud smacks as dozens of knee pads hits the floor. To my delight, I stood right up and watched with grim satisfaction all the skaters who were still struggling.

The beautiful veteran skaters whizzed through us so fast I could barely see them. They were insectile in their speed. I saw them tap several skaters, who left the rink.

"Left knee fall!" Whistle. Down. Up. "Rock star!" Whistle. Confused looks. Skaters who obviously had roller derby experience dropped to both knees simultaneously and the rest of us followed. The culling continued. So far I was still in. "Right knee!" Whistle. Down. Up. "Left knee!" Whistle. Down. Up. "Superman!" Whistle. Copying the experienced skaters, we dropped to our knees, then bellies, and stretched out our limbs. "You must be able to get up within two seconds to meet minimum skills requirements!" Beelzebabe shouted. "Right knee! Left knee! Rock star! Superman!"

"Gee!" Lauren panted, laughing. "I haven't skated in years. I think I'm doing pretty well." Her cheeriness made me want to throttle her. She didn't know how serious this was. She didn't appreciate the fatal gravity. I gritted my teeth and kept following Beelzebabe's whistles.

Sweat poured off me like my helmet had a faucet in it. Perspiration dotted the rink floor in a half-circle around my body.

"One hundred crunches! Twenty-five push-ups! Fifty squats!" Whistle. There were groans and gasps as the women tried to do as ordered. Another dozen women left the floor. "Sprint five laps!" Whistle.

Poison flitted amongst us as we clawed and swam our way through our laps.

"It's so hot!" I yelled.

Poison, looking as cool and crisp as a summer salad, stared at me with clear blue eyes. "Cope or die, sweetie. Feels fine to me."

When we finished our laps, sucking air like beached fish, Beelzebabe and the veterans skated to us.

"And then there were ten," Beelzebabe said, her laser green gaze making me writhe with pleasure and fear. "We will take six of you into our Fresh Meat program and the rest of you can keep working and try out again. Annie Maul?"

The willowy redhead skated forward and read the names off a sheet. "Lauren, Nickie, Amy, Kim, Gigi and…what is this? I can't read this." Annie squinted at the clipboard and showed it to Beelzebabe.

"Madeline, Madeline, Madeline," I chanted in my head.

"Starts with an M," Annie squinted.

"Meredith," Beelzebabe read. The skaters chosen whooped, cheered, and slapped hands. I fell to my knees. The other three rejects rolled slowly off the floor. Beelzebabe and the veterans skated off too. Lauren offered me a hand.

"Maddy, you can—"

"Don't." My voice was a punch. I stayed on the ground.

Lauren shuffled awkwardly, her borrowed skates clicking. "Well, listen, Maddy, I will quit. Fuck them. I just won't—"

My head jerked up, the pain in my face cutting her off mid-sentence. "Quit, don't quit, do whatever you want. But don't do me any favors. And don't do anything out of motherfucking *pity*! Leave me alone, okay?"

"I'll see you around." Lauren rolled off slowly and quietly, as if that would spare my feelings.

"Lauren, wait!" I called. "I'm sorry." Lauren didn't stop or turn but gave me a small wave.

I rested my forehead on the wood that had been so recently ringing with wishful wheels. I knew I needed to stand up but I just had to get a grip first. Just a breath or two. I heard skates sliding toward me so softly that I had to listen hard to make sure it was sound. I sighed from my buttocks and opened my eyes. Black skates, scuffed and worn with age and use, were close enough to kiss.

I dreaded to lift my gaze but the sight was irresistible. Those hard, muscle-curvy legs with pink argyle knee socks and hot pink booty shorts and a Hello Kitty baby tee stretched tight. The leopard green eyes. The shiny, short platinum curls not even damp with sweat.

"Get up." The words were harsh, but Beelzebabe's tone was as soft as kittens.

I stood and stared at the floor. "I was just leaving." I turned away, anger and sadness forcing me to feel a vast indifference for this woman and for derby.

"Come to my office, yeah?" Beelzebabe said.

I turned back so fast, I almost fell. I felt permission to stare at her. "Why?"

Beelzebabe shrugged. "Don't, then. But I know you will." She grinned, and it was so dazzling and seductive, I felt all my organs flip.

I turned and limp skated toward the bench. "Fine, whatever." I tried to make my voice breezy but it came out stridently squeaky.

"You hurt?" she asked, gliding alongside me.

"I have blisters that are bleeding."

Beelzebabe raised her chin, sniffing delicately. "No, they're not. Don't worry. Get some mole foam and better socks."

I reached the bench, sat down, and began tearing open all the Velcro straps.

"Just drop those in that bin in the locker room and leave the skates on the counter at the pro shop and then come have a drink."

"Everyone is gone already? It sure cleared out fast," I remarked, feeling uneasy that the rink was so quiet and it was just her and me, our voices echoing in the big space.

"Yes," Beelzebabe said, sounding like a hypnotic cobra. "Nice, isn't it?"

She smiled again and I thought I saw her eyes flash vermilion for a split second. I shook my head and looked again. Just the same poisonous neon green they always were.

"Don't you ever get spooked here all by yourself?" I asked, my voice involuntarily quavering.

Beelzebabe leaned close. Her skin smelled fresh and tangy, like salt that had just dried on a sandy beach. "Yes," she hissed with a hungry smile, "I do," meaning the opposite. She skated to her office. I followed, fear making me awkward, desire making me clumsy, and eagerness making me fall twice. At last, I reached the office and staggered into a chair and immediately removed the skates. It was over. I had wanted it, I had worked for it, and I had failed. I didn't know what I would do with this painful hollow, this dream in shards inside my empty heart.

"Here you are." Beelzebabe handed me a frosty can of Dew. It was so cold it hurt my fingers and the can's chill rose from it like smoke. Beelzebabe tapped her own can against mine as if we were toasting and said, "To disappointment, yeah?"

I set my can down. "I won't drink to that," I said frigidly. I had aspired to an audience with this woman and now I had it. Should I beg her? After all, she hadn't invited anyone else in here.

A smile twitched the corners of Beelzebabe's luscious mouth. "All right then, what would you like to drink to?"

"To achieved goals," I replied haughtily, snapped the top on my drink, knocked the can against hers, and gulped noisily. Beelzebabe watched me without moving.

"At least my toast will come true. You can count on being disappointed but you cannot count on achieving goals. Like tonight, yeah?" Beelzebabe took a long drink, then licked her lips and smiled like I imagined a happy shark would.

"About that..." I began.

"No exceptions," Beelzebabe said.

"But I was already tired from skating earlier."

Beelzebabe bared her teeth. "Are you making excuses?"

"No ma'am, but—"

"Good."

"To disappointment, then!" I swallowed the Dew, and it tasted bitter.

"Don't worry, I want you." Beelzebabe's voice was almost a growl.

"Then why? I thought I was as good as Lauren." I couldn't help whining.

"You're better than ten Laurens." Beelzebabe stood in front of me and knelt. Her feline green eyes were hypnotic. "Breathe," she reminded me. I gasped with a little hiccup. I was fully dressed but I never felt more naked than sitting still under that piercing green stare.

"I don't understand. Is this a game?"

"You're better because you have the hunger." Beelzebabe licked her lips again. Her gaze held me like an embrace. "Lauren and skaters like her are common and expendable. It comes too easy. They don't care as much. They don't work hard. They don't *want* it." Beelzebabe's cold index finger touched my lips. It felt so good against my feverish skin. Instinctively, I opened my mouth and her finger slid inside. I closed my eyes. When Beelzebabe began to pull out, I moaned and pressed my teeth on her finger and shook my head. I heard her laugh, but she let me keep her finger in my mouth. I caressed it with my tongue and sucked, savoring the briny flavor. I felt Beelzebabe put my burning finger into her cold mouth. My mind reeled with the surreality: my endless fantasies of this woman and here I was, a skewered servant. I melted, my waxen mind dissolving completely. Whatever she wanted, she could have. I would do anything for her. I was entirely hers. The feeling was so intense, I had to brace my feet against the floor to stay upright in the chair. My nipples were like hot marbles and my thighs were trembling.

"Please," I whispered to her finger, "please."

This time, Beelzebabe slid out. Then she clasped my hand in both of her cool ones and slowly pulled my finger from her mouth. "Yes," she answered, her green eyes glowing. "Yes. Just not yet, I think." She stared at me, the heavy weight of her gaze keeping me still. "But maybe just one thing first." She very slowly raised my shirt. She touched my throat and traced down my neck, my collarbone, my chest, to my sternum, goose bumps rippling over me in electric waves. "Breathe," she said. I couldn't. It was impossible to take my eyes off what this magnificent woman was doing. She closed thumb and forefinger around the clasp of my bra. One snap and it was open. I cried out. Beelzebabe's green eyes dilated and she tore open my bra and looked at my breasts. With excruciating care, she traced her fingernails around my nipples. They swelled and puckered into aching clits. I groaned and leaned my head back, my cunt throbbing. She kept teasing me until I was dizzy, her fingers tickling, pinching, torturing.

"I can't…stop, please," I managed to say, not meaning it.

"Stop?" Beelzebabe asked, grinning. "Okay, I'll do this instead." She pulled me from the chair and laid me on the floor with astonishing speed. She was on top of me, hard and heavy like stone. I closed my eyes again, surrendering everything. If she wanted to fuck me or kill me, I didn't care. I inhaled, sharp and quick, when I felt Beelzebabe's mouth on my nipple. It was cold like she had a mouthful of ice. She tugged and sucked and I came with an explosion. My fists pounded the floor. My arms flailed, knocking over the chair, and my legs quaked as if in a seizure. I didn't know this ferocious Madeline. I broke off two nails below the quick clawing Beelzebabe's back. I bucked and screamed, not recognizing anything: not my behavior, my desire, my orgasm, my shouting. I don't know all I said, but I do know I clutched Beelzebabe's granite body and repeated, "forever." I lay in her arms, trembling and gasping. She caressed me gently until my breathing slowed.

"God, who am I? What am I?" I laughed self-consciously, untangling my hair from under my spine.

Beelzebabe smiled to chill my dissolved jellybones into hardening and taking stiff shape again. "That depends." She kissed away the beads of sweat nestled at my breastbone. "You are delicious." Her eyes flared red briefly as if someone had taken a flash photograph.

Suddenly, I felt like a plucked chicken splayed out on a roasting pan. "Let me up, let me up!" I struggled to get free and to lower my wadded, wet shirt. Beelzebabe held me where I was. I thumped her shoulder and kicked. "What, are you on steroids? Get off me!"

"I thought this is what you wanted. More than *anything*. Derby or die." She smiled mockingly at me.

I stopped moving. "You're right. It is. Sorry, I just felt like a cat toy for a second. Is this an audition for the team?"

Beelzebabe laughed, shaking her head, her silver-white curls bobbing. "I picked you because I can spot potential."

"And?"

"And…" Beelzebabe took my hands and stretched them over my head and pinned them there. She smelled my skin and growled. Then she recovered herself and repeated softly, "And…you are ready to fully commit, yeah?" She rolled off me and pulled me on top of her. Her hands inched slowly from my rolled-up shirt to my ribs to my waist and then curved to hold my buttocks, still clad in polyester running shorts.

"Yes." My answer gusted out, all but creating wind.

"I sense that you have an unusual capacity to...give yourself completely to something." Beelzebabe squeezed and massaged me.

"Yes!" I cried, my eyes rolling back.

"That you have the courage and dedication to do whatever it takes," she continued, moving my hips in a subtle figure eight.

"Yes," I moaned, again drunk and befuddled by sensation.

"That you take your word very seriously and when you give it, you mean it," Beelzebabe whispered, removing her hands from my ass and inserting her cool fingers into the waistband of my shorts, playing with it, tugging at it, lightly caressing my stomach.

"Yes," I whispered.

"That you will do anything for the team, yeah?" she cooed. She brushed her fingers against the crotch of my shorts.

I quivered and whimpered. "Anything for the team," I repeated.

"Me too," Beelzebabe hissed. She rose halfway like a cobra and flipped us over. I was on my back again and I felt her tear the shorts from my body. She then hovered, her face just millimeters from mine. "I'll ask you just once. Do you want this?"

My heart was pounding so hard, my left breast pulsed with it. My legs were stiff and locked into place. I couldn't look away from her mesmerizing glow-in-the-dark green eyes. I realized how a hobbled bunny must feel right before the puma pounces. But between my hip bones—from my navel to my knees, I was a hot ocean. Waves of delight rolled from bone to bone, completely liquid. I tried to speak and only heard a click, so I blinked once.

"I knew it." Beelzebabe grinned and kissed a sizzling, frigid trail down my body. She deftly avoided my bucking cunt and when she reached my upper thigh, she placed her hand on my belly and pressed me to stillness. I waited, my mind whirling and soaring, not attaching to any specific thought. Beelzebabe lowered her cool mouth onto my smoldering clit and obliterated everything I knew. I felt the piercing pain of a terrible bite on my inner thigh but she slid two cold, hard fingers into my molten cunt and I split my own eardrums and stripped my throat screaming. The razor-stabbing ache of the bloody wound and the delirious ecstasy mixed and mingled and created an infinite desire for more, more, and more. The pain gave a delicious edge to the overpowering pleasure. They became indistinguishable. I wanted

Beelzebabe deeper, harder, sharper, softer, sweeter. If she wanted to eviscerate me, I wanted it too. If she wanted to eat me alive from breast to ass, I would open wide, surrender, and give her all I had. If she wanted to tear the flesh off me and fuck my bones, I would let her. I came and kept coming. I looked down and saw Beelzebabe's bloody, beautiful face. My orgasm possessed me like an insatiable demon. I swirled, in orbit. Finally, in a second or a decade, the ecstasy ebbed and I began returning. Beelzebabe soothed me, murmuring softly, petting me gently. She climbed on top of me again and kissed me passionately. I tasted my own blood and essence. After a few minutes, Beelzebabe stood up and threw my clothes at me. "Let me bandage your wound before you go." She got a first aid kit and dressed the bite.

"Now what?" I asked, hating myself for already worrying about where this was going and would she call me. What about the derby team?

"Now." Beelzebabe finished and smacked my leg. "You're on the team. You can skate like the rest of us."

"How?"

"You're a vampire and we can do anything."

I laughed, my voice hysterical. "Vampire? There's no such thing!" I continued laughing. "Even if there were, I'm not in the agonized throes of transformation."

"That's a myth we perpetuate to keep our numbers down. Becoming a vampire is a lot easier than playing derby," Beelzebabe replied.

I stopped laughing. I smacked my lips. "I don't have an insatiable thirst for human blood."

"That will come…but we've cross-bred with humans enough that we can also supplement our diets with regular food and drink."

"You didn't bite my neck."

Beelzebabe rolled her eyes. "I'm not here for Vampire 101. Why don't you run along and figure it out as you go?"

"But…"

"Here's a souvenir T-shirt." Beelzebabe handed me a red shirt from a box in the corner. "We're having a team meeting here tomorrow night. Come."

I left without another word, my mind ground zero after a nuclear blast. I slept better than I ever had in my life, like colliding with a coma.

I didn't wake up until I heard my cell, underneath my body. When I moved to retrieve the phone, I cried out; my bandaged leg was awake too.

"Hello?" I hoped it was Her.

"You're okay? Thank God." Dr. Mendez's voice was angry and relieved. She spoke to someone else. "She's there. I'm talking to her. Don't send the police." Then to me, "What the hell happened? Are you sick?"

"Why?" I stretched like taffy and moaned with pleasure. "What time is it?"

"Six. You missed the whole day of work. You've never been absent without calling."

"Six?" I sat up, alarmed. The team meeting was in an hour. "I slept for almost twenty-four hours?"

"Yes, are you all right?"

"I'm fine. Just really tired, I guess." I laughed. My throat was starting to feel dry, my tongue thirsty. "I'm sorry, Maria, I'll be in tomorrow."

"Okay, chica. We're just so happy you're alive."

I smiled to myself at that. "Yeah, me too. Bye."

I rose and showered and dressed carefully. I put on a plaid miniskirt, mismatched argyle socks, and a T-shirt that I sliced up. The T-shirt that Beelzebabe had given me was still in my bag. Maybe I should wear it. Oh, well, I was late. I could change at the rink. The bandage on my thigh was soaked through, but I didn't change because I liked that it was a badge.

At the rink, Josie wasn't there, or any of the other mortal skaters. Just the ten fierce, beautiful veterans. They all stopped talking when I approached.

"Well, well, well, if it isn't Beelzebabe's latest pet," a woman with long black curls snarled.

"Easy, Tatiana." Blonde Ice laughed.

"Don't think you're special," Tatiana said, raising her shorts to show me a scar on her upper inner thigh. I felt sick. "She will do anything for the team."

"Grow up!" Annie Maul ordered Tatiana.

"And shut up!" Blonde Ice added.

Tatiana growled to me, "She better be right about you." And then stalked away, bumping me hard.

"Forget about that bitch." Annie threw her arm around my shoulder. "One look from Beelzebabe and she had her U-Haul filled and ready to go."

I squirmed with shame, feeling sorry for Tatiana. "Are we gonna have a meeting or what?"

"All business, I like her already," Blonde Ice said.

"Attention!" Poison shouted. "Sit! Let's get started before everyone else arrives. We have a couple of new skaters."

Two? I looked around to see Beelzebabe walking in with her arm around a petite, auburn-haired beauty.

"My, that is one tasty dish," remarked a muscle-curvy skater called Blud Lust.

"Hi, so nice to see you all again." The woman smiled; her voice was pure Southern honey. I glared at her thigh and I could see the white bandage through the mesh of her torn black pantyhose.

Beelzebabe grinned. "This is Candace. Can I pick them or what?"

"Can she even skate?" I shrieked.

Everyone flinched. "Ruh-roh," mouthed Annie Maul.

Beelzebabe said smoothly as she and Candace sat, "So, to begin. Becoming a vampire and a derby skater all at once is a lot to handle. We're here to help. So don't worry. You probably have questions. Let's hear them."

"You're the devil," I murmured acidly.

Beelzebabe's fatal green stare of fury scared me. "What was your first clue?"

"But I thought…" I hid my sudden tears by staring at the ceiling.

"You didn't care what I was or what I did last night. But now that you see there are others, I'm Satan, is that it?" Beelzebabe's eyes narrowed and I could see her body tense as if to spring. I realized exactly how dangerous she was. She hissed, *"I asked you if you wanted this."*

"I should have been more specific!" I laughed deliriously. The other skaters patted me and muttered comforts. "It's just an adjustment." "You'll be fine." "Give yourself a while to acclimate." "Wait until you're on skates; this won't matter at all."

"Right. So I'm sure you girls are pretty thirsty. Skylar?" Beelzebabe called. From the pro shop, the thin guy with the track marks emerged carrying two IV bags of blood.

"Should be good stuff. I've been taking extra vitamins." He placed the bags on the table before Candace and me.

"What do I do with this?" Candace giggled.

"Drink it, pussycat," Blud Lust said.

"Ew, no, I can't. Not yet." Candace made a face and pushed it away. I unclamped the clear hose, stuck it in my mouth like a straw, and pulled hard. The salty, penny taste was exactly what I needed. The thick, hot blood satisfied every craving in every cell, nerve ending, muscle fiber, bone marrow, and hair follicle. In a few seconds, I drained the bag flat. I looked up to see everyone watching me with their mouths open.

"You were right about her," Tatiana said.

"I know." Beelzebabe smiled, one ice-colored curl dipping to her dark eyebrow, her gaze curling my toes. Her eyes made me weak and limp.

"Fuck that, let's skate!" I slammed my hands on the table, feeling a surge of power so intense that I knew I was indestructible. I could lift this rink right off the ground with one bare hand and crush it to rubble with the other.

"Slow down. We're gonna go over some basics." Beelzebabe stilled me with a fingertip on my wrist.

"You can't go in the sun without tons of sunscreen," Annie said. "You'll turn blue."

"From all the blood," Blonde Ice added with a snake smile.

"We're a breed of desert vampire who live all through Latin America and north to about Iowa. We don't travel because we are very interdependent with our local environment and we have evolved with it, so we can eat local foods on a limited basis. But outside our habitat, we are wholly dependent on hunting humans," Beelzebabe said.

"And we can drink Dew, thank God!" Blud Lust cracked open a bottle and chugged it.

"There is no God," Beelzebabe replied coldly.

"That's right, darlin', we are atheists," Poison told Candace with a smile.

"Almost as good as blood!" Blud Lust cried, crumpling the Dew bottle in one hand. Everyone laughed.

"But no matter how much human food you eat, it doesn't change our nature," Beelzebabe told me, stroking my hair. My entire body tingled.

"That's where Skylar comes in, don't you, baby?" Poison called to the pro shop where Skylar was changing plates.

He waved and called weakly, "Anything for the team."

"That's my boy." Beelzebabe beamed.

"Okay, about derby," Annie said. "We never get injured and we are, well, superhuman, so our challenge is to slow down and *not* use our advantages. *That's* what we like...to see how human we can make ourselves. To be as mediocre as we can possibly be is so much harder than you would think. But that's what we do." Annie laughed with a shrug. "The draw of derby is so strong, we'll do it no matter what."

"And the majority of our skaters are still human," Poison said.

"Who have no idea, and you better keep it that way," Blud Lust added.

"When some dumb shit doesn't wear a tampon, we put Vicks in our nostrils, so buy a jumbo tub," Blonde Ice said.

"What about sex?" Candace asked with a giggle.

"Hot stuff, you didn't get enough from Beelzebabe?" Blud Lust grinned. "Well, why don't we hook up later?"

"Honey, being a vampire is the best birth control there is," Blonde Ice cried exultantly.

"The best weight loss secret too," Poison said. "Ever notice there are no fat vampires? I used to have such an uncontrollable jones for Ben and Jerry's but now, all I have to think about is murder. Maybe I should write a diet book?"

"All vampires are rich too," Beelzebabe said. "When you have an eternity to amass wealth, it has a very nice way of accumulating."

"But it's not all sex and skating and glamour," Blud Lust announced. "Even vampires have to run errands, do laundry, and vacuum."

"And practice derby," Beelzebabe yelled. "Get your gear on!"

We all strapped on pads (you don't need them but must wear them for appearance's sake, Beelzebabe lectured) and laced up our skates. I withdrew the souvenir shirt from my bag and began laughing uncontrollably. I dropped it on the bench. I took one step on the rink and soared. I pushed and was airborne.

"Whoa, you need some practice controlling yourself, Maddy," Poison told me. "That's the hard part, looking like a human skater."

"So I went from helpless klutz to skilled, invincible dynamo and I have to pretend to be a klutz again?"

"That's about the size of it."

I leaped and twirled and skated so fast everything was a blur. I knocked other veterans on their asses and laughed with glee. I had never felt such delirious elation. No wonder they wanted to keep their members low, because why would anyone want to be human? I skated to Beelzebabe, screeched to a stop a razor's edge from her skate, and hugged her. "Thank you."

"You're welcome. Now rein it in, the other skaters are arriving." She pointed her chin to the crowd of derby girls entering. "Veterans! Don't hurt the fresh meat!"

"Yes, Captain." I grinned and skated laps very slowly. Gliding at a snail's pace felt comical and exaggerated, but I still passed a few human skaters. I saw Josie watching me carefully. I blew her a kiss and began doing backwards crossovers.

Lauren approached and I saw how truly awkward and hideous humans were. We skated a few laps together, me exhausting myself to stay slow and heavy with her.

"So, you're back." Lauren spoke awkwardly. "Did she make an exception?"

"No...I just had a private session with Beelzebabe," I hedged.

"Then you're on the team?" Lauren was jubilant.

"Yes, I am," I said proudly.

"Because you're *so different*! I can't believe it!" Lauren marveled.

"Yeah, Beelzebabe was really thorough." I felt my face form a seductive feline grin.

"Well, I need a lesson from her, then," Lauren stated. I sprinted to the bench, picked up the shirt, and gave it to Lauren. "Here, for you."

Lauren wobbled as she coasted and read the front aloud, "'My best friend became a roller derby vampire and all I got was this lousy T-shirt.' Huh?"

"Inside joke," I said.

"Funny," Lauren answered darkly. "So seriously, what happened? What's the difference?"

I saw how competitive Lauren was and how miserably hungry she was for derby.

"The difference is…that I will do anything for the team. And you won't." I did a lightning fast pirouette. "Will you?"

CONTRIBUTORS

JOEY BASS has been described as a prolific writer. While this denotes the quantity rather than quality of her work, she knows keeping at it is the best way to improve. After roaming up and down the West Coast of the U.S., she finally became civilised and is living in the U.K. with her partner.

RONICA BLACK (www.ronicablack.com) is an award-winning author and a three-time Lambda Literary Finalist. Her books range from romance and erotica to mystery and intrigue. Her latest, *Conquest*, is an erotic romance. Ronica lives in Glendale, Arizona, with her partner, where she enjoys a rich family life, raising a menagerie of pets and doing anything creative.

MEL BOSSA is a member of the Bi Writers Association. She lives in Montreal, where she is at work on a new novel.

VALERIE BRONWEN is a public health professional who lives and writes in New Orleans. A freelance journalist, this is her first published short story. She is currently working on her first mystery novel.

REBECCA S. BUCK (www.rebeccasbuck.com), from Nottingham, England, is the author of two full-length novels published by Bold Strokes Books, the latest being *Ghosts of Winter*, an April 2011 release. She is currently working on her next novel and has plenty of ideas for further works!

SAM CAMERON's (fisherkey.wordpress.com) young adult adventure *Mystery of the Tempest* features gay and straight teen detectives in the Florida Keys. Her work has also appeared in *Speaking Out: LGBTQ Youth Stand Up* and in numerous magazines and anthologies. She is the author of three science fiction novels and a Lambda Literary Award–winning collection of short fiction.

LESLEY DAVIS (www.lesleydavisauthor.co.uk) lives in the West Midlands of England. She is a die-hard science-fiction/fantasy fan in all its forms and an extremely passionate gamer. When her Nintendo DSi or 3DS is out of her grasp, Lesley is to be found seated before the computer writing.

JESS FARADAY (www.jessfaraday.com) is the author of *The Affair of the Porcelain Dog*, a novel of Victorian suspense. She lives and writes in the American West.

JANE FLETCHER is the author of ten speculative fiction novels, for which she has won Golden Crown and Alice B Readers awards. She has also been included on the Lambda, Foreword Book of the Year, and Gaylactic Spectrum shortlists. She lives in southwest England with her partner.

D. JACKSON LEIGH (www.djacksonleigh.com) grew up barefoot and happy, swimming in farm ponds and riding rude ponies in rural south Georgia. Her most recent book, *Call Me Softly*, is a tale of Southern lies and family secrets set in the polo fields of Aiken, S.C. Visit with Jackson at www.facebook.com/djacksonleigh.

L.T. MARIE is an athlete by trade. Born and raised in California, she resides in the Bay Area with her partner and two children. She enjoys three things: reading, writing, and Giants baseball. Her first book, *Three Days*, was released in the fall of 2011 by Bold Strokes Books.

CLARA NIPPER (www.claranipper.com) is a writer living in Tulsa, Oklahoma. Her book *Femme Noir* was released in 2009 and the sequel, *Kiss of Noir*, dropped in 2010, both from Bold Strokes Books. She is currently working on a new murder mystery involving a horndog homicide detective, tentatively titled *Murder on the Rocks*. Clara's hobbies include: fanatical gardening, candy-making for her artisan company, andyscandies.org, and skating under the name Cat Owta Hell for Tulsa Derby Brigade (www.derbystrong.com). Clara also enjoys wrestling plot lines into reluctant submission and collecting particularly creative rejection letters.

MEGHAN O'BRIEN (www.meghanobrien.com.) lives in Northern California with her partner Angie, their son, and various cats and dogs. She has written five published novels and many short stories, some of which have been featured in various BSB anthologies. Her latest novel is the paranormal romance/thriller *Wild*.

VICTORIA OLDHAM (www.victoria-oldham.co.uk) is a consulting editor, and relocated to the U.K. with her partner from California several years ago. She explores the rich history all around her and molds it into stories, mostly of the dirty variety. Her latest publication is *Girls Who Bite* (Cleis Press, September 2011).

WINTER PENNINGTON (www.winterpennington.blogspot.com) is the author of *Witch Wolf* and *Raven Mask*, the Kassandra Lyall Preternatural Investigator series, and *Darkness Embraced: A Rosso Lussuria Vampire Novel*. She can be contacted at Winterpennington@gmail.com.

L.L. RAAND is the author of the Midnight Hunters paranormal romance series (*The Midnight Hunt, Blood Hunt*, and *Night Hunt*). Writing as Radclyffe, she is the author of over thirty-five romance and romantic intrigue novels.

MERRY SHANNON (www.merryshannon.com) is the author of two Bold Strokes Books novels, *Sword of the Guardian* and *Branded Ann*. She is the recipient of two Golden Crown Literary Society awards and a ForeWord Review Book of the Year finalist.

NELL STARK directs the Writing Center at a small college in the SUNY system. Trinity Tam is a marketing executive in the music industry and an award-winning writer/producer of film and television. They live and write in New York City. Together they write the everafter series (www.everafterseries.com).

SHELLEY THRASHER has edited novels for BSB since 2004. Before then she was a college English professor and traveled the world every chance she got. Her short story "Paris Jazz" appeared in the *Gay and Gray* anthology in 2011, and BSB will publish her novel *The Storm* in late 2012.

Having grown up watching Grade A and Grade Z horror movies on *Shock Theater*, YOLANDA WALLACE has long been a fan of things that go bump in the night. This marks her first foray into paranormal fiction, but hopefully not her last. Her previous published works include *In Medias Res*, *Rum Spring*, and *Lucky Loser*. She can be reached at yolandawrites@gmail.com.

KARIS WALSH (www.kariswalsh.com) is a horseback riding instructor who lives in Washington. She is the author of *Harmony*.

REBEKAH WEATHERSPOON (letusseeshallwe.blogspot.com) is the author of *Better Off Red*, the first installment in the Vampire Sorority Sister Series. She lives in Southern California, but longs for the coasts of New Hampshire and Maine.

SHERI LEWIS WOHL lives in northeast Washington state. She earned her BA from Eastern Washington University and MA from California State University, where her master's thesis on the 1872 lesbian vampire story "Carmilla" was nominated for outstanding thesis of the year. When not working or writing, she trains for triathlons.

MJ WILLIAMZ has been writing professionally for almost ten years. She has over twenty-five short stories published, mostly lesbian erotica with a few horror stories and a couple of romances thrown in for good measure. Her most recent novels are *Forbidden Passion* (September 2011) and *Initiation By Desire* (January 2012).

ABOUT THE EDITORS

RADCLYFFE has written over thirty-five romance and romantic intrigue novels, dozens of short stories, and, writing as L.L. Raand, has authored a paranormal romance series, The Midnight Hunters.

She is an eight-time Lambda Literary Award finalist in romance, mystery, and erotica—winning in both romance (*Distant Shores, Silent Thunder*) and erotica (*Erotic Interludes 2: Stolen Moments* edited with Stacia Seaman and *In Deep Waters 2: Cruising the Strip* written with Karin Kallmaker). A member of the Saints and Sinners Literary Hall of Fame, she is also a 2010 RWA/FF&P Prism award winner for *Secrets in the Stone*. Her 2010 titles were finalists for the Benjamin Franklin award (*Desire by Starlight*), the ForeWord Review Book of the Year award (*Trauma Alert* and writing as LL Raand, *The Midnight Hunt*), and the RWA Passionate Plume award (*The Midnight Hunt*). She is also the president of Bold Strokes Books, one of the world's largest independent LGBT publishing companies.

STACIA SEAMAN has edited numerous award-winning titles, and with co-editor Radclyffe won a Lambda Literary Award for *Erotic Interludes 2: Stolen Moments*; an Independent Publishers Awards silver medal and a Golden Crown Literary Award for *Erotic Interludes 4: Extreme Passions*; and an Independent Publishers Awards gold medal and a Golden Crown Literary award for *Erotic Interludes 5: Road Games;* and the 2010 RWA Rainbow Award of Excellence in the Short/Novella category for *Romantic Interludes 2: Secrets*. Most recently, she has essays in *Visible: A Femmethology* (Homofactus Press, 2009) and *Second Person Queer* (Arsenal Pulp Press, 2009).

Books Available From Bold Strokes Books

Night Hunt by L.L. Raand. When dormant powers ignite, the wolf Were pack is thrown into violent upheaval, and Sylvan's pregnant mate is at the center of the turmoil. A Midnight Hunters novel. (978-1-60282-647-2)

Demons are Forever by Kim Baldwin and Xenia Alexiou. Elite Operative Landis "Chase" Coolidge enlists the help of high-class call girl Heather Snyder to track down a kidnapped colleague embroiled in a global black market organ-harvesting ring. (978-1-60282-648-9)

Runaway by Anne Laughlin. When Jan Roberts is hired to find a teenager who has run away to live with a group of antigovernment survivalists, she's forced to return to the life she escaped when she was a teenager herself. (978-1-60282-649-6)

Street Dreams by Tama Wise. Tyson Rua has more than his fair share of problems growing up in New Zealand—he's gay, he's falling in love, and he's run afoul of the local hip-hop crew leader just as he's trying to make it as a graffiti artist. (978-1-60282-650-2)

Women of the Dark Streets: Lesbian Paranormal by Radclyffe and Stacia Seaman, eds. Erotic tales of the supernatural—a world of vampires, werewolves, witches, ghosts, and demons—by the authors of Bold Strokes Books. (978-1-60282-651-9)

Tyger, Tyger, Burning Bright by Justine Saracen. Love does not conquer all, but when all of Europe is on fire, it's better than going to hell alone. (978-1-60282-652-6)

Wholehearted by Ronica Black. When therapist Madison Clark and attorney Grace Hollings are forced together to help Grace's troubled nephew at Madison's healing ranch, worlds and hearts collide. (978-1-60282-594-9)

Haunting Whispers by VK Powell. Detective Rae Butler faces two challenges: a serial attacker who targets attractive women, and Audrey Everhart, a compelling woman who knows too much about the case and offers too little—professionally and personally. (978-1-60282-593-2)

Fugitives of Love by Lisa Girolami. Artist Sinclair Grady has an unspeakable secret, but the only chance she has for love with gallery owner Brenna Wright is to reveal the secret and face the potentially devastating consequences. (978-1-60282-595-6)

Derrick Steele: Private Dick—The Case of the Hollywood Hustlers by Zavo. Derrick Steele, a hard-drinking, lusty private detective, is being framed for the murder of a hustler in downtown Los Angeles. When his brother's friend Daniel McAllister joins the investigation, their growing attraction might prove to be more explosive than the case. (978-1-60282-596-3)

Nice Butt: Gay Anal Eroticism edited by Shane Allison. From toys to teasing, spanking to sporting, some of the best gay erotic scribes celebrate the hottest and most creative in new erotica. (978-1-60282-635-9)

Initiation by Desire by MJ Williamz. Jaded Sue and innocent Tulley find forbidden love and passion within the inhibiting confines of a sorority house filled with nosy sisters. (978-1-60282-590-1)

Toughskins by William Masswa. John and Bret are two twenty-something athletes who find that love can begin in the most unlikely of places, including a "mom-and-pop shop" wrestling league. (978-1-60282-591-8)

me@you.com by KE Payne. Is it possible to fall in love with someone you've never met? Imogen Summers thinks so because it's happened to her. (978-1-60282-592-5)

Bloody Claws by Winter Pennington. In the midst of aiding the police, Preternatural Private Investigator Kassandra Lyall finally finds herself at serious odds with Sheila Morris, the local werewolf pack's Alpha female, when Sheila abuses someone Kassandra has sworn to protect. (978-1-60282-588-8)

Awake Unto Me by Kathleen Knowles. In turn of the century San Francisco, two young women fight for love in a world where women are often invisible and passion is the privilege of the powerful. (978-1-60282-589-5)